The
True Story
of Her Life

I Promise You

The
True Story
of Her Life

I Promise You

Rita Brei

Library of Congress Control Number: 2021900856

HARDBACK: 978-1-954673-17-5
PAPERBACK: 978-1-954673-16-8
EBOOK: 978-1-954673-18-2

Ordering Information:

For orders and inquiries, please contact:
1-888-404-1388
www.goldtouchpress.com
book.orders@goldtouchpress.com

Printed in the United States of America

CONTENTS

I dedicate this book to my best friend Dennis E. Bohner, who encouraged me to publish this book in English Language

INTRODUCTION

Many years ago an artist applied the final brush stroke to the portrait of a beautiful woman. The woman was very young, newly married, and as close to happiness as she would ever be again.

Somewhere in the Soviet Union, the portrait still exists, hanging, perhaps, in a museum. The image belongs to another time. After it was painted, the world the young woman knew was irrevocably altered by revolution, war, and bloody struggles for power.

The portrait caught a moment in a life. It captured the woman's expectations of a future that would fulfill the promise of the life she had known as a child. Her expectations never changed; her world did.

The woman who sat for that portrait lies buried in a nation that grew increasingly foreign to her while she lived. Long before her death, she ceased to resemble the woman in the painting. In her heart, however, she changed little.

Wanda Stanishevsky's story is one of a promise thwarted; the telling of it is a promise kept. Inevitably, the chronicle of Wanda's life becomes the story of many lives, including that of Rita Brei, who pledged to tell it.

Rita Brei

PART I

Only yesterday the sea had been quiet, peaceful; sailboats had drifted lazily and gracefully. There had been no sign of a storm.

But now it was impossible to think the sea had looked any other way.

Waves rolled in, one after the other, and broke with a crash on the cliffs.

They foamed and then left their foam among the seaweed on the shorecliffs.

Before the foam disappeared, more waves tossed new foam upon the old.

Although it was midday, the sky was dark, heavy and threatening.

A girl sat on a low slope. She watched the waves, but it was as if she did not see them. Her young face conveyed intelligence and beauty, as well as sadness and a woman's sorrow. Her silhouette against the backdrop of the sea seemed symbolic. The waves reached for the cliff where she sat, and the light spray flew up to touch her face.

What had brought her in such weather to the shore of the sea? Only a year before she had never seen the sea. She had been living in the ancient Polish city of Cracow. Today, like the waves, her childhood was passing before her eyes.

She remembered the early years when her governess took her to school and brought her home. They often went for walks in the park not far from their house.

They had lived in a beautiful house, covered with ivy. Behind it was a small garden. She recalled how guests often came to call. Her father was a lawyer, and he used to tell many stories about his practice, stories she had not understood at the time. Her mother, Pani[1] Rudzinskaya, she remembered as being young and beautiful. Her older sister, Sophie, had already graduated from high school and was studying music and voice.

When did it happen?

She had been eight then. The year was 1898.

She had been on her way home from school, her governess walking at her side holding her hand. As they approached the house, she had seen her mother being carried out on a stretcher. She had tried to run to her mother, but her governess had held her back.

"No, Wanda," she remembered her governess saying. "Here comes your father; let's go talk to him."

Pan[2] Rudzinsky was preoccupied and told the governess to take the child into the house while he went on to the hospital. Wanda did not understand what was happening. When she entered the house, several of the servants stood near the doorway. The horse-drawn ambulance pulled away and everyone tried to return to what they had been doing.

Soon, Sophie arrived and began a voice lesson. Wanda entered the room where Sophie stood by the grand piano, singing, as her teacher accompanied her. The song was a romantic ballad about love and tears, dreams, and happiness. Wanda listened for a few moments, then walked up to Sophie and touched her hand. Sophie stopped singing, and the piano fell silent.

"What's the matter with you?" Sophie asked. "Can't you see I'm busy?"

"They've taken Mama away to the hospital, Father's gone with her, nobody will tell me anything about Mama—and you sing!" Wanda, tears streaming down her face, looked up imploringly at here sister.

"You're confused. Mama is at a charity meeting. Nobody said anything to me about her being in the hospital."

Sophie excused herself from her teacher, took Wanda by the hand, and left the room. A maid was in the kitchen washing dishes, and Sophie asked her if she knew anything about their mother and where she was. The maid answered that Pani had taken ill after the meeting, that she had been carried out on a stretcher, and that Pan had also left. Immediately, Sophie dismissed her voice teacher, excusing herself for interrupting the lesson.

Sophie had just walked to the porch when she heard her father calling her. She went to him and he enfolded her in his arms, drawing her tightly to him. She heard his quiet sobbing. Sophie said nothing, but she sobbed uncontrollably.

"She's gone," their father said, "gone forever."

At the funeral, the 600-year-old Church of Our Lady was filled to overflowing. It seemed that all the inhabitants of Cracow had come to that corner of Market Square to pay their respects to Pani Rudzinskaya. The people, crowded outside the church, commented on what a sweet woman she had been, how God had called her to Him before her time, and how young her daughters still were.

The governess held Wanda's hand. Everyone all around was gloomy. Wanda looked up and examined the beautiful stained-glass windows in the old church. She did not comprehend her loss at all. It was quiet in the house after the burial. Everyone spoke in subdued voices. Even after a long time had passed, Wanda still wore a black mourning band on the sleeve of her coat. Her father and Sophie also wore the bands. Yet each of them adjusted to their loss in a very personal way.

When her mother was alive, Wanda had met her each morning, and her mama had sent her off to school with a kiss. Now, Wanda walked downstairs and saw only her mother's portrait. This mama always smiled, and Wanda would say to the portrait, "Good morning, Mama. I'm going to have breakfast now, and then I'm going to school."

On the way home from school, she walked in the park with the governess. Then she did her lessons, which helped her forget about her mother. But in the evening, on the way to bed, she would walk up to the portrait and, raising her eyes, say, "Good night, Mama, until tomorrow."

Sophie handled her grief differently. She was a tall girl with blond hair, light blue eyes, and an easy-going disposition. By nature, she was a romantic who not only read novels but lived them with the characters. Sophie was only eighteen at the time, and her mother's death affected her deeply. She would often stroke Wanda's hand and ask if she needed help of any kind. Sophie feared only one thing: that her father would remarry and they would have a stepmother.

At the time, that event did not seem likely, for their father had become reclusive; he spoke little and seldom went out. He withdrew almost totally. Each Sunday, when they all went to church, he stayed to pray until everyone else had left.

A year after their mother's death, Pani Rudzinsky's family removed their mourning bands, but it was obvious that Pan Rudzinsky's grief was growing deeper. Not a week went by that he did not go to the cemetery. Whatever the weather, he brought his wife flowers and stayed by the crypt for hours at a time.

Months passed, and life went on in a reasonably normal way. Sophie entered society, which meant she attended concerts, balls, and other entertainments. She had admirers, the most visible of whom was one Pan Kazimir.

One day Sophie told her father that Kazimir had proposed to her and wanted to talk with him. Several days later, sitting in the study with Sophie's father, Kazimir told Pan Rudzinsky that he and Sophie loved each other and were only waiting for his blessing to marry. Kazimir's parents had already approved their son's marriage to such a suitable girl as Sophie. Pan Rudzinsky gave his unqualified blessing. The betrothal lasted for several weeks, and during that time Kazik, as Sophie called him, was at their house almost daily.

To Wanda, Pan Kazimir was an interesting young man with a narrow mustache and a perpetually clean-shaven face. She watched him with great curiosity. For her this was something new. She secretly observed him kiss her sister after Sophie had escorted him to the door.

The wedding was a noisy, happy event. Sophie wore a dazzling white gown, and ten-year-old Wanda wore a lacy, rose-colored dress. Her wavy, light chestnut-colored hair was very long. With her hazel-brown, almond-shaped eyes and the beautifully proportioned lines of her face, everyone was compelled to stop and gaze at her. They compared her to her sister and said she would someday surpass in beauty all the young ladies of society. Their father listened with a smile to all the compliments paid his daughters. Wanda looked so strikingly like her mother that it caused him both pain and delight.

Sophie left for her honeymoon in Paris. After she returned, she and Wanda saw each other often. Sophie brought Wanda presents and always expressed an interest in how things were going in school.

Wanda attended a secular girl's school. She learned her subjects well but was far removed from the real world. Her governess, a devout Catholic, told her Bible stories and taught her always to pray at bedtime. Over Wanda's bed hung a picture of the Virgin Mary and Child, and above the table where she studied hung a crucifix.

Gradually, Pan Rudzinsky's grief passed, and three years after his wife's death he married an attractive woman, a widow who had never had any children. Wanda grew fond of her; she read Wanda stories about animals, fish, and plants. When her governess retired, Wanda spent all her free time in the company of her stepmother, Pani Maria. Her father was always busy, and Wanda only saw him evenings and on his days off.

Meanwhile, a son was born to Sophie. Once, when everyone had gathered for Pan Kazimir's birthday, he announced that he, Sophie, and their son were moving to Russia. He had been offered a lucrative business opportunity there, and they would be leaving in a month. Pan Rudzinsky had a long discussion about the move with Pan Kazimir. Later, while the family was on their way home, Pan Rudzinsky told his wife, "God grant him success. I won't like parting with my daughter, but they have their own lives to live."

Wanda remembered how they parted. She and Sophie cried, but Father was not so emotional. He merely said, "It won't do for me to give you a hug here, but you write to me often." The coach was loaded down with trunks, baskets, boxes and bundles. The four horses took Sophie, her husband, and their son far away from Cracow to distant Russia, to the city of Odessa.

Back in Cracow, it was autumn. Golden and scarlet leaves lent their warmth to chilly, gray days. It often rained. One day, as they returned from church, the Rudzinskys were caught in a downpour. At home, they quickly changed their soaked clothes and warmed by the fire. Maria told Wanda a story about a woodchopper, and Father smoked his pipe and read. Wanda laid her head on her stepmother's knees and Pani Maria stroked her hair. Warmth radiated from this woman; Wanda loved her soft voice and her tender hands.

After dinner Wanda drew pictures—she loved doing that more than anything else. She drew trees bending in the wind and clouds in the sky and took her picture to show to her stepmother. Uncharacteristically, Pani Maria was lying in bed. Wanda knocked timidly on the door and asked permission to enter.

"Please come in," Maria said. "I'm not feeling too well; I think I have a fever."

Wanda approached the bed and held out the drawing. Her stepmother looked at it and commented, "I like it better when you draw the sun. You've drawn today's weather. Looking at it, I feel cold."

For the next two months Pani Maria lay in bed. Wanda brought her drawings of happy things, sunny days.

Winter set in, and one cold morning Pani Maria did not awaken. Once again, everyone in the Church of Our Lady was dressed in black. Once again, there was a large crowd in the corner of Market Square. Many people said how they pitied Pan Rudzinsky, how he was such an unfortunate man to have lost two beloved wives.

Wanda was thirteen, and she cried bitterly. This loss she understood.

Two years passed, and Wanda finished school. By then, she was of above-average height. Her long braids, which reached almost to her knees, made her seem even more slender than she was.

A graduation ball was held at her school. All the girls had invited boys to attend. The parents sat along the wall and watched the couples whirl by. Wanda, however, had not invited a boy her own age; instead, she brought her father. In the years since Pani Maria's death he had changed. His hair was almost completely gray, his face had grown gaunt, and he looked ten years older than he was. The boys paid much attention to Wanda, asking her to dance, but she declined, choosing to stay with her father. The girls gathered around her, paying her compliments on her dress.

Pan Rudzinsky enjoyed the flattery that was being directed to his youngest daughter. He was very proud when everyone remarked that she was beautiful, a well-bred, and modest.

On the way home, the horses pulled the carriage at a slow pace, as if to extend a little longer the childhood that had already ended.

During this time, letters from Sophie continued to arrive. She had given birth to two more sons. Upon learning of her stepmother's death, she wrote a letter inviting her father and sister to come to Russia. But

Wanda had to complete her schooling, and Father had urgent business in Cracow and Vienna.

By the time Wanda's schooling was over, however, Pan Rudzinsky had almost given up his law practice. On the advice of his doctor, he began going every year to the best health resorts in Europe. He had a bad heart and had developed rheumatism.

The summer after graduation, Wanda was making sketches in the city park. She lived only a five-minute walk from the park, and she went often. Giant oaks cast their shadows on the walkways. Wanda loved the park. She loved Cracow.

As she sketched, she became accustomed to the curious who would come up and watch her. Several times she had noticed a young man watching her from a distance. Then one day he walked up to her and introduced himself as Pan Stefan. He was tall, with ash-blonde hair, brown eyes, and dimpled cheeks. He said that he knew her first name and where she lived. He also said that he had never seen such a beautiful girl and that it was dangerous for her to go walking and do her sketching alone.

Wanda grew flustered, and her cheeks reddened.

She thanked him for the compliment and said that she had known the park since early childhood. At one time she had walked there with her governess, but now she was old enough to be there alone. He said no more and bid her good-bye, but he continued stopping to visit her each day. Finally, he invited her to go boating. She received permission from her father, who was already acquainted with Pan Stefan.

Thus she set out on her first date. Her heart was beating more rapidly than usual. Her whole being was filled with a kind of exaltation. The Vistula River was clear, and, as they drifted, Stefan told her about himself.

"I've studied in Warsaw for three years," he said. "I have one year to go. In the beginning I wanted to be a history teacher. It's my best subject. But later I changed my mind and decided to study economics."

After boating, Stefan took her home. They said goodbye at the door, and he kissed her hand. She was fifteen; it had been her first date and the first time a young man had touched her hand.

Stefan was home for the summer, and he and Wanda saw each other almost every day. He was seven years older than Wanda, and she found him fascinating. He took her to the Kosciuszko Monument and showed her other historic places in the old capital of Poland, which at the time belonged to Austria.

"You were born and you've lived for fifteen years in Cracow," he told her, "but I can show you this city as you've never seen it before, from the perspective of its history."

Stefan was right. She had never really seen Cracow. His descriptions were colorful and interesting.

"Two huge mounds were built close to the city," Stefan said. "One was erected to the memory of Prince Krakus's daughter Wanda, who allegedly chose to drown herself in the Vistula rather than marry a German prince. The other was built in the nineteenth century in honor of Tadeush Kosciuszko."

He showed her the Roman Catholic Sigismund Chapel, built in the sixteenth century by Bartolomeo Bezecci, a masterpiece of Renaissance architecture. "No other city in Poland has so many historic buildings," he said, "and so many churches containing famous works of art."

On a visit to Market Square, Stefan pointed out the royal castle standing on the rocky hill of Wawel on the left bank of the Vistula near the heart of the old city. The castle was, he said, the residence of the Polish kings.

Through the summer, Wanda and Stefan were almost inseparable, but then their visits came to an abrupt end. Wanda's father announced to her that in two weeks they were going to Russia to see her sister. They would stay for two months in Odessa.

Pan Stefan came to bid her farewell. Wanda promised to write every week. They would be seeing each other in two months, so there was no need for passionate grief. To remind her of him he brought her a small, ivory Indian Buddha.

"This is a memento for you, so that you won't forget me—a talisman that will remind you that I await you and am bored. It will protect you against any kind of misfortune," he said.

"And so I shall remember that I have a good friend," she replied.

He bowed to her and then kissed her. The kiss was long and tender. She had never felt anything like it before. Her head began to spin gently. In her father's presence, Stefan kissed her hand before she climbed into the coach next to her father and they began their journey. There was warmth and sadness in her heart, warmth because of Stefan's lips, which she still felt, and sadness because she was going far from him.

Before long, her father diverted her from her thoughts. He happily talked about the impending meeting with Sophie. They stopped at a hotel for the night, the horses were changed at an inn, and soon they had reached the border.

At the border, a tall customs official said to Pan Rudzinsky, "You should be afraid to take such a beauty to Russia. They'll surely try to steal her there."

Pan Rudzinsky laughed, saying that Wanda was all of fifteen years old and would not allow herself to be stolen. At that moment, Wanda could have been taken for seventeen, the blush so complimented her face.

After several more days of travel, they arrived in Odessa. It was the summer of 1905. Sophie was happy to see her father and sister. They talked non-stop, trying to tell all of the news at once. At one point, Sophie turned to Wanda, saying that she would have a dinner party in honor of the arrival of her family and that she would introduce Wanda to several Polish young people in Odessa's high society.

After resting from the trip and having dinner, they all went driving along the boulevard in an open carriage pulled by a pair of horses. On either side, Wanda saw people strolling along the streets. The acacias were blooming, their scent drifting along the entire way. Reaching the sea boulevard, the family decided to walk for a while. There they joined still more of the strolling public. The people were finely dressed; the children played happily.

Eventually, they reached the seashore, and the sea stretched out before them. "What beauty!" Wanda exclaimed. "I love it here. In two months I won't want to leave."

But then she remembered Stefan and added, "We'll rest well, Papa, and then go back to Cracow to start work. Our Cracow and the banks of the Vistula River are also beautiful." Turning to her sister, she said,

"Sophie, don't you miss Cracow and Poland? Aren't you homesick for your native land?"

Sophie smiled. "A person is always drawn to home, but I have mine here, and I'm glad to see you at my home. You've brought with you a little part of Poland."

Later, they went out again for a stroll, this time without Pan Kazimir.

Lately, he had been traveling on business and was often away from the house.

In the evening, they drank tea and recalled childhood acquaintances.

Wanda was exhausted and fell asleep as soon as she lay down on the bed. She dreamed about Cracow and a beautiful lake with swans floating on it. They were black swans; only one was white. She and Stefan were boating and the swans encircled them. Then she dreamed of Pani Maria who complained that everyone had left her and that she was very lonely.

After awakening in the morning, Wanda had trouble recovering from the dream. When she came out of her room in time for breakfast, her face was visibly pale.

Concerned, her father asked, "Did you sleep badly?"

"No, I simply haven't recovered from the long trip," Wanda evaded.

At breakfast Sophie announced that the dinner party was set for Saturday. More than sixty people would be invited. Sophie ordered new dresses for herself and Wanda, who eagerly awaited the making of new acquaintances.

In the meantime, Father spent all his time with his grandsons. He went for walks with the oldest and told him about Cracow and Poland.

By Saturday afternoon, all the preparations for the ball had been completed. In a few hours the guests would arrive. Wanda put on her dress, an exquisite, cream-colored gown with lace and ribbons.

Her father stopped in to have a look at her. "Your dress is very becoming to you," he said. "You remind me of your mother; I first saw her when she was about your age. Now let's see how the young Polish aristocrats of Odessa have a good time."

After he left, Wanda pinned a flower in her hair. She looked in the mirror and she also realized the great resemblance between herself and her mother's portrait.

The guests began to arrive. Wanda and her father were introduced to each of the guests, many of whom seemed to be commenting about how charming Sophie's sister was. A threesome entered, and Sophie introduced them to Wanda. This is Pan and Pani Svitsky and their daughter Zosia. You girls should get acquainted."

Wanda noted that Zosia was rather attractive with pale blue eyes and blond hair. Wanda immediately liked her loquacious, out-going nature. Zosia promised to stop by the next day, and they made plans to spend the entire day together. Wanda immediately realized that her entire two-month visit would be filled if she and Zosia undertook this every day.

The ball was in full swing. The orchestra played and the couples whirled. They played Pan Rudzinsky's favorite dance, the mazurka. He came up to Wanda, nodded, and invited her to dance. He took her by the hand, like a gallant partner. He clicked his heels, raised Wanda's hand, and they began the dance. Wanda laughed, telling her father that he danced better than the young men. He noted that he had danced the mazurka many years ago and that he had not forgotten how.

Many young men, whose names she could not recall, asked Wanda to dance. One of them was Pan Dzhensky; Zosia had said that he was her boyfriend. When Wanda danced with him, she noticed that Zosia was keeping an eye on them. The dance ended and, having escorted Wanda back to her seat, Pan Dzhensky bowed and kissed her hand. When the music began to play again, he asked her to dance. Wanda saw Zosia winding her way towards them and then stopping when she saw that they were going to dance again.

"Zosia is your girl," Wanda said to Pan Dzhensky, "and I'm not at all comfortable that this is your second dance in a row with me."

"She's not my fiancee. We are not engaged," he replied. "We are simply good friends. I can't pass up the chance to dance with you. You are the queen of the ball. See how everyone is looking our way?"

Wanda laughed, but she enjoyed hearing compliments. She turned lightly, with graceful steps and fluid movements. She was in perfect bliss. What a wonderful ball! What excellent music! She was happier than ever.

How quickly the time flew! Soon the musicians were putting their instruments into their cases. The guests were dispersing, expressing their appreciation for the enjoyable evening.

Zosia walked up to Wanda. "So, tomorrow at eleven in the morning I will stop by for you. The evening was marvelous, wasn't it?"

"Yes, simply magnificent," answered Wanda.

For a long time she did not sleep, recalling again and again the evening that had just passed. Tomorrow she would write Stefan about the night.

Before going to bed, Father again took medicine; it was apparent that after the dancing he was tired. Wanda asked him about it, but he said the medicine was only to help him sleep better.

The next day, Wanda was waiting for Zosia when she arrived just after twelve. Zosia's small carriage was harnessed to a pair of horses. Wanda sat down next to Zosia, and the horses started off.

"To Derebasovskaia Street," Zosia said to the driver. To Wanda she added, "We own a large bookstore there where you can get the latest Polish literature."

The way from Pushkinskaia Street, where Sophie lived, to Derebasovskaia Street, where the bookstore was located, was a five-minute ride. In nice weather, one could walk the distance.

"Pushkinskaia Street is very beautiful," Wanda said, "so wide, and the architecture is amazing."

"Well, we're here," Zosia said. Turning to the driver, she ordered, "Come back in one hour."

"Why is the street called Derebasovskaia?" Wanda asked.

"He founded the city," Zosia answered. "He was a Frenchman, and his name was Derebas. You can find books about Odessa's history in our bookstore."

They entered the store. It was a single room with a great number of shelves filled with books. Zosia turned to the clerk and spoke in Polish: "Pan Mikhas, this is Wanda. She has just arrived from Cracow to stay for a while."

"I kiss your hand, Pani," Mikhas said, bowing low.

Wanda inspected the shelves, delighted with so many books of different sizes and shapes. She selected a small volume of verses by Adam

Mitskevich and a collection of stories by Eliza Ozheshko. Mikhas said that she could come any time for books since he lived there and would be happy to serve her.

Soon the girls said good-bye and left. As they strolled along the street, Zosia told Wanda that Mikhas was from a very well-known family that had fallen on hard times, so he was working for them and also was studying. They walked along the embankment and then returned to the bookstore where they stayed until the carriage arrived.

When they arrived back at Sophie's, Wanda thanked Zosia for her kindness.

Zosia promised to stop by in a few days. Thereafter, they met rather often.

Once, Zosia's friends invited Wanda to go sailing with them.

During much of her free time, Wanda read and sketched. She wrote letters to Stefan every week, as she had promised. However, there were only two letters from him.

One Saturday the girls went to the opera with Zosia's parents. The Odessa Theater of Opera and Ballet was the pride of the city, the most magnificent theater in Europe, both inside and out.

Wanda always enjoyed the theater and the ballet, but today she was worried because Father had not been well. The doctor had recommended a little less excitement. Wanda, returning from the theater, told her father how beautiful it was and that as soon as he began to feel better he must go with them.

She often went to the bookstore, and Pan Mikhas exchanged her books, as if it were a library. She was very interested in books about art, and Mikhas showed her many.

Wanda observed that Mikhas looked very ill. He often suppressed coughing; excusing himself, he would go to his room, which was just off the storeroom, and for a long time he would cough. His face was pale, and when he sorted through books his fingers trembled. He was nineteen or twenty years old, but his sunken cheeks and the dark circles under his eyes made him look older. To Wanda, there was something pitiful about his appearance. She saw how he fawned over Zosia, and it seemed understandable, since he was entirely dependent on her and her family.

One day Wanda went to the bookstore to take back all the books she had borrowed earlier. She and her father were leaving in a week. On the door of the shop was a sign: "Closed." She was disappointed because that meant she would have to make another trip to return the books, which were very heavy. As she stood there, she absent-mindedly turned the doorknob, and the door opened. Entering, she placed the books on the counter and turned toward Mikhas's room, wondering if he was there.

Wanda opened the door slightly. "Pan Mikhas, are you here?" she asked. "I've returned the books."

At first she saw no one. The thin window shades were pulled, but some light showed through them. Looking about the room, her eyes stopped at the bed. Pan Mikhas seemed ill and moaning, lying on the bed. She timidly went nearer.

Oh, Lord, what is this? Her eyes met the eyes of Zosia. She was aware of Zosia's loose, flowing hair before she noticed that Zosia was naked. So was Pan Dzhensky.

Wanda leapt away, throwing herself toward the door. Stumbling on the threshold, she fell, but she picked herself up and ran through the store and out into the street. She was choking; her tears seemed to be suffocating her. "Oh, God, why did I go in there? What should I do now?" she kept repeating. She was unable to run. She barely made it up the stairway to the house and then raced blindly to her room.

Once there, she paced about, wringing her hands, thinking, but not finding an answer. Suddenly, someone knocked, the door opened quietly, and the maid came in.

"Dear Pani, you already know. I see how sad you are. But everything will work out. You'll stay on here for just another short week, and then you'll be able to leave."

Wanda was puzzled. "What are you talking about? Why is it necessary to stay on? What has happened?"

"Your father is in the hospital. He went for a walk with one of the boys and just collapsed on the street. You know he has a bad heart. It's a good thing that Pani Sophie was at home. I'm sorry. I saw that you were crying and assumed you already knew."

Wanda did not stay to listen any more. She ran from the room and down the stairs. The maid followed her, saying something and gesturing with her hands. At the front door Wanda collided with Sophie.

"Everything is going to be all right," Sophie said. "Father had a heart attack, but don't cry. The doctor said that in a few days he'll be home. They must check him over thoroughly. Let's go into the house and calm down." She spoke rapidly, assuming an air of nonchalance. Wanda followed, staying close to her sister.

Wanda went on to her room. She fell on the bed and began to cry, burying her face in the pillow. What kind of day was this? Then she recalled how in her childhood her governess had taught her to ask God's help. She got off the bed, knelt down, and fervently repeated the words of a prayer. She asked The Mother of God to protect and save her father.

Rising from her knees, she felt relief. Now only one thing troubled her: that which she had seen in the bookstore.

In the evening, as Wanda and Sophie relaxed and drank tea, Zosia arrived unexpectedly. Wanda was unable to look at her. As usual, Zosia chatted merrily, as if nothing had happened. She told Wanda that some of her new friends wanted to plan a farewell party for her before her departure.

Wanda answered that this seemed unnecessary, since her father was in the hospital, and it was still not known when they could leave.

Zosia then began to relate the social news. If Wanda did not leave for two weeks, she could attend Marysa's wedding. It would be a big event, and everyone was already looking forward to it.

Wanda looked closely at Zosia's face. Nothing was visible on it. Zosia laughed unaffectedly and enthusiastically. For a moment, Wanda thought that the incident at the store had not really occurred. But when she met Zosia's glance, doubts evaporated. These were the same eyes.

Zosia said she would stop by in the morning and they would go to the French store since the dress she had placed on order was finished. Wanda did not refuse per se, but because of her father's illness, and her own sad mood, thought she would not go. However, Sophie urged her to get out of the house, saying that it would be better for Wanda not to be alone at this time.

The next morning the weather was nice. The driver stopped the horses at the French store and the two girls went inside. A little bell notified the sales clerk that customers had come in. A polite, middle-aged woman came out to meet them. Seeing Zosia, she beamed, pointing to chairs and inviting them to sit down. She went into the back room and soon came out, carrying a lilac-colored dress. Zosia took it into the dressing room and soon came out to model it for them.

"Do you like it?" she asked.

"Yes, very much," Wanda replied politely. "The color is very becoming to you."

After changing back into her regular clothes, Zosia picked out several items of lingerie. Then she instructed the saleswoman to have everything delivered to her home, and she and Wanda left the store.

They walked along the street, the cab moving slowly behind them. Zosia talked about many things, but not once did she even hint about yesterday's incident. Their walk took them to the bookstore, and Zosia took hold of Wanda's elbow and pulled her toward the door.

"You're not leaving yet, so take something to read."

"No, no!" Wanda protested. "My sister has many books, and I can read those."

Suddenly Pan Mikhas appeared at the door. "What is this? You don't want to come in? Welcome!"

He opened the door and Wanda timidly entered with Zosia.

"Come, I want to show you an interesting book about seventeenth-century Italian painting," Pan Mikhas said. "It has many illustrations, so it is very big and heavy and you'll have to look at it here."

He took the already-prepared book directly from under the counter and Wanda, having sat down on a chair, began to look it over. "It is very interesting and I shall look through it with pleasure," she commented.

"I am leaving," said Zosia. "Until tomorrow, all the best."

Wanda absent-mindedly nodded her head. She was so absorbed in the book that she did not notice that Zosia put up the "Closed" sign as she went out the door.

Mikhas began putting up books but kept looking in Wanda's direction. She looked up from the book and asked what time it was.

"It will soon be time for me to leave. I must go with my sister to the hospital and visit my father."

"What is wrong with your father?" Mikhas asked.

"Nothing too terrible. He had a heart attack, but he is already better, and the doctors say he will be home in a few days."

"Well, thank goodness everything will work out. It's a pity you must leave so soon," Mikhas continued. "You see, I passed my exam yesterday and wanted someone to celebrate with me."

"I am very glad," Wanda answered politely. "Accept my congratulations. Was it a difficult exam to take?"

"No, not very. I prepared for a long time. Now I am going on to the next course."

"What specialty have you chosen? What will you do after you have finished school?"

"I'm studying for the bar, but I still have a long time to study."

"My father was a lawyer. It would be interesting for you to speak with him. When he's home, I'll bring him here and you can discuss law."

"I would be very glad to make his acquaintance." Mikhas smiled. "If you wouldn't be offended, Pani Wanda, I would like for you to dine with me. I prepared it myself. Be so kind as to try it."

"I really don't know. My sister will be waiting for me. Well, all right. What is twenty minutes? It is an important occasion for you, and I would not wish to offend you."

Mikhas escorted her to the door of his room, and she timidly approached.

He opened the door before her. Entering, she stopped, unsure of what to do.

Glancing at the bed, she saw that it now had a bedspread on it. Again, she thought about how all this had appeared to her the day before.

On a table by the window were several cold dishes. Mikhas set two places and brought something hot.

Wanda sat down at the table. She felt uncomfortable. After pouring her wine, Mikhas poured himself a small glass of vodka. She pushed aside her wine, saying that she did not drink.

"Now what is this, Wanda? It's a very light wine. Drink to my success," Mikhas said and smiled warmly.

"All right," Wanda replied, "but only a little."

Raising her glass, she said, "To your future, Pan Mikhas."

He raised his glass in answer, said nothing, and drank the contents in a single swallow.

She drank half the contents of her glass. She liked the wine. It was pleasant and not strong. Mikhas poured himself more vodka, and Wanda drank the wine remaining in her glass. This time she toasted, "To friendship!"

Suddenly, it was as if Pan Mikhas were far away, and she was floating somewhere. The floor was moving under her feet.

She was aware of nothing else until she realized that she was lying stretched out on the bed. Pan Mikhas was sitting on the edge next to her. Looking around the room, she saw Zosia at the door. Behind her stood Pan Dzhensky.

Zosia said loudly, "We won't disturb them, Pan Dzhensky. Let's leave here. And you said Wanda was modesty itself."

They left, closing the door loudly behind them. Wanda looked at Mikhas. He was crying. She sat up, and Mikhas rose from the bed. He wiped his face, saying that it was his fault and God would not forgive him for what he had done. With difficulty, Wanda stood up; she could hardly move her legs.

"What has happened to me?" she said slowly. "What does all this mean? Did I get so drunk that I don't remember anything?"

She picked up her bag, which was lying on a chair, and directed herself toward the door. Mikhas, in silence, opened the door for her. Her head whirled, her legs trembled, and there was a fog in her head. After she stumbled from the store, she caught a droshky at the corner and climbed in with difficulty. Throwing herself back on the seat, she endeavored to reconstruct in her memory what had transpired.

Zosia's words now acquired another meaning for her. From the fact that Mikhas had wept and blamed himself, she understood that something irreparable had occurred.

"Oh, Mother of God, save me and have mercy on me! Why such punishment for me?"

Her soul froze. Fear seized her.

Arriving at the house, she paid the driver and he helped her down to the sidewalk.

There was a crowd of people at the house speaking in Polish and Russian. Wanda watched those who had gathered, not understanding what they were doing there. The people parted, making a path for her to pass through to the house. She heard only snatches of sentences. She wanted to run into the house, but her legs gave way and she fell.

She became conscious again while they were putting her on her bed. All around her were strangers. "What happened? Where is Sophie? Help me up." It seemed to her that she was screaming, but her lips barely moved.

One elderly woman, wiping her tears with a handkerchief, said that the Lord had taken Pan Rudzinsky away; it was, she said God's will. Sophie was at the hospital; she had left an hour ago, when she had learned the tragic news.

Wanda lost consciousness again. When she came to, she saw Sophie and a doctor. Sophie was on her knees beside Wanda's bed. She was crying. Wanda embraced her, and Sophie cried more loudly, saying that they were orphans now.

Someone called Sophie through the slightly opened door, and she rose and left the room. The doctor told Wanda he would give her another shot in twenty minutes and that she needed rest. Wanda listened to him in silence. Her temples throbbed. She could not think about anything. Her mind seemed to submerge into a fog, then emerge again.

Wanda's memories of the funeral were vague because she had fainted often during the ceremony. She had been held by the arms but did not remember by whom. She had wanted only to die, to be beside her father who had left her forever.

For several months Wanda could not leave her bed. She did not cry, as before, but instead withdrew and spoke little to anyone. The doctor visited her almost daily but could say nothing to console her.

Gradually, however, she began to recover. First, she was able to walk around the room. A few days later, she went to the cemetery with Sophie, who said she could go on the condition that she behave calmly.

As they walked along a path in the old cemetery, they could see many flowers on the graves. At their father's crypt, Wanda knelt slowly. She did not cry. With folded hands, she prayed silently, her lips pressed together. Sophie stood still, wiping away her own tears.

When they returned to the house, Wanda remained silent. That day she did not come down for dinner, preferring to stay in her room. Worried, Sophie called the doctor in the evening. When he arrived, he and Sophie walked into Wanda's room. They found her sitting on the bed, drawing something.

"How are you doing, Wanda?" the doctor asked. "What is it you're drawing?"

Sophie walked to the bed and looked at the sheet of paper. Wanda had drawn a crypt—the family's crypt. On the facade wall were oval portraits with inscriptions. On the left were the dates of her father's birth and death, and on the right was Wanda's date of birth.

Sophie burst into tears and said to the doctor, "What can I do with her? I don't have the strength even to look at it."

The doctor left the room with Sophie and returned alone. He brought a chair to the bed, sat down, and asked Wanda to listen to him. Taking the drawing from her hands, he set it aside.

"Your physical state does not worry me," he began. "It is your mood that frightens me. Has your father's death affected you so deeply? It seems to me there is something else. You asked your sister not to let your new friends in to see you. I am your friend and I want to help you."

Wanda did not speak, and the doctor continued.

"The picture you've drawn tells me you want to die. But you are not yet sixteen years old. Believe me, life is beautiful; everything is not as bad as you think it is now. You must live to preserve your father's memory. You must finish your education. You have your entire future ahead of you."

Wanda looked at him for a long time. Outside her window, the wind blew, and she listened to the rustle of the leaves. For a moment, she imagined that the doctor knew what had happened to her that awful day. No, she decided, he must never know, and no one must be allowed to examine her too closely.

The doctor noticed a change in Wanda's eyes. "You are right, doctor," Wanda said. "Physically, I am all right. It is only melancholy over leaving my native town, new impressions, my father's death—all of those things have had so strong an impact on me that I have been unable to cope. My sister should not be worried. I will try to get control over myself. Thank you, doctor, you have been very kind to me."

When the doctor left, Wanda lowered her head onto the pillow. She felt a change inside her that she did not understand. What was important, she repeated to herself, was that she stay calm and not cause Sophie undue worry.

Later that afternoon, she walked downstairs for tea. Taking her nephew onto her lap, she played and talked with him. When Sophie saw her, she was greatly relieved.

As the days passed, it seemed that everything was going better for Wanda although, as before, she refused to see her new friends. No matter how hard her sister tried to persuade her, she did not go to any parties. Wanda said that she was going to mourn her father for a year.

Wanda began taking Russian lessons because, at the time, she spoke only Polish and French. Sophie was often away with her husband on his business trips for a week to ten days at a time. Wanda studied and helped the governess teach and look after the children.

She often went to the cemetery by herself. Each time, a cabman drove her up to the gate, and she walked along the path of her father's grave.

Once, on a Sunday when it was cold, she was wailing, wrapped in a warm shawl and bending into the wind, when suddenly, someone blocked her way. She looked up to see Mikhas standing in front of her. She turned to walk around him, but he stopped her and held her by the arm.

"For God's sake," he pleaded, "listen to me. I am guilty and I know I am not to be forgiven."

Wanda tried again to move away.

"Please listen to what I have to say to you," Mikhas said. "I'm very sick. I have consumption, and I have very little time left to live. I want to explain. It is your right to choose whether to forgive me or not."

Mikhas coughed and put a handkerchief to his mouth. Wanda looked at him closely. He stood in front of her, his body shaking, his eyes glowing feverishly. When he took the handkerchief from his mouth, it was stained with blood. His face had grown even thinner. Concern overcame Wanda's anger.

"I've come to put flowers on my father's grave," she said, not knowing what else to say or do.

Mikhas released her arm, and she resumed walking. He followed her, coughing, and soon fell behind.

After she paid her respects to her father, Wanda walked silently toward the gate where the cabman waited. Mikhas accompanied her. He said he could not work anymore. He had been in the hospital, and he had to go back again. When they reached the cab, Mikhas seized Wanda's hand and begged her to listen to him. Wanda climbed into the cab and offered him the seat next to her. She asked the cabman to take them to the nearest cafe.

Ten minutes later, Wanda and Mikhas sat in a warm, cozy room. Wanda ordered a cup of tea for herself and a glass of hot milk for Mikhas. He held the glass in both hands, warming them. Wanda looked past him, trying to decide what to say.

"It looks like you've warmed up," she said, finally. I'm listening."

"Oh, my God," Mikhas sighed. "Where do I start? You know my parents are very poor, and I worked at Svitsky's shop. Zosia is very flighty and spoiled. For a year, she had been forcing me to sleep with her. If she didn't like something, she slapped me in the face and insulted me. When I tried to stop her she threatened to tell her father that I seduced her. It's not true. I was not the first for her. I was afraid to be associated with her because I knew what the consequences might be.

"One day, she told me I was to leave the shop on Wednesdays and Fridays from one until four. I was to hang a 'Closed' sign on the door and go study elsewhere. I knew she was with someone and that she arranged meetings in the room where I lived.

"I saw her once when she left the shop with Pan Dzhensky, and I realized he was her new lover. Then there was the day you caught her in my room. After that, she was afraid her parents and friends would find out.

"I returned to the shop at four o'clock, and she was waiting for me. She told me I would pay dearly if I refused to do what she asked. She brought some wine that I was supposed to give you. I thought I would simply be near you, but I drank too much. I was afraid everything would go wrong, and then Zosia would come in and there would not be the scene she had in mind. I was drunk and could not control myself."

"Don't say anymore," Wanda choked. "That is enough. I understand everything now. God will not forgive her for her malice."

Wanda rose. Mikhas covered his face. Tears fell from his hands onto the table, and he coughed.

"Sit down, please, I beg you," he said. "I know I will die soon. I want only your forgiveness."

"My forgiveness will not help you," Wanda replied sadly. "Let God forgive you. What you have done is not only a sin but also a crime. I was sick with grief for months after that day in your room. Father's death has left me here in Russia. I can't go back to Poland. I have been left alone in my grief. Do not ask me for forgiveness. God is your judge. And don't follow me, please. People are starting to notice us."

Wanda walked to the door without looking back. She climbed into a waiting cab and sat, crying quietly, as it pulled away.

When she reached home, Wanda decided it was good that Sophie was not there to see how upset she was. She spent the rest of the day with her nephews in order to divert her thoughts from what she had gone through that morning.

That night, Wanda prayed before going to sleep, asking that the Mother of God forgive Mikhas. For a long time she could not sleep. Mikhas's voice and his miserable appearance haunted her.

The winter was a cold one. Sophie and her family traveled to the Crimea. Wanda told them she did not want to go, saying she preferred to study. She had other reasons, though. She felt a change in herself. She was gaining weight and wore loose clothing to hide it. A frightening suspicion would not leave her alone, no matter how hard she tried to drive away the intrusive thought. In her soul, she knew she was pregnant.

The only person in the house besides Wanda was a maid, an elderly woman.

She bought everything necessary for them to live and did all the housework.

Wanda seldom spoke to her.

When the weather warmed a little in the second half of February, Wanda visited the cemetery. Walking down the path, she noticed a man and a woman approaching her. The man's face resembled Mikhas's, but he was older and taller.

Suddenly, Wanda realized they were Mikhas's parents. She met them, excused herself, and asked when it had happened and where she might find Mikhas's gravesite.

Mikhas's parents told her he had died a week before and pointed in the direction of his grave.

"Please pray for him," Mikhas's mother said. He was so young. He was a good son."

Wanda walked down the path to her father's grave, and on it she placed half of the flowers she had brought. She then found Mikhas's grave and covered it with the remaining blooms. As she stood silently, Mikhas's face appeared before her. Her lips moved in a quiet prayer.

Slowly, Wanda moved toward the gate. As she walked, she remembered how Mikhas had asked her in the cafe to forgive him.

"Yes, I have forgiven him," she thought. "He left this life forgiven."

She understood clearly that she was carrying Mikhas's baby, that the child was living inside her. No one now could help her. She could only wait for something vast and frightening to happen.

One morning in the middle of March, Wanda awoke feeling very ill. Her heavy body would not obey her. She staggered to the chair, picked up her shawl, and wrapped it around her shoulders. No one could be allowed to see her in that condition. She felt as though she would die soon.

Since her father had died, she had not written a letter to Stefan, although there were several from him. She could not write because she felt that whatever they had had between them could never be the same. When she thought about him, she felt as though her heart were breaking, and her eyes filled with tears.

No, she could not write to him, not after what had happened.

That afternoon, Wanda went downstairs, fixed a cup of tea, and told the maid that she would be gone for a few days. The maid nodded and walked to the kitchen.

Suddenly, Wanda felt a sharp pain in her stomach. She stood up and left the house. At the street corner, she got into a cab and told the driver to take her to the hospital.

At the small, private hospital where Sophie had given birth to her children, Wanda paid the cabman and entered the building. She spoke very little Russian, but the doctor spoke French, so they were able to communicate.

Wanda cried as she explained her misfortune to the doctor. She told him that, if she were to die, her sister must not know it happened during childbirth.

The doctor, a man about fifty years old, told her, "You must be as calm as possible. Don't worry. We will do everything in our power."

"How old are you?" he asked.

"Sixteen."

"What are you going to do with the baby?"

"I don't know. I live with my sister."

"Perhaps you would like to give the baby to a good home for adoption."

"What kind of home is it?"

"It is a very wealthy family. The woman has just given birth to a stillborn child for the third time. I will introduce you to her later. Right now, I will take you to the delivery room."

Nurses in nuns' habits laid Wanda on a table. During the delivery, Wanda lost consciousness. When she revived, she looked up into the nuns' faces. She heard the baby cry and the doctor say it was a healthy girl.

Wanda was lying in her hospital bed with the curtains lowered when the doctor came to see her.

"Well, everything is behind you now," he said. "In a few days you will be at home. Nobody knows that the baby is to be given away, except me. I want to introduce you to the lady who will adopt your daughter. She wants to see you. Today, you rest, and you will meet her tomorrow."

He left the room, closing the door behind him. In Wanda's mind, everything was confused. She dozed often, drifting away somewhere, and then awakening. She felt very relaxed and did not think about the baby, only that a terrible burden had been lifted.

The next day, the doctor showed Wanda to a room across from her own. In it was a lady in her early thirties, half lying, half sitting on high pillows.

The woman introduced herself to Wanda in Polish.

"I have heard that you are Polish, so we are fellow countrywomen," she said. "Come closer to me, child. You are so young. Yes, and you are beautiful, too."

She asked the doctor to leave them in privacy.

"Let us get to know each other, my dear. I am Countess Talchinsky." Wanda introduced herself, lowering her eyes.

"You have agreed to give me your daughter for adoption," the countess said. "I will be grateful to you all my life. You have saved me.

"Do you see these flowers?" She pointed to a bouquet of white roses.

"These are from my husband, Count Talchinsky. He gave me these flowers, thinking that I have given him a daughter."

Noticing Wanda's look of concern, the countess laid her hand on top of the girl's and continued speaking.

"Don't worry, my dear. You will be able to visit me and observe how your daughter grows up. Only you and I will know the truth. Do you agree to that?"

Wanda nodded her consent.

"Well, that's good," the countess said. "I'm glad to have met you. I will see you again soon."

Wanda stood up, thanked the countess, and walked out of the room. Her mood was greatly improved. Everything seemed much better to her.

After a few days, the doctor told her she could go home. He also said that the countess wished to see her before she left.

Wanda entered the countess's room. Beside the bed was a small crib. Lace curtains were lowered, so she could not see the baby. She approached the bed, and the countess motioned her to a chair.

"We will part now," the countess said, her excitement evident in her voice. "You will come to this address in three months. Do not come before then."

She handed Wanda a small slip of paper with an address written on it. Wanda looked at the countess and asked her timidly, "May I look at the baby now?"

"No, for God's sake," the countess protested. "The baby is sleeping, and I lowered the curtains to keep the light out."

Countess Talchinsky stretched her hand out towards Wanda.

"Give me your hand," she said.

Wanda did so, and the countess removed a ring from her own finger. It contained a large diamond, surrounded by smaller diamonds arranged to form a branch. She put the ring on Wanda's middle finger.

"This is a present for you from me," she said. "It belonged to my grandmother. Someday, when you are older, you will understand and appreciate what you have done."

She kissed Wanda on the cheek and Wanda left. She did not cry over the loss of her child, for she did not feel like a mother.

When Wanda was ready to leave the hospital, the doctor told her that the countess had paid all her expenses. He told her also that the countess was breastfeeding the baby by herself and that Wanda had been sent to her by God.

"Thank you, doctor," Wanda said, softly. "You have been sent to me by God, too."

Wanda walked out to the street and into a light drizzle. Wrapped in a shawl, she entered a cab and rode home.

A letter from Sophie was waiting for her when she arrived at the house. Her sister wrote that she and her husband would be home by the beginning of April.

Sophie's arrival helped divert Wanda's attention away from everything that had happened to her. The house was noisy, and life was proceeding at full speed. Wanda stayed busy with her nephews and helped Sophie around the house. She continued her Russian lessons and prepared herself to enter a college in the fall.

Spring had come. Trees blossomed, birds cried out near their nests, and the air was clean and fresh. Several times, Wanda and the family picnicked at the seashore, which was always crowded with merry people.

At times, though, Wanda went to the sea alone and crumbled bread for the hungry, noisy gulls. She sat at the edge of a path leading to the beach. She liked to look at the sea. It seemed to contain many enigmas, many unsolved mysteries.

Sophie sometimes gossiped, and if Zosia's name was mentioned, Wanda's expressions would change slightly. Sophie noticed, and soon she stopped talking about Zosia at all.

The ring on Wanda's finger was an object of attention and amusement.

Sophie said it was sheer luck to find such a ring on the street.

July arrived, and Wanda remembered that in a week she would go to the address the countess had given her. But through the spring and early summer, she had seldom thought about Countess Talchinsky and the baby. She struggled with two urges, the first to forget everything, as though it had never happened, the second to go see her child, although she knew the baby was no longer hers. As the time to decide approached, she thought more and more about her problem.

The next Saturday, Wanda went out and bought a doll. Later, she took a cab to within a block of her destination. From there, she walked, pressing the doll to her, filled with anxiety and fear.

When she was near the house, she stopped to look at her daughter's home. It was tall, a three-story structure. On the massive front door was a bronze lion's head. A ring passed through the lion's mouth.

Wanda stepped to the door and knocked. A butler opened it. Wanda gave him the countess's name, but he shrugged and said no such person lived there. Wanda showed him the address the countess had written down and looked at him questioningly.

The butler returned the piece of paper to her and said, "The address is right, but this countess has never lived here."

Wanda excused herself and retreated in confusion. For a moment, she stood still, and then she remembered that the people at the hospital might know where the countess lived.

At the hospital, she did not see the doctor who had taken care of her. A nun told here there was another doctor who could help her. Wanda recognized the nun as the nurse who had assisted the doctor when she had had her baby.

"No," Wanda said, anxiously, "I don't need another doctor. You can help me. Do you remember the name of the lady who took my baby?"

"You're confused, my dear," the nurse replied. "I don't understand what you're talking about."

"Do you remember me?" Wanda asked.

"Yes, I remember. You were hospitalized here. But I also remember that your baby was stillborn."

"You're confused," Wanda cried. "It was the countess's baby who was stillborn, not mine. Her room was right across from mine. I need only her last name. Perhaps I didn't remember it correctly. Countess Talchinsky ... that's how she introduced herself. I didn't find her at the address she gave me."

The nun seemed to be in a hurry.

"No, I haven't heard that name. Sorry, but I have to go."

The nun left, and Wanda stood, holding the doll. She left the hospital, walking nowhere in particular. It was a deception, she realized, all of it, and to herself she said, softly, "I have been cheated."

A strong wind began to blow. A thunderstorm was coming. Wanda's hat blew off and was carried along the street. She paid no attention to it and continued on. She walked toward the sea. On the brink of a cliff, she stopped, the wind buffeting her face. She stared at the sea, at its fury, and sank to the ground at the cliff's edge.

She held the doll in her hands, looked at it for a moment, and threw it into the sea. She watched as the waves grabbed it and carried it away. The doll disappeared in the gray abyss of the waves.

"The past doesn't exist anymore," she said to herself. "It sank to the bottom of the sea with the doll."

Wanda sat, watching the rushing sea, until the rain began to fall.

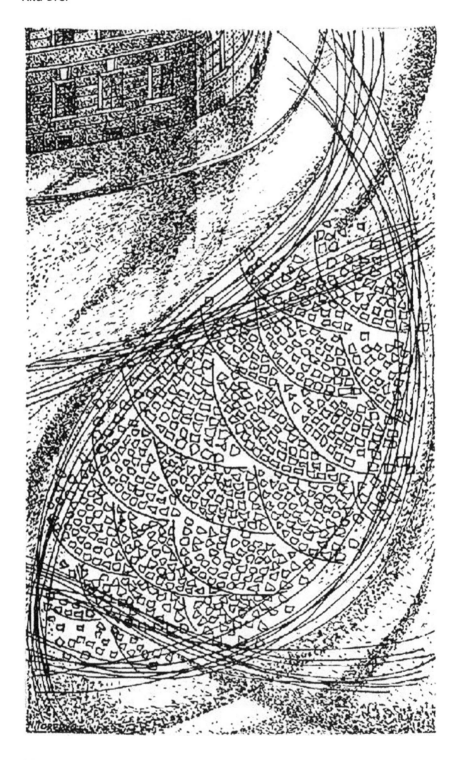

PART II

Sophie was at home when Wanda returned.

"Oh, my God," she exclaimed when she saw Wanda's condition, "you're soaked through! Where have you been?"

Sophie helped Wanda remove her cloak.

"You don't have your hat on. Your hair is soaking wet." She lead Wanda to the kitchen and told a maid to prepare a hot bath. "Quickly, remove all your clothes. You caused me a lot of worry. Have you been to the cemetery?"

"No, I was at the seashore when a storm hit."

"At the seashore in this weather? This is crazy! God forbid you should get sick again."

Wanda lay in the hot bath and allowed her mind to wander. Soon drowsiness overcame her. She followed her bath with a cup of hot tea, then went to bed, falling asleep immediately.

Several hours later she awoke, feeling fresh and vigorous. She found Kazimir reading a newspaper. Sophie and the children were in the other room. As Wanda approached them, she saw that an elderly woman was with them.

"Wanda, let me introduce you to Mrs. Khmelsky. She is leaving soon for Cracow and I have asked her to do a favor for me there. Our inheritance is being handled by Attorney Krier. Mrs. Khmelsky has been kind enough to speak with him and deliver my letter.

Wanda looked at the massive woman whose small eyes peered out from her fleshy face. For a moment, she was tempted to give her a letter to Stefan, but she drove the thought from her mind. Not now, she told herself.

"It's a pleasure to meet you. How long will you be staying in Cracow?"

"I will be there a couple of months. My husband has some business to attend to, and I plan to visit my mother and sister at their estate near Cracow."

"How long have you lived here?" Wanda asked.

"Six years already. I'm so homesick for my family that I can hardly wait to see them."

Soon the woman left and everyone went to the dining room for supper.

Kazimir said to Sophie, "I hate this Khmelsky woman, and her husband too. They are nouveau-riche boors, affecting aristocratic airs. What do you have in common with them?"

"They are going to Cracow, and I want them to deliver a letter to our lawyer. You always jump to hasty conclusions about people."

Wanda listened as her sister and Kazimir finished their discussion about the Khmelskys and began talking about their other acquaintances. Later, she went to her room and sat down to write a letter to Stefan. She had gone through so much that she did not know where to begin, how to explain the reason for her silence. She wrote a few lines, tore up the page, and began writing again.

Finally, she finished the letter. It was a one-page note:

Dear Stefan,

Please forgive me for my long silence, but there are many reasons for it. My father died, and I was sick for a long time. I am now living with my sister, but I do not have any friends. I am planning to go to college soon.

It is impossible for me to go to Poland alone because I am a minor. If my sister goes to Poland, though, I will go with her. Maybe we will see each other next year. Do you still remember me? I have very warm memories of you—you were so kind to me. I didn't think that everything would turn out the way it did.

Please write to me. I will answer your letter as soon as I can. I am sending this letter with Mrs. Khmelsky, and you can give her your reply, too.

Wishing you all the best, I am

Affectionately yours,
Wanda

She re-read the letter several times, then put it into an envelope and addressed it. She was still thinking of Stefan before she went to bed, picturing him reading her letter. She fell asleep, dreaming of him.

Mrs. Khmelsky came by two days later, and Wanda asked her if she could deliver the letter to her friend in Cracow.

"With pleasure," Mrs. Khmelsky replied, noting Wanda's beautiful handwriting on the envelope.

Sophie gave Mrs. Khmelsky her letter also. After the woman left, Sophie said, "It seems like Kazimir was right. There is something unpleasant about her."

"No, on the contrary," replied Wanda, "she is very kind. It was nice of her to take my letter."

Fall was upon them, but the weather was still very warm. On the college grounds, a noisy group of young men occupied the benches, and Wanda was among them. Her first week of college had already gone by. She found school and her art studies enjoyable, in spite of the fact that only three of the students were girls.

Time flew. Wanda took pleasure in her classes and pursued her studies with enthusiasm. She was often praised for her talent in art, for her ability to make sketches from nature, and her realistic renderings of her compositions.

Wanda's sculpture class was taught by an elderly gentleman. His office was cluttered with numerous statues, group compositions and sketches. She found herself fascinated by everything he talked about. An eighty-year-old man, she thought, but what a bright mind he still possesses! What rich experiences this man has had!

Wanda's class visited a museum of mechanical mannequins, the likes of which she had never seen before. In one room was a figure of a young sleeping beauty that appeared to be alive—her bosom moved as if she were breathing, and her head rotated slowly from side to side. A little devil sat on her chest, flicking his little red tongue. The figure was entitled "Nightmare," and the guide explained that the "lady" was experiencing a nightmare.

Another figure depicted an old woman. With her disheveled hair under her kerchief, she looked like a witch. She was holding an infant by the legs and throwing him into a blazing oven. The woman performed the act repeatedly. She had been given bastards to kill, and the scene appeared so life-like that Wanda felt suffocated. The countess's face flashed through her mind, then that of the old woman. She fell to the floor, unconscious.

When she came to in the entrance hall, she was surrounded by her fellow students. She apologized for the incident. The guide nearby said that many people could not watch these figures because they were so strikingly life-like.

When she arrived home, Wanda could remember nothing else about the museum. All she felt was a consuming weakness.

Christmas was coming, and Wanda was helping her sister decorate a Christmas tree while they waited for their guests.

"Whom did you invite?" Wanda asked.

"Just four families and one widower—Mr. Stanishevsky. He and Kazimir were once friends. His wife died three years ago during childbirth."

"Did the baby survive?"

"No, it died also."

"What a pity. He has lost both his wife and child. Have I seen him before in our house?"

"No, he left for Europe right after his wife's death, and has just recently returned."

"By the way, Sophie, I wanted to ask you if you've heard from Mrs. Khmelsky. She must be back by now."

"Tomorrow, when we're at church, I'll ask her friend about her. She should know because the Khmelskys asked her to look after their house."

The tree was almost completely decorated. Only six garlands remained to hang, and they had yet to fix the candles. Wanda enjoyed decorating the Christmas tree. She liked this holiday and was cheerfully dancing and whirling around with the children, singing Christmas carols. She had been invited to a party by her classmates, but she refused, having promised her sister that she would spend Christmas with her.

The whole family went to church together. It was packed with people, everyone dressed in their finest clothes. The men sat on one side of the church and the women on the other. Sophie and Wanda moved close to the altar and took their seats. Kazimir sat across from them with their two sons. The third son, only three and a half years old, was left at home.

Before the service, Sophie tried to find Mrs. Khmelsky's friend. Suddenly, she saw Mrs. Khmelsky and smiled and waved.

"Look, Wanda, there's Mrs. Khmelsky. We'll drop by her place after the service."

Wanda looked at the smiling lady, and the smile disappeared from the heavy face. "What's wrong with her?" Wanda thought. "She seems embarrassed."

The service began. The organ was playing, and the church choir sounded at once inspiring and solemn. Wanda prayed zealously as usual, but between prayers, her thoughts were carrying her away to her meeting with Mrs. Khmelsky, and what Stefan had written.

The service ended, and the crowd moved slowly to the exit. Mrs. Khmelsky waited for them in the aisle.

"How do you do, dear madam? When did you arrive?" Sophie inquired. "Last night. That is why I didn't have time to see you."

"You're probably tired after the trip. Why don't you rest and then come see us and tell us about Cracow, the news in Poland, and other business."

"No, I'm not very tired, and if you don't mind, I'll pay you a visit this afternoon."

"Do come. We'll wait for you."

Mrs. Khmelsky and Sophie continued to talk. Wanda stood beside them, and Mrs. Khmelsky seemed not to notice her, as if she were not there. Wanda controlled herself enough not to ask questions.

Kazimir had been sitting in a sled with his sons, waiting for his wife and sister-in-law. When they finally came and got into the sled, he asked what had taken them so long. Sophie said that they had met Mrs. Khmelsky and that she would come visit them after dinner to tell them about Poland. Kazimir said nothing.

All the way back home, Wanda thought about how she would be given the letter. In her mind, she already saw the letter clearly, its pages filled with writing.

During dinner she ate almost nothing. She was nervous, but she kept it to herself. How slowly dinner goes, she thought. After dinner, Kazimir left to take a nap, and the children were put to bed. Sophie and Wanda went to the living room to wait for Mrs. Khmelsky.

"It will be interesting to hear the lawyer's response," Sophie mused. "I wonder if it will be necessary to go to Cracow to draw up the inheritance?"

"If it were necessary to go to Poland, I would be glad to go. What about you, Sophie? Do you want to go to Poland?"

"I can't decide myself whether to go or not. It all depends on how things go for Kazimir's business. We can't possibly go to Cracow without him; the trip is too long and tiresome. I would like to go, though, just to see how things have changed."

At that moment, Mrs. Khmelsky arrived. Sophie offered her a chair and eagerly asked about the news from Poland.

"Here is the letter from your attorney. He's a German and seems to be a very intelligent man," Mrs. Khmelsky said, handing over the letter to Sophie. "Cracow hasn't changed much, but my mother has been feeling very ill, and my sister has her fair share of troubles. I left with an uneasy feeling in my heart that I would not be seeing my mother again," she lamented, pressing a handkerchief to her eyes.

"How old is your mother?" Sophie asked.

"She's 78 years old. She used to be so energetic, and I always thought that she would remain that way."

Wanda and Sophie exchanged glances. Mrs. Khmelsky turned to Wanda. "As to your letter, sweetie, I could not deliver it personally, because your friend had gone on a honeymoon trip. I left the letter to be given to him upon his return, so that he could answer you himself."

"Why did you leave the letter behind if you couldn't deliver it personally?" Wander cried. She rose and went to the door. Wanda heard Mrs. Khmelsky and Sophie talking in the background, but she went to her bedroom without looking back.

Her cheeks were on fire. Her feelings of bitterness and insult were suffocating her. "Kazimir was right," she thought, "she really is an unpleasant person." She fell on the bed and burst into tears, the pillow muffling her sobs. "Everything goes against me," she cried to herself. "Why am I so punished?"

Wanda calmed down enough to think of Stefan and how tender he had been to her. "Who is she, his new chosen? Is she beautiful?" Her tears slowly rolled down her cheeks. She was not sobbing anymore but continued to cry quietly. She found two of his letters and reread them. "Obviously, he didn't love me, if he could forget me so soon," she thought, and with that thought she felt more at ease.

Grabbing the statue of an Indian buddha that Stefan had given her, Wanda threw it out the open window to the garden below. She stood in front of the mirror and tossed her long braided hair behind her back. She thought, "Everyone thinks I am so beautiful, but why must I suffer so? Now Stefan is in my past." She walked away from the mirror with a thousand thoughts running through her mind.

Wanda's nephew knocked and entenred the room to study a new song with her. Christmas was just around the corner, and he and Wanda wanted to learn the song as a surprise for his parents.

Christmas Eve arrived. Wanda was in the living room with her nephews, greeting the guests in front of the sparkling Christmas tree. The children were dressed up in velvet suits and white shirts with ruffled fronts, solemnly surveying the scene. The guests continued to arrive, one after the other. They were friends of Sophie and Kazimir, and Wanda recognized most of them. Then a young man appeared that Wanda had not seen before. He was tall and blonde, sporting a small moustache. He introduced himself to Wanda as "Tadeush Stanishevsy." She liked the steadiness of his blue eyes.

They sat at the table side by side, Wanda quietly observing him. He had aristocratic manners and was very charming. When the formal celebrations of the evening had ended, everyone moved to the living room.

Music was playing on the gramophone, and couples danced under the glow of the candlelight from the tree. Wanda was dancing with Tadeush.

"You dance so gracefully," he remarked. "Have you studied dance?"

"Yes," Wanda answered, "we were taught to dance while I was still in school."

"When I came back from Europe, I heard that Sophie had a beautiful sister, but I did not imagine how beautiful."

"Thank you for the compliment," Wanda said, smiling.

"It wasn't meant as a compliment. You really are strikingly beautiful. You look like a Madonna to me."

Wanda blushed and lowered her eyes. She did not answer. Something had stirred in her heart—something she had not felt in a long time. She was flattered that such an elegant young man was so enamored of her.

Tadeush went on. "You are so well brought up and modest. Usually beautiful women are very spoiled and arrogant. I heard from Sophie that your mother died when you were very young and that your father died before his time. By the way, what do you do Wanda? What is your calling?"

Wanda told him about her passion for painting, her college, and her fascination with drawing which dated back to early childhood. Despite their age difference—he was about 11 years older than she—they understood each other very well. It was interesting for them just to talk to each other.

Sophie noticed Tadeush's interest in Wanda and whispered to Kazimir, "With God's help, it could be a brilliant match."

Kazimir replied, "He is not a fool. He realizes the unspoiled flower he has in his hands."

Tadeush invited everyone present to celebrate the New Year at his home. Only Sophie and her husband acceptd. Everyone else had already been invited to other parties.

When the time came to leave, Tadeush kissed Wanda's hand and said, "I thank you for the pleasant evening. It has been a long time since I've had such a good time. Till our next meeting, I will be glad to see you in my home." Wanda made a slight curtsy, her face lit by a happy smile.

As soon as the door had closed after the last guest, Sophie embraced Wanda and whirled around the room with her. "You can't even imagine what kind of man he is. He is intelligent, clever, very rich, young and a widower. What did you two talk about? I noticed that you impressed him."

Wanda just shrugged her shoulders, saying that they were just talking about different things.

"Don't draw hasty conclusions," Kazimir interrupted, "and most important of all, do not show that you are too interested in him. As to you Wanda, I'll tell you to be yourself—that's all he needs; I know him well."

After Christmas, Sophie and Wanda busied themselves selecting dresses for the New Year's party at Tadeush's. Sophie had forgotten to ask how many people would be at the party and was concerned about looking as good as everyone else. Wanda wanted to avoid wearing a bright colored dress, and she selected a light brown velour dress with a lace cape to wear. It was both demure and elegant.

New Year's Eve came at last. Wanda seemed completely calm outwardly, but inside she felt very anxious. Only her cold hands betrayed her state of mind. Wanda, Sophie and Kazimir climbed into the sled waiting for them at the central entrance to the house. With their fur coats shielding them from the cold night air, the three of them went off to celebrate the New Year.

As the sled glided across the snow, each of them was thinking private thoughts. What would this new year bring? What changes?

Tadeush met them at the entrance, wearing a well-cut black suit. Wanda was surprised that Tadeush himself, and not the butler, was welcoming the guests.

"Oh, we are the first!" Sophie exclaimed. "It's better than to be after everybody else."

"You are the first and the last, because I have invited nobody except you.

You are my only guests. How about that?" Tadeush smiled.

"I am very touched, Tadeush. That is very sweet," Sophie answered.

"What about you, Wanda. Do you like noisy company?" he asked.

"Oh, no, the fewer people, the more relaxed I am."

"Well wonderful! Now I know the ladies' opinion, and your opinion I already knew," he said to Kazimir.

Everyone walked to the living room, where a small Christmas tree stood near one of the windows. It was a huge hall.

"Please, make yourselves comfortable. I decorated the tree by myself because I have forgotten how to do this. I dismissed my butler and all the servants today. There is only a cook and one servant left.

"Sophie, I remember that you play Dvorzak well. Won't you play for us?"

"With pleasure, if I haven't forgotten. I don't play very often these days."

"I have music sheets that will refresh your memory."

Sophie went to the grand piano. She was still graceful and elegant; her figure had changed little in spite of having had three children. She played well. Wanda's eyes swept from the grand piano to the tastefully decorated hall. Sophie's house was considered to be elegant. She and Kazimir had their own carriage, a cook, a governess and a maid.

Tadeush's home was aristocratic. The feeling pervaded the house, yet it was not pompous.

Tadeush sat at the piano after Sophie had finished playing and performed several pieces by Schumann. It was obvious that he was an accomplished pianist. Sophie joined him at the piano to sing while he accompanied her. Kazimir joked that the next number was theirs—that he would play and Wanda would sing.

The four of them remained in the hall until dinner time. Tadeush recounted the stories of his travels through Europe. He had been to France, Germany, Switzerland and England. He had also spent a month in Poland before coming back to Odessa.

"My lawyer called me, so I was unable to visit Italy and Spain. Perhaps I'll be able to go next year."

The servant announced that the food was ready, and everyone was invited to the table.

They toasted the old year. Wanda sat next to Tadeush. She did not feel shy around him, but she still felt tense. She realized that she liked him, but fear gripped her. Her past still held her.

She saw again Mikhas's face just as it had appeared to her in the cemetery, Countess Gdansky's face and her hand as she removed the ring and handed it to Wanda—the price she had paid for Wanda's child. Wanda had gained her freedom but could not feel it. Many times she awoke, haunted by nightmares.

The last few minutes of the year were running out. As the new year drew near, they rose and lifted their glasses.

"We are drinking, ladies and gentlemen, to this new year," Tadeush said. "Let it be better than all the previous ones!"

The clock struck, and everyone held his breath. One, two, three … twelve. Hurrah! The new year of 1907 had arrived!

When the time came to leave, it was already morning. Everyone felt tired and slightly drunk. Parting with Wanda, Tadeush, kissing her hand, said that he was grateful to her for the evening and asked her if she would mind going to the opera.

"With pleasure," she answered.

Later, lying in her bed, Wanda fought sleep. She remembered Tadeush's piano playing, his laughter, and how he had touched her hand to his lips. Drowsiness finally overcame her, and she fell asleep, dreaming sweet dreams. … She was walking in a park in Cracow with Tadeush; then she was dancing with him in a spacious hall. She felt weightless, wrapped in his embrace. When she awoke, she still had that pleasant feeling, warm and tender.

In a few days, Tadeush came for Wanda, and they went to the theater. When they entered the theater, all eyes were on Wanda. Tadeush was a prominent and wealthy member of society, and his associations were always matters of interest. He had received numerous invitations to celebrate the new year but had refused them all. Now everyone understood the reason for his refusal. Everyone could see, not without envy, that this beautiful girl, as graceful and elegant as she was, could not have suited Tadeush better. He introduced her to a few acquaintances and saw the impression Wanda made. The young men were whispering as they passed: "She is as beautiful as a princess. What a lucky man. Where did he find her?"

Tadeush and Wanda walked to their box and took their seats. Wanda looked at the <u>parterre</u>[3] and saw a pair of binoculars pointed in her direction. She could make out the face of a blonde girl behind the binoculars. The girl took the binocular away from her eyes, and Wanda suddenly felt sick. It was Zosia! She was sitting in the first row of the <u>parterre</u>, next to an officer. Wanda felt so dizzy she could hardly control herself. She immediately looked in the other direction.

"What should I do?" she thought. "We must leave during the first intermission, because Zosia will surely make her presence known."

Wanda knew that such a spoiled and selfish person as Zosia would do anything to ruin her relationship with Tadeush. Wanda looked obviously nervous, her face blushing a deep red. Tadeush noticed something was wrong and asked her whether she was comfortable.

Don't pay attention to all the curious people," he chided her.

"It's just a little stuffy in here," she replied, fanning herself.

The performance had already begun, and Wanda listened inattentively, thinking about what she could use as an excuse for leaving after the first act. Just then, Tadeush bent over and whispered how charming she looked. She was dressed in a low-cut evening gown trimmed with elegant lace, with a double string of pearls wrapped around her neck. Her hair, piled high on her head, fell in luxuriant curls down to the middle of her back.

The first act was coming to an end. Wanda turned to Tadeush and whispered that she had a headache and wanted to leave during the first intermission. Tadeush nodded, and as soon as the curtain had been lowered, they moved to the exit. In the carriage on the ride home, Tadeush asked her what was wrong and if he could be of some help.

Wanda replied that she had noticed a certain girl in the theater hall whom she did not want to meet, adding, "Don't ask me about her, please."

"I understand you are upset. Where should we go now? It's still much too early to go home. Why don't we go to my place, if you don't mind?" Wanda did not mind, and they left for Tadeush's home.

He showed her his library, which contained several thousand volumes. Included were many unique editions and rare books. Tadeush told her that his father had started the library. In his youth he had been enthusiastic about collecting unique and rare books.

Tadeush and Wanda went to the living room for some coffee. Tadeush noticed how relaxed Wanda had become. Not a shadow of anxiety showed on her face. He realized that he liked her very much.

The clock struck eleven.

"It's time for me to go home," she said. "I'm very sorry I didn't give you a chance to listen to the end of the opera."

"Wanda, it was one of the best evenings I've had for many years. If you don't mind, I would like to look at your drawings tomorrow. I want to know better that passion of yours, your inside world."

"Of course you can look at them. There aren't many of my early drawings here—most of them were left in Cracow. Tadeush, I want to ask you to do something for me. Please don't mention to Sophie that we left the theater early. I don't want her asking any unnecessary questions because she is an acquaintance of that girl."

"I understand quite well. I won't say a word."

He escorted her home. When they reached the door, he bent down and kissed her on the lips. Wanda, being very shy, lowered her eyes.

I'll see you tomorrow," Tadeush said, kissing her hand. "Good night." Sophie was waiting for her. "Well, how was it? How was the opera? How about Tadeush? Are you happy together?"

"Everything is all right. He will be here tomorrow. He wants to see my drawings."

"Do you think he's in love with you?"

"I have no idea. I know that I like him, and it seems to me that he likes me, too. That's all I can say."

"That's a lot already. I'll pray to the Virgin Mary for you. I hope she'll listen to my prayers."

Tadeush arrived at two o'clock the following day. He and Wanda sat in the living room together, looking at her drawings and sketches. Tadeush was particularly interested in paintings and examined the album with special care.

"You have a natural ability to capture the environment around you. You are only lacking schooling. I think you made the right decision to study art. You have talent and you have to develop it. What are your plans for the future?"

"I will go to college for two years, and then I'll see. My professor has suggested that I go to Paris, but Sophie will not hear of me going there alone."

"She's right. You're only seventeen, and you shouldn't go alone, especially to Paris."

"As you see, my plans are limited. I think I'll benefit from attending college right here."

Putting the drawings aside, the two of them continued to talk for several hours. Sophie called them to eat. Wanda and Tadeush exchanged surprised glances, not realizing how quickly the time had passed.

Christmas vacation ended, and Wanda was back in college. She and Tadeush continued to see each other often. Sophie had no doubts that Tadeush was in love with Wanda and had serious intentions toward her. She tried many times to find out if Wanda loved him, but Wanda always gave the answer: "I like him very much; don't ask me about it all the time." Wanda couldn't confess that she loved Tadeush, even to her sister.

"Oh, how she loved him! She was pulled to him as though by a magnet. She had lost her heart to him a long time ago and could not imagine her future without him. She and Tadeush never talked about love, although they felt it. Tadeush often met her after classes, greeting her with flowers. It seemed to him that he had never loved another woman, that Wanda was his first love.

It was already springtime, the end of March. Wanda and Tadeush walked along the street, hand in hand.

Tadeush said, "I want to talk seriously with you. Let's go to my place if you want."

"As you wish. Let's go to your house," Wanda replied quietly.

Tadeush did not notice how pale she had become. She guessed what he wanted to talk about and knew that she would have to tell him her horrible secret. Fear possessed her. How she had waited for this moment, but how she had feared it at the same time!

Tadeush led Wanda into the small living room of his house. It was a cozy oval room with soft, plush furniture. Tadeush invited Wanda to sit down on the couch. He sat next to her and took her hands in his.

"I think you can guess what I'm going to talk about."

Wanda lowered her head and kept silent. He went on.

"I love you. These aren't just words to me. I feel them very deeply. When I leave you, I miss you all the time. You know, Wanda, I'm not a boy anymore. I'm 28 years old, and I've been married. I hardly knew my wife, but it seemed to me that I loved her. She died giving birth to our child, and the baby died soon afterward. I thought I would never recover from the terrible shock. After I moved abroad, I began to feel somewhat more alive, but I felt that my life would never be as before. When I met you, I felt immediately that you would be a new life for me. I love not only your beauty but your interests, your kindness, your character."

He brought her hand to his lips.

"I'm asking you to be my wife. If you love me as I do you, we will be happy together. I truly believe it."

He kissed her hand and looked into her eyes. Tears were falling from her eyes and streaming down her cheeks.

"What's wrong with you?" he asked. "Why are you crying? Have I offended you with my declaration of love?"

"Oh, no, you didn't offend me," she said softly. "I love you, too. I love you with all my soul, but I cannot be your wife."

Tadeush, astonished, held her hands and stared into her eyes.

"Why, if you love me? Who can forbid you to be my wife? You don't have parents, and Sophie wouldn't object."

"No, it's not that. I can't tell you the reason."

"You probably gave your word to someone else, and you can't break it?"

"I didn't give anybody any promises. I have nobody."

"What is it then? I want to understand. You love me; I love you. There's nobody between us who could stop us. And now you're saying you can't. What is it? Maybe I can help you."

"No one can help me. I have to go home. I can't talk anymore."

Wanda broke into tears. Tadeush pressed her to him, and she cried on his chest.

"Please tell me what's wrong. My heart is breaking from the pain." He stroked her hair, but she kept on crying.

"My darling, my only one, I beg you to calm down. You can say nothing, if you wish, but just don't cry."

Wanda began to calm down a little. Her handkerchief was wet, so Tadeush gave her his own. Finally, she started to talk.

"I knew I had to tell you sooner or later about what happened to me. You can decide for yourself whether I can be your wife or not.

"You remember that I asked to leave the theater during the first intermission? I was afraid to meet a girl who was responsible for my misfortune."

Wanda proceeded to tell him everything about what happened to her and how it coincided with the day of her father's death. She was no longer crying but speaking quietly, her voice trembling. She omitted only the part about the baby.

"Where is he now?" Tadeush demanded. "This man is a criminal who'll be held responsible for his crime."

"He's gone. He died a year ago."

"Oh, my God. This is unheard of. My poor girl, what you have gone through. Sophie knows nothing of this?"

"No, nobody knew, because our father died the same day. Nobody cared about me."

"Now I understand why you didn't want to meet that vile person. What meanness, what craftiness! You don't have to worry about a thing. I love you as before, even more now. How you must have suffered, alone, in your grief!

My love, my only one." He kissed her forehead, her eyes and cheeks. "Be my wife, I beg you!"

She smiled a little, and nodded. Having told him about that awful day, she allowed the part about the birth of her baby to go unspoken.

They left for Wanda's riding in a carriage, Tadeush kissing her hands, using the most tender words.

Sophie, as always, waited for her. She noticed Wanda's red eyes and, concerned, asked what had happened.

"He asked me to be his wife, and tomorrow he will talk to you."

"And you cried! Oh, Wanda, my dear! The Lord has answered my prayers. I'm so happy for you that I could cry too!" She hugged her sister, tears streaming down her face.

"You must rest. Tomorrow is a very important day. I must tell Kazimir the wonderful news."

Sophie, Tadeush and Kazimir discussed their plans for several hours. Wanda was finally called in when the official arrangements had been agreed upon. It was decided that the engagement should last a month, and that the time should be spent with only a close circle of relatives and friends. The wedding was scheduled for the fall, with a honeymoon trip to Italy to follow.

Wanda could not believe her good luck. She was to be married to such a noble man. Her heart trembled with excitement, but she was able to control herself and conceal her feelings.

The engagement party was held at Tadeush's house. The newlyweds were presented and declared to be a bride and bridegroom. Then Tadeush put the ring on Wanda's finger. The music began to play, and the couples flocked to the dance floor. The bridegroom was dancing with the bride, whispering tender words in her ear. Wanda lowered her head, blushing.

"All the men are jealous of me and keep telling me how lucky I am. They compare you to a mountain flower, tender and fragrant. We will be so happy together. I want you to be very happy with me."

"I'm happy already. I want this evening to be endless."

He pressed her to him, and she put her head on his shoulder.

The guests began to leave the party, one by one. Everyone wished the host all the best. The last ones to leave were Sophie with her husband, and Wanda.

"Well, Tadeush, now we are relatives," said Sophie, bidding him farewell. "I am glad to have such a brother-in-law as you."

Tadeush kissed her hand. "Thank you so much for giving me your younger sister." He kissed Wanda, and they parted.

In the carriage on the way home, Sophie was saying how there was so much business to attend to. There was not much time between April and August.

Time really was flying. Tadeush went to Europe on business. Wanda's wedding dress was ordered from Paris. Sophie was busy preparing the dowry for her sister, and seamstresses were working from morning until night embroidering linen. Monogrammed blankets were ordered from the nuns. When Tadeush came back from Europe, he had all the papers legalized for their trip to Italy.

One Sunday, Tadeush invited Wanda to his house and asked her what she would like to change, according to her taste. Wanda did not want change to a thing. The white bedroom set looked elegant against the light lilac colored walls.

When they were through looking over the house, Wanda and Tadeush went for a long, slow walk along the seaside boulevard. Tadeush talked, and Wanda just listened. The weather was wonderful, and there was a light breeze from the sea that made the summer heat more bearable.

They were approaching the monument of the Duke de Risheley in the center of the boulevard when someone suddenly blocked their way. They stopped, and in front of them was Zosia. Tadeush looked at Wanda and saw a pallor come over her face. She squeezed his hand. He understood at once who she was. He did not have time to ask what she wanted before Zosia started to talk.

"My name is Zosia. I used to be Wanda's friend, but for some reason, she got angry with me. I have heard that you are going to get married soon. Since I haven't received an invitation, let me take this opportunity to congratulate you. Mr. Stanishevsky, you honor Wanda by making her your wife. Her tastes haven't always been so fastidious. My former salesman friend. . ."

At once, Wanda swung her hand and with all her strength slapped Zosia across her face. The blow was so strong and sudden that Zosia lost her balance. She fell down, her hat rolling down the pavement. Tadeush bent over her and said, "My future wife has grown even more before my eyes. If she hadn't slapped you, I would have. I'd like to meet Mr. Svitsky and tell him something about his daughter's adventures."

Zosia lay slumped on the ground, supporting herself with both hands. Tadeush and Wanda passed around her and went on without looking back. They walked up to the end of the boulevard in silence, and then got into a carriage.

Wanda's hand trembled. Tadeush embraced her shoulders.

"Don't worry, my dear. She won't harrass you anymore. You can be sure of that."

The following Sunday they visited the cemetery. Wanda put flowers on her father's grave. She cried silently, her lips moving in prayer. Tadeush moved to a side pathway, so as not to disturb her. Finishing her prayer, Wanda rose from her knees and whispered, addressing the grave: "Daddy, I'm getting married; you would like him. You would bless us." She walked over to Tadeush, wiping her tears away with her handkerchief. Tadeush took her arm.

While they rode home in the carriage, Tadeush said, "It's difficult to lose one's parent when you're older. I was still very young when my parents died a tragic death. I have my uncle and his wife in Warsaw, and I call them father and mother. They never had children of their own. My uncle is my mother's brother. His wife is a very kind and noble lady. They're quite old, but I'm very close to them. It's terrible to even think that I'll lose them someday. But that's life, and there's nothing we can do about it. They'll be coming in two weeks, a week before the wedding. You'll have the opportunity to know them well."

"You never said they were your parents." Wanda said.

"I never had a chance to tell you about it. I mentioned to you what led me to Odessa, didn't I? When my uncle on my father's side died, he left me all of his fortune and the house, too. He was a bachelor and my father's only brother. I only saw him once in my life, when he came to Warsaw. I was seventeen years old then, and I was only twenty-one when he died. I didn't even know that he had left all his fortune to me. I moved to Odessa after he died, but thought I would return to Warsaw after the inheritance papers were legalized. But I like it here, and I began to sort out my uncle's business a little. So, I stayed. I go to Western Europe several times a year on business. After my wife's death, I stayed there for three years. I thought I would never come back. Then, my attorney called me, and I didn't mind at all that I came back, because I met you."

They arrived at Sophie's house, and he accompanied her to the door. "See you tomorrow, my darling," he said, kissing her.

Tadeush's aunt and uncle from Warsaw arrived a week before the wedding.

Tadeush brought Wanda to the house to meet them. Wanda felt very shy, but he cheered her up, saying that they were old darlings and that she would like them.

A doorman opened the door and Tadeush and Wanda entered the hall. His parents rose to meet them.

"Let's get acquainted! This is my fiancee, Wanda. These are my honorable parents."

Wanda curtsied and came over to greet them. Everyone moved to the living room.

"We are so happy that our son has made such a good choice," said Tadeush's mother. "When did you leave Poland? Where did you live there?"

"I came here two years ago from Cracow."

"I used to visit Cracow often," Tadeush's father said. "What is your father's name?"

"Vladek Rudzinsky. I came over here with him to visit my older sister."

"Is your father a lawyer, by chance?"

"Yes, he was a lawyer. He died a few months after we arrived."

"I knew him well. We met several times. I heard that his beautiful wife had died. Please accept my condolences, young lady. Your father left a good memory behind." To Tadeush, he said, "Your fiancee is from a good family, and that is important to us. Besides, she is also a beauty."

Tadeush smiled, and Wanda was embarrassed. Tadeush's mother took Wanda by the arm and led her on a tour of the house. "Let the men talk without us. I want to see how my son lives here. To tell you the truth, we have never been here before. We didn't come for his first wedding. My husband was against that match."

They walked from room to room. The dining room table was being set for dinner, and Tadeush's mother thought the food smelled delicious.

"I certainly do like this house. It's as nice as the one we have in Poland." They went back to the living room, and soon a servant announced that dinner was ready.

The dinner proceeded very pleasantly. They all praised the cook, the choice of food, and especially the girl Tadeush was taking for his wife.

Sophie invited all of them to dinner the next evening. As Wanda's older sister, she felt responsible for the wedding. Furthermore, with their parents gone, she felt the added burden of being both mother and father to Wanda. As the wedding drew closer, Sophie grew more worried.

Sophie supervised everything for the dinner at her home, right down to how the table was laid. When the preparations were complete, Wanda came down from her room to see Sophie.

"Oh, Wanda, I'm more nervous than I've ever been," Sophie said. "I can imagine how excited you are. During my wedding preparations I was not so nervous, probably because I was younger then, and father was still alive."

"Sure, I'm nervous. It's only natural. But with Tadeush I'm sure of myself. He gives me strength. I can't even describe my feelings to you. It's more than love. Oh, Sophie, I'm so happy I could embrace the whole world."

"You look much calmer than I am. How can you stay so calm? You have father's character and mother's looks. Turn around. Let me look at you. Everything fits well. I like your dress. The cherry color suits you." Sophie talked rapidly, as usual, trying not to forget anything.

Soon, Tadeush and his parents arrived. The two families sat in the living room and got to know each other better. Tadeush took Sophie's younger son in his arms. Wanda had noticed before that when he was at their house, Tadeush liked to talk to the children and bring them gifts.

Tadeush leaned toward Wanda and said, "He has always been a patriot and wants all Poles to live in Poland."

Kazimir said that he thought they would move to Poland the next year but, noticing Wanda's inquisitive look, added that he did not know for sure.

As they left, Tadeush's parents thanked Sophie and Kazimir for an evening well spent and for the excellent dinner. Tadeush's mother embraced Wanda.

"Be sure you rest, my darling. It is a great event you are going to have in a week."

When the door closed after the guests, Wanda retreated to her quarters. Walking upstairs, she overheard Sophie ask Kazimir when they were going to Poland and why he had not said something about it before. Wanda did not wait to hear the answer but entered her room.

A maid knocked at the door and asked whether Wanda needed any help undressing. Wanda said that she did, and the maid came in. The maid was a middle-aged Polish woman, but she was very energetic.

"Ah, young lady, how lucky you are," she said, unbuttoning Wanda's dress. "A person so young and beautiful as you could get even a prince. I watched today as I was helping serve dinner. How happy they all were that young master is taking you for a wife! And you were a flower among them all!"

Wanda smiled, saying nothing.

"You've been quiet ever since you've been here," the maid continued. "I haven't heard a loud word from you. The Lord rewarded you with a good character. He gave you happiness too. I pray for you and for Sophie's family so that you will always be in good health."

"Thank you, Hannah, you are a kind woman." When she had undressed, Wanda let down her hair, and Hannah left, bidding her good night. Wanda stood in her nightgown in front of the mirror and combed her hair. It was very long and thick. She was always receiving compliments about her hair, and Tadeush delighted in it.

Her hair combed and braided, Wanda went to bed and read. She found herself thinking about many things and was unable to catch the meaning of what she was reading. She put the book aside and turned the lights off. She could not fall asleep. She lay awake, remembering everything, and trying to drive away the bitter memories. Her wedding would be in six days. Then, she and Tadeush would go to Italy.

She had never even dreamed about it. When she studied Italian paintings, she admired the genius of the Italian artists. Now she would have the opportunity to visit the homeland of Leonardo da Vinci, Raphael, and Michelangelo.

Finally, she fell asleep. She dreamed of an orchard. The fruit trees were blooming. She was walking along a path, and her mother was walking toward her. How long it had been since she last saw her! She looked exactly like her portrait and surprisingly like Wanda herself. Her mother was smiling. Coming to Wanda, she took her by the hand and they walked together. Wanda asked, "Where is father? I want to tell him that I'm getting married."

"He knows everything, my child. We are so happy you are marrying a noble gentleman. Here is my wedding gift to you."

She opened a box and took some bracelets from it. They were a set of women's silver bracelets with different patterns on them. There were seven of them. Wanda's mother put them on Wanda's wrist herself and Wanda looked at them, fingering them one by one. She looked up to thank her mother, but for some reason she could not hear her own voice.

Wanda woke up. It was still early. She looked at her wrist where the bracelets had been and nothing was there.

"What a strange dream," she thought, "and how vividly I saw Mama and those bracelets." Now she was fully awake. She did not tell anyone about her dream.

The wedding day arrived. The ceremony was to be held in a large Polish church, and the reception would follow in the banquet hall at Tadeush's house. Eighty people had been invited, despite Wanda's objections. Sophie said there would be a lot of offended people anyway, so the number could not be less.

One of the maids, with two girls helping her, dressed Wanda. Two children, Sophie's son and the five-year-old daughter of an acquaintance, were to carry Wanda's train.

Finally, Wanda was ready. A carriage waited for them at the main entrance. Sophie looked Wanda over one more time, giving her last minute instructions.

Just then, someone knocked at the door. A messenger from the post office came in and held out a parcel addressed to Wanda. Sophie read the label but saw no return address. A maid cut away the paper and handed the box to Wanda. As she opened it, all eyes were upon her.

Suddenly, Wanda's face grew pale. She reached into the box and took out some silver bracelets. She looked for a card, but nothing was there. Wanda stood motionless, not saying a word.

The bracelets were exactly like the ones she had seen in her dream.

"Sophie, how many are there?" Wanda asked, her voice shaking.

"Seven. It's a lucky number. It's just strange that we don't know who sent them. Well, it's time to get in the carriage." No one had noticed Wanda's excitement.

The church was crowded. All the seats were filled. Tadeush stood waiting for Wanda. Taking her arm, he walked her to the altar.

"You worry too much," he whispered. "Your hands are cold. Calm down. It's only a ceremony."

"Yes, for some reason, I am worried." Wanda continued walking, keeping her eyes down. Her nerves were strained to the limit. She was oblivious to the stares of all the people in the church. The question hammered relentlessly in her mind: "Who sent the bracelets?"

At the altar, the priest asked them questions, and Tadeush and Wanda answered. It seemed to Wanda that the ceremony would last forever. At last, they were declared man and wife. The recessional march began, and Wanda and Tadeush turned to walk back down the aisle. Flowers were thrown at their feet. Someone outside was handing out money to beggars. They were congratulated from all sides. Sophie and Tadeush's mother were crying. Wanda and Tadeush got into the carriage and drove off to the reception at their house. The guests began to arrive in carriages decorated with flowers. The tables in the banquet room were arranged in a U shape, with two seats in the center for the bride and groom.

The guests took their seats. When Tadeush and Wanda entered the hall, everyone rose and greeted them with a boom of applause. The newlyweds took their seats, with Tadeush's parents on Wanda's side and Sophie and Kazimir beside Tadeush.

Champagne flowed and toasts were declared. The newlyweds kissed each other. The next toast was to the parents. Wanda again recalled the bracelets. Sophie put a handkerchief to her eyes, saddened that her parents were not alive to see Wanda's wedding.

Dinner was coming to an end. Strains of music could be heard in the next hall. Couples whirled around the dance floor, and the newlyweds disappeared without being noticed. Tadeush carried Wanda in his arms to their bedroom, her arms around his neck. Wanda was gripped with fear. Tadeush circled around the room with her and laid her down on the bed.

He tried to unbotton her dress. Wanda stopped him. "Please turn off the light. I feel shy."

The light was turned off. She forgot about everything. Nothing existed anymore; everything that surrounded them disappeared. They were alone in the world.

Morning light penetrated the curtains. Wanda awoke to see Tadeush looking at her, smiling.

"Today, my dear, we are going to Italy. Are your bags ready?"

"Yes, Hannah helped me pack them. Everything is ready."

Tadeush embraced her and whispered, "I wanted to tell you that I was the first one for you. That boy obviously had just been sitting beside you, and you were only frightened by it."

Wanda moved from him, her eyes wide open.

"Why are you looking at me like that? It's true!" He embraced her, pressing her to his body. She looked across his shoulder and the image of the countess and the crib where the baby lay flashed in front of her. She had the ring on her finger—she lifted her right hand and looked at it. It had happened, all of it, and she could not erase it from her memory.

Tadeush pressed her to him once more. "My love, my only one, I am the happiest man in the world." He kissed her all over, and she cried without making a sound. "Why are you crying? Have I insulted you?"

"No, my darling, I'm crying from happiness." Wanda mouthed a silent prayer: "Oh, mother of God, preserve and forgive. You have protected an orphan. I am so grateful to you." Then, she remembered the bracelets.

"Tadeush, I forgot to tell you that yesterday, before we left for the church, a messenger brought a package with my name on it. There was no return address. Inside was a box with bracelets in it, seven of them. They were women's bracelets, silver ones. Who could have sent them to me?"

"Probably, you have a secret admirer. You haven't seen all the rest of the presents yet. Maybe there's something interesting there also."

"Maybe," answered Wanda, thinking that it was just a strange coincidence. The steamer was due to leave at four o'clock, and they had only a few hours to get ready.

They looked over the presents before they said good-bye to their families. There was a variety of gifts: sets of china service, silver, crystal, figurines. All were elegantly wrapped, with cards bearing the names of people who had sent them. Only the little box containing the bracelets had no name.

Tadeush examined each of the bracelets, trying to find at least some clue on them. Finding nothing, he put them on Wanda's wrist.

"It doesn't matter who they're from. They're beautiful and elegant, and if you like them, wear them."

"Put them back in the box, please. They're a little heavy, and I won't take them to Italy. I want to put on a gold bracelet, the one that you gave me."

He took the gold bracelet from a velvet case and put it on her wrist.

"I'm very glad that you like it," he said and kissed her tenderly.

They did not have to say goood-bye at home because everyone wanted to go to the seaport. The sea was absolutely calm. Everyone commented on the good weather and hoped it promised Tadeush and Wanda a happy voyage.

Wanda wore a white lace dress and complemented her beautiful attire with a white purse and a white umbrella. Tadeush wore a white suit, white hat, and white gloves.

"Such a beautiful couple," said Tadeush's mother, bending toward Sophie. "I just can't take my eyes off them."

"They'll fly away now, just like two butterflies," Sophie said, sadly. "The steamer will carry them far from Odessa. Our honeymoon was in Paris. It was Kazimir's idea. I think it will be much more interesting for them in Italy."

"My darling," Kazimir said, "I remember you were fascinated by Paris. We went to the opera so often that I offered to move so we could live across from the theatre someday. You already forgot."

"No, I didn't forget. I liked Paris, but it seems to me that Italy is more romantic for newly married couples."

The steamer sounded its horn, and the newlyweds and their families parted. Sophie embraced Wanda and told her not to worry about anything. After an exchange of handshakes and kisses, Wanda and Tadeush were on deck, waving to those who had been left on shore.

The steamer gave two more piercing wails and sailed slowly away from the dock. Above the ship, seagulls cried. Wanda showed Tadeush how the gulls landed on the water, how skillfully they caught fish while on the wing.

"I like the sea very much," Wanda said. "It holds so many mysteries. What about you, darling?"

"Yes, the sea is romantic, but it can be severe. It is difficult to cope with. Still, there is nothing more beautiful. In Italy the sea is warmer, and it has a different color. I've read that at the shore of Capri the water is turquoise blue."

"Will we be on Capri, too?"

"Yes, we'll visit the south of Italy."

The day was ending, and they walked to their cabin. Later, while they sat in the restaurant, Tadeush told Wanda about Germany and Switzerland.

"Now," he said, "I have my wife, my dear Pani Stanishevskaia.

She smiled, and he bent down and kissed her hand.

What did she lack? She had everything that anyone could dream of. She was seventeen years old. She was beautiful, healthy, very rich, and she had a husband who worshipped her. What else could one demand from life? She was happy, content with everything.

But why could she not laugh? Why did she always catch herself? It had all happened too fast, too unexpectedly. Only a short time ago she had been miserable. She had felt no bond with the baby who had been taken by the countess. But the fact that the baby existed somewhere prevented her form being completely happy. Tadeush had been sent to her by God himself, and she loved him with all her being.

The sea was calm throughout the voyage, without even a small storm. They arrived in Italy after a few days. There, on that unfamiliar land, Wanda began to feel better.

The songs of gondoliers in Venice, melodious and beautiful, filled the air as the boats passed along the canals. It seemed that everything was filled with song. The Square of Saint Mark, with its wonderful, ancient cathedral, delighted Wanda.

They were in the square early one morning when Wanda, running, shouted to Tadeush, "Catch up with me!"

He reached her, took her in his arms, and, swinging her in circles, kissed her. She was seventeen years old, and now there was no shadow of sadness in her beautiful eyes.

"Tadeush, my dear, Venice is a miracle of nature. We will certainly have to come back here."

It was time to say good-bye to Venice. They were on their way to Florence. A carriage was loaded, and they bade farewell to Saint Mark's Square, gondolas, and gondoliers.

As they approached Florence, Wanda again was in high spirits.

"Here in Florence the great artists painted their immortal works," she said. We'll be able to see the originals."

"You like to draw, my dear," Tadeush answered, "and it has a special meaning for your. I have an idea. I just don't know whether you will like it or not. I would like to find an artist here in Florence who will paint your portrait. What we must know is how much time it will take."

"I like your idea. It will give us a memory of Italy that will last all our lives."

"And it will be a memory not only for us, but for our children and grandchildren."

Wanda smiled, laying her head on his shoulder. How happy she was with him!

They arrived in Florence at dark. Porters unloaded the carriage, and Wanda and Tadeush walked to the hotel. After a brief rest, they went to the restaurant. There, a very young Italian sang and played the guitar. He walked among the tables and sang in a warm voice.

When he reached the table where Wanda and Tadeush were sitting, he bent toward Wanda and asked, "What song do you want me to sing for you, bella donna?"

"Tadeush, what is he asking? I don't understand."

"He asked, 'What is it you wish for me to sing for you, beautiful lady?'" Tadeush did not understand Italian very well and did not speak it at all. "Tell him to sing something from a Giuseppe Verdi opera."

"Oh, madonna, you like Verdi! I will sing an aria from "Rigoletto" for you."

He began to sing. He had the voice of a professional. Everyone in the restaurant listened to him with pleasure. When he finished the aria, everyone applauded.

He again leaned toward Wanda and asked, "What else do you want me to sing? What would you like to listen to?"

Wanda grew embarrassed and looked at Tadeush. He was smiling.

Without waiting for an answer, the Italian started to sing another aria. He stayed by their table. Everyone in the restaurant watched the scene, waiting to see how it would end.

"Tadeush, let's leave. Everybody's looking at us," Wanda said, taking Tadeush's hand.

"Calm down, my dear," Tadeush said. "It does you credit. You are the most beautiful woman here, and he is singing about love and beauty for you. There are always a lot of gapers everywere."

The singer finished and, lowering his guitar, continued to look at Wanda. Then, shaking his head, he said, "Bella, bella."

Wanda again asked Tadeush if they could leave, and they rose to go. The Italian started talking very quickly about something, gesturing them to sit, and he left their table. But they moved to the exit without looking back.

"What tempers those Italians have. Did you see how his eyes glittered?" Tadeush asked. "A little bit longer, and I would have become jealous."

"Yes, you're right. So many emotions. So many gestures. But the voice— that is what's important. Perhaps the climate promotes it."

When they arrived for breakfast the next morning, the restaurant was filled with people. The singer from the night before sat at a table drinking coffee. Noticing them, he rose and walked to meet them. He spoke rapidly, placing his hand on his chest and lowering his head.

"It seems as though he's apologizing for yesterday's incident," Tadeush said. "But I don't know that for certain."

The Italian took Wanda's hand and put it to his lips. Tadeush called for a waiter.

"Do you speak anything besides Italian?" Tadeush asked the waiter. "I speak French, if you wish."

"Wonderful. Please translate. What does this young man want?"

The conversation between the two Italians was brief, half of it consisting of gestures.

The waiter translated, smiling, "Marcello says that he has never met such a beautiful girl. Last night, he composed a serenade and wants to sing it, if <u>signore</u> doesn't mind."

"Tell him I do mind. We want to have a quiet breakfast and then go to a museum. He can sing as much as he wants during the evening."

After listening to the translation, Marcello bowed and left their table.

"You see, my dear. They are ready to sing serenades for you early in the morning, and newly composed ones at that. What do you think about it?"

"I'm afraid of him. His eyes are glittering, just like Othello's. I only like his voice. I think I'll remember these Italians and their tempers for a long time."

After breakfast, they went to the museum. Wanda walked slowly from painting to painting, writing in her notebook. She gave her opinion, excitedly, about almost every work. When they had examined several halls, they left the museum, leaving further sightseeing for the next day.

Tadeush approached a museum attendant and addressed him in French. "When does the museum close?"

"We're open today until two o'clock," the attendant answered in rather good French.

"Could you recommend a good artist? I want him to paint my wife's portrait."

The attendant looked at Wanda.

"I'd want the portrait of such a beautiful woman as your wife to decorate our museum."

Wanda became embarrassed, but she thanked him for the compliment.

"I can name several artists," the attendant continued, "but you had better go to Maestro R. He's one of the best portraitists in the city."

"How can we find Maestro R.?"

"I can send a note to him by messenger. Tell me your name and where you're staying. Also, tell me when you are available."

"Thank you very much. I appreciate it. Here is the information you need," Tadeush said, writing everything necessary on a piece of paper. He handed the paper to the attendant.

The attendant, an elderly man of obliging appearance and good manners, looked little like an Italian. Well-fed and slightly round-shouldered, he was suited to the role of a priest. Even his quiet voice resembled that of a servant of the Church.

Tadeush and Wanda were walking toward the museum exit when the attendant called to them.

"I am sorry, Signior Stanishevsky, my name is Roberto Manelli. I forgot to introduce myself. I don't think Maestro R. knows any language except Italian. I can be of service to you."

"That's very kind of you, Signior Manelli," Tadeush said.

"Just call me Roberto, if you wish."

"It's all right with me, Signior Manelli," Tadeush said, smiling. "Tell me, where did you study French?"

"My mother was French, and I lived in France almost every summer at my grandmother's. When I was a young man, I lived in France for several years."

"Now I understand why you speak French so well. Thank you again for your service."

They left the museum on foot and continued walking.

"My darling," Wanda said, "let's have dinner in a different restaurant, and then we'll go to our room unnoticed."

"It's a good idea," Tadeush replied, "but our young singer will be very upset. Whom will he sing his serenade to?"

"Let him think we're not in the hotel. You're joking, of course, but I'm afraid of him."

"What are you afraid of? As long as I'm with you, nothing will happen to you."

They entered an open-air cafe. The atmosphere was pleasant there. Across from the cafe was a square, in the middle of which was a small fountain. Doves were pecking crumbs thrown by pedestrians and drinking water, unafraid of the fountain's splashing.

"Look, Tadeush," Wanda cried. "What a beautiful view!"

Wanda was as happy as a child with everything, and Tadeush very much liked that quality in her. After ordering wine and a light supper, the newlyweds sat and listened to the music. An elderly fiddler played, his violin crying mournfully and the bow shuddering. He walked to their table and started to play a rhapsody. Tadeush gave him some money and thanked him for playing.

After supper they went for a walk. They walked slowly, Tadeush holding Wanda's arm and she carrying a small umbrella. They were noticed because they were a beautiful couple. Tadeush wore a light colored suit and hat, and Wanda wore a light lilac-colored dress decorated with lace. The air was clear, and they walked, enjoying nature.

Only when it was growing dark did they return to the hotel and go upstairs to their room. No one was in the entrance hall, except clerks. Music could be heard from the restaurant, but soon that sound, too, subsided. The windows of their room faced the courtyard. The night was warm and quiet.

Tired from walking, they rested on the sofa. Suddenly, below the windows in the court, they heard a guitar, and Marcello started to sing his serenade.

"It's very strange," Tadeush said, shaking his head. "He saw that you are a married woman. I could understand this if you had been with your parents."

Wanda walked to the window and looked from behind a curtain in order not to be seen. She saw Marcello singing and people peeking from their windows to see who it was and to whom he was singing. She moved away from the window.

"Tomorrow we'll move to another hotel," she said.

"You're right," Tadeush said, "This singer could start a scandal because I could lose my temper. Come to me, my dear."

He placed her on his lap and put her head on his shoulder. Pressing a finger to his lips, he gestered for her to be silent. They sat in silence and listened until the serenade ended.

The singer's voice died away, and he disappeared as suddenly as he had appeared. The stillness of the night returned once again.

"I've listened to him," Wanda said, "and I think he is singing about our love, yours and mine. I am the happiest person in the world because you are here. Are you happy?"

"It's very difficult to convey in words how happy I am, how much I love you," Tadeush answered. He pressed her to him, took her in his arms, and carried her to the bedroom. Outside was the warm night of Florence.

Tadeush woke up first in the morning and decided to go to the manager with a request that they be moved to another hotel. After his morning shower, he dressed and looked at Wanda. Her long hair lay scattered on the pillow and framed her face and shoulders. Her face, with its faintly flushed cheeks, was as tender as a peach. Her mouth was open slightly like a small child's. How beautiful she was! He stood, admiring her, and was immeasurably happy.

Wanda stirred, awakened, perhaps, by his stare. She opened her eyes.

"You've dressed. Have I slept long?"

"No, I just got up early, and I was watching your sweet sleep. I'll go find out about moving to another hotel while you get ready."

Tadeush approached the clerk at the front desk, but had no time to ask for the manager before he was handed two envelopes. He opened the first one. In it was a note from Signior Manelli. He wrote that Maestro R would be at the hotel by eleven o'clock. Signior Manelli would accompany him and they would be able to arrange everything.

Tadeush opened the second envelope to find two folded pieces of paper. On one were the notes of a song; the other contained the words of a serenade and signature—Marcello.

"Restless Italian," Tadeush thought as he returned upstairs to the room. He gave up looking for the manager because Signior Manelli and the artist would be coming.

After breakfast, Tadeush and Wanda met the artist and interpreter in the hall. The artist, Maestro R, was a man of medium height and dark complexion in his early forties. He looked at Wanda with his light hazel eyes and, his stare fixed, seemed to be mentally transferring her image to the canvas.

After the ceremony of introduction and exchange of compliments, Maestro R said it would be his pleasure to paint the portrait of Signiora Stanishevsky.

"It is an honor for me to paint such a lady," he said. "It isn't often an artist comes across such a model."

They agreed that he would start to paint at ten o'clock the next morning, and the artist left.

Tadeush spoke to Signior Manelli. "Can you tell me where we can find a hotel closer to the artist's studio?"

"Certainly. My pleasure. If you are free, we can go now." The three of them left to see the new hotel.

"Signior Manelli, would you be so kind as to translate what's written here?" Tadeush asked, giving him the piece of paper with the words of the serenade on it.

"Signior Manelli translated:

SERENADE

Where are you from, oh beautiful star
That pours out bright love?
The passion of the love I feel
Is unequalled in its immeasurable might.
To someone else fate has given you.
Beside you there is no place for me.
Before I lose all self control
Please show your face, that I may see.
Is this your husband or your master?
I envy him incessantly.
Be merciful, oh my redeemer.
To your decision I will agree.
Where are you from, oh beautiful star
That pours out bright light?
The passion of the love I feel
Is unequalled in its immeasurable might.

Marcello

"What is it?" asked Signior Manelli, handing the sheet back to Tadeush. "You wouldn't believe it. A young singer wrote it for my wife. Yesterday night he sang it underneath our windows."

"Oh, these young people. They're absolutely ill-bred. They have no decency. You could complain to the manager of the hotel about the disturbance."

"I think that after we change hotels his passion will subside."

Tadeush and Wanda moved the same day. The new rooms were luxurious and only a block from Maestro R's studio.

The next morning, at ten o'clock, they arrived at the artist's studio. Wanda wore a velvet, cherry colored dress, with a large decollete, exposing her shoulders. The decollete was framed by lace fixed by an elegant brooch.

Maestro showed them some of his works. They agreed that the portrait's size should be twenty-four by thirty inches.

The artist sat Wanda in a chair and several times adjusted her posture. At last, he chose a position he liked. In her hands, Wanda held a half-opened fan, and her hands rested on her lap. Tadeush sat and watched how Wanda posed. The corners of her mouth curved in a little smile.

"Tell me, how long will it take?" Tadeush asked, carefully selecting his words so the artist would understand him.

"Two or three hours a day for eight to ten days, total," the artist answered, simultaneously showing the numbers with his fingers.

"Very well, that suits us."

So they would have to stay in Florence for about ten more days. Wanda thought he would paint it more quickly because of her own experience as a painter. But what she had seen in the studio had not resembled her work. It had shown the mastery of a great artist. People's faces looked alive; it seemed they would start to talk and come to life from the portraits. She could not paint like that. His paintings left the impression that even the air had been reproduced.

"You know, my dear," said Wanda, leaning on Tadeush's arm as they left the studio after the first sitting, "I will never paint again after what I have seen here. It is art; what I do is merely a craft."

"Oh, no, you have everything ahead of you, and even though I can't guarantee that you'll paint as he does, you'll do well."

Each morning, after breakfast, they went to Maestro R's studio. Sometimes Tadeush watched, and sometimes he read. After the sitting, they dined and walked. At night they listened to the music, but they did not see Marcello.

On the eighth day, the portrait was almost complete. The mastery of the artist was visible in the painting. Wanda's eyes looked pensive and her mouth held a little smile. Everything had been reproduced, down to the smallest detail. Even the carving on the fan was visible, and so too was the countess's present, the beautiful ring on Wanda's middle finger. Soft creases of velvet shimmered in rays of light. With a few additions to the background and several more strokes, the portrait would be ready.

As they were leaving, Wanda noticed sketches lying on a table.

"Look, Tadeush, these are sketches of my portrait. There are several of them. Why did he draw them?"

"I think he doesn't get a model like you very often. When we're gone, I believe he'll paint one more portrait of you."

The portrait was ready and carefully packed. Signior Manelli was present to translate the words of appreciation that were exchanged when Tadeush paid the artist. Tadeush and Wanda said good-bye to the maestro and Signior Manelli and left the studio, taking the portrait with them.

A road coach stood in front of the hotel while several men loaded baggage —trunks, traveling bags, suitcases. Soon, Wanda and Tadeush would leave for Milan. They were in good spirits. Tadeush was very satisfied with the portrait. So, farewell to Florence, a wonderful world of art!

As she was climbing into the coach, Wanda saw Marcello leaving Maestro R's studio.

"Look, Tadeush, isn't that our singer who just left the artist's house?"

"Yes, it's him. I didn't think they knew each other. Get in, my dear, it's time for us to go."

A short block separated the hotel from the artist's studio, and it was clear that the man was Marcello. They were in the coach, and Wanda wanted only one thing—to get away as soon as possible. Marcello reached the coach, removed his hat, and looked at Wanda, smiling. He walked into the hotel and reappeared in a few minutes. He crossed the street rapidly and disappeared from view.

The coachmen and servants took their places and the coach started to move.

Suddenly, they heard someone calling for Signiora Stanishevsky.

Tadeush looked out the window and was given a letter. He closed the door and the coach started to roll, gaining speed. He removed a sheet of paper from the envelope, unfolded it, and read:

> Dear Signiora Stanishevsky,
>
> I beg forgiveness for my impertinence. I want to tell you that your beauty conquered me. I ordered your portrait from Maestro R and will be able to enjoy you forever.
>
> Be as happy as you are beautiful.
>
> God save you!
>
> Your humble servant,
> Marcello

Tadeush and Wanda were silent for a moment. Then, embracing Wanda's shoulders, Tadeush said, "You know, it seems to me that he fell in love at the first sight. It can't be held against him. He was so in love that he was ready to do anything. Somehow, I feel sorry for him. Believe me, such feelings are not possessed by everyone, only by a few. I couldn't feel that way, no matter how much I loved you. Somewhere I read about such unexpected feelings. Usually they end tragically because people can't keep them under control and risk everything, even their lives. Have you seen his eyes? I feel sorry for him from the bottom of my heart."

"What do we do now?"

"Nothing. We left in time. He will have your portrait, and I will have both you and your portrait. But you remember this situation. It deserves to be remembered. Now we are going to Milan for just three days."

Milan greeted them with pouring rain. They went to their rooms and rested after the journey. The incident with Marcello had somehow disturbed their honeymoon.

Wanda thought about what Tadeush had said and tried to compare the feelings of both men. But she could not because she did not quite understand. Tadeush thought about how he loved Wanda with all his heart and how he could never have been seriously in love with her had she belonged to another. Perhaps he did not love her strongly enough and she realized it. He was clearly upset.

Because of their moods and the weather, Milan did not impress them. They attended the opera twice and visited the cathedral. Then they left for Rome.

They spent a week in Rome. The hotel where they stayed was located near the Trevi fountain. Near the fountain a light carriage harnessed to two horses waited for them each morning to take them sightseeing. How many cathedrals there were! Each was more beautiful than the one before. The best artists and architects had painted and decorated the ceilings and walls of Rome's cathedrals. Every day they visited another.

Once, as they were leaving a cathedral after the service, Wanda said to Tadeush, "It seems to me I am closer to God here. Tomorrow we'll be in the Vatican. I have never dreamed that I could be there."

"And I have dreamed of seeing Italy. As you can see, my dream came true, and, what's more, it came true with you. I thank God for everything. The most important thing is that you are happy with me."

"I'm very happy. I can't think about anything else. You are my life!"

Their hearts were flooded with joy. Wanda spoke the truth. After everything she had gone through, she could not believe she could be so happy. As much as she was able to love at seventeen years of age, she loved Tadeush. He had become everything to her, replacing her mother and father, whom she had missed so much before. She thanked God for her happiness in the first words of her prayers.

The Vatican made an indelible impression on them. The Sistine Chapel—it was a special wonder of human genius! Wanda was delighted with everything she saw. St. Peter's Cathedral and the square in front of it were majestic. People stood, struck by the majesty, and spoke in low voices. Wanda made notes of the names of artists and sculptors who had created the masterpieces. Before leaving for Sorrento, they visited Tivoli. It was just an hour's drive from Rome. The ancient castle was half destroyed, but the fountains had been preserved, and there were many of them in Tivoli. Everything was different than what they had seen before.

They spent only one day in Sorrento, and in the morning they were taken by a small schooner to the island of Capri.

The sea was calm at first, but soon it grew stormy. The schooner was tossed about in the waves. Wanda felt giddy and sick. Tadeush held her with one arm and grasped a rail with the other to prevent them from falling. They were surrounded by tourists. Shouts could be heard, now from the front, now from the rear. Someone lost his balance and fell to the deck. At last they landed, passing safely between two cliffs.

For a few hours Tadeush and Wanda rested until they recovered from the rolling and pitching of the ship. Then they set out to explore the island.

Capri overflowed with greenery and flowers. A steep road carried them upward, far above the sea. The horse walked slowly and the young people had an opportunity to look around and see everything. From where they sat, the view was splendid.

"Look, Tadeush," Wanda said, "this island is a garden. It's just a paradise on earth here."

"The air is clean," Tadeush answered. "It's easy to breathe. I like it very much, but I could never live on an island because it's separated from the mainland."

"Admit it, my dear, sometimes one wants to be far away from all the events of the world."

"Yes, I want to be on the most distant island. But only with you. Frankly, this one is too civilized."

After sightseeing, they had dinner on the terrace of a restaurant, enjoying the wonderful view of the sea. A young Italian began to play his guitar and sing. Neither he nor his voice resembled Marcello, but both Wanda and Tadeush at once recalled him. This man was singing about the sea, about mermaids and how one of them took his heart with her to the depths of the sea. In the restaurant, different languages could be heard: German, French, Russian, and English.

"You can see, my dear," Tadeush said, "how many tourists this island attracts. But it seems that only we speak Polish."

They spent two days on Capri, and then they were on the way to Sorrento and back to Odessa.

As they returned from the island, the schooner sailed gently and smoothly, sliding across the water. The sea was no longer stormy.

Farewell, Italy! They carried with them warm feelings about the hospitable and wonderful country. The way back was also quiet, without any storm. Tired and happy, they arrived at the Port of Odessa.

PART III

Sophie and Kazimir met them at the port. Wanda had faithfully sent postcards from every city in Italy, so her sister and her husband were well informed. Nevertheless, Sophie overwhelmed Wanda and Tadeush with questions. They had no time to reply before she asked new ones.

"The main thing is that you have arrived safely," Sophie said at last. "Now you must rest at home."

They all rode to Tadeush's house. Tadeush and Wanda handed out the presents they had brought for everyone.

"And now the best of all," said Tadeush, and he unrolled Wanda's portrait. Sophie began to cry and, pressing a handkerchief to her eyes, said, "Ah, Wanda, how much you look like Mama! But her portrait was done in stricter tones. Kazimir promises me that soon we'll go to Poland, and I will bring Mama's portrait over. Then we'll see how greatly you two resemble each other."

Wanda's portrait was placed in a gilded frame and hung on the hall. The memory of Italy and of the wedding trip would stay with them forever.

Wanda was happy. Tadeush was very attentive and concerned about her. He agreed that she would continue her college studies. She was taking Russian language lessons and art classes. One of the rooms in the house was filled with her works, including Italian landscapes.

If Tadeush was gone and she was not studying, she spent her time with her sister. Wanda loved her nephews. She walked with them in the park, attended children's plays, read to them, and drew for them. They were also very attached to her.

Time was flying. It has been a year since Wanda had married. She and Tadeush celebrated their anniversary with relatives and close friends. They received presents from Tadeush's parents in Poland. Tadeush presented Wanda with a beautiful necklace of gold and precious stones.

Once, Sophie and Wanda were shopping in a children's clothing store, and in a whisper, Sophie asked, "Don't you plan to have children? Excuse me for such an impertinent question, but we are sisters."

"I know Tadeush wants to have a baby. I see how he plays with your children. Of course I don't mind the question. I just haven't been able to get pregnant yet."

"If you want, I'll take you to my doctor for an examination."

"I need Tadeush's advice. I can't make the decision myself."

"Your husband is busy during the day, and I'll go with you. What are you afraid of?"

"It's simply that Tadeush must know about it."

"Well, ask him. I don't think he'll object because I'll go with you."

Sophie was right. Tadeush was glad that Wanda would go to the doctor with Sophie.

"Generally," he said, "you don't have to worry about it. We've been married only a year. We'll have children yet."

But Wanda worried not because something might be wrong with her, but because she recalled, with horror, another hospital and another doctor's examination. She was afraid that the experience by itself would take her back to her previous state of mind, when she had been ready to die because of everything she had gone through. Just thinking about it had turned her hands and feet cold.

Finally, Sophie persuaded her to get a check-up, and they walked together upstairs to the doctor's office on the second floor of the hospital. Wanda knew that the doctor was "a very nice old man," as Sophie had put it.

The doctor told her that it sometimes took a few years to get pregnant. If, even after that time, she was not pregnant, it would then be necessary to examine her husband.

Wanda was not particularly worried. She and Tadeush were happy. Not a single cloud darkened the horizon of their family's happiness. Often, Tadeush took her with him when he traveled on business.

The departure of Sophie and her family for Poland was approaching. Wanda spent all her time at Sophie's playing with her nephews. She was very close to them, and it was difficult for her to comprehend that they were going away. She did not know when she would see them again.

"Oh, Wanda," Sophie said, comforting her, "such a husband as Tadeush won't allow you to be bored. He's so responsive and caring."

The day of departure came. Sophie, Kazimir, and their children were going by train. The luggage had been loaded, and all of them stood near the car, talking.

Sophie embraced Wanda. "Next year, I think, you'll have your own little one, if God permits, and you can move to Poland."

They both cried, pressing handkerchiefs to their eyes. Boarding had been announced, and everyone hurried. Standing on the platform, the sisters embraced each other once more, and Sophie entered the car. Kazimir helped her up. The train started to gain speed and in a few minutes disappeared around a curve. Wanda still waved after the train was out of sight. Tadeush walked over to her and put his arm around her shoulders.

"Now I have only you here, my darling," Wanda said through her tears. "Calm down, my dear. I'll be going to Europe in a few months, and you'll go with me. We'll stop in Poland and visit them."

"Thank you for reassuring me, Tadeush. Now I'll wait for our departure." For the next few days, Wanda tried to think about other things, but she could not. She felt sad. Almost every day she thought about Sophie and her nephews. She continued to attend college. In her free time she took part in charitable organizations.

As time passed, circumstances developed that prevented Tadeush from going to Europe. Letters came from Sophie, and Wanda answered them regularly. Tadeush and Wanda were invited to receptions, and they received people at their house. Wanda described all the details to her sister.

She had been married two years. She was nineteen. Their second anniversary coincided with an invitation to a masquerade ball. Wanda and her good friend, Yasia, were discussing what they would wear for the masquerade. Everyone was to wear a mask during the first part of the ball and would remove the mask for the dance. Prizes would be awarded for the best dancing and the best costume. Then the queen of the ball would be selected.

Wanda picked a "Mary Stuart" dress, and Tadeush was to wear a prince costume. Three weeks before the ball, Wanda ordered the masks and costumes. A few days before the masquerade, they were delivered.

A maid helped Wanda put her costume on, and Wanda knocked on Tadeush's door.

"Come in," she heard her husband say. "It's open."

She walked into his study and stopped. Tadeush rose to meet her. "Splendid!" he said. "You look just like royalty. And where is my costume?"

"It's in the box. You can put it on, and we'll rehearse."

"It's impossible to take my eyes off you. Is this my wife?"

He walked to her and kissed her. She had to lean forward because her skirts were so wide.

"It's interesting to think about how they kissed and hugged in those days, when it was impossible to approach a sweetheart. They must have met their lovers in their regular attire. What do you think, my dear?"

"I think the 'air kiss' was invented then," Wanda answered, laughing. Tadeush found the box with his costume and went to change. Wanda waited for him in the living room. He returned wearing a black velvet camisole and beret. A high collar prevented him from turning his head.

"I wonder how they were able to walk in such inconvenient clothing?" he asked, looking at himself in the mirror.

"That's why I wanted you to practice—to get used to it," Wanda answered.

She stood beside him at the mirror.

"Euzef is wearing a gypsy costume, baggy silk trousers and a loose blouse tied up with a belt, and an earring. I'd trade with him. What could be better than free movement."

"When the masquerade starts, you'll see, my dear, that my selection was the best. There will be a lot of gypsy costumes, but I think no one will have costumes like ours."

"In that case, your highness Mary Stuart, let's go to the hall and begin to learn how to walk without getting in each other's way."

They laughed, joining hands and looking at each other.

They tried to dance, and it was not a bad attempt. The dance was a mazurka they both loved, and it had been written for dancers in clothing like theirs. They walked around in the costumes for a little while longer, Tadeush bowing and Wanda curtsying.

The day of the ball arrived. The maid fixed Wanda's hair and, having placed the last lock in place, said, "Pani, you do, indeed, look just like a queen. You are even more beautiful than you are in the portrait. It's simply impossible for anyone to take his eyes off you. It really has to be God who gives such beauty to a human being, I must say."

"You are kind, Marisa, thank you. My hair turned out well. You have good hands."

Marisa walked out of the room. She was a large girl with reddish hair and freckles. She had very light colored eyes without lashes and almost without eyebrows. She was very hardworking and honest. She had worked for Tadeush and Wanda for two years.

Tadeush and Wanda arrived at the masquerade ball at six o'clock. Many carriages had already arrived, and people wearing masks were descending from them. The ladies walked in the company of their cavaliers. The scene glittered with the variety of costumes.

Tadeush and Wanda walked into the hall. Before them walked a short lady wearing a gypsy's costume.

"You see, my dear," said Wanda, "there will be so many gypsies that Yasia and Euzef will make up a camp. Look to your left. There's another pair."

As they climbed the stairs, a lady in a domino costume was descending towards them. Her face was almost covered, and she wore a cap. Still, Wanda recognized her. It was Zosia. This time Zosia did not stop Wanda and quickly ran downstairs. The meeting disturbed Wanda, but Tadeush noticed nothing. She walked on, supported by Tadeush's hand.

Many people were already in the hall when Tadeush and Wanda entered. Couples wandered up and down, sat on sofas, and drank beverages carried about by servants. The orchestra played an introductory march and then fell silent. A speaker asked for everyone's attention.

"Ladies and gentlemen," he began, "it is requested that all present approach the jury by couples when your number is called." He named the members of the jury and described the first three prizes for costumes and then the prizes for dancing. "When our evening of dancing is over, you may remove your masks. Then the queen of the masquerade ball will be announced, along with her first and second maids of honor."

Everyone applauded, the orchestra began to play, and the applause died away. As the music played, numbers were called, and couples approached the jury and moved off to the side. The jury completed its review, the orchestra played a waltz, and couples circled.

Wanda noticed "domino" again. Zosia stood with someone in the costume of the chess king. Wanda saw that Zosia had not taken her eyes from her and Tadeush.

"Will we try to dance, my darling?" Tadeush asked.

"I'm a little tired. This costume is heavy, and I'm not used to being so tied up in a corset."

They walked to a sofa and sat down. Wanda fanned herself and watched the couples. Yasia and Euzef joined them. Neither resembled a gypsy very closely. Both had very light colored skin and blue eyes.

"Give me your hand, my beauty," Yasia said, "and I will tell your fortune. I will tell you what awaits you."

Wanda relinquished her hand, laughing.

"A surprise waits for you, and if you will grace my hand with silver, I will tell you more."

"Tadeush, my dear, give her a coin. Let her tell my fortune."

"I have only large ones," he joked, "and if you want to know your future, I'll tell it better than any gypsy woman."

"Listen to him, Wanda. He takes my bread from me, and he claims still to be a prince."

They watched the masquerade, joking with each other and laughing.

The speaker asked for attention once more.

"Now the winners of the costume competition will be announced."

The hall became completely silent, and the speaker continued, "The first place prize goes to the costumes worn by couple number seventeen, by Mary Stuart and the prince. ... Second place, number twenty-four. ..."

But Wanda heard no more. She saw only that everyone present was looking at her. She squeezed Tadeush's hand.

Yasia leaned towards her. "I did tell your future, that a surprise was waiting for you. You see, I really can tell the future."

"It's good that we're in masks," Wanda said. "I'd burn up otherwise. My face is on fire."

The speaker continued, "Ladies and gentlemen, you may remove your masks now. The ladies are asked to pass by the jury in sequence of their numbers. Then the dancing will continue, and, at the end of the ball, the queen and her maids of honor will be declared. So, ladies, get ready."

Again, the music played slowly, and the ladies passed by the jury in order.

The review ended and the speaker said, "Let's dance, ladies and gentlemen.

Be merry!"

The orchestra played a mazurka, and Wanda and Tadeush rose to dance. The beautiful couple drew the attention of everyone present. When the dance was over, Tadeush and Wanda returned to the sofa.

They sat and watched the dancers, Wanda searching for one couple in particular. She saw the "domino" and the "chess king." They danced with their masks still on. Other couples had retained their masks, but the majority had removed them. Someone danced out of rhythm, obviously drunk. Shouts were heard, first from one side, then the other. Someone's foot had been stepped on. After about ten minutes, order was restored. A few very drunk couples had been escorted out of the hall.

The speaker again asked for attention.

"Ladies and gentlemen, let me have your attention, please, one more time. I'll now read you the jury's decision. The queen has been chosen. She is lady number seventeen, Wanda Stanishevsky. She is nineteen years old. The first maid of honor is number twenty-three, Maria Palensky, twenty-one years old. The second maid of honor is number fourteen, Olga Zgeba, twenty years of age. The queen and her maids are asked to approach the jury."

All three were given certificates rolled to resemble ancient scrolls. Wanda unrolled hers and read: "This diploma is given to the Queen of Beauty, Lady Wanda Stanishevsky, at the Ball of Count N., on August 10, 1909."

The queen and her maids, all young and beautiful, smiled happily. The maids of honor stood on each side of Wanda, each possessed her own kind of beauty—Maria, a brunette with blue eyes, and Olga, a blonde with hazel eyes.

The three were presented with figurines of the "Three Graces," produced at the Kyznetsovsky china factory. Wanda also received a crown, which was fixed in her hair.

Everyone applauded the winners. Tadeush walked to Wanda, embraced her, and kissed her.

"Let's get acquainted, Wanda," said Maria Palensky. "This is my husband, Stanislav. My darling, this is my queen."

Wanda curtsied, and the two couples exchanged compliments.

"We've been married for three months," Stanislav said.

"And here you are," said Tadeush, "Maria is already the first maid of honor."

"How long have you been married?"

"It's our third year, now. We celebrated our second anniversary. Now my wife is the queen, which makes me the king."

They all laughed, everyone joking about the selection of the queen and the maids of honor.

Olga Zgeba had gone elsewhere, and they did not see her.

The close of the masked ball was announced. Everyone moved toward the exit. Wanda removed her crown and gave it to Tadeush. She kept the certificate. Maria and her husband walked behind them.

Near the exit, Wanda noticed Zosia. She was still wearing her mask. Suddenly, Zosia started to walk briskly in Wanda's direction, forcing her way through the crowd. Wanda's hands began to tremble, and she dropped her certificate. She bent down to pick it up, but her wide skirts prevented her from bending far enough. At the same time, Tadeush bent and picked the certificate up. Before Wanda could straighten, she heard Maria cry out behind her.

Everything happened so fast that it was impossible to understand what had occurred. Maria's hands flew to her face. She was screaming. Suddenly, she stopped crying and fell into her husband's arms. She was surrounded by people, all of them shouting. Someone yelled, "Stop 'domino.' She threw something in her face."

But it was useless to look for Zosia. She climbed quickly into a carriage where the "chess king" had been waiting for her, and they soon disappeared around the corner.

The injured were rushed to a hospital. Maria's face had been badly disfigured by acid. She was blind.

Wanda was close to a nervous breakdown. She knew it was Zosia who had thrown the acid. And she knew Zosia had intended the acid for her. Only because she had bent down had that poor woman become the victim.

The next day, Wanda and Tadeush visited Maria at the hospital. She was in critical condition. Stanislav had stayed with her from the beginning. Wanda could say nothing.

"Who could have done it?" Stanislav cried. "She didn't have any enemies. It's just madness. Why did such a tragedy happen to us? Her mother is coming tomorrow. I sent a telegram. How will I explain it to her?"

Stanislav wept, holding his wife's hand. Wanda laid flowers on a table, and she and Tadeush left.

After walking a block, Wanda stopped. Tadeush looked at her. She was crying. He embraced her and pressed her to him. Without speaking, he stroked her hair.

"I should be in that hospital instead of her," Wanda choked.

"What are you talking about? Calm down."

Wanda repeated her words again and again, weeping. Tadeush could do nothing to comfort her. At home, he led her to an armchair, knelt in front of her, and took her hands in his.

"I beg you, calm down and explain why you think you should have been the victim, instead of Maria."

"Zosia did it. I saw her. She was wearing the domino costume. She pushed her way through the crowd toward me. I dropped the certificate and bent down to pick it up. Everything happened so fast. Zosia splashed acid in Maria's face because Maria was walking behind me. That's all."

Tadeush rose. "Let's go to the police at once. That bitch must be arrested immediately. Why did you keep silent about it? Why are you afraid of her?"

"You can see for yourself. She's capable of anything. Yes, I'm afraid of her." Wanda began to cry again.

At the police station, Wanda took out a complaint against Zosia. Tadeush added what he knew about her. When the police went to the Svitsky's, Zosia was not at home.

"Where is your daughter?" one of the officers demanded.

"She has been gone for two days, and we don't know where," Zosia's mother answered, frightened.

"Tell me, what costume was your daughter wearing at the masked ball?" the officer asked. He prepared to write down the answer.

"A domino costume," said Zosia's mother.

"What does all this mean, officer?" Zosia's father interrupted. "Why are you asking all these questions? Has something happened to her?"

"We have witnesses who saw your daughter splash sulphuric acid in a woman's face at the masquerade."

"Oh, my God!" cried Zosia's mother. "It can't be. Maybe it was someone else."

"We have a lot of witnesses," the officer answered. "Someone wearing a domino costume threw acid. There was only one costume like that at the ball. Your daughter's acquaintances identified her. Would you tell us who she was with? Who was wearing the chess king costume?"

No, Zosia's parents did not know whom she was with.

The Svitsky's home was placed under surveillance. Zosia would be arrested as soon as she reappeared.

Wanda went through a lot during those days. She thought about many things, but her thoughts returned often to what had happened. Tadeush, seeing what she was enduring, decided to surprise her.

"In a week, my dear, we're going to Germany. We'll stay there about a month and a half, and then we'll go to Poland to visit my parents and your sister."

Tadeush was right. The plans diverted Wanda and encouraged her. She was busy buying presents for everyone. Tadeush had given her so little time, only a week. Marisa helped her. They went shopping together. Eventually, they had brought everything for the children. They had still to buy for Tadeush's parents and for Wanda's sister and her husband.

September was a golden season in Odessa. It was afternoon. Wanda and Marisa rode in an open carriage. There were few pedestrians on the streets. People did not go for walks at that time of day. The cabman drove slowly.

Suddenly, Wanda saw Zosia. She was walking, holding a white umbrella. A few steps behind her walked a man carrying a suitcase. They were headed toward the Svitsky's home.

A strange feeling seized Wanda. She wanted to shout, but she could not. She grasped Marisa's hand and whispered, "That's her. She must be stopped."

Marisa looked around, not understanding.

Wanda said to the cabman, "Slowly follow that lady with the white umbrella."

He nodded. Wanda watched Zosia, not taking her eyes away from her. Zosia approached the main entrance of her home, folding the umbrella. The man with the suitcase stopped. Wanda watched as two men came up to Zosia. One of them blocked her way to the house; the other addressed the man who followed her.

The carriage stopped, and Wanda observed what was going on from a distance.

Zosia looked back at her companion, weighing the situation, and then started to run. But she was intercepted immediately by one of the policemen. He grabbed her arm, spoke to her, and led her back to the entrance. Zosia submitted, lowering her head. Then, an instant later, she dashed toward the street. The heavy traffic prevented pursuit. Zosia, running, glanced back the way she had come. At the same time, a team of horses galloped around the corner.

Wanda covered her face with her hands and heard a shout. Passers-by screamed. Wanda opened her eyes on a terrible scene.

Zosia lay in the dust of the street, trampled by the horses.

"Let's go home," she said in a very low voice.

At home, Wanda felt sick. Her hands trembled. Her head was on fire. She lay down on the bed, and Marisa helped her undress.

Tadeush walked into the bedroom. He noticed at once that Wanda was upset.

"What happened? Calm down, my dear, I'm with you."

He sat on the edge of the bed and took her hand. She stopped crying, but she shivered. Her face was pale.

"Tadeush, I saw how she was trampled by the horses. It happened across from her house, when she started to run."

"My God, why were you there? You shouldn't have seen such a horror."

"We were going shopping."

Wanda explained what had happened. Then she added, "You see, my darling, this is my punishment. It seems I was doomed to be a witness to her horrible death."

"Please, try to forget about it. Do something to get your mind off it. We'll be gone in three days."

Tadeush did not tell her that Maria had died. He had seen it in the newspaper.

Wanda spent a restless night, leaping up in her sleep and crying. In the morning, Tadeush sent for a doctor. The doctor gave her a shot and she fell asleep.

"Don't worry," the doctor told Tadeush. "She's very upset, but everything will be all right. She'll sleep now, and then she'll feel better."

After seeing the doctor out, Tadeush went to his office. There was business to be taken care of before he and Wanda left.

Yasia arrived to see Wanda and walked straight to the bedroom, even though Marisa explained that the mistress was sleeping.

"You sleep so late," Yasia said. "You can't imagine what happened." Wanda awoke and looked at Yasia fearfully. It was noon. She had slept for about four hours.

"Look at today's newspaper." Yasia gave the paper to Wanda. On the page were two photographs of Zosia. In one, she was a smiling, handsome young blonde. In the other, she was lying, dead, run over by horses.

Wanda turned away and said nothing.

"Listen, it says here that she was the only heiress to a fortune. What else did she need?"

"I know what she lacked," Wanda said, raising herself slightly from the bed. "She lacked kindness, a love for her fellow creatures, a trust in God, a respect for her parents. All that cannot be bought. She was so spoiled. She did what she wanted to do. I feel sorry for her parents, but no one can help them." Wanda's voice was strained, and Yasia, seeing how upset she was, hurried to leave.

It was necessary to put off the trip to Germany until Wanda recovered.

After a few months, she felt better, but she was still easily frightened. Urgent business sent Tadeush to Europe alone, and Wanda agreed that they would go together the next year.

During the time that Wanda was by herself, she did a great deal of drawing, doing sketches by the sea. Once, while she was painting a seascape, a woman and a child sat beside her on the bench.

"What is your name?" Wanda asked the child.

"My name is Timosha. I'm four years old, and a few months." He became shy and pressed his face against the woman.

"May I sketch your son's face?" Wanda asked. "He has a wonderful expression."

"I'm his governess, but you may draw him. And you, Timosha, sit up straight."

Surprisingly, the boy sat straight, and Wanda sketched his features. Soon, the governess took the boy away to feed him. Wanda finished the portrait without them. Then she had an idea.

"What if I did an album of children's portraits?" she thought.

Wanda walked home contented. The first portrait was complete. While Tadeush was gone, she would be able to do several more. She was no longer sorry that she had been unable to accompany him to Europe.

In three weeks she drew six children's portraits and a few landscapes. The weather was good. The sun shown every day, and it was warm. All of her portraits were of children between three and six years old, and all of them were charming.

Once, on a Sunday, she went to church. She did not go often because there was a chapel in the house, and she could pray there any time. On that day, she saw Pani Svitsky, Zosia's mother. She had difficulty recognizing her. Pani Svitsky's hair was white, she had grown thin, and she had developed a nervous tick.

"Poor Pani Svitsky," Wanda whispered to herself.

When she arrived home, Wanda looked at the portraits of the children she had painted.

"What will they bring to their parents?" she thought. "Joy or sorrow? Each will have his own fortune."

Two years had passed since she and Tadeush had married. But still there were no children. Tadeush said nothing about it, and Wanda was ashamed to talk to him about it. How she would love to have a little baby of her own!

If the baby were a boy, he would look like Tadeush. And if it were a girl, she would look like Wanda. She dreamed and waited for Tadeush. Then she received a cable. Tadeush would be back at the beginning of December.

Early one morning, while Wanda was still sleeping, Tadeush arrived and entered the bedroom quietly to avoid waking her. But Wanda awoke at once and rushed to meet him.

"I missed you so much," Tadeush said. "I'll never go alone again. I'll send my manager or take you along." he embraced her and kissed her passionately.

"And I missed you very, very much. I needed you. Have you been to Poland? Have you seen all my relatives?"

"No, my darling, I was in Germany all four weeks. I had a lot of business to take care of."

After breakfast, Wanda opened the gifts Tadeush had brought her and was delighted with everything. Tadeush sat on the sofa and admired her. She was his Wanda again, her face alight with joy. How he loved her! He was always amazed by her childish delight and adult reasoning.

Following a month of separation, they were together almost all the time.

Tadeush joked that they were having their honeymoon again.

The new year was approaching, and the first snow fell. Sleighs glided along the streets, the bells on the horses' harnesses ringing. Children played in the snow, building snowmen. Winter brought special memories of Cracow to Wanda. There was always more snow there, and it stayed longer. She remembered how she used to go to the skating rink in the park. Ah, how long ago it was!

"It'll be Christmas soon," Tadeush said one day at dinner. "I want to give you a diamond ring. We'll go to a jeweler, and you can pick the one you want."

"What are you talking about? I have a lot of rings already."

"Well, then, what would you like? I'll buy you anything you desire."

"What I want isn't for sale," Wanda said, smiling. "Perhaps I'll be able to get it even if it can't be bought."

"And it can't be gotten, either, because I want a baby. A little, warm baby." Wanda was relieved to have finally said what had been on her mind. "You're right," Tadeush said. "We really need a baby. You'll make a good mother. I can imagine you with a little one. But it seems to me that it's early for you to be worrying about it. We'll certainly have children, and not one, but several. While we don't have them, what would you like to have for Chirstmas?"

"All right, let's go to a jeweler. I don't have a ring with a pearl in it. Maybe we'll be able to find something unique."

"I'm glad you agree with me. We'll go tomorrow, after breakfast."

They rode to the jeweler's in a sleigh. A light snow was falling. The store was located on the main street. In less than twenty minutes, they were climbing the stairs of the jeweler's. The salesman, an amiable, middle-aged man, met them.

"What can I do for you?" he asked.

"What can you show us from your pearls? We're looking for a ring," Tadeush said.

Wanda selected a ring set with one large pearl, with little branches of small diamonds shooting out from it. Tadeush liked her choice. The jeweler measured Wanda's finger.

"In a day, my lady," the jeweler said as he took his leave, "your ring will be delivered to you."

After thanking him, Tadeush and Wanda walked to the exit. A salesman opened the door for them.

As they were going down the stairs, Wanda saw a man and a woman climbing down from a sleigh. The woman held the hand of a girl, four or five years old. The girl wore a luxurious fur coat, muff, and hat. Wanda looked at the woman, and her heart began to beat faster. There could be no doubt. It was the countess. And it meant that the little girl was the baby whom the countess had taken from Wanda. Their eyes met. The countess looked straight at Wanda, and they recognized each other.

Trying not to betray her shock, Wanda got into the sleigh. Tadeush was talking about something, but Wanda did not hear him. When they reached the end of the block, she asked that the sleigh halt.

"What happened, my darling?" Tadeush asked.

Wanda tried her best to smile. "I want to walk by myself. You go home, and I'll be there soon. Don't look so surprised. I beg you, my darling, let me walk. And please, don't ask questions. I'll explain later. Now, help me down."

Tadeush helped her descent from the sleigh and honored her request that he not ask any questions. The sleigh carrying Tadeush turned the corner, and Wanda started to walk quickly toward the jewelry store.

From a distance, she watched as the countess's husband helped her into the sleigh. The girl was already inside. Wanda increased her pace and reached the sleigh, almost running.

"Wait, please. I want to talk to you." Wanda said, catching her breath. "Get in, dear," the countess said to her husband, "and tell the driver to get the horses going."

"There's a girl here," the count answered. "What does she want?"

"Don't pay any attention. She's a crazy woman. I've seen her somewhere." The sleigh started to move, and Wanda realized that her hope of seeing the child was slipping away. Later, if she had asked herself what made her do what she did next, she could not have answered.

As the sleigh gained speed, Wanda ran after it. Running was difficult because of her long skirt, fur coat, and high-heeled shoes. She began to feel short of breath. The sleigh sped forward and turned onto Rishelevsy Street. Wanda kept on running but stopped when the sleigh turned the corner. She lost her balance and fell down on the street, hurting her knees. She tried to get up, but the pavement was slippery, and she fell again and again.

Finally, someone helped her to her feet. Limping slightly, she walked towards the sidewalk, leaning on the person's arm. When she reached the sidewalk, she heard the man who had helped her address her by name. She did not understand at first what he was talking about, and he repeated himself.

"Mrs. Stanishevsky, a cabman is waiting for me at the corner. I'll take you home, if you don't mind."

"How do you know me?" Wanda aksed, looking at the stranger.

A rather young man in a military uniform gazed at her, smiling slightly. "I've known you for a long time, even before your marriage. I had the pleasure to see you at the masked ball after your marriage."

"That's strange. I've never seen you before, and I don't know your name," Wanda said, shaking snow off her skirt. She could not see her knees but felt sharp pain.

"Captain Vladimir Chernov," the man said, introducing himself.

"Thank you, Mr. Chernov, you have been very kind. And now I have to go. Please, don't follow me. I have some business to take care of before I go home."

"I apologize for the personal questions, but why are you alone? How could your husband let you go out alone in such weather? You could be run down by horses."

"You're right. Your question is an immodest one. Allow me not to answer it. Good-bye, Mr. Chernov."

Wanda walked with difficulty towards the jewelry store. It was good that it was located on the same side of the street.

Chernov stood for several minutes, watching as Wanda slowly moved away. Unnoticed, he started to walk after her, giving a sign to his coachman to follow him.

Wanda walked into the jewelry store, and the owner approached her.

"Did you forget something, madam?" he asked.

"Yes, I intentionally dismissed my sleigh, and I want to ask you to select a pocket watch with a chain—as a gift for my husband for Christmas. It's going to be a surprise."

"At your service, madam," he said, and showed her a selection of gold watches of different makes.

Wanda picked a watch and asked that it be engraved. Then, as if it were an afterthought, she asked, "Could you tell me, by chance, who that lady was who came in with her husband and child? Her face is very familiar to me."

"Of course I know her, madam. That was Countess Gdansky."

"I took her for someone else. Would you tell me where she lives? Then I'll know for sure whether or not it's she."

"I'll take a look. I have my clients' addresses on file. Here's their address. They live on Rishelevsky Street, number thirty-two. Mr. and Mrs. Gdansky rarely come to Russia. They live somewhere in the south of France. But when they do come, the countess likes to visit my store."

"Thank you. She's not the same lady."

Wanda walked out. The owner of the jewelry store had rendered her a valuable service. But now she felt severe pain in her knees, and her nervousness had not left her. With difficulty, she negotiated the stairs and looked around for a cab. Suddenly, she noticed Chernov.

"Let me take you home," he said, approaching her. "My sleigh is at your disposal."

"Thank you, but why are you here again?"

"I was waiting for you. I knew that sooner or later you'd come out of the store."

Wanda looked at him, smiling a little.

"You are very kind, Mr. Chernov, I'll accept your favor."

"It is you who does the favor to me." Chernov gave his driver Wanda's address.

"You know exactly where I live," Wanda said anxiously. "How long have you been watching me?"

"Come now. I don't watch you. It's just that sometimes I look at you from a distance. I think I've known you for four or five years, in spite of the fact that you've never seen me."

"How can you watch me without being noticed?"

"It's my secret. But don't worry. I'll never harm you. I'm thankful that you finally gave me an opportunity to render you at least some small service."

Wanda looked at him and said nothing, thinking that the next day she would go to the Gdansky's house and that immediately, she needed to go to bed. She closed her eyes, and Chernov continued to look at her as she leaned back on the seat.

"I remember when you were married. I was in the church and envied your husband. I've never seen such a beautiful bride as you were."

"I first met you in the late spring of 1907, I was on vacation, my last one before I graduated from the military academy. I came to Odessa to visit my mother. I've always loved the Black Sea, and this is the best place for me to think. You see, I write poetry, and my muse speaks to me most clearly on the seashore.

"That day, I'd finished a poem, and when I returned to the boulevard, I saw you. I couldn't take my eyes off you. You came from nowhere. I'm ashamed to confess I followed you at a distance until I found where you lived."

Wanda listened to him, and her cheeks were on fire. He had distracted her thoughts from what had just happened. She did not ask any questions, feeling the pain in her knees and wishing only to get home as soon as possible.

The sleigh came to a stop, and Chernov said, "We've arrived already." Carefully, he helped her down from the sleigh and followed her to the door.

"Have a merry Christmas," he said. "Be always happy. May your eyes never be sad."

"Thank you very much again," Wanda said. "Perhaps you'll come in? I'll introduce you to my husband."

"No, thank you, not now. I have a question for you, though. Tell me, please, do you wear those bracelets? Do you like them?"

"Oh, my God. So it was you who sent them. I racked my brains over them, thinking it was some kind of mystery. I liked them. They're very elegant. But without knowing who sent them, I was afraid to wear them. I could ask you a lot more questions, but I don't feel well." It's time for me to go to bed. Thank you again."

Chernov kissed her hand, bidding her farewell, and Wanda knocked on the door.

Tadeush was sitting in the living room reading a magazine when Wanda came in. He rose to meet her, seeing how unsteadily she walked.

What's the matter with you darling? I couldn't understand what it was that made you decide to take a walk."

"Oh, Tadeush, I fell and hurt my knees. It's very slippery outside. Don't ask about anything, my dear. I'll explain everything to you later. Right now, help me lie down."

Tadeush called for a maid, and both Tadeush and the maid helped Wanda get undressed. When her stockings were removed and Tadeush saw her knees, he shook his head and said, "How did you manage to get up by yourself? You battered your knees so badly that there isn't an unmarked spot on them. All the skin is removed. We'll have to call a doctor."

Tadeush washed her knees and put compresses on them. He put her in bed, covered her, and sat down beside her.

Wanda tolerated the pain, not crying once. The sharp pain left her, but her knees continued to ache. The maid left to call a doctor.

"You've surprised me with all this, of course," Tadeush said. "Perhaps I'll understand when you tell me about it. But right now I'm in total ignorance."

"You promised not to ask. I'll tell you later."

The doctor came, gave Wanda a shot, and prescribed medication for her knees. Wanda enervated. Tadeush lowered the blinds and left the room.

The events of the day flashed across Wanda's mind. She saw the face of Countess Gdansky, fear in her eyes. Wanda understood that the countess had told her husband a fabricated story about some madwoman in the maternity ward, insuring herself against the possibility that Wanda might find her by accident. Wanda realized she had done the wrong thing. She had no right even to come close to the countess. She suddenly felt sorry for the woman, imagining what it would be like to live in constant anxiety. Neither of them had ever really been happy. Each of them had a deep secret that could not be revealed to anyone.

Then Wanda remembered the officer, Chernov. "He's a nice young man," she thought. "But what does he want from me? I'm married. And yes, the bracelets. What does it all mean? I dreamed that my mother brought me the bracelets in a box. Now I can wear them."

Wanda's mind began to wander, and she fell asleep.

Wanda awoke in the morning. Tadeush was not there. She tried to get to her feet, but the pain in her knees prevented her from even bending her legs. She remained in bed for almost a week. A nurse applied lotions and bandages.

By the end of the week, the snow had melted and the sun was shining. In two days it would be Christmas, but it was like spring outside, as it often was in Odessa at that time of year. There was often hardly time to harness the horses to a sleigh before it was time to unharness them again.

When Wanda felt that she was able to walk, the first thing she wanted to do was visit Countess Gdansky. She would make certain that she would not be recognized.

A half hour after Tadeush left for his office, she put on a coat and a hat with a veil. This time, she would think everything out carefully in order to avoid what had happened before. She developed a plan for what she would say, how she would introduce herself, how she would behave. She had only one goal: to see the child.

Wanda went to the store and bought a box of hand-painted Christmas tree ornaments. Then, a block from Countess Gdansky's house, she let the coachman go.

"Wait here for thirty minutes," she told him, and went on foot.

She read the numbers on the houses until she found thirty-two. It was a three-story residence, displaying the beautiful architecture of the last century. As she climbed the stairs of the front entrance, she heard a buzzing in her temples and felt a dryness in her throat.

She knocked. A doorman answered.

"May I see Countess Gdansky?" she asked. "It's a business matter." The doorman shook his head.

"No, madam, they are not at home."

"I'll leave this box, then, and come back again, when they're at home."

"I don't think that will be soon, madam. They left almost a week ago to travel abroad."

Wanda could not believe her ears. "What's going on?" she thought. "I won't see her again." The thought angered her.

In a voice that betrayed both her confusion and her hopelessness, she said to the doorman, "Take this box. They are Christmas tree decorations. I brought them for the countess's child. But now it doesn't matter."

She turned to leave, but the doorman said, "Madam, you may come in. The countess's aunt lives here. If you will wait, she will be back soon."

Wanda walked into the hall and stopped.

"What is your name, madam?" the doorman asked. "And what business do you have?" He was an elderly man with a full beard.

"Madam Stanishevsky," Wanda said. "I'm an artist. I paint children's portraits. I'm supposed to have an exposition, and I want to do the portrait of the Gdansky's daughter. I was advised by one of our mutual friends that the child is simply charming. But now I see it's impossible. If there is a photograph, I could do it. I'll return the photo."

"There is a small photograph in Count Gdansky's study. You can go in there. I'll show you."

Wanda followed him. The count's study was to the left of the entrance hall. The doorman opened the door and let Wanda in. It was a large room, paneled with wood, with bookcases, leather chairs, and a large, polished table. It reminded her of Tadeush's study.

The doorman walked to the table and showed Wanda the child's photograph. The girl had blonde hair, large, dark eyes, and dimples in her cheeks.

"She's a beautiful child," Wanda said. "It's a pleasure to see such a face." She tried to smile. "What's the girl's name?"

"Her name is Marina. You are right, madam. She's a beautiful child, but very sick. She has a cough. Something is wrong with her lungs. A doctor advised them to live in the south of Franch permanently. So they've left. It is unknown when they will return to Odessa. The count will come back, but as for the countess and the girl, I don't know. The countess's aunt says it will be at least three years before they come back here."

"I want to wait for the countess's aunt to return," Wanda said, "so I can ask for the photo. When I've finished the portrait, I'll bring it back. It will take only a few days. The holidays are coming, but, even so, I will return it no later than the first week of January."

"You may take the photo, madam, and bring it back to me. The countess's aunt doesn't even enter this half of the house. You have a kind face. I see that you need to paint the portrait very much, and I will take your word for it. Let me wrap the photo up for you."

"You can't imagine how grateful I am to you. I'll most certainly bring it back to you. You can trust me."

He nodded and gave Wanda the photo. She pressed the packet to her and went out through the open door. At the front entrance, she stopped and took fifty rubles from her purse.

"This is for you for Christmas," she said to the doorman. "Thank you very much."

"Thank you, madam. You are very generous. God bless you." To the doorman, whose salary was fifteen rubles a month, it was a lot of money.

Wanda walked quickly down the stairs, despite the pain in her knees. The cabman waited for her at the corner. She went home, gazing throughout the trip at Marina's photo. Tears flowed down her cheeks.

At home, she calmed down somewhat and at once began work on the portrait. After a few hours of work, the sketches were ready. She had captured exactly the girl's looks and smile. But she added something, as well, giving the little girl in the portrait an expression showing some anxiety.

By Christmas, the portrait was complete, and Wanda placed it in a row with the others. She now had at least the face of her child. Despite the suffering the portrait had caused her, she would never agree to part with it for anything.

Wanda and Tadeush had invited guests for Christmas. The dinner progressed amidst a gay, pleasant atmosphere. Tadeush offered to show the guests the portraits Wanda had painted. Everyone was delighted with the children's faces. One of the guests, Professor Polansky, looked at the portrait of Marina for a long time. Then he turned to Wanda.

"How were you able to reproduce this girl's facial expression so exactly? She smiles, but there is an adult's sadness in her eyes. It's a very interesting face. This portrait deserves attention. You have talent."

Wanda blushed as everyone applauded the professor's statement.

"It wouldn't hurt for your wife to get Italian or French training in painting," the professor said to Tadeush. "Think seriously about my words. She has innate talent."

The guests parted late.

The next morning was Christmas, and Tadeush opened the gift Wanda presented to him—a gold pocket watch with a chain. On the watch lid was an inscription: "To my beloved Tadeush on Christmas, 1912. Your wife, Wanda."

"I ordered this surprise from the jeweler when I returned to the store," Wanda said smiling.

"Yes," Tadeush said, "I will remember this gift. It cost you bruised knees, and you've suffered so. You are still a child, a grown-up child, and I love you very much. I have a surprise for you, too. I want you to study in France. We'll go there together. We'll spend a month there. Then I'll get back to my business, and you'll stay as long as necessary to study. Professor Polansky will write a letter to his good friend, an artist whom you'll be able to work with in his studio. Well, what do you think of my surprise?"

Wanda embraced Tadeush and said, "My darling, my love, God himself gave me you as a husband. I'm the luckiest woman in the world."

They talked about the trip during breakfast. After they ate, Wanda left for the orphanage. For more than a year she had sponsored the children in the orphanage, which was located at the monastery. On Christmas Eve, she had delivered a whole cartload of presents that she had purchased, wrapped, and labeled with the children's names.

Such joy her work created! The children gathered at the tree. They sang and danced, holding hands, and Wanda enjoyed the celebration with them.

She had painted the portraits of the children in the orphanage, too. She loved and pitied the orphans, and on that Christmas morning, she had kind words for each of them.

Back at home, Wanda felt fatigued, but she did not lie down to rest. Instead, she sat down to write a letter to Sophie. She wrote that they would see each other for sure. She wrote about her upcoming trip to Paris, and she explained that she had been promised an exposition of her paintings.

Wanda wrote a very warm letter to her sister. She had not seen Sophie and her family for a long time and lived in the hope that she would again embrace them all.

The tickets were booked for April. Wanda bought herself new dresses in a French store. She was going to Paris for the first time. How much joy she felt! How much hope!

She would take only a few of her works, those she considered the best.

Among them would be the portrait of Marina.

Professor Polansky had written the letter of recommendation to his friend. At the beginning of April Wanda visited her father's grave. The day was warm. She sat down on a bench in front of the crypt, holding flowers in her hand. She had always talked to her father as if he were still living.

"Dear father," she said, "I'm going to Paris. I'll be an artist. If you could only know how happy I am. You'll be the only one I miss. When I see Sophie, I'll give her your regards. She asks in her letter whether I visit your grave. What a strange question. If I didn't see you, I would miss something." Wanda rose, put the flowers down, said good-bye to her father, and walked to the path. She had walked a few feet when she heard steps behind her. Turning, she saw Chernov. He wore his uniform. Wanda stopped and looked at him in astonishment. Chernov came up to her and greeted her.

"Here we are, meeting again. I thought there would never be another chance."

"What are you doing at the cemetery, Mr. Chernov?"

"My mother died exactly a year ago, and I came to visit her grave. And you have been to your father's grave?"

"You know even that?"

"At the entrance I noticed your cabman and realized you were here, but I thought you were with your husband."

"No, I always come to see my father alone because I want to feel free. Besides, Tadeush doesn't like to go to the cemetery. Do you have brothers or sisters? I see you've come alone for the anniversary of your mother's death."

"No, I don't have anybody. I was the only son, unfortunately."

They walked slowly down the path to the main exit and talked as if they were old friends. Wanda told Chernov that she was going to France, and he was sincerely happy for her. They came to the cab and stopped.

"Would you come to visit us some time? I want to introduce you to my husband," Wanda said, giving Chernov her hand in parting.

"No, it would be embarrassing for me. In what capacity could you introduce me?" Chernov asked, shrugging. "Farewell, Wanda. Have a safe trip and have a good time in Paris."

"Thank you, Mr. Chernov. You are a good, kind friend. I don't have so many friends. If you ever need anything and I can be of help, I'd be glad to do a favor for you. Good-bye."

"Good-bye, Wanda. I'm glad to hear that from you."

The cab pulled away. After it had traveled some distance, Wanda looked back and saw that Chernov still stood, looking after her. She waved to him and he waved back.

Wanda felt strange. She had seen him for only the second time, but it seemed to her that she had known him for a long time. He was so courteous and well-bred. She knew she liked him. And why should she not? In the eyes of society, Vladimir was a hero and would be liked by any woman. Wanda reasoned with herself. She loved Tadeush, and no one could take his place in her heart.

At dinner, Wanda told Tadeush that she had met an acquaintance at the cemetery.

"What's his name?" Tadeush asked. "Perhaps I know him."

"His name is Vladimir Chernov. He's an officer." Wanda described Chernov's appearance.

"No, I don't recall him, but his last name seems familiar."

Wanda did not mention that it was Vladimir who had sent the bracelets to her as a wedding gift. She did not know herself what prevented her from telling Tadeush about it.

The day of their departure for France came. They sent a letter to Cracow in order to be sure they would be met there. For the first time in many years Wanda was leaving Odessa. She had grown used to the city that had brought her first grief and then happiness.

They drove to the railway station. Acacia was blossoming everywhere, emitting an intoxicating odor. Wanda looked around at the city they were leaving for a time. Yasia and Uzef came to the station to see them off. As always, Yasia chatted a good deal. She was very lighthearted, able to endure nothing serious, completely Wanda's opposite.

"I am so envious of you," Yasia said. "You go to Paris and all over Europe, and we go to Petersburg this summer. My cousin lives there, but I've never been there. Wanda, my dear, do write to me at least now and then."

"I'll write to you about my impressions, for sure. I promise."

The two women embraced. The boarding had been announced, and Tadeush took Wanda's elbow.

"Let's get into the car, my darling," he said, "or the train will leave without us."

He helped her ascend into the car. The whistle sounded and the train moved ahead. They stood at the door and waved until the station disappeared from view. Then they walked into the car. They were traveling in a first class compartment. It was the first time Wanda had traveled by train, and she found the seats soft and comfortable. She liked it on the train. She sat at the window and watched as the suburbs of Odessa flew past.

"Tadeush," she said, "I feel as though this train has torn us away from the city and carried us away like a particle of dust. Do you feel like that?"

"No, I've never thought of it that way. But I travel by train very often. How did you get here from Poland?"

"By carriage. My father didn't want to go by train. I remember he said he didn't like the knock of the wheels and the whistle."

"I'm thinking about being with you in Paris and how you'll conquer the Parisian beauties with your beautiful look."

They were talking in low voices, and Wanda suppressed her laughter because across from them sat a lady in black with a veil covering her face. Beside her sat her maid.

Wanda and Tadeush were both speaking Polish, although Tadeush spoke very good Russian and Wanda was quite fluent. They were uncomfortable speaking their native language with someone sitting across from them.

After about ten minutes, the lady asked Tadeush in Polish, "Would you tell me what time it is now?"

Tadeush told her and then added, "I didn't think you spoke Polish. Let me introduce myself. I'm Tadeush Stanishevsky."

The lady introduced herself as well, lifting her veil a little.

"I'm Baroness Ronsky. My maiden name is Densky. It's hard to believe that you are Polish and we're traveling in the same compartment."

They started to talk. It turned out that they had quite a few acquaintances in common.

"I'm going to Warsaw," the baroness said. "And where are you going?"

"We're going to Cracow and then to Paris," Tadeush answered.

"I'm leaving Russia forever," the baroness said. "My husband died a month ago. I have a nephew in Warsaw. He is the only relative I have left. God didn't give us children, but I'm not complaining. My husband and I traveled a great deal. He had a brother who lived in Odessa, and that brought us there. We lived in Paris for four years. They were the best years of my life."

Baroness Ronsky turned out to be a good conversationalist, and the talk went on until they reached the border. They passed through the customs inspection, and the train crossed the border.

"Farewell to Russia," the baroness said. "I'll never come back here. You are young. You have all your lives in front of you. My charge d'affaires told me that we're in troubled times now. The children of our former friends went to America. My advice to you is to get out of Russia and, if you can, out of Europe entirely. I'd leave myself, but at my age there is nothing to go for."

Wanda listened to the baroness with interest. Tadeush talked to her about politics and it was clear that she understood it. They continued to talk, passing the time. Finally, the train arrived in Warsaw. The baroness stood and turned to Wanda.

"Farewell to you, sweetheart," the baroness said. "I wish you the best. I enjoyed just looking at you during the trip."

She then addressed herself to Tadeush.

"Listen to me. Take your beautiful wife away from Russia. Go to America. Someday you'll remember my words. Well, good-bye now. I had a good time."

The conversation with Baroness Ronsky had not lasted long, but Tadeush and Wanda would remember her as an interesting traveling companion.

"Why was she talking about going to America?" Wanda asked.

"It's my understanding that mostly unfortunate people go to America, poor people who have nothing to lose," Tadeush answered. "We're quite well off here. We have considerable accounts in European banks, so we have no reason to go."

The train approached Cracow. Wanda held her breath. She looked out the window and saw Sophie and Kazimir and the children. If the children had not been standing next to Sophie, Wanda would not have recognized them.

The sisters embraced each other, crying. Wanda's nephews called her Pani Wanda. How they had grown!

They arrived at the house. Wanda had been born there. Her childhood and adolescence had passed there. Returning took her breath away. Almost nothing had been changed in the house. She remembered everything, down to the smallest detail.

Tadeush saw the portrait of Wanda's mother and looked back and forth at the picture and Wanda.

"There is a great resemblance," Tadeush said. "But you are slightly different. Besides your mother is older in this portrait than you are now."

Sophie declared that she had arranged a reception in honor of her sister and her husband to be held on Saturday.

Wanda went to her room and called to Tadeush. "Look," she said, "there are my early drawings."

They stood, looking the sketches over, and Wanda was transported back to her childhood.

On Saturday, everyone dressed up for the reception. By six o'clock in the evening, the guests began to arrive. Sophie introduced them to her sister and her husband.

"Sophie," said one of the guests, "your sister is a beauty. If she lived in Cracow, she would be the most beautiful of all the women."

"I don't think we need to move here," Tadeush said, laughing.

At the table Sophie announced, "My sister from Odessa, from the southern Ukraine, received a first prize for her beauty. They say, and not for nothing, that the women of Poland are the most beautiful in the world."

Wanda shyly listened to the compliments. A servant came in and told Sophie that Pan Stefan and Pani Isabella Shkabsky had arrived. The new arrivals were seated to Wanda's right. Wanda's heart beat faster. She had not knows that Sophie knew them.

A long time ago, Wanda had been in love with Pan Stefan. It had been the first time she had experienced those feelings, but she still remembered. How she had cried when she had found out he was married! Over time, all of her feelings toward him had disappeared. But now she was excited. The feeling was strange.

Stefan had changed little. His wife was very pretty, but slightly overweight. Because they were late, they said hello from a distance. If they had arrived before dinner, Wanda might have revealed her excitement, but, as it was, no one noticed. And Wanda had learned how to control herself.

After dinner, Stefan found a moment when Wanda was left alone. His wife was talking to Kazimir. He approached her, smiling, and whispered, "You used to be a beautiful girl, but now you are simply like a goddess. I enjoy looking at you."

"Don't, Stefan. This isn't quite proper of you."

"Why, I'm only telling you what I see. Do you have children?"

"No. Tadeush says I'm still a child myself," Wanda said, laughing. "Do you?"

"Would you believe we have five children and my wife is pregnant with our sixth. She's a fierce Catholic. All these years, I remember her mostly pregnant."

"You're a happy father. You have a big family. That isn't bad, is it? Besides, you obviously don't mind having so many children."

"No, I wanted to have two, but not everything depends on me."

Wanda shifted her gaze from Stefan to Tadeush. Of course, she had never loved Stefan as she loved Tadeush. No, she would never trade places with Stefan's wife. Wanda sat down on the sofa, and Stefan asked permission to sit beside her.

"Sit down, please," Wanda said. "Tell me, how is life in general? What's new?"

"Wanda," he answered, "I want to tell you something. If you can, simply hear me through because I don't know if I will have a chance to see you again. I received your letter when I returned from my wedding trip. I cried like a little boy. I still keep your letters. They're all that's left for me from you. Do you still have the talisman, the Buddha?"

"No, I threw it away when I got the message that you were married."

"I didn't know anything about your misfortunes. I thought you had just forgotten me, had started spinning in the whirlwind of society. It's a pity that we have neither the time nor the proper conditions. I could tell you a lot."

"It's good that we have neither the time nor the conditions," Wanda answered, "because everything has happened for the best, Pan Stefan. The years I've been married have been the best years of my life. I'm very happy, very happy with him. We're going to Paris. Tadeush is giving me a chance to study painting."

"Surely, possessing a woman such as you, he would fulfill all your wishes. What's more, you are not capricious. You are smart and talented."

"Thank you for the compliments. I have to go." Wanda got up from the divan. "Our conversation grew lengthy," she said as she walked away.

Wanda joined Tadeush and they walked to the ballroom to dance. Wanda thought about how happy she was as Tadeush's wife. What someone had once said was true: "There is no higher blessing than to love and to be loved."

Dessert and champagne were served. Sophie picked up a wine glass and asked for attention.

"Ladies and gentlemen," she said, "I propose a toast for our guests, for my dear sister and her husband, and for our being together once again."

Everyone toasted and drank.

"I'll ask another toast," Stefan said. "Let's drink, ladies and gentlemen, to Wanda's talent and to her success in art in Paris. The Polish intelligentsia is proud of you."

The toast was made suddenly. It was obvious that Stefan was quite drunk. Of course, everyone joined the toast. Wanda was very embarrassed. People approached her and she thanked them.

The evening came to an end. The guests departed. Stefan and his wife were the last to go.

"Dear Wanda," Isabella said, "if I have a daughter, I will give her your name. I don't think Stefan will object."

"I'm very touched," Wanda said, "Thank you."

Wanda gave her hand to Stefan, smiling. He kissed it and gave her a long look. He was not smiling.

When the door closed behind them, Wanda siged with relief. The meeting with Stefan had left her with an unpleasant feeling. It seemed to her that if they had not met, Stefan would have remained happy in his own way. But it could be that she was simply sentimental.

The day came for Wanda and Tadeush to leave Cracow. Wanda parted with her sister and her nephews, promising that when she and Tadeush returned from Paris, they would visit again. This time, there were no tears.

They spent only two days with Tadeush's parents. Wanda liked the small, cozy estate. Tadeush's father was ill and bedridden. His mother was all right so far, but because of her husband's illness, she was very tired. Tadeush was upset. He loved his parents very much.

"Wanda," Tadeush said, "they are the dearest people. Even though I don't live with them, they are always in my heart. It will be very difficult for me to lose them. Now I see that it will be soon."

They said farewell to Tadeush's parents and rode in a cab to the railway station. Tadeush was silent all the way, and Wanda did not disturb him. She understood.

They arrived in Paris early in the morning. A cab took them to the hotel, and they sat in the open vehicle, looking around. Wanda squeezed Tadeush's hand.

"I'm in Paris," she said. "It isn't a dream."

"No, my dear," Tadeush said, "you're in Paris with me. I promised I'd fulfill your desires."

The hotel was plush, with marble, mirrors, velvet. Bellmen in uniform were at their service.

Tadeush sent a note to Professor Truse, notifying him of their arrival and where they were staying. They agreed to go to his studio in a week. In the meantime, they had a chance to see the sights of Paris. They visited exhibitions and museums. Tadeush served as guide. he knew the city well and was able to keep his bearings.

One night, they attended a performance by a famous dancer. She was young, beautiful, and graceful. Her style and ability amazed them.

"There is something unusual about her," Wanda whispered to Tadeush during the performance. "I'd like to paint her portrait. Everything about her is ideal."

"You're ideal, too," Tadeush answered, "but you're not a dancer. Seriously, though, it's the last day of her tour in Paris."

"What a pity. I'll probably never see her again. She even has an unusual name."

"It's probably a pseudonym," Tadeush said, "but it sounds good— 'Mata Hari.' It's Turkish or something."

The dancer was stunning. She was almost naked. Only a thin veil covered her body. She twisted like a snake. Tadeush and Wanda had never seen anything like it.

The next day, they visited the studio of Professor Truse, which was located in a very picturesque and quiet part of the city. It was in the outskirts of Paris, far away from the noise and confusion. They were met by the professor himself, and he led them into the studio. Wanda showed him her drawings, and he started to examine them.

Professor Truse was about sixty years old, of medium height, with a nicely clipped, small beard. He was very elegantly dressed.

After he had looked at the drawings and sketches, he sat down across from Wanda and said, smiling, "I will gladly work with you. You certainly have talent. Some of your works are simply excellent. This portrait of a girl, for example."

He took Marina's portrait in his hands. "There is nothing to add," he said. "It is a good work. Your lessons will be held three times a week."

The professor showed Wanda some of his own works and orders for portraits and other paintings.

"You will be my assistant," he told her, "and some of the work you will do by yourself."

Wanda was very satisfied. She liked everything about Paris—the pofessor's studio, the parks, and the people who walked in them. She was very happy.

Wanda's lessons began. Tadeush saw her off to the studio, and returning to the hotel, kept himself busy with business correspondence. He was happy that Wanda would be able to improve her talent.

When Tadeush brought Wanda back from the studio, she told him about her experience, about how her work was going, about the professor and his assistants. One of the assistants had worked there for five years.

"The professor has had forty years of practice as an artist," she said. "He is well acquainted with the Italian school of painting because he lived in Italy for twenty-two years. And, what's most important, I'll paint portraits and other subjects, still lifes and landscapes."

"That's good," Tadeush said, "but soon you'll have to go on alone. It's time for me to go back to Odessa. It's been almost two months since we arrived her."

"Wait a week or two more."

"You must understand, Wanda. You spend seven or eight hours a day in the studio. I've already been all over Paris. I could be a guide, but my accent betrays me. And I have urgent business to take care of."

Of course, Wanda understood, but she was used to being with him during all her spare time.

"When you were gone to Germany," she said, "I missed you. But it was different then. I was at home. Everything was familiar. Our friends visited me. I spent my spare time at the orphanage. So time went quickly while you were gone. But now it's different. You'll be gone for months. I'll be here in a strange city with strange people."

At the hotel, Wanda became very upset and refused to go to dinner.

"What are we going to do, my darling?" Tadeush chided. "You're still an absolute child, and I don't want to leave you. I'll have to write a letter to my manager and tell him to keep informed about the business. I'll stay with you for about three more months. After that, we'll see."

"You are my angel," Wanda said, embracing and kissing him.

Once, while she was painting a seascape with a sailboat on the open sea, Wanda began to think, for the first time, that she was afraid of being alone in the world. She had been with her father, then with her sister, now with Tadeush. The very thought of being alone made her fearful. What was she afraid of? Loneliness or people? Both, it seemed. She realized that in three months she would have to interrupt her studies at the studio.

Three weeks before Tadeush was to leave, Wanda said to him, "Your stay here is coming to an end. What are we going to do?"

"I've thought it over," Tadeush answered, "and I think I've come up with something. It will be necessary to find a companion for you. It's important that you not be left alone. As for me, I have to go. I have urgent business to attend to, something I have to decide myself, without the manager."

"But we don't know anybody here. Who will recommend a good companion."

"Don't worry. I talked to Professor Truse. He has recommended a respectable lady. You'll meet her tomorrow."

Wanda slept badly that night. She still thought about how she would have to be without Tadeush for a long time. She was so attached to him. What kind of person would the woman be? They would be together for such a long time. Wanda awoke frequently and looked at her husband.

"My dear, my love," she thought, "if I could express in words how much I love you. No, I won't be able to be alone. Nothing and no one can replace you. If we had a child, I would give my attention to him, but, as it is, you're the only one I have."

She fell asleep again.

Wanda's worries were groundless. The woman Professor Truse introduced them to was very pretty. She was about fifty years old. Her name was Madam Simona. She was a good conversationalist. Wanda would not be bored with her.

"I'm a widow," Madam Simona said, "and I don't have any special worries. So I'll be able to take care of you."

"That's wonderful," Tadeush said. "I'll be eternally grateful to you, Madam Simona. I'm sure the two of you will get along well."

Wanda tried to stay calm, at least outwardly. Madam Simona occupied the adjoining room. As they were eating dinner together for the last time, Tadeush tried to encourage Wanda.

"There's an acquaintance of mine here," he said. "She's a countess by origin, and he is a grand duke. We've vacationed together in the south of France. If you want, I'll introduce you. He's a cousin of Czar Nikolay."

When Tadeush mentioned the word "countess," Wanda started. The thought came to her that Countess Gdansky was in Paris, and that Wanda would surely see her.

Tadeush had no chance to introduce Wanda because the duke and duchess rose from their table and walked to the exit. Already, Wanda was thinking that she would, indeed, see Marina.

At the railway station, Wanda controlled herself well. She did not cry. But she asked Tadeush, over and over, when he would be back.

"I'll come back by Christmas," Tadeush said. "It's only four months. Time will pass quickly. Write to me about everything, in detail."

"Oh, yes," Wanda replied, "I'll write often, as if I were talking to you. You're right, time will fly."

They said farewell, and the train carried Tadeush away. As soon as the train disappeared, Wanda began to cry. She was simply unable to suppress her tears any longer. Madam Simona comforted her, telling her there could be no reunions without separations.

When they had returned to the hotel, Madam Simona tried to divert Wanda, but she failed.

"My dear," Madam Simona said, "We've talked about this already. your husband didn't go off to battle; he went home on business. As for you, you're visiting Professor Truso's studio, and you must be happy and not cry."

"But today I want to be alone," Wanda answered. "I must have time to gather my thoughts."

"All right, but only today. I'll wake you tomorrow morning. You rest now." Madam Simona left the room, closing the door behind her. Wanda lay on the bed with her eyes closed.

"I must get control of myself," she thought. "I must think this through. I have to find out where the countess lives. But how will I explain to Simona who the countess is and why I'm looking for her. It's good that Tadeush isn't here. Otherwise, I wouldn't be able to do this."

In the morning at breakfast Wanda asked, "Madam Simona, have you heard the last name Gdansky—a husband, wife, and a little girl."

"I don't recall it. I have a good friend, Madam Rushena, and she knows half of Paris and all the high society. I'll introduce you to her."

Madam Simona did not keep Wanda waiting long. The next day, Wanda made the acquaintance of Madam Rushena, a tall slim woman, wearing pince-nez. She was the opposite of Madam Simona, who was short, stout, and rosy as an apple. Madam Rushena reminded Wanda of a teacher she had once had. The teacher had been a cold person, and Wanda had not liked her very much.

The three women sat at a table in a small cafe, drinking coffee. Madam Rushena asked, "What can I do for you?"

"I would like to know whether or not you are acquainted with Countess Gdansky," Wanda responded. "She and I are from the same city."

"Yes, I have seen Count Gdansky with his wife and a little girl. If we're talking about the same Gdanskys, then I've seen them twice, once at my cousin's home and again at a reception given by an old marquise. I remember that at my cousin's they had a child with them, a beautiful girl. But, as I remember, a doctor has advised them to rest in the south. It seems to me they live in Nice now. Sometimes they come to Paris. During one of their trips here I met them. That's all I can tell you, my dear."

"Didn't I tell you?" said Madam Simona. "Madam Rushena knows all the high society of Paris. Do you want to go to Nice to see the Gdanskys?"

"No, it isn't worthwhile for me to go to see them. But if they come to Paris, I'd like to meet with the countess. It must seem like a surprise, though. She has known me since I was sixteen. I got to know the count later," Wanda lied.

"Good," said Madam Rushena, "as soon as I know that they're coming, I'll let you know. I haven't seen them in more than a year, but I'll find out when they're coming to Paris and where they'll be staying."

"I'll be very grateful to you, Madam. You will be doing me a great favor." Madam Rushena bowed and left, explaining that she was in a hurry to take care of some business.

"Her husband was a minister," Madam Simona said. "He died a year ago and left her a nice fortune. She still gives receptions and she's still invited into the circles of high society. Her son lives in England. He holds a high post in the French embassy."

"If it's not an intrusion, do you have a family?" Wanda asked.

"No, it's not an intrusion. My husband died eleven years ago. He also held a prominent post, but his was in the Parliament. I also used to give receptions and was a part of society. But now, except for Madam Rushena, I communicate with almost no one. When my husband died, it turned out that he left me almost nothing, except debts. I knew he played cards at night, but I was sure it was only an innocent pastime. As it was, he had bonded our entire fortune, even my dowry. A few days before he died he'd lost everything. We didn't have any children, and I was in a disastrous situation. Thanks to Madam Rushena, I was able to survive. She supported me during the hard times. I was forty-two when it happened. I kept a lingerie shop for eight years and never remarried. Recently, I sold the shop. I'll be able to live a modest life on the money. Now you know everything about me, Wanda. And you're so young that you have nothing to tell. You've studied, gotten married, and you're only twenty-three years old. Did I guess right?"

"Yes, you're right," Wanda smiled. "Nothing has happened in my life that's worth mentioning."

Wanda wanted to believe what she had said. She wished simply to forget her past so that it would be as Madam Simona had presented it. But how could she forget? She should not even try to, because she was seeking an encounter with Countess Gdansky.

Soon, Wanda received the first letter from Tadeush.

"My dear, my love," he wrote, "as soon as the train took me away from the station, I started to miss you. I saw your sad face in front of me. My heart was torn with pain. I beg you, write to me often. It is good for you to be in Paris. It will make you stronger to be far from me, and, above all, the professor's lessons will be useful to you. You are my smart girl. You understand everything. Remember that you are always with me, my love, and that we will meet again soon. I will stay in Germany for two weeks, and then I go back to Odessa. Be careful."

The letter was signed, "I love you, your Tadeush."

Wanda's spirits rose after she read the letter. She was working with great interest in Professor Truso's studio. His assistants invited her for supper or to attend the theatre, but she politely refused each time. Madam Simona always waited for her after the lessons, and they went everywhere together. Wanda had a good opportunity to learn the language by conversing with Simona.

Wanda wrote a letter to Tadeush describing how she was spending her time. She wrote that Madam Simona gave her no chance to become bored. At the end of the letter, she added, "Thank you, my dear, for everything you are doing for me. God save you. With love, your wife, Wanda."

Once, toward evening, Wanda and Simona were sitting on the balcony. There was no wind, and the weather was warm but not stifling as it was after a rain. Rain had fallen in the morning, but the sun had come out at noon. As she sat there, Wanda enjoyed observing the pedestrians.

"I would like to paint pictures of life in Paris," she said.

"You are so young and talented," Simona said. "Really, God does give everything to one person and nothing to another. Take me, for instance, I've never had any talent."

"Why do you say that? Everyone has a talent for something. It's necessary only to concentrate one's attention on it."

"My dear, I'm already fifty years old. If it wasn't there when I was young, it's not going to be at all."

"You told me once that you are a good cook. That's also a talent. Not everyone can cook. I can't. I don't even know how to start."

"When I was in your position," Simona said, "I couldn't cook. But life forced me to learn and I came to like it."

A messenger from the hotel came and brought a note. Madam Rushena informed them that she would be there the next day at five in the afternoon.

"That's wonderful," Simona said. "We'll all dine together. She has obviously found out when your acquaintances are coming."

Now Wanda had something to think about. She mentally sorted out all the versions of how she would meet with the countess. Of course, if Tadeush had been there, they would have gone to some reception. But no. She would have betrayed herself then. Above all, it was necessary to find out where the Gdanskys were staying and try to see the child from afar.

Wanda fell asleep late and woke up very early. She did not go to the studio but drew in her album. Usually, she showed her pictures to the professor and he noted his criticisms the next day. But that day she could not concentrate. Even though she had been telling herself that she had no right to come close to the child, she felt differently. The baby had been hers, had grown inside her, was a part of her own body. She belonged to Wanda more than she could to anyone else.

Finally, at five o'clock, Madam Rushena arrived. Wanda looked at her and again, involuntarily, recalled her old teacher.

"Have dinner with us, my dear," Simona said to Madam Rushena.

"I don't feel like dinner right now," Madam Rushena answered. "Maybe later. Meanwhile, we can sit down and talk. I have some news for you, and it isn't very pleasant."

"What is it?" Wanda asked. "Has someone taken ill, and the Gdanskys can't come?"

"It's not that," Madam Rushena said. She asked Simona for a glass of water, drank it, took a breath, and continued. "It's a tragedy. The Gdanskys' girl died. It turned out she had consumption. It happened more than a month ago. A good friend of mine was at the funeral. When she rested in Nice, she always visited the Gdanskys."

Wanda was paralyzed, speechless. The lady continued her terrible story. "But that isn't all. There's big trouble with the countess. They keep her in a special sanatorium. My friend tells me that she went with the count to visit the countess in the sanatorium. She said it was difficult to recognize her. She looks like a madwoman. She calls to the child all the time. She keeps saying to her husband, 'She gave me the child, and she took her back. Pay her any amount of money, just so she gives Marina back.' You know, my friend came back devastated. I feel terribly sorry for the count. You can, of Course, go see him. I think he'll be glad to see you."

"No," Wanda said, rising, "I have nothing that will help him. Oh, my God." She bowed slightly and went to her room. Falling on the bed, she burst into tears. Her child was no more. There was no more of her little darling. She had never been able to know her, to hold her in her arms.

Someone knocked at the door. Wanda did not answer.

"Will you come to dinner with us?" Simona called.

"No, go without me," Wanda answered. She rose from the bed and began a letter to Tadeush.

My Darling,

Come, if you can, and get me. I will not be an artist anyway. I have had enough lessons to understand that. I cannot be without you anymore. I miss you very, very much. Write to me, please, to tell me when you will be able to come. I love you.

Your Wanda

When he received the letter, Tadeush sent a telegram informing Wanda that he would be in Paris on July 15. Three weeks remained before his arrival, and Wanda counted the days.

Three weeks passed, finally, and Wanda met Tadeush at the railway station.

She pressed her cheek to his, crying.

"You've lost weight," Tadeush said. "Oh, Wanda, you shouldn't have been left alone."

"Everything will be all right, now that you've come."

Before they left for Odessa, Wanda saw a gynecologist. He found a small, inflamed area and said that it had prevented her from becoming pregnant.

The doctor, an old man of less than medium height, prescribed medicine for her.

"Take one of these each day, madam," he said, "and I guarantee that in less than a year you'll be pregnant."

Both Wanda's and Tadeush's spirits rose. They were young, good looking, and rich, and they had their entire lives in front of them. What else could they desire? Now they had hope that they would have a child, a child that, as Wanda liked to say, would be "soft and warm."

They did not stop in Poland on their way back, but went directly to Odessa.

Tadeush had urgent business to attend to.

With them, they carried Wanda's sketches, drawings, and paintings, her memories of Paris.

PART IV

Wanda met with her friend, Yasia. They had much to tell each other, impressions to share. What had Wanda experienced? There were many things, both new and interesting. She had been in Cracow and had seen her sister and her family. Paris had become very close to her and, at the same time, very distant.

Wanda talked about everything, except her latest experience. Only to God Himself could she tell what grief she had had to go through.

Yasia listened, holding her breath. Of course, Wanda had been in Paris! And she, Yasia, had been to Petersburg. She had something to tell, too. She had had two secret dates with a handsome officer.

Wanda opened her eyes wide, listening to Yasia. Then, in bewilderment, she asked, "Don't you love Yuzef?"

"Of course I love him. But this was just a flirt, a fleeting passion. This feeling picked me up and carried me away." Yasia's voice was deep, throaty.

"And how far did it carry you away?" Wanda asked in astonishment. "Well, what can I say?" Yasia said, shrugging. "I was very much in love with him, but it happened so unexpectedly that I didn't have time to think about anything."

"You didn't answer my question. How far did your 'fleeting passion' go?" Yasia grew shy. "It went far. If Yuzef had known about it, he would have killed me. I share it with you only because I have no one else to tell. Don't judge me too severely. It can happen to anybody. Tell me, in all this time, have you had an affair with someone?"

"No," Wanda said, shaking her head. "There has been no affair. My only affair is with Tadeush, and I want it to be endless."

"But you're so pretty. It seems to me that men must be pestering the life out of you. When we happen to be with you socially, I notice that men just can't take their eyes off you. Don't you notice it?"

"I notice it, and I'm used to it, used to compliments. But I don't give preference to anyone. Besides, I don't want to be a bigger sinner than I am. My other sins are enough."

"Don't say it like that, Wanda. We're all sinners. One sin, more or less—it doesn't matter."

"It's you who thinks that. I have another opinion. When did you last confess, in a church."

"Last week. Why?"

"Did you tell your priest about your sin? Did you admit your sin, as a Catholic?"

"No, I don't even want to admit it to myself. But I prayed and asked the Lord to forgive me my sin."

Wanda did not answer. She thought a moment, understanding Yasia, because she herself had not been telling everything in confession.

"All right, Yasia," Wanda said, smiling, "let's talk about something else. This could come to a quarrel, and I don't want it."

"You're right," Yasia agreed. "Tell me, where are you going to celebrate Christmas?"

"We haven't talked about it yet. I don't know. Do you have any suggestions?"

"If you want, we can have it at our place. Our parents won't come this year."

"We still have time to talk about it. We have a lot of time before Christmas," Wanda said. "Yasia, tell me, how many years have you been married?"

"It's been five years this summer. Why do you ask about it all of a sudden?"

"Because you don't have children, and I'm wondering whether you still don't want them or if there's another reason you don't have them."

"You know, I've been checking with the doctors for three years now, and all of them say I'm healthy. But Yuzef doesn't want to be examined. He says he's healthy. Frankly, I'm not very worried because Yuzef never brings the subject up. It's my mother who insists on it all the time. She wants to have grandchildren. Why don't you have children? Is there a reason?"

"Before I went to Paris, I didn't know for sure why we were childless. It turned out that I had to have some treatment. The doctor guarantees that we'll have children. I'll have to have an examination after Christmas. It'll be three months after the treatment."

"I'll go with you, Wanda. It's time for me to go for an examination. For some reason, I feel bad."

"If you don't feel good, you don't have to wait. You can go any time. I'll go with you if you want."

"Good. Will you tell me when you're free? We'll go to my doctor."

"I think any day next week except Wednesday and Friday will be fine because on those days I'll be going to the orphanage. I haven't seen the children for a long time. With the holidays coming, I'll have to prepare something."

They agreed on Tuesday. Wanda would pick Yasia up, and they would go to the doctor.

While Wanda was talking to Yasia, Tadeush was talking to Yuzef.

That evening, at supper, Tadeush smiled and said to Wanda, "Yuzef was telling me how he and Yasia went to Petersburg. She stayed with her cousin, whom he can't tolerate, and he rested in Petergof at his friends'. They saw each other only on Sundays. We couldn't do it that way. Right, my dear?"

"Of course not. But Yasia didn't say anything about that. It's strange," Wanda answered, pensively.

"And what could she tell you? That her cousin has an eye on her husband. He told me how she sticks to him. But she is so unpleasant that she disgusts him. And Yasia, the silly woman, doesn't see anything. He also told me how well he was spending his time in Petergof with a young lady. I asked him if he loves Yasia. He said that, of course, he loves her, as his wife. But that doesn't prevent him from having an affair sometimes."

Wanda looked at her plate and did not answer. Now she understood better the relationship between Yasia and Yuzef. She did not tell Tadeush that Yasia had also been unfaithful. She understood that it was a woman's secret and that no man would approve.

"Don't even think about letting on that you know something when Yuzef is around. There's no need for Yasia to know anything. He told me about it man to man."

"You don't have to warn me, Tadeush. I wouldn't say anything to anyone about such a thing."

Wanda visited the orphanage. The children gathered around her, and she was happy in their company.

It was a Catholic orphanage. Some of the pupils, having reached the proper age, were preparing to become monks or nuns. They were going to monasteries and convents. Wanda was present, sometimes, at the ceremonies held when the young orphans departed to follow their religious lives, and her feelings were mixed.

On Tuesday, she met Yasia, as they had agreed, and the two women went together to a doctor. Yasia was the first to be examined. After about thirty minutes, Yasia came out of the office. Wanda looked at her and noticed red spots on her face. Yasia sat next to Wanda but had no time to say anything because the doctor called Wanda's name.

It was Wanda's first visit to this doctor. She had her own physician, and decided to go to this doctor only because of Yasia's recommendation. The doctor asked questions, and a nurse wrote down Wanda's answers. After the questions were asked, he began to examine her.

When Wanda had dressed and was sitting in his office, the doctor said, "Your condition isn't so bad. There is almost no inflammation. You still have to undergo treatment for two or three months. Then everything will be all right."

Thanking him, Wanda left, thinking, "Again, I must wait for months. Everyone is comforting me."

In the waiting area, she approached Yasia, and they walked to the exit.

Wanda offered to go for a walk because the weather was good. Yasia agreed.

"Well, tell me," Wanda said when they reached the street.

"The doctor said that I'm three months pregnant. I felt that something was wrong with me, but I couldn't believe it." Yasia spoke excitedly.

"How lucky you are. If the doctor had told me that, I would have flown like a bird. What a surprise this is for Yuzef."

"You don't understand. Remember, I told you I met an officer in Petersburg. The whole month my husband was in Petergof, we saw each other sometimes, but there was nothing between us. It's been two and a half months since we returned from vacation. So I got pregnant in Petersburg. What's more, we've been married for six years, and I've never been pregnant in all those years. Now you understand what I'm afraid of. If he does the calculations, how will I be able to explain it?"

Yasia's cheeks were on fire. Wanda looked at her with concern. Several minutes passed in silence.

"It seems to me that you are worrying about nothing," Wanda said. "Yuzef won't notice two or three weeks. Control yourself. Behave naturally, as if everything is supposed to be this way. Make him happy and don't tell him about the time. Tell him that it has been two or three months. Then you'll see that I am right. Everything will be fine."

"Oh, Wanda, I am a great sinner. I'll have to pay yet, and for a long time, for my sin."

She started to cry, wiping her eyes with a handkerchief. They were walking along a quiet street; there were few pedestrians.

Wanda stopped. "Calm down. We might meet someone we know who will interpret your tears as he wants. And remember, you don't want to seem upset by your pregnancy. Let's go sit in the park. When you calm down, we'll go on."

It was the end of November. Yellow leaves spun and fell. It was still warm. If it were not for the color of the trees and the carpet-like covering of leaves underfoot, one would think it was the end of summer.

Wanda and Yasia walked down the path in the park, cleared the leaves off a bench, and sat down. Yasia did not cry anymore. She stared in front of her, her eyes directed at a point just beyond her feet.

One more secret had found its place in Wanda's soul, but this time it was someone else's secret.

A few days later, Wanda found out that all was well. Yuzef was happy about the news and told Yasia to take care of herself. Her tears he took for tears of joy. That was good. Wanda was happy for her friend. But she was upset that her own treatments had, as yet, had no results.

The Christmas holidays and the new year of 1914 were approaching. They decided to celebrate at Yasia's, with only a few couples.

Wanda ordered a dress in the latest fashion. As she left the store, she thought she saw Chernov standing across the street. A cabman waited for her at the corner. She got into the cab and turned to look at the place where the figure had been standing. No one was there. Wanda thought it was her imagination. She had not seen him for a long time, and after all this time, she could have been mistaken. But she clearly remembered their last meeting before her departure from Paris, when she had met him at the cemetery.

Greeting cards awaited Wanda at home. She looked them over, some from acquaintances, one from Sophie. She picked up a small card printed in gold. It contained a handwritten note: "Merry Christmas, Happy New Year! Yours Truly, V. CH."

"Well, well," Wanda thought. "All of a sudden he decides to send a greeting card."

She no longer had any doubts about whether she had imagined seeing Chernov. He had been there. Without fully realizing what she did, she hid the card.

Christmas at Yasia's passed merrily. Yasia was the target of many jokes. Someone said that she must have been eating for three people; it looked as though she were expecting twins. Yasia behaved so naturally that no traces of her former anxiety could be seen.

Wanda decided that women have a well-developed ability to keep secrets. The year 1914 arrived. What would it bring to these happy people? When the toast had been proposed and everyone had made wishes, Wanda had made only one: a baby. She wanted the Lord to send her a baby; that was all she lacked.

The winter was, as always, unstable. Now it snowed, then it rained, and at the end of February an early spring came.

In March, Yasia gave birth to a baby boy. The birth was without complication, and the baby, the doctor said, was very healthy.

Yasia was supposed to go home after a few days. Her parents arrived because it was their first grandchild. Wanda bought a present and waited for her friend impatiently. Yuzef called on Wanda and Tadeush, and they all went together to bring Yasia home with her child. Yasia had not changed at all.

Yasia's parents were waiting for them. The baby boy was sleeping when they arrived. He had a dark complexion. Yasia and Yuzef both had white skin.

When the baby was uncovered, Yasia's mother said, "He's so swarthy, just like my father was."

Her mother's statement took a load off Yasia's mind. Her son was as swarthy as the handsome officer.

"Well, then," she said, "let's name him in honor of my grandfather, since they resemble each other."

Wanda watched the scene. She was content for her girlfriend. Everything had gone very well.

When Tadeush and Wanda were on their way home, Wanda asked her husband whether he had liked the baby. He answered that the baby was charming. A week later, Wanda visited a gynecologist who told her she was pregnant.

She could not believe it, and she asked him to check one more time.

The doctor smiled and said, "My dear, this is not the first time I've seen you. I'm sure you're pregnant, and you have been for about two months. You'll give birth in September or October."

At home, Wanda waited for Tadeush, looking often at her watch. Finally, she heard him come in. She walked toward him.

"Let's go to the study," she said. "I have to tell you something."

When Tadeush closed the door behind them, Wanda rushed to embrace him, crying with happiness.

"We're going to have a baby. I'm pregnant. The doctor said I'll give birth in September or October."

Tadeush guided her to the sofa, sat beside her, and kissed her. He kissed her eyes, cheeks, and forehead and then pulled her head down and rested it on his chest.

"I've been waiting for this, and I've been afraid. The two feelings have always struggled in me. I've been waiting for those words with pain in my heart. And now it's done."

Tadeush told her that no other man could be happier than he. He told her that from then on he would be with her during almost all of his free time. Only once more, at the end of the summer, would he go to Germany to legalize the papers that would sell his business to his manager.

"It will be my last trip, my dear. I'll need no more than two weeks to take care of these matters. Everything will be excellent, my love, just as you want it."

Filled with happiness, Wanda said, "I begged the Mother of God, and she heard my prayers. Oh, Tadeush, tomorrow I'll deliver donations to the orphanage and the monastery."

It was a day in Wanda's life worth remembering. She wrote a letter to Sophie, describing her joy.

Almost every week, Wanda was at Yasia's, playing with the baby, knowing that soon she would be playing with her own baby. Tadeush asked her constantly how she was feeling. He went with her to see the doctor. He watched over her every move.

Spring passed and summer was drawing to a close. In August, Tadeush left for Germany. Wanda was in the seventh month of her pregnancy. She felt well, but Tadeush, in telling her good-bye, kept reminding her to take care of herself. He left orders for the servants to look after her.

They said farewell at home, and a cab took Tadeush to the train station. Wanda passed her time in the garden. The roses were blooming, giving off a wondrous fragrance. She lay in the arbor, reading her favorite books.

One evening, after supper, she was bored, awaiting Tadeush's return. It had been a week since he had left. A telegram arrived, saying that he had arrived safely.

One morning, she awakened, and, after her morning toilet, she started for the garden. She was having breakfast on the veranda. While serving the meal, a servant said, "Oh, Lord: I was at the market this morning. They were saying that war has begun."

"What? What a thing to say," Wanda answered. "Please call Nicholai for me."

Nicholai had been a servant in the house since before Tadeush and Wanda were married. He was not a young man, but he had a strong nature. He came to Wanda on the veranda.

"You called me, madam?"

"Yes, Nicholai. Go down and bring me today's paper."

Wanda had finished breakfast when Nicholai brought the newspaper. On the front page Wanda read that war had indeed broken out. The citizenry was requested to remain calm.

"Oh, my God," Wanda whispered, "if only Tadeush had come back earlier. He's still in Germany." Her hands grew cold, and she dropped the newspaper on the floor.

"Be calm," she told herself. "For the sake of our baby, I must not get excited."

But she could not dispel her anxiety. Fear gripped her heart. She left for Yasia's and there found a complete absence of worry.

"Why are you acting this way?" Yasia asked. "Yusef says this is a brief alarm, that everything will soon be settled."

"God grant that it will be," Wanda answered. "Tadeush is in Germany, and I'm waiting for a telegram. It should come any time. I'll go home. Maybe there's already a message waiting for me."

Wanda hurried home, but there was no telegram. The servant said that a gentleman was waiting for her. The matter was important.

In the parlor, Wanda found Chernov. He stood to greet her.

"I beg your forgiveness for just dropping in on you," he said, "but you no doubt have heard that war has started."

"Yes, I heard, and I read about it in the paper. Sit down, please, and tell me your opinion. How serious is it?" Wanda sat down across from him.

"It is very serious, dear Wanda. Otherwise, I would not have troubled you. The military authorities are better informed about the situation. I know you are expecting a baby, so I wanted to inform you and your husband. You can move in time deeper into Russia, a little further from Europe. The military action may spread throughout Europe."

"Thank you very much for your concern, but, unfortunately, my husband is in Germany. He should be coming home in a day or two. I'll tell him about your attentiveness to us. I'm very grateful to you, Mr. Chernov."

"So your husband is in Germany. You must be worried. Just how did it happen that he left when you're in this condition? Pardon me for asking such question."

"He went to sell a business to his former German manager, Shtolz. This was to be his last trip to Europe, he said. Now I'm worried about his safe return."

"Everything will be all right. You don't have to feel that way. When will he return?"

"In two or three days. I'm expecting a telegram no later than tomorrow."

"So you still have some time. I'll stop by the day after tomorrow, if you have no objections."

"Please. You're always welcome. I would be most grateful." They said goody-bye, and Wanda escorted Chernov to the door. "God sent him," Wanda thought. "I feel a little better now."

She slept well that night. In the morning, she again looked through the newspaper. Events were disturbing.

Wanda spent the entire day in anticipation, but no telegram arrived. Yasia came to visit, and Wanda was diverted for a few hours. After her friend's departure, however, Wanda grew even more pensive.

"What can I do?" she asked herself over and over.

Before going to bed she prayed again. Then, lying there, she placed her hand on her stomach. The baby was moving wildly, and Wanda told it that Papa would soon arrive and all the worry would be over. She fell asleep. It was a restless night. She dreamed, and her dreams awakened her.

The next day, the long-awaited telegram arrived. Tadeush informed her that he would be coming home on the twelfth. Wanda looked at the date the telegram had been sent. The seventh—rather a long time for a telegram. Obviously, it had been delayed somewhere.

Today was the twelfth. That meant Tadeush would soon be there. Wanda ordered everything to be made ready for his arrival.

The maid combed Wanda's hair and placed two thick braids around her head. Wanda thanked her, telling her that she could not remember when she had awaited the arrival of her husband so impatiently.

Dinner was ready, but Tadeush was not yet there.

"Apparently, the train has been delayed," Wanda thought.

Evening drew near. It was getting rather dark. Wanda continued to wait for her husband, not wanting to eat dinner without him.

She called the servant. Nicholai came immediately because he had not yet gone to bed.

"Nicholai, go to this address and deliver this note from me. If they tell you to wait while they compose an answer, then wait. Here's the note and the address."

Nicholai bowed and left, taking the note to Chernov. Wanda had written: "Most esteemed Mr. Chernov: I need your help. My husband sent a telegram, saying that he would be here today, but the day has ended without his arrival. Perhaps you know someone who manages the railroad. Please advise, as I am very upset. Tadeush had already sent a telegram on the seventh, but it arrived only this morning. Please forgive me for bothering you at such a late hour. Respectfully, Wanda."

Nicholai rang, and Chernov himself opened the door. After he read the note, Chernov asked Nicholai to wait for a minute while he got his hat. He was going back with Nicholai to see Madam Wanda.

On the way, Chernov told the servant, "I have a request of you, my dear man. Aren't you the one who gets all the mail for the Stanishevskys?"

Nicholai nodded, and Chernov continued. "Beginning tomorrow, you keep all letters or telegrams sent to Madam. At the end of the day, when I come over, give them to me."

"I can't do such a thing," Nicholai answered, hesitantly. "I work for the Stanishevskys."

"Understand. This is for her own good. She is with child, and she must not get excited. If something bad happens, and she should see it written in a telegram. ... Now am I understood?"

"I understand. But it will be like deceiving Madam Wanda. She is so kind, so gentle."

"This is not deception, Nicholai. There is war now, and anything can happen. Her husband is in Germany."

They approached the house. At the entrance, Nicholai said, "All right, Mr. Chernov, I'll keep the mail, but only if Madam Wanda doesn't meet the postman at the door."

Wanda was waiting in the parlor. Chernov walked in and greeted her. "You are very kind to come, when it turns out I'm alone at such a time,"

Wanda said, as if she were apologizing.

"Now what do you mean by that?" Chernov asked. "I am always at your service. It is an honor for me to be of use to you. I don't know the train schedule exactly, but I believe they have been detained or hindered in some way. Tomorrow, for sure, I'll find out and give you a full explanation. Now you must rest. You look tired."

Wanda nodded submissively. "You're right. It could be that the trains have been detained. Once again, please pardon me for disturbing you. I think everything will be cleared up tomorrow."

Chernov promised to find out everything he could as soon as possible and took his leave.

The next day, before noon, Chernov learned that there had been a train wreck in Germany and that the train had been headed for Russia. But it was not known whether Tadeush was on that particular train.

When he arrived at Wanda's home, Chernov asked if a telegram or other news had come. There was nothing.

Wanda was waiting for him, and could only look at him inquiringly, not quite able to ask the question. Chernov began to talk immediately.

"Don't be upset. Trains from Germany are being detained, and it is still not known when they'll be running on schedule again."

He was telling the truth. After the accident, the trains could not run. "Perhaps, dear Wanda, you can give me the address of your husband's former manager. I want to send him a telegram personally. When we get an answer, we'll clear up everything."

Wanda retrieved an envelope from Tadeush's study and silently held it out to Chernov. As he left, Chernov once again tried to calm her with assurances that everything would be all right.

PART V

Nothing happened as Chernov had planned.

A telegram arrived for Wanda at night. She read it and fainted. The maid laid her on the sofa with difficulty. Wanda moaned but did not open her eyes. Soon Nicholai brought the doctor.

The doctor asked the maid whether Madam Stanishevsky had any relatives in town. She answered that she did not know, but she recalled that Nicholai had once brought Mr. Chernov.

The doctor sent for Chernov. Vladimir arrived and introduced himself as a friend of the family.

"Listen to me, my friend," the doctor said to Chernov, "this is a terrible tragedy. Poor Madam Wanda is losing the child she has been wanting all this time. She is bleeding badly as a result of her fall. Now it is necessary to fight not for the life of the baby, but for her life."

They rushed Wanda to the hospital. Her condition was critical.

Later, Vladimir learned that the telegram was from Tadeush's manager, Shtolz. He had informed her that Tadeush had perished under unexplained circumstances, and he expressed his condolences.

Vladimir was not allowed to see Wanda because of her condiition. The loss of her husband and child and the loss of a great deal of blood had drained Wanda's strength and her will to live.

For a long time, the doctors fought to save her life. Apparently, she was fated to live, for she began to recover.

After a month, Vladimir was allowed to see her. A pale, very thin Wanda looked at him without speaking. Vladimir kissed her hand.

"They told me that you'll soon be home. Does that mean you're better?" he asked, trying somehow to begin a conversation.

"I don't want to go home," Wanda said quietly. "I want to go to Poland, to my sister."

"Dear Wanda, just now that is not possible. There is a war on. I have come to tell you goody-bye. I'm leaving for the front. I'm an officer, and my place is there. If you only knew how I have hated to leave you under these circumstances."

"Don't leave. Stay with me, if only for a little while. I'm completely alone. Why am I being punished so? I want only one thing. To die. Let the Lord take me. But no. I live so that I may suffer. Where will my strength come from, Vladimir?"

He held her hand in silence. So much grief had been hers. His heart ached for her. What could he do to help? He was going to the front.

"I'll be able to help you move further into Russia," he said. "I have a small estate. A comfortable house and clean air will return your strength to you. I have a week yet, and I could take you there."

"Thank you, Vladimir. I have no one left who is as close to me as you. If you go to the front, the only thing left for me to do is pray for you. I don't want to be alone all the time. It has occurred to me that perhaps I may be of use here as a nurse."

Before his departure for the front, Vladimir visited Wanda at her home. She was sitting in a chair, dressed in a black dress and a black veil that covered her hair and shoulders.

"I've come to say good-bye," he said. "I leave to join my unit in the morning. I'll write to you, if you don't object."

"What do you mean, object?" Wanda answered. "I had intended to ask you about that. My friend Yasia was here today. She came to tell me that she and her family are leaving for somewhere in the Riazan district. She invited me to go with them. But I don't want to go anywhere, only to get stronger and help in a hospital."

"You've made the right decision. You should be with people."

They said farewell. Vladimir kissed her hand, and then he looked into her eyes. He saw that life was returning to her.

Hospital work occupied all of Wanda's time. Most often, she was on duty at night so that she would not have to be alone at home. Frequently, she spent her days working in a shelter, helping orphans. Each Sunday she went to morning mass at her church. She considered becoming a nun. When she spoke with the priest, he told her to enter the sisterhood if her heart told her to.

But her heart had not found peace. Whenever she found herself alone, all her thoughts returned to what had happened and she asked herself, "Why am I living?"

Time, and time only, separates us from events. In our memory a trace remains, but with time the events are not so keenly felt.

Wanda often lost track of time. Life returned to her, but something vague possessed her. She received letters from Vladimir. They always arrived very late. In one letter, Vladimir told her that everything was quiet and peaceful, but Wanda doubted that nothing had happened during the several weeks it had taken for the letter to reach her.

The year 1916 arrived, and Wanda was still working at the hospital. The work tempered her. She felt that she could help, that she was needed.

Following an interruption of several months, a letter from Vladimir arrived. He wrote from a hospital. He had been wounded in the leg, and he would be mustered out for home soon. Wanda read through the letter many times. What good fortune it was that he was alive, this man who had grown so close to her and who had stayed by her. She had heard nothing from Sophie.

Vladimir came home in mid-summer. When they met, Wanda did not recognize him at first. They had not seen each other for almost two years. He had grown very thin, his cheeks were sunken, his moustache was gone, and his sideburns were beginning to turn gray.

But when he said, "Well, now I'm home," Wanda immediately knew him. She pressed herself to his chest and cried for joy. Vladimir held her with one hand. In the other he carried a cane. He was lame from the wound.

"Let me look at you, dear Wanda. You've kept your youth well. You're such a beauty."

"You're joking. It seems to me I've grown older by many years. It not only seems like it; I feel it."

Wanda wore a dark dress. A single long braid of hair fell down her back. Her rather severe appearance actually made her look older, but she was, as before, sweet and lovely.

Wanda and Vladimir saw each other often after their reunion. He told her about the front, and she told him of events at the hospital.

Once, Vladimir asked, "Are you still sketching?'

"No," Wanda answered, "I can't even think about it. It seems as though that was a part of my past life, and it's gone, taking everything I had with it."

"It doesn't have to be that way, dear. Life continues. You're still a fine young woman, and a beautiful one."

"I beg you, Vladimir, talk to me about something else. So, what do you think? Will the war end soon?"

"I think they must conclude it. So much innocent blood has been shed. What will you do when the war is over?"

"I'll become a nun. I want to find peace, to be closer to God."

"You what? How can you even consider that? You're not serious. You'll change your mind."

"What is left for me in this life? What can I hope for? What awaits me? If I could go to my sister in Cracow, then maybe things would be different."

"Oh, Wanda. I look at you and I understand that except for you I have no one else in the world. I've known you for a long time. I've seen you happy and I've lived through your grief with you. I've had only one wish—to be near you. Don't think about a convent, and you don't have to go away. I think you know I've loved you all these years. At the front I lived for only one hope—to see you again."

Vladimir fell silent and looked at Wanda, waiting for her reaction.

She had listened to him, standing by the window with her head lowered.

She raised her eyes, tears falling down her cheeks.

Vladimir embraced her, his hands on her shoulders.

"Don't cry," he said. "I have no wish to offend you. Would you rather I left?"

Wanda's shoulders quivered. She spoke through her tears. "Don't go. You really are the only one I have."

They sat down on the sofa. He took her hands in his and kissed them. Wanda was quiet. She was thinking that fate had chosen to give her still one more chance at life. But did she want it?

That evening, they drank coffee and talked until midnight. When Vladimir left, Wanda knew she was no longer alone. She knew her life was in his hands. The past was gone. Only memories remained, memories of happiness and grief. They would remain with her forever.

Two years had passed since the terrible events. She was alive, her health was good, she was twenty-six years old. In the hospital, she helped the sick. On her days off, she spent time at the orphanage with the children. She felt that people needed her. And there was Vladimir, the closest friend she had.

For several days, she checked the mail after she arrived home from the hospital. Finally, there was a letter from Vladimir. He had not come over because he did not want to disturb her. He had decided to write. It was easier to lay out his ideas on paper.

He wrote:

"Dear Wanda, I understand I do not have the right to upset your peace of mind. I saw your reaction to my confession of love. I ask of you only one thing. Do not enter a convent. You are still so young. The war will end and your life will be restored to order."

"Why have I decided to write to you? It would be awkward for me to look at you and tell you that I love you and only want to be with you."

"Be my wife. I hope someday you will accept. If you have no feelings for me at all, and after my confession you still believe you want to enter the convent, it is your life and you have the right to lead it as you see fit."

"I will know if there is no letter from you that your answer is 'no.' But if you have some feeling for me, and you agree to be my wife, write, if only a short note."

"I beg your forgiveness for disturbing you. I am an officer, and I know how to control myself. But with you my boldness forsakes me."

"If there is no answer from you in two weeks, I will leave for the front. Good-bye, dear Wanda."

"Your devoted Vladimir Chernov. December 5, 1916."

Wanda read the letter several times. She did not cry. It seemed to her as if she had been waiting for this, somehow, subconsciously. Of course, for her, no one could replace Tadeush. She liked Vladimir, and it was difficult for her to be alone, so difficult to be alone.

She would answer him tomorrow. She had to collect her thoughts. But, late that night she was already composing her note.

She wrote a brief reply:

"Vladimir, come. It is already several days since I have held you. Thank you for your letter. Wanda."

A week later, Vladimir and Wanda were married. The wedding was held in the church and attended by a few friends of Vladimir's and acquaintances of Wanda's. They decided to live in Wanda's home.

It was Tadeush's house, where Wanda had spent her best years. During the time she had been alone, she occupied only two rooms and the kitchen. She never entered the remaining rooms. The maid had left long ago to move to the country, and Wanda had found herself spending less and less time at home. A woman came in only to clean and cook.

When Vladimir moved in, they engaged a full-time maid.

Vladimir's house was sold, and he and Wanda decided to build a summer house, a dacha, right by the sea, once the war was over. The year 1917 drew near.

Wanda was satisfied with Vladimir. He was considerate, easy-going, and affable. He was at the height of bliss. Before, he could not have believed that Wanda would be his wife. His happiness was endless.

In February, Vladimir was recalled to his unit as a result of the February Revolution. When he returned home, he told Wanda of the events in St. Petersburg. The czar had abdicated the throne. What would follow?

A provisional government was announced, but in Odessa little changed.

Only the newsboys in the streets cried out about the sensational news.

By March, Wanda knew that she was already pregnant. She did not have the same feelings she had had three years earlier. She was not joyous as before. Fear overcame her, and she was unable to subdue the feeling.

It was spring. The acacias and lilacs were in bloom. She and Vladimir were sitting at the seashore, and he said, "Wanda, I'm thinking about what we should name our child."

"Don't think about it dear. Let him be born first. There are a lot of names. We'll pick one of the best."

"No, I want to tell you, if you don't mind."

Wanda was silent, and Vladimir continued. "If it's a boy, we'll call him Tadeush, and if it's a girl. ..."

Wanda stopped him, placing her palm over his mouth.

"I beg you," she said, "don't say it, though you've already said it. I'll only add that if we have a daughter, we'll give her the name Maria, in honor of Saint Mary."

In June the dacha was ready, and in September, Wanda gave birth to Maria. The little girl was born healthy, and everything went very well. Wanda's face shone with her indescribable happiness. She wept tears of joy.

Vladimir clutched her hand in his. What joy! What happiness! Wanda had given birth to his daughter. They would have a son and another daughter. They would have a family, large and happy.

The next year, Wanda would be with her daughter by the sea.

Little Maria looked very much like Vladimir. Wanda wanted to nurse her daughter by herself, but she did not have enough milk, so they hired a wet nurse. The nurse's name was Zina. She was about twenty-five years old and had a son about two months older than Maria. The boy was her second child. Zina's mother was looking after the older child, and Zina and her son lived at the Chernov's. Her husband had been taken into the army before the child was born.

Vladimir left often to work with his unit. During the daytime, Wanda was busy with her daughter or with housekeeping. She always waited for dinner until Vladimir came home. Even if he was very late, she did not dine without him.

One night, Vladimir came home early. He was pale.

"What happened, Vladik?" Wanda asked. "Are you all right?"

"Yes, I'm all right, my dear. It's Russia that's sick. The revolution has taken place. The Bolsheviks have seized power. The provisional government has been arrested."

"What's going to happen?" Wanda asked in horror, taking his hands in hers.

"We'll fight the mutineers. I am an officer, and my place is in the army. The soldiers will support us. Calm down, my dear. You're trembling all over. We live in a time of disturbance, but everything will be all right. You'll see." Vladimir ate quickly and left to join his unit again. Wanda was left holding little Maria and praying to God to save her little one, to allow the child to grow up knowing her mother and father.

"I beg you, my Lord," Wanda whispered. "Don't leave her an orphan, as I once was. I've had to go through so much in my life. My God, everything is in your power. Bless and forgive."

She put Maria in her crib and walked to the living room. It had been a long time since she had looked at the newspapers. Not since she had married Vladimir had she studied them. She sat down at the small table where the newspapers lay and started to look them over.

Odessa's Leaf, The Monday News, Odessa Theatrical Review: all of them carried front page news about the revolution. Wanda turned page after page. There was war in Europe, events in Poland, France, Germany. The planet was on fire. How long would it go on?

A note was brought late that night telling Wanda that Vladimir would not be home. He returned the next day.

"What's going to happen, Vladik?" Wanda asked. "What can we do?"

"Calm down. We'll think of something. The army is disciplined. The officers have been well trained. The uprising will be suppressed. It will only take time."

Vladimir Chernov, who was an officer in the czar's army, believed what he said and would remain faithful to his duty.

The year was 1918. Red flags flew at every intersection in Odessa. The Reds were masters of the city.

Wanda received a note from Vladimir. He wrote that he would come for her soon, and they would go abroad. For now, she and Maria should not go out on the street. It was dangerous.

Wanda had not seen Vladimir for several months. He and his unit had retreated before the coming of the Reds.

Wanda was praying passionately, on her knees when someone knocked loudly on the door. She walked to it and asked who was there.

"In the name of the Revolution, open up, or we'll break the door."

Wanda opened the door and stepped back to the wall, out of the way. Four people came in, three men and a woman.

"How many people live in your house?" one of them asked.

"My husband, my daughter, and myself. My husband is at the front right now."

"What front? Where does he serve? Where is his unit? What's his last name, first name?"

"I don't know where his unit is. I know that he's been at the front since 1914. He's an officer."

"Everything's clear. Your husband is White. He's an enemy of the Revolution, and with enemies we have little to talk about."

"Oh, no. He isn't an enemy. He's Russian. Chernov, Vladimir Nikolaevitch. We have a little girl. She's less than a year old."

"How many rooms do you have here? Hey, Stepa, go count on the second floor. We'll look on the first."

Wanda walked to the baby's crib and took Maria in her arms. She held the child, watching the unwanted guests walk from room to room. The one called Stepa went downstairs and then reported how many rooms were there.

The same day, strangers were settled in each room of Wanda's home. She had only one room on the first floor. There was noise in the house. Songs were sung; shouts rang out from one floor to the other. Wanda made her way to the kitchen for a drink of water.

"Hey, let the lady through. Look at that dress she has on. Don't you want to swap it for soldier's boots?"

They shouted something else in her direction. She filled a carafe with water and went to her room.

"Oh, my God," she thought. "What will I do? When Vladik comes, will I survive all this? To whom do I look for protection?"

The shouting and pounding frightened her. They were building partitions.

Someone yelled at her.

"Hey, lady, why are you sitting in your room? Come out and help the working class. Or are you afraid to get your little hands dirty?"

"Leave her alone," someone said. "Don't you see she's frightened to death? She has a little child."

"Why are you taking the side of the bourgeoisie? I suppose they've had pity on folks like us?"

There was a knock at the door. Wanda opened it.

"Why are you sitting in here locked up?" one of the intruders asked. "We're not beasts. We're humans too. Don't be afraid of us. We haven't come to kill you. And don't hang on to your baby so. Nobody will hurt her. Go to the kitchen. We've cooked some soup. There's enough for you, too."

"Thank you, I'll go now. I just want to put my daughter to bed."

The door was closed. There was nothing else to do. Hunger takes its toll; it is necessary to eat something. Some boiled milk was left for Maria. More milk was supposed to be delivered the next day. The important thing was not to oversleep. Wanda would have to go out to meet the delivery woman.

Wanda walked to the kitchen. Something steamed in a big bowl. They poured out some soup with potatoes in it onto a plate for her and then cut off a piece of bread. She thanked them and started to return to her room.

"Why won't you eat with us? Are you too fastidious?"

"You aren't bothering us," another voice added. "Sit down and eat like everybody else."

They made room for her at the end of the table, and Wanda put her plate down and sat. She could not swallow. She felt the stares fixed on her. She had to overcome her feelings. There was nothing else to do. She started to eat, chewing slowly.

"That's better. Eat. Nobody will take it from you."

Wanda awoke early the next morning. She dressed quickly and left the house through the back door. She walked around to the front and waited for the delivery woman. She noticed a sign attached to her door.

"Revolutionary Committee of Working and Farming Youth," it read.

So that was who had settled in her house. The whole committee. How long would it last?

The milkwoman had not arrived. Pedestrians began to appear. Wanda paced back and forth in front of the house, carrying the milk cannister.

Suddenly, behind her, someone called to her in a low voice. It was Vladimir.

He put a finger to his lips. "Be quiet."

Vladimir wore his military overcoat and boots, but his epaulets were gone and his head was bare.

"You've come for us," she cried. "I'll go get Maria."

"No. Not now. We must wait until night. We'll leave then."

They entered the house through the back door. The members of the committee were still asleep. Vladimir removed his coat, and Wanda saw that he was still wearing his uniform.

"Darling, take your tunic off. Get changed. I'm afraid they'll see you." Wanda did not know that she had been watched from a window, that members of the committee had seen her come in the back door with Vladimir. To them, everything was clear. She was the enemy and she had brought an enemy home. It was now necessary to call the guards and conduct search.

Vladimir had not time to take his tunic off. He stood beside the crib, watching his daughter sleep. Wanda stood next to him. He put his arm around her shoulders, and there was a knock at the door.

They kept silent. The knock repeated, louder.

"Open up right now," a voice said. "We know you're hiding someone in your room."

Vladimir opened the door.

"She isn't hiding anyone," he said. "I am her husband, and I have come home. As far as I can remember, it is our home."

At the door stood two armed men. Behind them stood members of the committee.

"Come out of the room, White Guard. Cover your epaulets, you White Guard rat."

"I won't go anywhere. I live here. This is my family, and I have come home."

"Let's take him, men. It seems he doesn't understand nice talk." Instinctively, Vladimir reached for his holster. Everything happened in an instant.

A shot exploded, then a second. Vladimir fell. He was dragged by his feet over the threshold. Someone took his wrist and checked his pulse. "Gone."

"What have you done?" Wanda screamed. "Why did you shoot? He hasn't hurt anyone. You animals. Why did you kill him?"

Wanda fell on Vladimir, weeping bitterly. Someone lifted her from him and took her to her room. Maria lay in her crib, crying. Wanda ran to her.

"My little one. My dear little girl," she cried. "Now we are all alone in the world. They killed him before my eyes. Vladik is no more. You don't have a father."

Wanda wept, stroking the baby's head. The child looked at her with wide, round eyes.

Soon, Wanda was notified that she would have to move out. She would be able to take what she could carry and leave immediately. Her room had been searched but nothing had been found.

On the street, Wanda found a cab. The cabman helped load her baggage. Her portrait had been wrapped in a sheet along with her drawings. She had been allowed to take them. That was all. Farewell to a home, a place of comfort once, a place of terror now.

"Where are we going, lady?" the cabman asked. "I don't know. Go straight ahead. I'll remember."

She searched her memory, trying to recall where the wet nurse lived. "Go to Alexandorvsky Street. I remember the house." Fortunately, she found where Zina lived.

"Wait here," she said to the cabman. "I'll be right back." She knocked. Zina's mother opened the door.

"Wanda, what is it? You're as pale as a ghost. Come in. I'll call Zina." Zina was already walking toward them.

"Wanda," Zina asked, "has something happened to Mashenka? Is she sick?"

"No, my dear Zina. She's all right, thank God. I'll explain everything later.

Would you let me spend the night with you? My baggage is in the cab." They walked out to the street. The cabman helped unload the baggage and carry it into the house. Zina's mother served tea. Mashenka was fed and put to bed.

Wanda shuddered as if she had a fever.

"What happened?" asked Zina's mother. "Calm down. Why did you leave home?"

"I didn't leave. I've been driven out. They killed Vladik before my eyes." Wanda wept. Zina and her mother cried, too. Zina walked over to Wanda, wiping her tears away.

"Control yourself, Wanda," she said. "You must be healthy for Mashenka's[4] sake. Take care of yourself. You have to be strong. There's nothing we can do."

Wanda stopped crying. She was staring in front of her without seeing. Then, quietly, she said, "They didn't give me a chance to bury him. They just killed him and dragged him away. Why didn't they kill me, instead of leaving me to watch it all? Why didn't I become a nun? I wouldn't have known this grief. Why has God turned away from me? Who can answer me?"

Wanda's final words were strained, almost a scream. She began to cry again.

"Wanda," Zina said, "these are such awful times. So many innocent people are perishing. You have Mashenka. Take care of her."

Wanda wanted to stand up, but her strength had left her. She fell to the floor, unconscious.

When she regained consciousness, Wanda was lying in bed. A doctor sat beside her. Zina and her mother stood at the foot of the bed.

"You're all right, now," the doctor said. "You have to have some rest, a long sleep. Take this medicine. It's a sedative. I'll come to see you tomorrow."

Zina escorted the doctor out.

At first, Wanda could not comprehend where she was. She took the medicine and fell asleep. Outside, rain poured down and thunder roared. Lightning flashed. It seemed the storm would never end. Nature would finish what people had started.

By morning, however, the storm had subsided. The streets were washed, and the air smelled of ozone, a clean odor. Wet red flags hung from buildings, reminding everyone of who the masters of the city were.

Wanda remained in bed for several days. Zina acted as her nurse, while Zina's mother took care of the children.

"Zinochka, my dear," Wanda said, "how can I ever thank you? I still have my gold watch, my necklace, and my ring. They didn't take all of it; they couldn't find everything. If you can, sell these things and buy whatever you need."

"Now, now," Zina replied, "we aren't that bad off. We have enough food for now. I was at the city market this morning and bought everything we need. It's most important that you get well, gather your strength. Mama and I watched you while you slept. You're so beautiful, we couldn't take our eyes off you. I remember how good you've been to me. I felt as though your home was my home. And Mashenka—she's like a daughter to me. After all, I fed her at my breast. Don't worry, we won't leave you in your trouble. Nikolai will be back soon and everything will be all right."

"Where is your husband now, Zina? Has there been a letter?"

"Yes, there was a letter a week ago. He's in a hospital. He received a slight wound. He writes that he started to have difficulty hearing. Otherwise, he's healthy, and he'll be sent home soon."

"That's good. Things will be easier for you. I'm glad."

After a week, Wanda was able to get up by herself, but she was still very weak. She watched Mashenka and Anton sit in a crib together and play.

"What's going to happen to me now?" she thought. "I must get control over myself. I must survive for her sake. Things can't go on like this for long. There will be a change. I must try not to think about it."

A month after that terrible day, things did change. The Reds retreated from the city, and the flags were removed. The city was in a state of anarchy. No one knew for certain who was in power.

Wanda, Zina, and Zina's mother, Elena, went to Wanda's home to see what had happened to it. The place had been badly vandalized. Windows had been smashed, and the door hung fully open. They walked inside. It was obvious that those who had departed had had little time to destroy more. All the furniture was in place, but there were some boxes stacked on top of the grand piano.

Wanda began to cry.

"No, I'll never come back to this house. Never."

Wanda rented an apartment in the building where Zina and her mother lived. It consisted of only two rooms and a kitchen. She did manage to get some furniture transferred from her house. She now lived alone with Mashenka. It was time to put life back on its proper track.

Zina's husband came home from the hospital. He had been made completely deaf by a concussion, but he was alive. He could do some manual labor. Before the war, he had worked as a joiner. He had built all of Zina's furniture with his own hands.

Wanda had no more acquaintances in the city. They had all disappeared, either abroad or to other towns. Many of them had run away in panic, not knowing where they were going. Wanda had stayed, waiting for better times, and had found herself in this small apartment. What would she do? How would she make a living?

PART VI

Wanda began by selling her necklace. With the money she recovered she paid her rent six months in advance. Stepan and Zina helped her stock up on food. She had a sack of potatoes, flour, oil, and honey. She was prepared for the winter. Little by little, she learned how to cook. She remembered those times when she had a cook, a maid, and a governess. Now, she had to be cook, maid, and governess at the same time. But she was also a mother for Mashenka, tender, gentle, and very careful. Motherhood gave her strength and spirit.

Soon the foreign "Entente" left the city, and red flags flew again. Soldiers marched in rows down the street, singing marching songs.

For a short time the Reds had been replaced by Greens and then by Whites. Wanda had had a chance to go to Konstantinopol, but had not used it. She was afraid of new troubles because of the small child she had to care for. The last steamer sailed, and the next morning the Reds entered the city, this time to stay for a long time.

The year was 1919. Wanda was able to find a job in a hospital. She helped with bandaging and looked after the patients. Elena watched Mashenka. The girl was growing up a quiet child. It seemed she understood that it was very difficult for her mother to be alone. Wanda's only concern in life was to see to it that Mashenka remained healthy and did not go hungry.

A year passed. Zina and her entire family left for Nikolai's aunt's village. It was the beginning of a hard time for Wanda. She could not go to the hospital for a full day because no one was available to look after Mashenka, so she lost her job.

Of all her jewelry, Wanda had only the ring given to her by Countess Gdansky. She did not want to part with it. Perhaps, she thought, everything would be all right. But the miracle did not happen. She was unable to find someone to care for the child, and there were no jobs anywhere.

Once, on a warm, summer-like fall evening, Wanda put Mashenka to bed and went outside to the street. She was wearing a skirt and close-fitting blouse. She did not care about her appearance, but she was gifted with natural beauty. Her waist was still slender, her skin retained its tender color, and her chestnut hair, with its natural curls, was thick and long. As she walked alone down the street, people noticed.

Zina had said to her once, "Cover your head with a kerchief, and then you will be less conspicuous." She had taken Zina's advice, and that night a kerchief covered her hair, her shoulders, and part of her face.

There was a cafe on the corner. Music was playing, and drunks were shouting. Wanda opened the door. She smelled drunkenness, cigarette smoke, and something sour. Nausea rose in her throat. She walked into the cafe and up to the bar. A man in his early thirties stood behind it.

"What can I do for you, madam?" he asked. "Do you have a part-time evening job for me?"

"What do you do during the day?"

"I have a small child. I'm alone. My husband died."

"What can you do? Do you sing, dance, play?"

"No, I can't do anything like that. Perhaps I could wash dishes or clean tables."

"Show me your face. I can't see you behind that kerchief."

Wanda removed the kerchief. Her face burned with shame under his examination.

"Well," the man behind the bar said, "I can hire you as a waitress. The job is from six in the evening until two in the morning. The wages aren't very large, but you'll be able to earn good money with your looks. You can start tomorrow about four. I'll show you what to do. By the way, what's your name?"

"I am Wanda Stanishevsky." She could not let anyone know she was the wife of the dead White officer, Chernov.

Wanda thanked the barman and walked out. Her cheeks still burned, and she was shivering. She thought about what the man meant when he said she would be able to earn good wages with her looks. She had not even asked him how much she would be paid.

The next day, Wanda asked her neighbor to look after Mashenka and hurried to the bar. The place was empty. The man she had talked to the day before stood behind the bar.

"Come here," he said. "I'll show you what your duties will be. How old are you, Wanda?"

"Almost thirty."

"You look younger."

Wanda smiled.

"Yes," the barman continued, "you're so young and already a widow. It's the war. Nothing can be done about it. How old is your child?"

"She's three and a half. She was born in 1917."

"Let's get to business. Your duties are to take orders from customers at the tables, come to me, and tell me what and how many have been ordered. Then, when you get the order, you'll take it to the table. The job isn't hard, but you'll have to be on your feet all the time, and the people who come here are mostly rabble. You'll have to listen to all sorts of things."

"I'll try. I don't have any other choice. What's your name? You haven't introduced yourself."

"My name is Grisha."

"Are you the owner here?"

"No, everything here is under the control of my mother. She has owned this establishment for many years. After the Revolution, it was closed, and then they permitted us to open it again. We live right here, on the second floor."

Grisha turned out to be a talkative man. It was obvious that he liked Wanda. He told her that his father had died long before the Revolution and that he and his mother lived together. He was thirty-two years old and had never been married. Wanda was content that he did the talking because she did not want to talk about herself.

By six o'clock customers had begun to fill the cafe. Another waitress, a big woman about forty years old, was also working. She wore her hair piled high on her head, and her voice was coarse from smoking. It seemed that she was well known in the cafe.

"Hey, Verochka," someone shouted from a table by the window. "Come here, baby."

Verochka walked over with a free and easy gait, her hips swinging. She blew her cigarette smoke into the face of a fat customer. He smiled and gestured for her to sit on his lap. Verochka sat down and embraced his fat neck.

Wanda watched the scene unfold. "My God," she thought, "is it possible that I'll have to behave like that. No, I won't do it."

Just then, someone shouted, "Hey beauty, take our order."

Wanda walked to a table where three men sat. It was clear that they had come to the cafe immediately after work and without changing clothes. Their clothes were dirty, and their hands and faces were dark with grime.

"Are you new here?" one of them asked.

"Yes, this is my first day. What would you like?"

"Don't rushus, baby. Let us take a look at you. You're too pretty. It isn't very often we meet such a beauty, is it, fellows?"

They all laughed. Wanda was clearly very uncomfortable. "Bring a glass of vodka for each of us and a snack, for starters."

Wanda turned around, heading for the bar. One of the men at the table reached out and patted her buttocks. She turned around sharply, her face reddening. Tears filled her eyes.

"Never do that again," she said. "I'm not a streetwalker."

At the bar, she handed the order to Grisha. He looked at her face.

"Relax, Wanda. I warned you about that. You'll have to get used to it or quit."

"It's better that I quit now. This isn't for me. I'd be better off doing the dirtiest most difficult kind of work, but not this."

She turned quickly, removed her apron, and walked out of the cafe.

The night was warm. Leaves drifted slowly to the ground. Gradually, Wanda slowed her pace.

"I must survive this difficult time," she thought. Tomorrow, I'll go to a jeweler and sell Countess Gdansky's ring. That's all I have left."

She calmed down a little. When she arrived home, she retrieved Masha from her neighbor and took her for a walk. The little girl held her mother's hand and walked by herself. She did not ask to be carried, but she did ask many questions: "Why is this so? What's the name of this? What is it?"

Later, after Wanda put Masha to bed, she relaxed completely. The next morning, about ten o'clock, someone knocked on her door.

"Who's there?" Wanda asked.

"It's me. Grisha. Open the door, please."

"How did you find me?" Wanda asked, opening the door for him.

"Very simple. You told me where you live, and once I knew the building, it was easy to find the right apartment."

"Come in, Grisha. Sit down. This is my daughter, Masha." The little girl stood, pressing herself against her mother's legs. Grisha sat down and spoke first.

"I came to tell you that it was your right to walk out of the bar because you're a decent, honest woman. I'm very embarrassed that it happened the way it did. But I warned you."

"It's not your fault, Grisha. Thank you for your concern, but the job is really not for me."

"No, it's not for you. You're young, beautiful, well-bred. You can arrange your life."

"I don't even want to think about it. I need to sell something and then just wait. Everything will settle down, and I believe I'll find a job."

Grisha looked around the room. Above the sofa hung Wanda's portrait.

Grisha stood and walked closer to the painting.

"Is that you, Wanda? I can't take my eyes off it. When were you painted?"

"I was seventeen then. It was a long time ago, a very long time."

"You're beautiful now, too. Only you look tired. It seems as though you don't get enough rest."

Wanda nodded.

Soon, Grisha left. He walked to the door and asked, "What are you going to sell, Wanda? That is, if it's not a secret."

"It isn't a secret. I have only one ring. It's all that remains from my past. I've kept it as long as I could. It's very precious to me. But now I have no choice."

"Will you show it to me?"

Wanda took the ring from her jewelry box and gave it to Grisha.

"No, Wanda. Don't sell this ring. It's very beautiful, and you treasure it. I'll try to help you. For now, good-bye."

Grisha left, closing the door behind him. Wanda held the ring in her hand. The huge diamond shimmered with all the colors of the rainbow. It was a very unusual ring, and it was all that Wanda had.

She walked to the window. Outside, it was raining. Only a few pedestrians passed by. Wanda thought about Grisha's words. How could he help her? She understood that Grisha pitied her, and that meant that he was a good man. He had found it in his heart to be concerned about Wanda and Masha. Probably, he would give her an opportunity to work in the kitchen instead of in the barroom.

That was Wanda's thinking, but Grisha was considering something quite different. Wanda had impressed him very much. She had, in fact, captured his heart when he had first seen her. But could she care for him?

A few hours later, Grisha knocked again on Wanda's door. She opened it, surprised by his second visit. His arms were filled with packages and boxes.

"These are for you, Wanda. Help me. Where can I put them?"

"What are they, Grisha?"

"Some food. May I take it to the kitchen?"

"Yes, please. But why did you bring all this?"

Wanda led the way to the kitchen, and Grisha followed her. On the table, he placed bread, butter, sausages, milk, and other food. Then he gave Masha a bar of chocolate.

"Tell me, Grisha," Wanda said, "why did you bring this food? I feel so embarrassed. Why are you so kind to us?"

Grisha looked at her. "Let me put it this way. You don't have anybody to take care of you, and I don't have a family. I just like you, and I decided to help you."

"Thank you very much, Grisha. When I find a job, I'll pay you back. Thanks again for your help."

"It's all right, Wanda. Don't worry about anything."

After that evening, Wanda began receiving packages of food and money through the mail. In the beginning, she was embarrassed about taking help from Grisha, but after a while she grew used to it.

Russia was in a severe depression. People begged for a piece of bread on the streets. It was easy for Wanda to become accustomed to a better life and to Grisha's visiting at least twice a week. Masha became attached to him because he brought her toys and candy. Wanda watched them play hide-and-seek and other games. Another six months passed.

Once, on a Sunday afternoon, Grisha arrived at Wanda's apartment about six o'clock.

"Aren't you working in the cafe today?" Wanda asked.

"No, I hired a man to replace me. He's a good bartender. I hired him temporarily, and I'll see what happens."

Wanda went to the kitchen to prepare supper. Grisha took Masha onto his lap, wrapped his arms around her, and read her fairy tales.

Soon after supper, Masha went to bed, and Grisha and Wanda sat on the sofa, talking. Grisha had never asked Wanda about her past or about Masha's father, but he had decided that this evening he would find out more about her life. He also wanted to ask her about her feelings toward him.

Grisha was shy. He could not start the conversation. Finally, he took Wanda's hand in his and said, "Tell me about yourself. I want to know as much about you as you'll let me."

Wanda looked into his eyes and smiled.

"No, Grisha. There's no need to talk about the past. It's gone forever. Let's talk about the present and the future. Someday, I'll tell you, but not now."

Grisha's eyes were as blue as the sky, and he looked at Wanda with childish trust.

"How do you feel about me?" he asked. "Do you like me, at least a little?"

"I like you very much. No one is closer to Masha and me than you are.

You're a very noble man."

Grisha ventured further. He kissed her hand. Then, taking her by the shoulders, he pulled her to him and kissed her lips. It was a long kiss.

Wanda realized that the time had come to pay the price for all Grisha's kindness toward her. She knew she did not love him. Only her feelings of gratitude held her. But Grisha loved her. To him, she was something extraordinary, far above any other woman he knew.

Grisha stayed the night. Wanda could not refuse him anything. When she awoke, Grisha was not beside her. She went to the kitchen and found him preparing breakfast. He met her and embraced her.

"I love you," he said. "Be my wife. I'll be a good father for Masha." Wanda's heart stopped. She understood that this was the best thing that could happen to her. But she felt no love for him, not the kind she had felt for Vladimir, and certainly not the feeling she had for Tadeush.

Wanda had no time to reply. She saw Masha standing at the entrance to the kitchen. The girl was smiling.

"Grisha," she said, "you live here for good now."

"You must ask your mother if she'll permit me to live here."

"Mother, mother, let him live with us. I'll play with him. We'll be happy." Mashenka tugged at Wanda's robe.

"All right. Grisha may stay, if he wants to."

"Thank you, mommy. Grisha, finish the fairy tale you were reading to me yesterday."

"No, my dear," Grisha answered, "we'll have breakfast first. Then I have to go to work. When I come back, I'll finish reading to you."

So Grisha, Masha, and Wanda began a new life.

Wanda tried not to think too much about it. It was necessary to survive, to raise her daughter. She realized that she had little choice.

A few months went by. Masha became very attached to Grisha, and Wanda knew she had to get used to it. Her letters to her sister in Poland were not answered. She still hoped that when the war was over she would be able to leave for Cracow with Masha.

In the beginning, Grisha told Wanda he wanted to marry her. Wanda told him that they should wait until the war was over. After a month, Grisha stopped talking about marriage. Wanda was content. It was good that he did not insist, as time would show.

"I want to introduce you to my mother," Grisha said once. "I have to warn you that she doesn't like other women. She's been a widow for a long time. She raised me alone with my uncle. And there's one more thing I have to tell you. She holds on to old traditions. I left all that behind long ago, but my mother is in her sixties, and she has her own beliefs."

"What are you saying?" Wanda asked. "I don't understand. What traditions are you talking about?"

"Ah, Wanda. I watch you always praying before you go to sleep, just as you've taught Masha to do. You're Catholic. You have your own religion and traditions. You've never asked me who I am, what family I came from, and what I believe in."

"My husband, Masha's father, wasn't a Catholic. But he was an extremely decent and noble man."

"Yes, I understand that. But it's different in my case. My mother is Jewish, and my father was a Jew. I think you understand it's not the same. As I told you before, I have the best intentions toward you. I won't find anybody better than you, but I have to overcome one difficulty. I have to persuade my mother that you are my very life, and that is the truth."

Wanda said nothing. She could find no words. She had not imagined that Grisha was a Jew. He had blue eyes, fair hair, a straight nose. What would she do now? How would everything turn out?

"Why are you silent, Wanda? I don't think anything will change between us."

Wanda shook her head. "I don't know how your mother will react to your relationship with a Catholic woman."

I'll arrange everything. I told you only so that you'll know what's going on."

After their conversation, many things changed. Grisha became gloomy, and Wanda asked no questions. Once, he did not show up for two days. At first, Wanda thought that his mother had forbade him to visit her. Masha asked again and again why Grisha did not come. Wanda told her that he had been working. She was too shy to go to the bar to find out what had happened to him. She was, after all, only a mistress to him.

It was 1921, a time of hardship and hunger. Wanda did not fully realize how bad things were until her own and her child's welfare was threatened. They were helpless again, in need of food.

"If Grisha doesn't come tomorrow," Wanda thought, "I'll go to the bar. It can't be that he just left without saying anything."

She did not have to go to the bar. There was a knock at her door, and she opened it to an elderly woman whose head was wrapped in a gray kerchief. The corridor was dark, and Wanda could not see the woman's face.

"Whom are you looking for?" Wanda asked.

"I'm looking for you. Your name is Wanda?"

"Yes. Who are you?"

"Can I come in?"

"Please."

The woman walked straight into the room.

"I am Esther," she said, "Grisha's mother. May I sit down somewhere? We have to talk."

"Please, sit down on the sofa. Would you like to take your coat and kerchief off. I'll hang them up."

Esther unbuttoned her coat, slipped her kerchief down onto her shoulders, and sat down. Wanda took a chair in front of her. Masha was asleep, and Wanda closed the door to her room.

"It's cold outside," Esther began. "The wind is strong. Grisha is sick. He has a high temperature."

As she spoke, Esther stared at Wanda, obviously studying her.

"What does the doctor say?" Wanda asked. "Is it a cold or something more serious?" Wanda's face showed her worry.

"The doctor doesn't know yet. We'll have to wait a while."

"Can I do anything to help?"

"Yes, you can give me a hot cup of tea."

"With pleasure. I'll put a pot on the stove right now. I just made fresh tea." Wanda went to the kitchen. Esther stood and walked to the portrait.

"What a beautiful Polish woman," she thought. "No wonder my son lost his head over her."

Wanda put the tea on the table and brought some cookies and jam.

"Sit down at the table," she said to Esther. "It's more comfortable there." Esther took a seat at the table and held a cup with both hands as if to warm them. She looked past Wanda. The two women sat in silence for about five minutes. Finally, Esther placed her cup back on its saucer and spoke.

"My son sent me here. He gave me the address and asked me to get to know you. We've had a lot of discussions about his affair with you. I had nothing against my son staying with you, helping you and your child. I have nothing at all against you. Grisha's right. You impress me as a decent woman. But don't get me wrong. My son is a Jew and will never marry a Catholic. It doesn't matter how beautiful you are."

Now it was Wanda who looked straight into Esther's eyes and spoke. "Well, I don't insist on marrying your son. It was his proposal, not mine. As soon as the opportunity comes, I'll go to Poland to my sister. You don't have to worry. I won't tie Grisha to me. I'll always be grateful to him for his kindness toward me. Tell him to get well and never to come to me again. I'll never consent to be his mistress, and my child should not grow used to him. That's all. As you can see, I have no claim on him."

Esther stood, put on her coat and kerchief, and started for the door. At the door, she stopped and looked back.

"I was sure you were different," she said, "that you wanted to marry my son. But I see I was mistaken. Good luck to you."

Esther walked out and closed the door.

Wanda stood looking at the closed door, as if Esther had not really left and would come back in. She was crying. What would happen now? She had been comfortable when she knew there was a man in the house. But she was alone with her child again. Then she began to regain her composure. The Lord is gracious, she thought. He would not permit her to wander aimlessly with the child.

Two weeks after Esther's visit, Wanda was returning from the store and met Grisha. He stopped her and held her by the arm.

"My mother told me everything about your conversation," he said. "She liked you. …"

"But not enough to let you marry me," Wanda interrupted. "I can see you're quite well already."

"This is the first day I've been up. I have malaria. Up until now I've been shaky. That's why I didn't go to your apartment and decided to meet you here. I was afraid I could infect Masha if I held her. Does she still remember me? She hasn't forgotten, has she?"

"Of course she remembers you. All the time she waits for you to come back. And because of that I don't want you to come back ever. I don't want my daughter to get used to you and then realize I'm your mistress."

Wanda removed her arm from his grasp.

"I have to go, Grisha," she said. "Thank you for everything. Be healthy and happy. You are a good man. I'll have only good memories of you. Now, good-bye."

Wanda walked toward her apartment building, and Grisha accompanied her. "Wanda," he said, "I love you. I only want to be with you. I'll try to persuade my mother that times are different now. It's been almost four years since the Revolution. It's time to forget old prejudices. Just give me time. I can't do it all at once."

Wanda stopped. "Listen, Grisha. I'll never marry you. If there's an opportunity, I'll leave for Poland. You must try to forget about our relationship. What has been will never be again."

Wanda continued to walk toward her building. Grisha followed her for a few more steps and then stopped.

Wanda went home and fed Masha, but she could not eat. She cried, not knowing the reason for her tears at the time, whether they were the result of being alone to care for Masha or the pain she had caused another person.

A surprise awaited her that same day. A letter from Sophie came through. Wanda read and re-read it. She kissed the pages and said, over and over, "Thank God all of them are alive, healthy, and waiting for us." This time she cried with happiness.

She put all of her papers together, her birth certificate, and her marriage license that said she had wed Tadeush Stanishevsky.

At the city police station, she was given forms to fill out for emigration. She was told that, because she was a Polish native, she could leave after going through all the formalities.

It seemed that everything was going her way. She wrote Sophie, telling her that it had already been four years since Vladimir had died and that she was alone with Masha. The only dream she had was that she and Sophie would meet again as soon as possible.

The days Wanda spent waiting for permission to leave seemed long. She did not know that a very different fate awaited her. Before long, she realized she was pregnant, and a visit to the doctor confirmed her suspicion. The doctor saw her fear and her tears. He found out the child had no father and listened as Wanda explained that she had to go to Poland to her sister.

"You could have an abortion," he told her. "You're only seven or eight weeks pregnant."

"No," Wanda sobbed. "I'm Catholic. I can't kill a life. This is my child." She went home, feeling empty.

"What can I say to my sister?" she thought. "She knows I'm a widow for four years. Oh, God, what can I do? What will Grisha do if he finds out this is his child?"

Wanda began to cry again. Questions flooded her mind, but she felt helpless to answer any of them. She wept and did not see her daughter approach her and begin crying as well. Wanda's tears stopped when she saw her daughter's.

"Don't cry," Wanda told Masha. "Everything will be all right. We'll be leaving this city soon."

"Is Grisha coming with us?" Masha asked.

"No. He's sick. He can't go."

Masha began to cry again. Wanda took the little girl onto her lap and hugged her tightly, stroking her hair.

"All right," she said. "Tomorrow I'll go see Grisha." Masha danced with happiness.

Soon, Wanda began looking for a new apartment and found one. The place was on the opposite side of the city and was less expensive. She had enough money to live on for only one month, and she spent some of it to move. She told her neighbors she was going to Poland to see her sister. She even showed them her visa.

To Sophie she sent a letter explaining that the government would not let her go, that she had to wait.

Wanda purposely told the neighbors that she was going to Poland. When Grisha came to see her a month later, the neighbors told him where they thought she had gone.

Grisha sat on the stairs, held his head, and began to cry. He loved Wanda and Masha, and now he had lost them forever.

When Grisha returned home and told his mother that Wanda had gone to Poland, his mother told him how sorry she was. But in her heart, she was glad this beautiful Catholic girl would not stand in her son's way. Now he could marry a Jewish girl.

Esther put all her energy into working through a matchmaker who had found a wealthy, twenty-five-year-old girl. The girl's father had a little store, and he was able to offer an adequate dowry. Esther was satisfied. All she had to do was talk to Grisha. She succeeded easily. Grisha told her he no longer cared because the woman he loved had gone. He would please his mother.

"All right, Mama," he said, "you can see your grandchildren as you've always wished."

The bride's name was Rosa. She was plump and had thick lips, entirely the opposite of Wanda.

Grisha's mother told him that life must go on. She was right, he knew, but Wanda would be a part of his life forever, a dream that had never come true.

Meanwhile, Wanda looked for a job, any job, for any salary, but could find none. No jobs were available, even for men. It was a time of severe depression.

Once, she heard someone say that people were needed to repair the railroad. When she arrived at the yard and saw how young girls pulled the ties, she realized she could not do the work because of the baby. She left without filling out an application.

Back at home, she decided she would have to sell the countess's ring. "This is the only thing left from my past," she thought, "but it's the only way to stay alive. I must find a buyer."

She found a jeweler, an old man with pince nez glasses. The jeweler examined the ring and said, "This is a very unusual ring. Who was the owner?"

"Countess Gdansky. She gave me this ring in 1906."

"Oh, I knew the Gdanskys. Nice people. Where are they now?" He was whispering. "Did they run away from Russia"

"No, they left long before the Revolution, before 1914."

"I can tell you, madam, that this ring is worth a lot of money. The diamond is no less than four carats, clear water. But I cannot buy it from you because I haven't enough money. I'm an honest man, and I have a reputation. It's not in my nature to cheat people. I'd like to help you. Will you give me your address? I'll let you know when I find a customer. People are emigrating now. Perhaps someone will be interested in the ring."

Wanda agreed and gave him her address. She was glad to find this honest man, someone remaining from the old days.

A few days later, the jeweler sent his delivery boy to Wanda to ask her to come to his store with the ring. She took the ring and followed the delivery boy.

A buyer sat in a back room in the shadows, and Wanda did not see him. She gave the jeweler the ring and sat down to wait for him to return from the back.

After fifteen minutes, the jeweler told Wanda that the customer liked the ring. He told her the price offered and that his commission would be twenty percent. Wanda did not believe the price. The jeweler told her that she must give her word to say nothing about the deal.

"Oh, no, never," Wanda answered. "I'll tell you the truth. There's no one left for me here. I'm alone."

"If you agree, you can have the money right now."

"Certainly, I agree, and God bless you. If not for you, my daughter and I would have starved. Times are very hard now. People are dying on the streets. ..."

He would not let her finish. "Can you wait? I'll be right back."

The jeweler returned to the back room. He came back with money, a great deal of money in a briefcase. When he opened the case, Wanda saw that it was stuffed with bills.

"Would you like to count it?" he asked.

"No, no. I trust you. Why would I need to count it? I appreciate it. Thank you very much. You can't imagine what you've done. For three days I've had no heat in my apartment. I had no money for firewood. May I go now, sir?"

"Yes, madam. Good luck to you. Few people are left from the old days. I thank you so much, too. I have a very good commission. As I told you, I have a good reputation. People have known me for years and know they can count on me. Good luck again, madam. Good-bye."

The jeweler nodded politely, and Wanda left, holding the briefcase tightly against her breast. She walked along the street and tears streaked her face. Few people were on the street, and no one paid any attention to her.

When she arrived home, Wanda collapsed on the couch and cried for everything, for the good and the bad in her life.

Masha called to her from another room, "Mama, I'm hungry."

Wanda could not hear her daughter over the sounds of her own sobs. She noticed Masha only when the girl plucked at her sleeve. Masha was barefoot and in her nightgown. She had wrapped a shawl around herself for warmth.

Wanda took Masha onto her lap. "What happened, my love?" she asked. "I thought you were asleep. Did I wake you up? Let's get you dressed. You could catch cold."

"Mama, why are you crying?"

"I won't cry anymore. Now I'll make you something to eat. Go get dressed."

She took Masha to her room and then went to the kitchen. First, she hid the money where no one would find it, keeping only enough for necessities. She put cereal on the stove to cook and went to see the porter for firewood. An hour later, she and Masha sat close to the stove. The fire warmed them, and Wanda felt much better. She knew she had enough money to survive with her daughter. She also understood that she could not go to Poland before her child was born. Later, she could explain to her sister that she had adopted the child after someone died. It was plausible; many parents died, and there were many orphans. Anyone not yet dead would be glad to give up a child for adoption so it could survive.

In the evenings, when Wanda put Masha to bed, she tried to read because she could not think about anything anymore. It was not easy.

Her situation would not let her forget. She knew she could change nothing.

"Why have I not died or gone mad?" she thought. "Why do I have to survive and suffer?" She asked herself many questions, but there were no answers. She could only tell herself, "This is God's will." God had given her this baby and the strength to bear it and care for it. She had a responsibility, and she would live up to it.

A few times, Wanda received requests from the authorities that she come and sign the papers for her visa. Each time she received the notices, she began crying and hid them in her desk.

When the baby was due, Wanda found a lonely woman who would look after Masha. She explained that she was a widow.

Wanda gave birth to a boy. The labor was easy; there were no complications. In a week, she was home. Vera was very helpful to Wanda, and she agreed to stay on for three months until Wanda regained her strength.

Wanda named her baby Gregory. On his birth certificate, she put the father's name as Vladimir, only because she wanted the baby and Masha to have the same father.

Everything was going as Wanda had planned. She and the baby were fine, the baby growing healthy and strong. She took the request to the authorities and tried to explain why she had not come before. She said she had had to wait for the baby to be born. They put her son's name on the paper and told her to return in two weeks. She could not believe her good luck.

As she walked home, Wanda thought, "I'll send a letter to Sophie explaining that I adopted the baby. I know it's a lie, but it's a white lie."

She rushed home, so happy that she saw nothing and no one. She also hurried because she had to feed Gregory.

Someone called her name sharply. She stopped, breathing heavily. She turned around and saw Grisha. Her heart beat rapidly.

"What can I say to him?" she thought.

Grisha walked up to her and took her hand.

"What's this all about?" he asked. "Now I see. You left me for somebody else."

"No, Grisha, I've looked for no one and found no one. After I talked with your mother, I understood you would never marry me. That's why I changed apartments, to be far away from you. It's true that I'm going to Poland. All this time I've been waiting for a visa."

She lowered her head and saw a wedding ring on Grisha's finger. He was aware that Wanda had seen the ring.

"Yes, Wanda, I'm married. I pleased my mother. She'd like to have grandchildren."

Wanda looked into his eyes, and Grisha began to cry.

"Good luck, Grisha," Wanda said. "I wish you good luck from the bottom of my heart. You are a good man. I will remember you and everything you've done for me. Now, I have to hurry. Masha is home alone."

She pulled her hand from his, but he took hold of hers again.

"Don't go," he said. "If you go now I'll never see you again. I love you, Wanda. I understood that more after I married. I understood what I had and what I lost. Let me come to your home and say good-bye to you and Masha before you leave for Poland."

"No. Never," Wanda blurted. "For a long time, Masha remembered you and talked about you. But now she no longer talks about you. Please don't come and hurt her again."

"All right, Wanda. If you don't want me to come, I won't. Calm down. I didn't mean to upset you. Perhaps you just need my help."

"Thank you, but I don't need anything. I sold what I had, and I have enough money to live until we leave."

Grisha put her hand to his lips and started to kiss it. Wanda pulled her hand away.

"Don't," she said, softly but firmly. "It will be better for both of us. You're married now; you have your own life to live. Let me go, please. In a week, when I go back to pick up my visa, I promise you we'll talk before I leave." Wanda turned around and walked quickly to a trolley stop. A minute later, the trolley arrived, and she was gone.

Grisha stood and watched the trolley leave. Then he turned and walked slowly home. At home, he went to his office and remained there, not emerging for dinner. Rosa knocked on his door and told him several times that she had prepared his favorite dishes. But Grisha did not respond.

"If you're sick, my dear," Rosa said, "I'll call the doctor." Grisha said nothing.

Rosa called Esther. She told her she had never seen Grisha this way before.

Esther knocked on Grisha's door.

"Grisha, this is your mother," she said. "Please open. What happened to you, my son?"

Grisha did not answer.

"All right. We have to call someone to break down the door," Esther said. Grisha opened the door and told his mother to come in. "I would like to talk to you," he said, "and to you alone."

Esther entered and closed the door.

"What happened to you?" she asked. "You're pale. Do you have a fever again?"

"No, mother. I saw Wanda. She didn't go to Poland. She just moved across town because she wanted to please you by leaving my life."

As Grisha talked, he paced the room. Esther sat on the sofa and followed him with her eyes. He stopped in front of her and resumed speaking.

"I love Wanda. Why have you never understood what is best for me? I'm your only son, and you have always told me there is but one wish in your life —to see me happy. Do you call this happiness? I have lost the woman I love and cannot live without. And I have to live with a woman I don't love and have never loved. Answer me. Everyone comes to you for your wisdom. You solve people's problems. Why can't you help me, your own son?"

Grisha broke down in tears, placed his handkerchief to his eyes and strode to the window. Esther walked up behind him.

"Calm down, son," she said. "This will pass. You have only known Rosa seven months. It's a very short time."

Grisha turned sharply and grabbed Esther's shoulders.

"Oh, mama, mama," he cried. "You still don't understand what you've done. I was always a good son and tried to please you. No, you are wrong. I'll never get used to Rosa because I don't want to. I love Wanda, and I will do everything in my power to stop her from leaving."

"You can't do that. What will people say? You agreed to marry. No one dragged you by the hand into this marriage."

"I wanted to please you. I didn't care because I had lost Wanda. Mama, try to understand. I'll die without her. Today, I saw her for only ten minutes, and I know I need nothing else in life but her. I'll do anything. If you want to help, help. Otherwise, stay out of my way."

Esther looked at her son in awe. Grisha turned and abruptly left the room. He walked in the park until very late. Then he sat in a cafe trying to decide what to do. But nothing came to mind. Before him he saw her eyes full of tears as if she were begging him, "Don't follow me. Let me go."

He arrived home late and very drunk. Rosa sat fully clothed waiting for him. He passed her as if she were not there, but she stopped him.

"Grisha, what's wrong? No one will talk to me. No one will explain what's happened."

He stopped in front of her, looking at her with bleary eyes.

"Go home, Rosa, to your father," he said, very clearly. "I'm not a good husband. I'm not a husband at all. I don't love you."

He walked to his office, but Rosa followed him.

"Grisha, my dear, has somebody hurt you? You're a good husband. I love you."

Grisha turned to her.

"Go home tomorrow. And now, go to sleep."

"I'm not going without you. We'll go together." Rosa took hold of Grisha's hand.

"You are stupid, Rosa," Grisha said, wrenching his hand away. "I'll tell you now what I might not tell you tomorrow. Listen to me, and listen well. I love another woman. I'm still in love with her. Our marriage was a mistake. I loved this woman before I met you. You're still young. You can put your life together. You'll meet someone else."

Grisha slammed the door to his office. He staggered to the sofa and lay down without removing his shoes. He heard Rosa crying in the other room but ignored her and fell asleep. In the morning, Esther woke him.

"My God, Grisha. You slept in your clothes, even your shoes. Wake up. I'll help you now."

Grisha was disoriented. Soon, however, he sat down and recalled everything that had happened the night before.

"Mama, make me a cup of coffee. I have to hurry. What time is it?"

"It's eleven o'clock. What's your hurry? What's come over you? This woman is only bad luck for you. Just what we need, a Catholic woman."

"Shut up, now," Grisha screamed. "And never say anything bad about Wanda again. When she left she gave me my freedom even though I didn't ask for it. She didn't ask me to marry her. She held her daughter by the hand and I knew they had been hungry many times. I will not forgive myself if I lose her again."

"This is how you speak to your mother? What happened to my kind, sweet son? Only because of this woman can you speak to me this way."

"Stop right there. I asked you for a cup of coffee. This conversation has gone too far. I have a headache. Don't talk to me about anything anymore."

Esther went to the kitchen and said nothing more.

Before Esther had awakened Grisha, she had talked with Rosa. She asked her to go to her parents' home for a few days until the situation had been resolved. But as Esther made coffee, she began to realize that the problem could not be solved.

"What will happen?" she asked herself. "What will happen?"

After Wanda talked to Grisha, she went home and began breastfeeding Gregory. As she listened to the sounds of Gregory nursing, she looked at him and thought, "You are my sorrow, and you are my sin, but I love you. You are my little son. You will grow up without a father, but when you are grown, I will tell you, only you, who your father was and everything about him."

Tears fell from her eyes. Gregory began to cry, and Masha, hearing his cry, came from the other room. Wanda placed her son in his cradle and brushed her tears away.

"A little while longer and we will leave this place forever," she thought. "We'll start a new life, and everything will be different."

Wanda waited for Monday when she would go for her visa. Waiting made the time go slowly. She tried not to go out because she was afraid she might meet Grisha. Vera bought all the necessities for her and walked in the park with Masha.

Wanda was right. Grisha was searching for her, but finding her was not easy. Her name was Stanishevsky, according to the address bureau, but she had kept Tadeush's name because she had not seen her first husband die and had no death certificate. This was a war, a revolution, and no one could afford to worry about formalities.

Grisha, however, remembered that Wanda needed her visa. So he went every morning to the visa office. He did not know what day she would come.

One morning, he saw Wanda as she walked into the building. She did not see him. He followed her and listened as she talked with the officer.

"You have two weeks to leave the country," the officer said.

"I think one week will be enough," Wanda answered.

When she left the building, Grisha followed her, and when she reached the end of the block, he called to her. Wanda waited for him.

"I must talk to you," Grisha pleaded. "Please wait." Wanda stared at him in astonishment and fear.

"What do you want, Grisha? We've already talked about everything. Let me go. I beg you one more time. I wish you the best in your life with your wife."

"I have to talk to you. I must. Don't go, for God's sake. Listen to me. I know I can't live without you. I don't have a life without you. I love you deeply. I'll divorce Rosa and marry you. I swear."

"Oh, no!" Wanda cried. "God, no. Let me go. It's all I want from you. I'll never be your wife. You know that. I'm a Catholic, and I'll remain a Catholic. Let me go to my sister. I never did anything to hurt you."

"I know that," Grisha said. "You're so very kind. This was my mistake. I tried to please my mother. But now I'm trying to be a man, not her little boy anymore. I tell you, if I can't have you, I don't need life any longer."

Wanda was terrified. Grisha held her hands, kissing and squeezing them.

All she could think to do was run away. She spoke shakily.

"Listen, Grisha. They've given me two weeks before I have to go. We have enough time to talk this over. Please, solve your problems with your wife. Later, when you're free, we can see what happens."

"Can I visit you during these two weeks."

"No. You must give me your word that you will not come over. After two weeks, if you're a free man, I'll make my decision whether or not to stay."

"I can't be without you. Don't make me promise not to see you."

"Come now, Grisha. You were without us for over a year. What are two weeks to you? I'm serious. We need this time for both of us to think."

"All right. Where can I see you after two weeks?"

Wanda wrote her address on a piece of paper, handed it to Grisha, and said, "Give me your word you will not come for two weeks."

"I promise. But now, let me kiss you."

Grisha held her and kissed her lingeringly on the lips.

"Grisha," Wanda protested, "shame on you. This is a public street. People are watching us."

She pushed him away.

"I don't care about these people. They can see how I love you, and I'm not ashamed. I'm proud of it."

"All right, Grisha. I'll see you in two weeks. Now I must go. Please don't follow me."

Grisha nodded. Wanda crossed the street to the trolley stop. She turned and looked at Grisha. He stood in the place she had left him.

"This is good," Wanda thought. "In a week, I'll be gone. In two weeks, he'll come, and we'll be gone. I know I've lied, but it's the only way."

Wanda entered the first car on the trolley. She did not see Grisha leap onto the steps of the second car, just as the trolley pulled away.

When Wanda left the trolley at her stop, Grisha, hidden, followed her. He watched her walk to her building and open the door. He was satisfied. Now he could go home.

"I know where she lives," he thought, and I know she intends to leave in a week. I'll come every day."

He walked back home, and, as he walked, he thought, "I don't know that I have the right to hold Wanda here, not to let her go, but I know my life means nothing without her. She is all I have."

Before the revolution, Grisha had studied economics and business in Germany. He had one love affair then, but had been very young, so he had almost forgotten the feeling. He understood that his feeling for Wanda was different, very strong and deep. He blamed no one else for his misfortune, only himself and circumstances.

He arrived home. No one was there. He spoke to himself, "This is good. I need to rest a little. I don't need anyone bothering me right now."

He lay down on the sofa and fell asleep immediately. Esther woke him. "Son, where have you been? We've been looking for you all over."

"What time is it?" Grisha asked. "How long have I been asleep?"

"It's two o'clock. When did you go to sleep?"

"At eleven. Why were you looking for me?"

"Your Uncle Simon and I have been to the park and the cafe and to see some of your friends, but we couldn't find you."

"Now you see I'm at home, and it doesn't matter where I've been," Grisha said, holding his head.

"Son, we have to talk. Tell me, how do you feel? Can I call your uncle?"

"Why are you talking to me? We have nothing to discuss. Nothing will change. I'm in good health, and my mind is very clear."

"Your Uncle Simon is like a father to you. He sent you to school in Germany. You've always respected him. This is only for your good. Will you listen to him?"

"All right," Grisha answered, as he stood up. "He can come in. I'll listen to what he has to say."

Uncle Simon entered the study. He was a little man of very slight build with red hair. He had been a widower for many years. His wife had died without leaving him any children, and he had not married again. He and Esther were brother and sister and also very good friends. When Esther's husband died, Grisha was eleven years old, and Uncle Simon became a father to him. Uncle Simon was very well educated. He had always wanted his nephew to be educated and well-mannered.

When Uncle Simon walked into the study, Grisha began pacing the room. "Sit down, please," Uncle Simon said, "and listen. Try to understand what I'm saying."

Grisha sat in a chair and looked at his uncle. Simon stood in front of him and spoke.

"You're a grown man, and I have to talk to you as if you were a teenager. You've always been a good son and a good nephew. Your mother and I were proud of you. I understand Rosa wasn't your choice, but when we introduced you, you agreed to marry her. She's your wife by law, and your behavior is indecent."

Grisha tried to interrupt, but his uncle silenced him with an upraised hand. "Let me finish what I've started. Later, I'll listen to what you have to say. Your mother and I are so ashamed of your behavior. If you were eighteen, this conversation could be expected. But you're over thirty years old and must try to understand other things. The financial situation in our family is very bad now. We have no money left, but Rosa's dowry has helped us get back on our feet again. So what now? You're married less than a year and you just throw her out of the house because of this woman. …" Grisha did not let him finish.

"Don't ever talk about her that way," he said, harshly. "She's the woman I love. She's everything to me. My life. The meaning of my life. I know I was wrong about Rosa, but she's young and rich, and with her money she can marry again soon."

Uncle Simon broke in loudly.

"How can you talk like that? She's still your wife. Raising your voice won't help. It will change nothing."

"If you and my mother try to keep Wanda and me apart," Grisha continued, "I'll kill myself. Do you hear? I'm serious. I want nothing else in my life. I can be a laborer, and I can make enough to support us. I don't need a mother or Rosa's money."

"You talk like this? I don't believe what I hear. You're no hero. What happened to you? I don't recognize you anymore."

Grisha stepped close to his uncle and looked into his eyes.

"You're right. I've changed. But I've changed only because I'm deeply in love. I can't explain this feeling to you because perhaps you've never loved in your life. If I'd not met Wanda, I'd have lived my whole life never knowing this feeling."

Grisha's uncle looked at him as though he'd never seen his nephew before.

This was not the same Grisha—calm, kind, soft-spoken.

"Calm down," he said to Grisha. "All right. Can you tell me more about this woman? Perhaps then I could understand you better."

"Her name is Wanda. Why do you always call her 'this woman?' Mother saw her, and she found nothing wrong with Wanda except she is Catholic. Wanda is beautiful, soft. If you could see her lovely brown eyes. … I can't explain.

Uncle Simon shook his head.

"You can't even explain who she is, where she came from, what her family is like. All you can say is 'she's beautiful.'"

"Why do you need to know her place in society? The revolution made everyone equal. But if you want to know, she's from a rich, aristocratic family. She was born in Poland and came to Odessa with her father when she was fifteen. Her father died and she lived with her sister. Later, she married and had a little girl. Her husband was killed in the war. That's all I can tell you about her. She has suffered enough. She has lived through sorrow and, what is important, I love her. She's the only one for me."

"Yes, her story is not a happy one. Try to understand me. I believe you. Maybe Wanda is a good woman. But what I know is that you still have a wife, and you can't just scratch her off. She's a human being. Try to talk to her. Maybe Rosa will understand. I don't know what else to say."

"That's fine. Don't say anything. Let me be the judge of my life. Not you. Not my mother."

"You know, Grisha, maybe I should talk to Wanda. Maybe I can find out what might happen between the two of you."

"Oh, no. This is enough. Mother talked to her, and you know the end of that story. You've talked to me, and that's enough. Now our conversation is over."

Uncle Simon stood, looking old and stooped, and walked slowly to the door. Grisha watched him leave, and when his uncle closed the door, he said to himself, "I believe he understands me now."

He felt much better after talking with his uncle. He thought no more about him; his thoughts dwelt entirely on Wanda. He saw himself holding her. He saw Masha on his lap. No, he could not live without them. Why should he wait for two weeks? He had to go now to talk to Wanda about everything.

Grisha walked along the street, filling his lungs with fresh air. He did not bother with the trolleys. He felt exhilarated.

When he arrived at Wanda's building, he asked the man sweeping the sidewalk where Wanda lived.

"Second floor, apartment four. But who are you?"

"Thank you, I'm a relative," Grisha answered, and he hurried to the second floor. He knocked at the door of Wanda's apartment.

Vera opened it. She held Gregory in her arms.

"Yes? Who are you looking for?"

"I believe this is the wrong apartment. I'm looking for Wanda. She has a little girl, Masha. Can you tell me where she lives?"

"She lives here. I just help her because she's alone."

"Where is she now?"

"She went to the store. But who are you?"

"I'm a friend. My name is Grisha."

"Come in, please. Sit down."

Grisha walked inside and saw the familiar furniture. He sat on the sofa and asked, "Where is Masha?"

"What time is it? She should be awake. She's asleep in the bedroom."

"No, no. Don't wake her up. I can wait."

Vera went to the bedroom, put Gregory in his cradle, and returned.

"Your name is Gregory. Wanda's son has the same name." Grisha stood, and his eyebrows rose.

"This is Wanda's son? I thought he was your child."

"Oh, no," Vera said, smiling. "At my age, a little child? Now I understand. You haven't seen Wanda for a long time. Did you know her husband died before her son was born? It's such a pity. Her husband died and never saw his little boy."

Grisha was shocked. He sat down again on the sofa. His heart beat rapidly.

This was news.

Masha awoke and called for her mother. Vera answered, "Your mother's not home. This is Vera. We have a guest. Come here, Mashenka."

The door opened slightly, and Masha peeked out. She recognized Grisha right away, although she had not seen him for more than a year. She wore pajamas and was barefoot. She ran to him and threw her arms around his neck.

Grisha hugged her tightly.

"I knew you'd come back," Masha said. "I missed you. Have you seen my little brother yet? He's so tiny and so cute. We're taking him with us to Auntie Sophie's. And will you come with us, too?"

She looked at Grisha, then, and saw the tears in his eyes. He could not speak. He understood only that Wanda had had his son and it was the answer to all questions. She would be with him. Now everything would be the way he wanted.

Masha laid her head on Grisha's shoulder.

"Mashenka," Vera said, "come, baby. You must dress. You're still in your pajamas."

She took Masha's hand.

"Grisha," Masha asked, "will you still be here when I come back?"

"Oh, yes. I'm waiting for your mother. I'll be here."

Vera could not understand why this friend of Wanda's was crying. Maybe he felt sorry for her, alone with two children.

But Grisha had stopped crying. He was no longer sad but excited. He had a son.

When Masha returned, she was dressed.

"Do you like my new dress?" she asked Grisha.

"Oh, yes, Mashenka. It's beautiful. Could you show me our little brother? I haven't seen him yet."

"Let's go," Masha answered.

She took Grisha's hand and led him to the other room. The little boy was babbling and smiling. His tiny hands were free, and he held a rubber toy, beating against his blanket.

Grisha stood, holding Masha's hand, and watched his son. Yes, this was his son. The same blue eyes, blonde hair, fair skin.

"These are my children," he thought. "This is my family. This is where I belong."

At that moment, he heard Vera's voice.

"Wanda, you have a guest. He came to see you before you leave."

Grisha turned and saw Wanda in the doorway. Her eyes were wide with shock. She held bags of groceries but dropped them to the floor.

Grisha tried to help her with the bags, and Wanda stooped at the same time.

They looked into each other's eyes. Grisha spoke first.

"I was wrong. Please, let me talk."

Wanda turned to Vera.

"Vera, please take Masha to the park for an hour."

When Vera and Masha had gone, Wanda sat down on the sofa and began to cry. Grisha sat down beside her and put his arm around her shoulders.

"Don't cry," he said. "Everything is behind us. Why didn't you tell me you were going to have a baby? Oh, Wanda, how can you make it through all this by yourself? I'll always be with you. It doesn't matter what happens. You can count on me. If only you would try to understand how I love you."

Wanda rested her head on his shoulder and cried quietly. After a while, she wiped her tears and looked at Grisha. She shook her head.

"Why did you come early?" she asked.

"I couldn't wait. Understand me. I could think of nothing else. I love to see you, to hear you, to be with you. You asked the impossible of me. Before, I saw you and understood you hadn't left Odessa. Now, I know you want to leave before two weeks, maybe only because you found out I'm married. But please tell me, why didn't you let me know I have a son?"

"Your mother doesn't want a grandchild from a Catholic woman."

"I'm my own boss," Grisha said. "My mother has her own life. If she wants a son, and doesn't want to lose him, she'll try to understand me."

He took Wanda's face in his hands and began to kiss her.

"You're mine forever," he said. "You, or death. I see no other way."
Wanda was devastated, powerless.

"I'm finished," she thought. "I can't leave the country."

To Grisha, she whispered, "What have you done, Grisha, to your
life and mine? What can we do now?"

"I need only one word from you," Grisha replied. "Tell me you want
me to stay. Tell me you want your children to have a father. That's all I
want from you. I'll take care of everything else."

"I want to go to my sister. Let me go. Later, you can come to Poland
and we'll see."

"No. Now that I know I have a son, I'll never let you go. Your sister
has her own family. If you go to your sister with two children, at first
they'll be happy to see you. But what about later? Without a husband.
Without a father for your children. Do you call that happiness? Your
life is here. I'll be a good husband for you and a father to the children.
Try to think now, and answer me."

Wanda cried quietly, saying nothing. Grisha walked to the other
room, took Gregory in his arms, and brought him to Wanda.

"Look at him," he said. "He has a right to have a father. What
happened to his parents is not his fault."

Grisha sat down next to Wanda and held Gregory in his lap.

"He understands," Grisha said. "He's smiling at me."

"Oh, sure," Wanda replied. "He recognized you right away. When
he was born, I saw he looked just like you. You see, he hasn't let me
forget you."

An hour had passed. Vera and Masha returned from the park.
Masha stood next to Grisha. Wanda went to the kitchen and asked Vera
to help her with dinner.

Grisha held his son in one arm and put the other around Masha.
He could not remember when he had been so happy before in his life.

They ate dinner together as they had before, Wanda, Grisha, and
Mashenka. As Grisha ate, he glanced often at Wanda, and he saw that
even though she seemed calm, she was still upset.

That evening, they sat on the sofa. Grisha held Wanda's hand to
his lips. "Try to understand me, my love" he said. "I don't want to hurt

you. Please tell me, what's better for you? To be with me, a husband and father to your children, or to be alone again and not know your future?"

"I was so close," Wanda said. "My visa is in my hand. My sister is waiting for us. What can I say to her now? I know the children need a father. You're right about that. But I'll say again what I said in the beginning. You're still married. You're not a free man."

"Wanda, my love, you're the only wife for me in this world. You've given me a son. Tell me, what greater bond could exist before man and God?"

"But you have an obligation. You're still married."

"I believe my obligation is to raise my son. That is what is most important to me."

"Grisha, you're repeating yourself. By law, you're still married, and that's important to me. Now, go home. It's too late. I'm tired. You're tired. Too much has happened today."

"Why do I have to go? My son is here, and so is the woman I love. I don't want to go. I don't want to leave."

"Yes, Griha, this is your son and my sin, and I will ask forgiveness for that for the rest of my life. You can't stay here."

"All right. If that's what you wish. But let me sleep on the sofa."

"No. I don't want to discuss this anymore. You're not a child. You must understand. I have neighbors who know I'm a widow with two children. They won't know whether you're sleeping in my bed or on my sofa. I would like to keep my reputation before we get married."

"Fine. I'll do everything you say. I'll get a divorce, and we'll be married in a civil ceremony. I'll rent an apartment in another part of town. All the neighbors will know is that I'm the father of two children. Do you like that?"

"First, take care of your divorce. Later, we'll see," Wanda said, smiling. Wanda walked Grisha to the door. He stopped at the door and said, "Wanda, give me your word that you won't leave before I return. You're everything I have, and I want to know that if I come tomorrow, I'll see you again."

"You're not coming tomorrow. You're not returning before you're free. I already explained that, and I don't want to repeat myself."

Grisha turned sharply.

"You want to leave without telling me," he said. "I know you've planned this from the beginning. Tell me the truth. Don't lie to me."

"No, I'll not go without telling you. I don't want to lie to you. You may come after a few days and tell me what's happened. Don't worry. I'm not leaving now, but I hope, if you can't be free, you will not hold me here. I have only two weeks. Now, good night, Grisha."

They kissed, and Grisha left her.

Wanda slumped against the wall, her eyes closed, and thought, "Two weeks are not enough for him. He'll not hold me here. We can go."

The next morning, Esther told Grisha that Rosa's parents would not let her return to him.

"That's wonderful," Grisha answered. "Things are simpler than I thought they'd be."

"How can you talk like that?" Esther protested. "This is a shame. This has never happened in our family before. If you were uneducated, simpler, you would have kept your wife."

"Mother, you're starting all over again. I don't want to hear this anymore. I must leave."

"All right, you can do what you want. But I'm sure you'll never give me grandchildren."

"No. You'll have grandchildren. I promise you."

Esther left the room, brushing away tears, and spoke softly to herself. "Sure, this Catholic will give you children. She already has a child."

Things went unexpectedly smoothly and quickly for Grisha. Rosa signed the divorce decree because she recovered her dowry. They had no children and no property to divide. Grisha received the divorce decree on the fourth day. He did, however, bribe the clerk to hurry the process along.

He tucked the decree granting him his freedom under his arm and knocked on Wanda's door. She opened it, saw his elated look, and understood there was no hope that she would leave.

Wanda felt her body tense; she felt cold.

"Can I come in?" Grisha asked. "Where are my children?"

"Come in and sit down, Grisha. They went for a walk with Vera. What happened?"

Wanda knew what his answer would be.

"You can see," he said, and he handed her the decree. "I'm a free man. Soon I'll be a slave again for the rest of my life."

Wanda read the decree, her heart beating fast. She had no hope that she would leave Russia.

"Nothing happens the way I want it to," she thought. "Nothing happens the way I will it to happen."

"How could you do this so quickly?" she asked Grisha. "I remember some friends who divorced. But it took a few months."

"You forget. Times have changed. This is a civil marriage. We have no children. Both sides agreed. The revolution made it very simple."

"Yes, you're right. Everything is simple, and different."

"I kept my word. Now we can marry. Do you, Wanda, agree to marry Gregory Vinar?"

"Yes, I do. Do I have a choice?"

"No, you don't. You can do only one thing. Be my wife."

A week before Wanda would have been free to leave Russia, she married Grisha in a civil ceremony. The children took his name—Maria Vinar and Gregory Vinar. Wanda, however, kept her last name—Stanishevsky. No matter how Grisha begged her, she would not change it. Tadeush was still alive in her heart. She had not seen him buried.

Soon, Grisha found a job in a factory. It was not difficult for him because he knew about business and economics. The government had taken the bar his mother had owned. Esther shared an apartment with her brother. She had to accept Wanda because she did not want to lose her son. She had discovered she had a grandson, and she did not need to ask who Gregory's father was. She saw her son as a little boy in Gregory's face.

"What character Wanda has," Esther said to Grisha. "She bore your son and would not tell you. Other women would have begged you to marry them if they were pregnant."

"When you get to know her, she will be like a daughter to you," Grisha replied. "She's soft, well-bred, well educated and, I might add, beautiful. What's most important is that I love her and the children, and I'm very happy."

"Yes, my son. I'm glad you're happy."

For Wanda, things were going well. When they married, they changed apartments and lived in Bolshaya Arnautskaya. The apartment had three rooms, a private kitchen, and a balcony on the second floor. Grisha made enough money.

Wanda sent a letter to her sister explaining that the government would not let her go. She received a letter from Sophie. Her sister was sad, but she was glad they could write to each other.

"In one letter, Wanda told Sophie she had married a good man. She added, "Nobody can take Tadeush's place in my heart."

A year later, Wanda wrote, "I have a little son named after his father, Gregory."

It was 1924. Wanda was thirty-four years old, Grisha thirty-seven. They were young, healthy, full of energy and plans. Soon, Masha went to first grade. Sometimes, Wanda cried very quietly when she received a letter from Sophie.

"Oh, God," she thought, "I want so much to see my sister and Poland. But most of all, I want to go to Poland and take my family with me."

She knew it could not be. Uncle Simon died and Esther lived alone. Grisha would never leave his mother, and Wanda could not ask him to. She was happy. Grisha was a good father. Masha called him Papa. He spent all his free time with his family. They had a few friends from Grisha's factory. Everyone believed the two children were his.

Life went on. After her brother's death, Esther visited her son's family almost every day. There was peace between Wanda and Esther.

"Grisha was right," Esther thought. "She is an angel."

And Wanda thought, "Grisha is right about his mother. She feels the same toward both children. But Masha is a good girl. She's so nice to Esther. She calls her 'my dear Granny.'"

Once, they had guests for Grisha's birthday. One of his friends walked up to Wanda's portrait and said, "I see, dear Wanda, that before the revolution you were not of poor society. Who were your parents?"

Everyone looked at Wanda. She remained calm.

"My father was a well-known lawyer in Cracow. My mother died when I was eight years old. What did you mean, 'not of poor society?'"

"Exactly what I said. Your father was not a laborer. Your mother was not a laundress. Your clothes show it."

"What's so surprising? I was seventeen then."

"No surprise. But now it is very important to be from the proletariat. Yes, my friends?" He looked around the room.

No one spoke. No one could add anything to what he had said.

"My friends," Grisha said, loudly, "sit down and eat. This is my birthday. That's what you came for."

Everyone sat, but no one was comfortable. Esther had taken the children to her apartment before the guests arrived. Grisha was glad, because she would not have kept quiet.

The evening showed Grisha and Wanda what kind of friends they could have. Grisha did not know why, but soon all his co-workers began talking about him and asking him questions.

"Is it true your wife is from the bourgeoisie?"

Grisha answered only that the revolution had made everyone equal.

One morning, his boss called him into his office.

"Tell me, Grisha," the boss asked. "How long have you been married?"

"I have a daughter seven years old and a son two and a half. But why do you ask?"

"That means you were married before the revolution."

"Why are you asking me questions about my private life? It has nothing to do with my job."

"In our society, as you know, we are building socialism. Your private life and your social life are everyone's concern."

"Can you tell me what is your concern?"

"Oh, someone told me you were hiding your past from us."

"That's nonsense. What can I hide? I was born in Odessa. My mother's still alive. You can ask her."

"Where did you receive your education?"

"In Germany. Why?"

"You see, if you're just from a poor family, you could not have gone to Germany to be educated. Do you speak German?"

"Sure, but I don't understand what this is all about. Lenin lived outside the country. But that aside, what's the matter with getting my education outside the country? I live here, I work here, and I have done nothing to harm my country."

"I'm not sure about that. Where did you meet your wife? In Germany? And you brought her here?"

"I don't have to answer you. This is my private life. You can fire me if you don't like my work. But no one can pry into my private life."

Grisha stood, said no more, and left the office. He went home.

When Wanda saw him, she was surprised.

"What happened?" she asked. "Are you sick?"

"No, my dear, I'm fine. It's my boss and the people around him. They're sick."

He told Wanda about the conversation with his boss.

"Oh, Grisha, I don't like it. Did you see the newspaper? Maybe it would be better if we went to Poland for good."

"How can you say that? You know my mother will never leave. She always says, 'I was born here and I'll die here.' No, my dear, we must do something else. I'll go to work tomorrow and try to find out exactly what they want from me. But I have a feeling I'll have to look for another job."

"That won't be difficult for you. You know your business."

"I don't know what this is all about. It's nonsense. What do they want from me? They asked me about my education in Germany. ..."

"Calm down. Don't be nervous. You've started smoking too much again." The next morning, Grisha arrived at work, and the secretary gave him a piece of paper. He read it.

"In the best interest of the company, you have been relieved of your position as of January 20, 1924."

Grisha walked out to the street. He could not get enough air.

"The scoundrels," he thought. "They fired me without thinking that I have a wife, two children, and an old mother to care for."

He was choked with fury, but he understood he could do nothing. He did not go home. Instead, he went to his mother's. When Esther met him at the door, she said, "I'm glad you're here. I'd almost left. But why are you here?"

"I came from work. I've been fired for no reason." He handed her the dismissal.

"What's this all about?" Esther asked. "Why? Maybe because you're a Jew?"

"No, they didn't say that. My boss talked about my past and my education in Germany."

"Oh, my God. What will you do now?"

"You know, Mama, Wanda has a proposition. We could go to Poland. Maybe it's the best thing to do in this situation."

"I'm surprised at Wanda. She's still talking about that. All right, you can go and leave me here by myself."

Esther put her handkerchief to her eyes.

"Ah, Mama, nobody's leaving you here. You'll come with us."

"You know, son, I'll never leave. As long as I live, I live here."

"We won't go anywhere without you. You don't need to worry. But I must look for another job."

Grisha walked home. He told Wanda he wasn't feeling well and lay down on the sofa. After an hour, Wanda tried to wake him.

"Grisha, wake up," she said, touching his hand. "I've fried some potatoes.

Let's eat.

He did not answer. He lay on his side and did not move. Wanda tried to rouse him, nudging his shoulder.

"Grishenka, my dear, what happened? Open your eyes. Masha, call someone, please."

Masha went to call the neighbors. The neighbor from across the hall came over and saw Wanda on her knees, crying.

"What happened? Can I help?"

"I don't know," Wanda sobbed. "I can't wake him." The neighbor, an older lady, unbuttoned Grisha's shirt.

"It looks like he's fainted," she said. "I'll go call an ambulance." Wanda continued to cry and to try rousing Grisha.

"Grisha, please wake up, I beg you. Open your eyes. Oh, my God, what happened to you?"

Wanda laid her head on his chest, sobbing loudly. The ambulance arrived. The attendants pulled Wanda away, and the doctor, a woman, began to examine Grisha.

"What happened to him, doctor?" Wanda sobbed. "Please help him. We have two children. He loves them."

"Calm down," the doctor said. "Get a hold of yourself. We have to take your husband to the hospital. We'll do everything in our power."

Two attendants put Grisha on a stretcher and carried him to the ambulance.

Wanda followed them.

In the hospital, Grisha died, never regaining consciousness. The autopsy showed he had suffered a heart attack.

Oh, grief! On the same day the whole country was in mourning— the leader of the Russian revolution, Vladimir Illyitch Lenin, died also.

But Wanda did not grieve Lenin. She, Wanda Stanishevsky, had lost, again, someone very close to her.

Esther seemed to turn to stone. Her lips closed tight, and she shed no tears.

She looked at her son's face. It was difficult to tell what she was thinking.

The coffin was lowered into the ground. Esther was held by both arms. She only moved her head from side to side, her lips moving without sound. Wanda sobbed. Vera put her arm around Wanda's shoulders and talked to her soothingly. When Wanda looked into Grisha's coffin, she saw the faces of Tadeush, Vladimir, and Gregory. She fainted.

A strong wind blew. The winter was unusually cold. The snow lay on the ground for more than a week, and the temperature was twenty degrees below zero, centigrade. It was unusual weather for Odessa. It was cold outside, and just as cold in Wanda's heart. What could she do with two children by herself?

After the funeral, everyone went to Wanda's apartment. It was warm there, thanks to the porter. He pitied the poor woman alone with two children. The porter's wife had stayed with Masha and Gregory during the funeral. She prepared a samovar of tea to warm the guests.

Esther took her grandson on her lap.

"My little boy. You're my little angel. What has your father done? How could he leave us like that?"

Gregory wrapped his arms around Esther's neck and kissed her on the cheek.

"You lovely child. You're my only one. I can't live without you. You're all I have. Wanda, you can't leave for Poland. You can't take my grandson with you. Can you?"

At last, Esther began to cry.

"Calm down," Wanda said. "Don't say anything. When you cry, the children cry."

Gregory started to cry and held out his arms to Wanda.

"Esther, stay here with us tonight," Wanda said. "I know it's not easy to be alone. We can stay together."

Esther agreed. She stood, staring out the window.

"Oh, God," she said. "It's so cold, and my Grishenka is lying in the cold ground. It's not right. Children are supposed to bury their parents. I thank you, Wanda. You gave me my grandson."

Wanda remained silent. She put the children to bed and asked Esther to go to bed. Esther lay down in Wanda's bed, and Wanda covered her with a blanket. Then Wanda sat alone in the living room with her thoughts.

"Alone again," she mused. "My poor children. I have to raise them without a father. Maybe I should leave Russia because, except for bad luck, I have nothing here."

She continued to think, lying on the sofa. "We'll take Esther to Poland. She has no one here. Tomorrow, I'll write to Sophie and ask her what to do."

Wanda fell asleep on the sofa, fully clothed.

The next morning, she did not write to Sophie because Gregory was ill. He was running a high temperature. She called the doctor who prescribed medication and said the little boy had a cold.

Esther was beside herself. She took Gregory's temperature every fifteen minutes. When he slept, she put her ear to his chest to be sure he was still breathing.

"Don't worry," said Vera, who came for a visit. "Children don't grow up without any illness."

Esther made chicken soup and tried to feed her grandson, but he did not want to eat.

"He's very, very ill if he won't eat chicken soup," Esther said, crying. "This is serious."

Wanda suggested that Esther take Masha to her apartment in case the illness were contagious.

"What are you talking about?" Esther cried. "How can I leave my grandson? Here's the key to my apartment. Take Masha and go."

"I'm his mother," Wanda replied. "I can't leave my child."

"All right. You can keep Masha in another room until Gregory feels better." Vera solved the problem. She would take Masha. They prepared clothing for Masha, and she and Vera left. The weather had improved, and transportation was available again.

Esther and Wanda stayed with the sick child. The pediatrician came the next day and diagnosed the illness as mumps. Everyone felt better. They put a warm compress on the swelling, and Gregory's fever fell. His sickness had diverted Wanda and Esther from their unexpected grief. After a week, the little boy felt well.

Esther went home, but she visited every day. She complained constantly.

She had no appetite, could not sleep well, and had terrible headaches.

"You must go to the doctor," Wanda said. "You need to take care of yourself."

"Yes, you're right. I'm waiting for warmer weather. Then I'll go to the doctor."

A month after Grisha's death, the streets were slushy and a cold wind blew. Usually, Esther visited each morning about ten o'clock. But it was already noon, and she had not come. Wanda began to worry and decided to go see if Esther were ill.

Wanda knocked on Esther's door, but there was no answer.

"Perhaps she's gone to the store," Wanda thought, as she turned to leave. Then she noticed a light under the door of Esther's apartment. She knew Esther never left the light on when she was gone.

Wanda knocked harder. Still there was no answer. The nieghbor, a middle-aged woman across the hall, opened her door to investigate.

"Excuse me, have you seen Esther today?" Wanda asked.

"Usually, she goes for milk in the morning. But I didn't see her today." They called the porter. He came with a ring of keys. After a few minutes, the door was opened.

Esther lay on the sofa in the living room. She was clothed. One shoe was on the floor, the other on her foot. Wanda walked closer. The neighbor and the porter followed.

"What happened to you?" Wanda cried. "Oh, no, not this again." Esther was alive. Her face seemed lopsided. Her left eye was wide open.

"I believe she can't talk," the neighbor said. "I'll go call Dr. Vlasov. Poor woman, she just lost her son."

Wanda sat down at the end of the sofa.

"We'll wait for the doctor," she said through her tears. "You must live. You must be healthy. We need you."

Esther looked at her, speaking with her eyes. Wanda answered the silent question.

"Gregory is fine. He slept through the night and has had his breakfast." Esther closed her right eye. Wanda tried to control herself and not cry.

Tears fell from her eyes. She stood and put her handkerchief to her face, turning toward the window. She began to pray.

"Oh, Saint Mary. Make a miracle. I beg you."

She sat down in a chair near the window and watched the people on the street. Everyone had his own problems.

"What can we do now?" she thought. "I can't go to Poland and leave Esther here in this condition. And I can't take her." She wept silently.

There was a knock at the door, and the doctor arrived. She saw a man about thirty-eight or forty years old with pince-nez glasses. He was of average height and build. He took off his coat and rubbed his hands together to warm them. He walked to the sofa where Esther lay.

"Please," he said, "only close relatives can stay. Everyone else must leave." Wanda stood near Esther's head.

The doctor started to examine Esther. When he finished, he said, "Please come with me to the other room. I need to talk with you."

Wanda and the doctor went to Simon's room, and the doctor asked her, "How are you related to her?"

"I'm her daughter-in-law. Her son, my husband, died months ago."

"It is necessary to take her to the hospital. She has had a stroke. The left side of her body is paralyzed. Her right side is partially affected.

We must check her. Please accept my sympathy. Her condition is very serious."

He put his hand on Wanda's shoulder and continued, "I'll call the ambulance, and you can go with us. Be calm. Life is a struggle. This is truth. You're still young. I saw how you worry. Tell me, do you have other close relatives?"

"No one, except my children," she answered. Again she began to cry.

The doctor looked at her, thinking, "She is a very beautiful woman. She looks so elegant. Her features are classic, irreproachably beautiful."

The doctor was an artist. He spent all his free time painting. Now, he looked on Wanda as a subject for his art.

The ambulance arrived and took Esther to the hospital. The doctor and Wanda walked to the ambulance. In front of the building, the curious had gathered. People were always curious about such events.

Wanda arrived home late that night. Vera had been worried.

"Vera, I really appreciate what you've done for me," Wanda said. "My misfortune has repeated itself. I thought I had suffered enough, but I was wrong." She explained everything that had happened.

"What will you do now?" Vera asked. "How long will Esther be in the hospital?"

"I don't know, but it won't be very long. Tomorrow, they will consult. We'll know after that."

"I'll help you as much as I can. I understand it's difficult for you," Vera said as she left. "Tomorrow, I'll come over and stay with the children. You can go to the hospital."

Wanda walked over to her.

"God bless you, Vera. You're very kind. I'll never forget this." Wanda put the children to bed and went to the kitchen to prepare tea.

After three weeks, Esther's condition had not changed. The hospital asked Wanda to take her home. Doctor Vlasov called Wanda.

"I can help you put your mother-in-law in a nursing home because you need to take care of the children," he said.

"Oh, no," Wanda replied. "I'll not put her anywhere. She can stay with us. She'll get better more quickly."

"You're not only beautiful, but you're also very kind, sympathetic. Rarely does one person have all those qualities."

Wanda did not answer. What could she say? She had heard it so many times, but the words had never helped her. Fate had slapped her. Her fate was far worse than the fate of those who were not beautiful, kind, or sympathetic.

The doctor seemed to read her mind.

"'Don't be born beautiful; be born lucky,'" he said. "Do I understand your thoughts?"

"Yes, doctor. You're right."

"Please give me your address. I'll visit your mother-in-law. I have to see my patient."

Wanda thanked him for everything.

A few hours later, Esther was transferred to Wanda's apartment. Wanda prepared a bed for her, the same bed Esther had slept in for many years. Next to the bed she placed Esther's dresser. She had to sell the rest of the furniture because the government took Esther's apartment.

The days seemed endless. Day after day, Wanda worried and cared for the two children and Esther, who lay like a vegetable. Wanda spoon-fed her. Esther heard and understood, but she could not speak. When Wanda asked a question and the answer was "yes," Esther closed her eye. If the answer was "no," the eye remained open.

Doctor Vlasov visited as he promised every week. He saw how Wanda kept everything neat and clean and how she took care of her mother-in-law.

"Tell me, Wanda, when do you sleep? You look tired. You have to rest because you might become ill."

"No, I'm strong. Four hours of sleep a night is enough for me. But soon I must look for a job. My money's almost gone. Vera can look after Gregory, and Masha is starting school."

"What kind of job will you be looking for?"

"I don't know yet. I can paint. But I haven't done it for a long time."

"Really?" I'm an artist, too. What kind of painting do you do?'

"I paint landscapes and sometimes portraits."

"May I see your work, if it isn't secret?"

"Of course. I can show you my paintings. They're in a box in the other room."

As the doctor walked toward Wanda's bedroom, he saw her portrait.

"You look so young there," he said. "How old were you when it was painted?"

"Seventeen. The portrait was done by a famous Italian artist."

"It looks like magic. You can see even the air in this portrait."

"Oh, doctor, I don't like to talk about it. This portrait is all I have left from my past."

She showed him her sketches and portraits of children.

"You have a real talent," he said. "You are a real artist. I believe you can find a job very easily."

Wanda heard a noise from another room. "Excuse me," she said. "I'll be right back."

It was Esther. Wanda walked to her bed and asked, "Do you want some water?" Esther held her lips tightly closed and kept her eyes wide open.

"Is something bothering you?"

Esther closed her eye, meaning "yes."

"Is the bed uncomfortable?"

Esther did not respond. Wanda adjusted her pillows and sheets. She saw Esther moving the fingers of her right hand. Wanda understood that something was wrong.

"I'll call the doctor. He's here and he can check you. Do you want that?" Esther did not want it. Wanda called the doctor anyway.

"Give me your hand," Doctor Vlasov said to Esther. "I'll take your pulse." Esther's hand did not move.

"Maybe she's had another stroke," he thought. He checked her, but found nothing different.

Doctor Vlasov left. Wanda had understood Esther well, almost instinctively.

"You don't like this doctor?" she asked Esther.

Esther closed her eye.

"But why? He's a good doctor. He's an artist, and he promised to help me find a job."

Esther blinked rapidly. It meant she did not like the situation at all.

"You don't want me to go to work? We have money for only a couple more weeks. I have to find work."

Esther closed her eye, and Wanda understood the conversation was over. After a few days, Doctor Vlasov stopped by and told Wanda, "Odessa Opera Theatre is looking for a set designer. I recommended you to the director. You can go for an interview. They are waiting for you."

It was the best Wanda could hope for. The director hired her. Her schedule was convenient. She could work any time as long as the sets for the opera or ballet were completed.

Doctor Vlasov visited her several times at the studio. Wanda told him each time how much she appreciated what he had done.

"If not for you, doctor," she said once, "I wouldn't have this job. It's interesting and exciting work."

Doctor Vlasov smiled. "Someday, you'll do something for me."

Six months later, Wanda's life had grown stable and comfortable. She worked in the theatre studio. Masha went to the first grade. Gregory started kindergarten. Esther was partially recovered. She could sit up and move around with help. She had started talking a little.

Once, while Wanda was brushing Esther's hair, she said, "A little more time and you'll be well. I'm so happy to see you recovering. You'll be back to normal soon."

Esther took Wanda's hand and kissed it.

"Thanks," she said, and tears fell from her tired eyes.

"Don't cry," Wanda said. "You shouldn't get upset. You need to be calm in your condition."

Wanda remembered a different Esther, overbearing and stubborn, and Esther's gratitude touched her heart. How grief changed people! It was difficult to believe this was the same Esther who said she would never accept a Catholic.

The year was 1927. Life was much better. NEP, the New Economical Political system, was at its peak. People had small stores and bakeries. Farmers brought meat, vegetables, and fruits from the country to the city market. Odessa had almost forgotten that kind of life. Nightlife was different. Cabarets and restaurants were open.

Wanda started receiving orders for business signs. She made a good living. One night, she had just put the children to bed and was fixing Esther's bed. "I don't believe it," she said. "I don't need to worry about tomorrow anymore. I make enough money that I can even save a little.

We have everything we need. What's important now is that you recover. Doctor Vlasov said you'll be walking by yourself in a few months." Esther spoke with difficulty, but Wanda could understand her.

"I don't want this doctor anymore. Tell him not to come. I feel better."

"What do you have against him? He found a job for me. He was the first to help you when you got sick. I hope we can appreciate what he's done. I saw before that you don't like him. Can you tell me why?"

"He comes because he likes you. I see how he looks at you."

"That's nonsense. He's married. He has two children. He's never shown an interest. He's a gentleman. Esther, you're wrong about Doctor Vlasov. All men look at me like that."

"I don't know. Maybe. But you're beautiful, and I saw his look."

"Calm down, Esther. I'm thirty-seven years old. I'm a widow with two children. I have more important things to worry about."

"Look at you. You look twenty-five. You haven't had an easy life, but it doesn't show on you."

Esther was right. Nobody could tell Wanda's age. Her skin was smooth and soft. Her light brown eyes and long lashes, the curve of her lips, and her long, thick hair had not changed in fifteen years. All those years, people had noticed her.

Esther was right about Doctor Vlasov, as well. He was in love with Wanda. He thought about her constantly. Her quiet, gentle nature had changed his life. He understood it was infatuation, like a schoolboy romance. He tried to control his feelings, but Esther saw them clearly.

Wanda had not thought about Doctor Vlasov until Esther mentioned her opinion.

Once, when Wanda had completed a private order, she showed Doctor Vlasov her work.

"It's excellent," he said. "You have very good taste. I'm proud of you." She glanced into his eyes and saw, for the first time, how he looked at her.

It was not merely a friendly look. She felt it, but did not show what she felt. "Wanda, I have two tickets to the opera. My wife and children are staying at our dacha. Can you come with me?"

"Oh, no, I can't do that. How would it look? I have to put the children to bed and help Esther. I have a lot of responsibilities. I'm never free in the evenings."

"You're such a young and beautiful woman. You've buried yourself in this kind of life. You have no boyfriends. Work and home, home and work: no one would believe it's all you do."

"I don't understand. What's wrong with a woman who's a widow having a life like that?"

"Oh, nothing is wrong with it. But life is passing. You don't want to marry again?"

"I've never thought about it. No, I don't want to marry. Who would want someone else's children and mother-in-law?"

"You don't know how much you're worth. A young man who was never married would be happy to have a woman like you for his wife."

"What's he implying?" Wanda thought. "Maybe he plans to introduce me to someone."

"Dr. Vlasov," she asked, "why are you so sure? I think young men want young girls."

"I'll tell you why. If I weren't married and I were twenty years younger, I'd ask for your hand. I repeat. You don't know what you're worth."

He lowered his eyes and, for a few moments, remained silent. The entire conversation had taken place in the theatre's basement studio.

"Can we go to a cafe and have a cup of coffee?" he asked. "I'll answer your question for you. It's daytime. You don't need to worry if someone sees us."

"All right. I'm a little hungry."

Doctor Vlasov ordered coffee and pastry. Wanda began to eat, thinking about what he might say. She had a feeling what he would say, and thought, "Oh, God, take this away. I don't need this."

Doctor Vlasov spoke. "If you wish, Wanda, you can have a different life. Just imagine. You could have a maid. You wouldn't need to work. You could have everything you want. All of it is in your hands."

"Maybe you've found me an old, old rich man?"

"No, just the opposite. I can't imagine you and an old man together."

"Perhaps you will explain how I can change my life. It's an interesting picture you've drawn for me."

"This is not easy, but I'll try. First, I love you. These aren't just words. This is a very deep feeling. In my forty years, I've never faced such a tragedy. If you could only know how I think about you all the time. I wanted to keep this a secret, but I couldn't. It's larger than I am."

"Doctor, you're married. You have children. How can this happen? You're right, this is a tragedy. What can you offer me? You've not decided to leave your wife and children."

"No, I can't do that. At least not now."

"If I understand you, you're offering to make me your mistress."

"Why do you put it that way? I love you. You're alone, and I believe you like me. We spend time together and enjoy each other's company. We're not hurting anyone."

"How about your wife? You're cheating on her. How will you share yourself with two women?"

"You don't know my wife. You can't understand. My marriage is more like a business arrangement. We don't love each other. My wife is free to do what she pleases. She has everything she needs and asks for nothing more."

"This is strange. What can I tell you? If you weren't married, I might think about accepting a proposal. But what you ask me to do now is not in my nature. I'll never understand the relationship between a married man and another woman. And remember, I'll never be anyone's mistress. I'm free, and I like being free. Thank you for everything you've done. I'll try to pay you in my own way. ..."

"Stop, Wanda," Doctor Vlasov interrupted. "You didn't understand anything I said. I love you deeply. This is serious. I can't imagine my life without you. And now you give a lecture about how a married man can't have a relationship with another woman? Can you understand? If I hadn't met you, my life would be different. I'd be free. Remember, nothing can stop me. You'll be mine. There is no choice for you. You're human and have been a long time without a husband."

"Doctor Vlasov, I thought you were different, but I was mistaken. Now you're trying to frighten me. I don't believe you can do it."

"You can call me Konstantin, or Kostya, for short. To you, I'm not Doctor Vlasov," he said, smiling. "And frankly, I don't know what to do. I've never felt this way before. I think I could do anything to make you mine. You see, I'm very honest with you."

"I don't need your honesty. This is what I want. Don't come to see Esther anymore. I can find another doctor. This conversation is over."

Wanda stood and walked toward the exit. Doctor Vlasov left money on the table and followed her. On the street, he took her arm.

"I didn't mean to insult you," he said. "I didn't think the conversation would go this far. Forgive me, please. I have to see you again."

"No. You have to get used to not seeing me." Wanda looked into his eyes. "Try to understand. I'm not looking for adventure. If I want to be married, I can find someone who pleases me. But right now, I don't need anything like that. For the first time in my life, I'm standing on my own feet and doing what I want with my life. Why should I throw everything away now and become someone's mistress?"

"Oh, Wanda, I've really insulted you. It hurts me to hear what you say. Maybe I can change this situation. Just don't tell me you don't want to see me again."

"What else can I say?"

"You're a very kind person, and you won't just throw me aside. I'm your friend. You don't have many friends."

"You're right. I have almost no friends. After my husband's death, I realized I didn't need friends. Yes, I'm kind and soft, but those qualities have worked against me. Believe me, I'm trying to change. I'll never again be kind to those who harm me."

"I don't believe you. I know you. I count on your indulgence."

"Let me go home. This conversation has gone too far."

"Yes, you're free. I'll not hold you. But give me your word that you're not angry with me and that we'll still be friends, like before. I'll not make any more assumptions."

"No, it's not easy to believe. Look at your eyes. If you won't assume things about me, I'll not assume things about you. Good-bye, doctor."

"Please, call me Konstantin."

Wanda smiled, turned, and walked to the trolley stop.

"Oh, damn," Doctor Vlasov thought. "How could I talk to her like that? I should have been more delicate. Now it will be hard to change this, but I must try. I will approach her differently. What a woman. She's a goddess. I would do anything for her."

He walked slowly down the street, looking at his feet, thinking about his next move.

Wanda arrived at home, feeling tense. Esther looked at her and noticed that something was wrong.

"What happened, Wanda? Did you lose your job?"

"Oh, no, thank God. I'm just tired, and I have a headache."

"Lie down and rest a little. I believe something's bothering you." Wanda did not answer. She went to the kitchen to prepare dinner.

A week passed. Wanda heard nothing from Doctor Vlasov and did not see him. She felt, however, that he was watching her.

"This is good," she thought. "I believe he understands now that I can't do what he asks."

Leaving the studio one afternoon, she opened the door and saw Doctor Vlasov coming into the studio.

"Hello, Wanda," he said. "Are you leaving?"

"Yes, I've finished my work for today."

"Would you like to have a cup of coffee with me?"

"No, I wouldn't. I still taste the coffee from last week."

"Why do you talk like that? I promise you, everything will be different now. Do you believe me?"

"I'd like to believe you, but I don't want coffee and the same conversation again."

"All right. If you don't want coffee, would you like to have lunch with me? I'm hungry. How about you?"

"It's the same, coffee or lunch. During lunch, we have more time. Do you think I'm naive? After our last talk, I don't like being with you. Do you understand?"

"No, I don't. I give you my word, I'll never talk about it again. What I want is only to see you, to look at you. We have a lot in common. We could talk about anything. Would you please have lunch with me?" Doctor Vlasov smiled.

"What can I do with you? You won't quit. I'll give you one more chance."

"She'll be mine," Doctor Vlasov thought. "There is no doubt. But I need to be more careful."

They sat at a table in the restaurant. Soft music played. A waiter took their order. Vlasov talked about art and music.

"Do you play the piano?" he asked Wanda.

"No, I don't. My sister played. Sophie was a very good pianist. Once, she thought to make the piano a career, but she got married, had three children, and it became just a hobby."

"If you were in Poland, I would never have met you."

"That's the best thing that could have happened to me. I had hoped to leave. Once, I had a visa in my hand. But circumstances kept me here."

"That's wonderful. Everything happened for the best. You'll never regret staying here."

"Are you serious? What's so wonderful? I lost my husband. I have two children and a mother-in-law on my hands."

"You misunderstand me. I meant it's wonderful I met you because. ..."

Wanda interrupted him. "You're starting again. Can we please change the subject?"

"All right. I promise, no more."

The waiter brought wine. Konstantin raised his glass and said, "I propose a toast: to the most beautiful woman I ever saw in my life."

He drank his wine quickly and poured another glass.

"My second toast: I also propose a very good friendship. You can rely on me."

Wanda smiled and said nothing. Doctor Vlasov said nothing more about love or friendship during the rest of the meal. He took her home, kissed her hand, and they parted.

Doctor Vlasov thought his new tactic was smarter. After a few months, he believed, Wanda would be his.

Even though Wanda claimed not to be naive, she was. She could fall easily into Doctor Vlasov's trap. His plan went much farther.

Konstantin talked to the theatre director and asked him to give Wanda fewer and fewer jobs. He knew that soon she would ask him again for help.

"The end justifies the means," he thought.

He did not think of his actions in terms of subterfuge or meanness. He did not want to harm or shame Wanda. All he wanted was for her to be his mistress, and he would pay any price.

As she received fewer and fewer jobs, Wanda began to worry. Konstantin invited her to dinner, and she accepted.

"Konstantin," Wanda said, "there is not much work for me at the studio. I just have enough to pay my bills. Perhaps you know someone who needs an artist."

"Certainly I'll help you. Tomorrow, I'll ask some friends."

Wanda began painting for Konstantin. He gave her the subject, and she painted. In time, he found people who were interested in buying the paintings, or he gave them to a gallery. He made no money, but he was not looking for it. All he wanted was to become closer and closer to Wanda so that someday she could not survive without him.

Konstantin did not visit Esther for some time. She felt much better and began to move about on her own and help Wanda. Wanda never mentioned Konstantin's name to Esther. If Wanda had dinner with Konstantin, she asked him not to take her all the way home, but to drop her off a block away.

Once, Wanda gave him one of her paintings and said, "I've finished this in time. What is my next job?"

"I'm sorry," he answered. "I have nothing now. You'll have to wait. Here is the money for this job."

"Thank you very much. This will be enough for a whole month."

The month was almost over, but Konstantin had no new work for Wanda.

She began to worry. She would have to look again, day after day, for a job.

She started to think again about going to Poland.

One evening, she approached Esther carefully with the subject of Poland. She was surprised when Esther said, "Yes, Wanda. We should go."

The next day, Wanda went to the authorities and asked for a visa application.

"Have you been asleep, citizen?" the officer asked. "Emigration was stopped long ago. Now you must live here."

Wanda could not breathe. "I have a sister in Poland," she said. "I was born in Cracow. You can check my papers. I've already had a visa once."

"I repeat. Emigration is over. We don't have that office anymore." Wanda walked out to the street, tears streaming down her face.

"It's over," she thought. "I'll never see my sister and her family again. Some power has cursed me. When I had a visa, I couldn't go. Now I can't get a visa when I can go. There is no hope now."

She made her way to the studio and dried her tears. She walked to the director's office. He sat at his desk, writing.

Wanda tapped on the open door.

"Come in, Wanda," the director said. "I didn't see you. Are you upset?"

"I need a job. Maybe you can help me. I have two children and a mother-in-law to care for. I see you've hired new people, yet you say there is no work for me. Do you dislike my work? You've never told me so."

"Calm down, Wanda. Sit down. I liked your work." The director stood and walked around the desk. "But now we have a different situation." He did not look at her and was silent for a minute. Then, he asked her, "When did you last see Vlasov?"

"About a week ago."

"He has so many connections. It's better if you contact him. He can help you as no one else can."

Wanda stood without speaking and walked out the door. The director stopped her.

"This is Doctor Vlasov's phone number. Maybe it will help you."

He gave her a card with the number on it. Wanda thanked him and left.

It was spring, 1928. The scent of acacias permeated the air. Wanda walked slowly down the boulevard, wandering aimlessly. If someone were to ask her where she was going, she would be unable to answer. She sat on a bench and looked around. The sea lay before her, flat and blue like the sky. Seagulls chattered on the water. It was midday, and few people were about. Wanda calmed down. She did not cry anymore, but she thought, bitterly, that she had to ask Konstantin for help. He was her one hope.

The next day, she called the number on the card. It was Doctor Vlasov's clinic. Wanda heard Konstantin pick up the receiver.

"Hello, this is Wanda."

"Hello, Wanda. I haven't heard your voice for some time. Over the telephone, your voice is even softer. What can I do for you?"

"I need a job. Do you have anything for me?"

"I'm sorry. There is nothing. But let me think about it. When can I see you?"

"I'm free during the day. The children are in school."

"All right. Can I meet you at eleven o'clock in the same cafe where we had coffee? Do you agree?"

Wanda sighed. "Yes, I'll be there at eleven."

"Good. See you tomorrow. Good night, Wanda."

"Good night."

Wanda was at the cafe fifteen minutes early. She wanted to prepare herself.

She could think of nothing.

Konstantin arrived and saw Wanda sitting at a table, drinking coffee.

"Either you're early, or I'm late," he said.

"No, you're on time."

"I'm glad to see you, Wanda. You look so sad. Everything will be just fine, believe me."

Wanda smiled and said nothing.

"That's better," Konstantin said. "I like your smile. What will we order? Do you like French toast? They prepare it very well here."

"All right. It doesn't matter to me. I'm not very hungry."

Before the waiter brought the order, Konstantin talked about the weather, politics, a new musical at the theatre. Wanda listened and thought, "He's very intelligent, an interesting conversationalist."

They ate slowly, talking, in no hurry to go anywhere.

"Do you have anything for me?" Wanda asked, as she pushed her plate away.

"Yes, as a matter of fact, I have a very unusual job for you. I can show you tonight, about six o'clock. I'll pick you up, and we'll go to the place. If you have time tonight. If not, we can schedule it for another time."

"No, I can go, at seven. Esther will stay with the children. But what kind of job is it? Can you explain?"

"No, I don't want to tell you before I show you. But you will be painting." They talked a while longer and then parted. Konstantin reminded her that he would pick her up at seven.

On her way home, Wanda thought about Konstantin. He seemed a good person. She understood she had no one else who could help her.

At seven o'clock, Konstantin was waiting for Wanda down the block from her apartment. He opened the door to let her in and started the car.

"How are your children, Wanda?"

"They're fine, thank you, growing fast. How are yours?"

"They're still at the dacha. I'm so busy I haven't had time to visit them. One more month, though, and they'll be home."

"Where are we going?" Where is this job?"

"Don't rush. You'll see. It's just a few more blocks."

After ten minutes, the car pulled up and stopped in front of a beautiful mansion. In the building lived artists, musicians and some Communist Party members.

Konstantin and Wanda walked to the second floor. Konstantin opened the door for Wanda, and they entered a beautiful apartment, four large rooms with a balcony overlooking the street. A high ceiling made the rooms seem larger.

"Whose apartment is this?" Wanda sked. "It's mine, but you must work here for me."

"What do you mean?"

"I want you to paint a mural. I have some sketches I'd like to show you."

"I've never done anything like that in my life."

"You can start, and we'll see how it looks. One room I'd like to be Oriental, another room Greek, and the other two we'll decide about later."

"Where do I start?"

"Put a background on the walls. They're smooth and flat. All the paint you need is in the kitchen. You can start in the living room. I want it to be Oriental, banzai trees and exotic birds, butterflies, all in light pastel colors. That's the basic idea. Do you like it?"

"Yes, I do. When can I start?"

"If you wish, tomorrow morning. Here's the key. Everything here is in your hands."

He gave her the key and an envelope.

"This is an advance. You'll receive the rest when you finish the job."

He took Wanda home. She asked no questions. She thought only about the unusual work and how she would begin. Before they parted, she thanked him again.

At eight o'clock the next morning, Wanda began working. She prepared sketches for herself. She had complete freedom of imagination. She started with the background, soft green fading to light blue from floor to ceiling. Next, she painted the banzai trees. In the distance, she painted tiny, Oriental structures.

A few days later, she finished the living room. She called Konstantin, and he said he would come after lunch.

"This is excellent," Konstantin said, when he saw Wanda's work. "I can't imagine anything better. Do you like it, Wanda?"

"Yes, I do. It was very exciting. What's interesting is that you can never take this picture away."

"Now you can start on the bedroom. What style would you like there?"

"I'll do anything you say, but tell me what you want."

"You have very good taste. You understand the subject much better than I do. Tell me, what style did you use in your bedrooms before the revolution, if it isn't a secret?"

"It's not a secret at all. All our bedrooms were in a French style."

"Wonderful. You can use the French style here, too."

"But we had no pictures on the wall. The walls were covered with heavy silk fabric. Only the draperies and the furniture made the style."

"Oh, I understand. I can find that kind of silk for the wall. Somebody else can do that job. But you can help me choose the color."

"I can't know what color until I see the furniture."

"You could help me look for furniture in an antique store."

"Of course I can, but I thought you would move the furniture from your apartment."

"No, no, this apartment will be completely different. Tomorrow, at ten o'clock, I'll pick you up if you're free, and we can look for furniture and fabrics."

"All right, I'll be ready at ten. I don't think I'll need this paint anymore. I'm finished. Tell me, what kind of furniture do you want in the living room?"

"I didn't tell you? I ordered a full set from a Chinese dealer. I believe you'll like it when you see it."

"What will you do with the office and the children's room?"

"The wood paneling in the office needs to be refinished, and the children's room. ... I need to think about it. How would you decorate a room for your children, Wanda?"

"Don't ask me. Only a mother can choose for her children. Everyone has a different taste."

"I'd like to make it a surprise. Can you decorate the room as if it were for your children?"

"All right, if you wish. But I have to know how old your children are and what hobbies they have."

"As I told you before, try to imagine it's for your children. The daughter is older, the boy is young, close to your children's ages."

"Fine, I'll prepare sketches and show you. I didn't know your children were the same ages as mine."

Konstantin did not answer, as if he did not hear Wanda's last words. He walked to the window. It was midsummer.

"What do your children do during the day when they're not in school?" he asked.

"Oh, they stay with Esther. She walks with them in the park. Or they play with the neighbor children."

"What doctor is looking after her? She refused my help."

"She wanted no doctor, categorically. She didn't even want to talk about it."

"It's all right with me. She's an adult and knows how she feels. I just thought she had another doctor."

"No. It's her opinion that she doesn't need any medical help."

"Remember, Wanda," Konstantin said at last, "be ready at ten o'clock tomorrow."

"I'll be ready. See you then."

But nothing happened as they had planned. When Wanda returned home, she found Esther lying on the floor. The children were not at home; they had gone to the playground with the neighbor children.

Wanda picked up Esther's hand to check her pulse. There was none. She opened the door and called for help.

The ambulance came in about fifteen minutes. The doctor pronounced Esther dead. At the hospital, the autopsy showed that Esther had had a second, fatal stroke.

PART VII

The funeral was held a few days later. There were few people, some neighbors and acquaintances. Wanda wept; one more person very close to her, who was there when she needed her in a lonely life, was gone.

Konstantin met Wanda in front of her apartment building when she returned from the funeral.

"Please accept my sympathy," he said. "I'm so sorry. Esther refused medical help. We just talked about that a few days ago."

"Thank you for your concern," Wanda replied. "It is my misfortune. Everyone close to me dies when I most need them."

"Maybe I can help you somehow. You can rely on me. You know I'm your friend."

"No, thank you. I don't need anything now. I won't be able to work on your apartment for a few days. I need to be alone."

"I won't hurry you. You can call me when you're ready."

"Thank you very much. I'll always remember your kindness."

"As I told you, I'm your friend. Your sorrow is my sorrow."

He gave her an envelope and said, "You spent money for the funeral. Here is payment for the work you've already done. You'll receive the rest when the job is finished."

"I don't need this money now. I still have what you gave me before I started."

"If I give it to you, take it. I know what kind of job you're doing."

"Thank you, but now I must pick up the children from my neighbor's. Vera is out of town. I'll call you later. Good-bye now."

"Good-bye, and have a good rest. Pull yourself together. I'll wait for your call."

"Now, Wanda," Konstantin said, "you can pick out everything you want for the living room."

"What about the price? How much will this cost?"

"Don't worry about the cost. We'll reach an agreement."

"All right. If money's no object. Take down a list. I'll tell you what you need."

Wanda chose a sofa, two end tables with lamps, a coffee table, a painted screen, two leather floor cushions, and a small, but beautifully designed, Oriental rug. Choosing the fabrics for the bedroom walls and installing them took two more weeks. Finally, the apartment was ready: living room, bedroom, children's room, and office. Even the kitchen had been retouched. Wanda walked from room to room one more time. Everything looked elegant, rich, and in very good taste.

In thirty minutes, Konstantin would arrive, and she would give him the key. Her job there was finished. The money she received for the unusual project was enough for her and her family for some time. Later, she would decide what she needed to do.

Konstantin came.

"Hello, Wanda. You say everything is finished?"

"Hello, Konstantin. In my opinion, you can move in any time. Here's your key. Thank you for your support and the unusual work."

"Don't rush, my dear. Sit down. We have to talk."

They sat in the living room, and Konstantin gave her a folded paper.

"This is a legal document giving you the right to live here. Familiarize yourself with it."

Wanda opened the document and began to read. She read it over several times and looked at Konstantin questioningly. He smiled and took her hand.

"You've gone through so much grief, Wanda," he said. "Now you can enjoy life. This is yours. Don't look at me as if you're afraid. I'm not asking you for anything. I don't want to be paid. If sometimes I come for a cup of coffee, or I need someone to talk to, you won't throw me out."

"I don't understand this. Why have you done this for me? You have your family, and I feel very ashamed."

"I've taken nothing from my family. I've done this especially for you because you've been a large event in my life. You can't imagine what you mean to me. But as I promised, I won't talk about my feelings again. I'll be quiet now. Anytime you're ready to move, I'll find people to help you."

"Oh, God, what is this?" Tears streamed down Wanda's cheeks. She placed a handkerchief to her eyes. "Why did you do this without asking me? All I want is a job and a chance to make my own money to support myself and my children."

"Calm down. I can't stand to see your tears." Konstantin kissed her hand. "For God's sake, please quiet down. Believe me, this is the best thing that could happen to you. I'm leaving now, but remember, I'm your best friend. I'm the only friend you have. Good night, Wanda. Now you have a phone in your foyer. If you need anything, give me a call."

Konstantin walked out, closing the door behind him. Wanda was left sitting on the sofa with her handkerchief clutched in her hands.

She sat a while longer without crying. Then she stood and walked again from room to room. When she entered the bedroom, she stopped and looked at the bed.

"Most likely, I'll have to share this bed with him," she thought. "Of course, I'll have to pay for everything he's done for me."

Wanda had no way out. Again her life was in someone else's hands.

Soon, Wanda moved to the new apartment. A few days afterward, someone knocked on her door. When she opened it, she saw a simply dressed, but very clean, middle-aged woman.

"I have a recommendation from Doctor Vlasov," the woman said.
"Please come in," Wanda invited. "What can I do for you?"

"Doctor Vlasov told me you're looking for a housekeeper. I can come at eight o'clock in the morning and stay as long as you need me. The people I worked for before knew Doctor Vlasov very well."

"Why did the doctor tell you about me?"

"He said you're a widow with two children, and that you are an artist, and that you studied art with him in the same studio."

"Yes, that's true. How about payment?"

"The doctor gave me the money for three months that you had given him to find you help. Don't worry. I'm good with children. I can cook and clean and do laundry. I worked for my last employer since 1915. He was a professor. They moved to Moscow, and I didn't want to go.

I have an apartment. It's small, but it's mine. Nobody in my family is still alive."

"You can see the apartment now, and I'll introduce you to the children."

"Very well. I haven't worked for almost two months. I'm not used to being without work."

"What is your name?" Wanda asked.

"I'm sorry. I forgot to introduce myself. I'm Varvara Steponovna. You can call me Varia, if you wish."

"Children!" Wanda called. "Come here. I want to introduce you to your new babysitter. Her name is Varvara Steponovna."

Everything was going well for Wanda. She had no worries about food or money. The theatre studio called her and offered work for a few hours a day. She took the offer happily. She felt better because she was doing something on her own.

Two months passed before Konstantin called.

"Good evening, Wanda. How do you feel?"

"Good evening, Konstantin. Everything is wonderful. Thanks so much for everything. Did you know I've started working at the theatre?"

"You have to work. It's a new law. I'm very happy for you. Your voice sounds different. Now you sound alive. I have a question. When and where can we celebrate your happiness and good mood?"

"I don't know. I think it would be best if I prepare a dinner and invite you over."

"Fine. I accept. I'll bring a bottle of champagne. Tell me the day and time."

"I don't know. What day is most convenient for you?"

"How about Saturday at seven, three days from now? Is that all right?"

"Yes, fine, but maybe a work day is better for you."

"Saturday is best for me and for you. Good night, now, till Saturday."

"Good night."

Wanda put the phone down. She was apprehensive.

"I've waited for that call," she thought. "I knew sooner or later he would ask to come over. I know I must accept him as a good friend. I have to ask him about his wife, his children, his practice. I'll let him talk about everything but his feelings. Perhaps that will work."

Wanda paced the living room, thinking. The children slept. Varia had left at six o'clock.

She could think of nothing more. She picked up a book and started reading.

But her mind would not concentrate on the printed words.

Wanda fell asleep very late, still apprehensive. She liked Konstantin. He was a gentleman, and she appreciated everything he had done. Only one thing about him bothered her. He was married and had children. She had never faced that situation before.

On Friday, Wanda asked Varia to help her with dinner.

"I am having a special guest tomorrow," she said to Varia, "and I need your help."

"All right. I can go to the city market. Tell me what you would like to prepare."

"You can buy a fish and a young turkey or duck for the main course. We'll get something for an appetizer at the store."

The next morning, Varia helped Wanda in the kitchen. By four o'clock, almost everything was ready. The duck was in the oven, and Wanda told Varia to go home.

Exactly at seven, Konstantin knocked on the door. Wanda opened it. "Good evening, Wanda. I haven't seen you for a long time. You look charming."

"Thank you for the compliment. Come in. Sit down."

Konstantin sat on the sofa. "You have heaven on earth here," he said. "You're a part of everything around you. Where are your children?"

"They're playing in their room. They've had dinner, and I've told them not to disturb us."

"How have you raised the children by yourself and disciplined them?" Wanda sat in an armchair facing him.

"And your children behave differently?" she asked.

"Yes, indeed. Very differently. They're spoiled, whining children."

"How could that happen?"

"My wife and the nannies take care of them. I haven't had time to see them. When I go to work, they're asleep, and when I arrive home, they're asleep. Only sometimes on the weekend when I'm home do I see how wild they are. I've tried talking to my wife, but she won't listen. She says they'll change when they grow up."

"How old are your children."

"My daughter is fifteen, and my son is twelve."

"They're not little children. They should understand how to behave."

"You're right, but it's not like that."

"How long have you been married?"

"I see you'd like to know everything about me. I'd enjoy more talking about you."

"All right. Dinner is ready. Come and sit down at the table."

"Fine. I think the champagne is cool."

Konstantin had brought a bottle of champagne, and Wanda had put it on ice. They ate dinner, sitting opposite each other. Konstantin raised his glass. "I'd like to propose a toast. Hold your glass. To the happiest evening of my life. To the woman I worship, to her beauty, to her charm, to her happiness. To you, Wanda!"

They touched glasses. Wanda's face burned. She was smiling shyly. They drank the champagne.

"Now I'd like to propose a toast," Wanda said. "I'd like to drink this champagne to you, Konstantin, to your kindness, to your understanding, and to your humanity. To your happiness, Konstantin. You deserve it."

"I so appreciate toasts like that, and I drink with pleasure. I hope everything you wish for me comes true."

They ate an appetizer and Wanda brought the hot meal.

"You're an excellent cook," Konstantin said. "Everything tastes so good."

"Thank you, but Varvara Steponovna helped me."

"By the way, how is she? Do you like her?"

"Thank you very much. She's a kind, nice woman. I'm very happy with the way she cares for the children."

"Very good. I told you everything would be just fine."

They ate slowly, talking of many things. Finally, dinner was ended, and Wanda carried the dishes to the kitchen. Konstantin followed her.

"Let me do the dishes," he said. "You can go put the children to bed."

"No, I can do everything myself. I've already prepared the hot water. You can relax in the living room. I'll be in soon. You're my guest." Wanda smiled at him.

Fifteen minutes later, the kitchen was clean. Wanda put pastry and a tea service on the table.

"Now I'll put the children to bed. When I'm back, we'll have tea." Konstantin nodded. He leafed through some magazines. Wanda returned soon.

"The children are washed and in bed. Now we can have tea." They sat at the table, and Wanda poured the tea.

"Try my pastry," she said. "It's apple. I baked it this morning."

"I'm full, but because you baked it, I'll try it."

"How do you like it?"

"This is delicious. It's not sweet at all. I must have one more piece. To all your qualities I can add that you are a good cook."

"How about your wife? Does she like to cook?"

"I don't know. But I don't think so. We have a housekeeper to do the cooking. She cooks well."

Wanda smiled and said nothing. They finished their tea and sat together on the sofa. Wanda understood that the time had come when she would have to pay him back for his kindness. She saw how he looked at her.

"What are you thinking about now, Wanda? Can you tell me, or is it a secret?"

"I'm thinking about you, how noble you are."

"I'm not noble at all. Everything I've done for you I've done because I love you. Now you may ask me what I'm thinking about."

"All right. What are you thinking about, Kostya?"

"I want to kiss you, if you will let me. If you feel anything for me." Wanda looked down. Her hands lay in her lap. She smiled.

"Your silence is consent," Konstantin said. "Your natural shyness won't let you answer me."

He pulled her to him and kissed her on the lips. It was a long kiss. Wanda felt her head spin slightly. No man had touched her for a long time. This kiss was decisive. She put her arms around him, an Konstantin knew she now belonged to him. He picked her up, carried her to the bedroom, and placed her on the bed. Her heavy, braided hair spilled over her shoulders.

"How beautiful and charming she is," he thought.

He could not pull his eyes from her. He understood she wanted him no less than he wanted her.

"Oh, God, what time is it?" Wanda asked in a panicked voice.

"It's still very early," Konstantin answered. "Five o'clock. What are you frightened of?"

"The children could wake up. It's already late. When did you wake up?"

"About fifteen minutes ago. I just watched you sleep. You're so beautiful.

You're like a goddess. I love you madly. Tell me, do you love me?"

"Only last night you told me silence is consent."

"No, I want to hear it. It's important to me to hear it."

"Yes, I love you. You're my last love. This is not just love. I believe this is something more."

"That's all I want to know. I will love you with all my heart and soul. I will do anything for you. My heart belongs to you. You're my wellspring, my oasis."

"I don't understand what you're talking about. You have a family. How can you manage?"

"We can talk about that later. But now I want to make love to you again." Wanda did not think about his family anymore. She gave herself to him.

It was Sunday morning. The children woke up and were ready for breakfast. Konstantin had left before they awakened. Wanda had breakfast with them. She felt tired, but happy. She did not know what her future with Konstantin would be. She knew only that she was happy with him. She was thirty-nine years old, but she felt much younger. Masha was eleven and Gregory was seven. Life had smiled on her one more time, and she understood it was the best thing that could happen to her. In her memory, she saw her past. When Tadeush was gone, Vladimir came into her life. When Vladimir was gone, Grisha came into her life. Now, when Grisha and his mother died, Kostya came.

"I believe it is God's will," she thought, "that I not be alone. I have to accept life as it is."

Everything would be so wonderful if Kostya were free. But now, I don't know what will happen."

She sighed deeply because she knew she could decide nothing alone.

Konstantin began coming three or four times a week. Sometimes he stayed overnight or left very late. Wanda never asked any questions. The children called him Uncle Konstantin, and Wanda called him Kostya.

It was the end of December. It would soon be the new year of 1930. Konstantin brought food from the delicatessen.

"This is for us for New Years," he said. "I'll be celebrating with you." Wanda smiled and asked no questions.

"I love you much more than before," Konstantin said to her. "I feel no pressure from you at all. You're never hysterical. You never ask questions. You are very dear to me."

He held her close and placed her head on his chest.

"It's impossible not to love you," he continued. "I'm only afraid that someday you'll want a family, a husband, and you won't want me anymore. When I think about that my heart shrivels and my hands freeze. I'll never give you to anyone. Never. Do you hear me?"

"Why do you talk about this?" Wanda chided. "You know it will never happen. I like things as they are. I'll never make plans again. I've had plans before, but they've never come true. I've learned to take life as it is. I have everything I need, beautiful children, a fine apartment, and a man I love who loves me. What more can I ask?"

"Oh, Wanda, I hope it will always be this way."

"Something is bothering you. What happened?"

"It's nothing specific, but something worries me."

Before the new year, Konstantin's wife had gone to visit her sister in Moscow, and she had taken the children. Konstantin was happy. He felt free and came to see Wanda every night after work.

They celebrated the New Year by candlelight and soft music. They danced together. It was New Year's Eve, and everyone made his own wishes. Konstantin wished the evening would never end, but Wanda remembered the New Year's Eve with Tadeush. She felt she was dancing with him again. She lived in the past and did not think of the future.

Konstantin wanted to forget his past and to see Wanda in his future, as his wife. It was his greatest wish. He was very serious about his wish, but he told no one, not even Wanda. What did the year 1930 promise?

During dinner, Konstantin explained that his private practice would be closed soon. He had a large office—six rooms—an assistant, Ukimov, and a nurse, Nadezhda Ivanovna Kaiser. He had many patients because of his excellent reputation. He had graduated from the medical academy in Moscow in 1915. After the revolution and the war, his patients changed, but he still had many from middle and upper class society.

"What will you do if they close your practice?" Wanda asked.

"I'll work in a clinic. I still have many consultations over there. My patients will still be my patients. I've heard they are closing not only private practices but also all private businesses. Now they're talking a lot about collectivizing farmers' land. The entire harvest will go to the government. The farmers will keep just enough to survive. It's a new movement. Nobody knows yet when it happened or how. All I know is that the farmers who have lived on this land for generations, whose fathers and grandfathers have given their sweat to the land, have lost it."

"Yes, it's not simple," Wanda said. "What happens to the people who refuse to give up their land?"

"I don't believe anyone asks. They just take it."

Their talk was interrupted by the ringing in of the new year on the radio. They prepared to say good-bye to the old year with a toast and then to toast the New Year. It was five minutes before midnight. Kostya poured the champagne.

"You can wish for everything you want in the next five minutes," he said, "and all will come true. I, too, can wish."

Wanda closed her eyes and made her wish: "I wish everyone health and happiness," she thought. "Everything else is in God's hands."

"I wish to be with her and only with her," Konstantin thought. "I want her to be my wife."

The clock began to strike: one, two, three ... twelve.

"Happy New Year!"

"Happy New Year!"

They kissed each other, feeling happy and excited.

During 1930, Konstantin began working in the clinic. His private practice was closed. He made enough money to support two families. He stayed overnight many times at Wanda's apartment. Sometimes, he arrived at ten or eleven o'clock at night and left at six in the morning. Wanda was reluctant to ask him about what his wife thought about his almost never being at home. Wanda could not understand the relationship between Kostya and his wife. It was very strange to her. Sometimes Kostya looked very worried when he came. When Wanda asked what had happened, he said, "I'm just a little tired." But Wanda saw it differently. She saw it as the effects of his double life.

In reality, it was not as Wanda supposed.

Outside of his medical practice, Konstantin was very familiar with smuggled goods. For many years, he had known people in the business. Through their hands passed gold, diamonds, foreign currency, narcotics. In the port, these people knew what they had to do. Konstantin's wife knew everything about his activities. She had introduced many of the people to him. Konstantin remained on the sidelines, issuing orders concerning the movement of people and goods. A great deal of money passed through his hands. His family wanted for nothing. He made enough to support his own family and Wanda's family. Smugglers visited him as if they were patients, and he told them what to do. The black market was booming. Konstantin left home when he wanted and returned when he wanted. His wife knew he was a busy man.

Once, Konstantin tried to talk to his wife about a divorce.

"How can you think about that?" she exploded. "We have children."

"Can't you understand?" he answered. "It will be better for us. I could still be a father to them. We have nothing between us. Do you enjoy that kind of life?"

"Yes, I have my life; you have yours. But you're my husband by law, and you will be for as long as I wish."

"How can you dictate to me? You haven't worked a day in your life. I'll support the children, but not you. And I will not live here anymore."

"Fine, but think. If I go to the authorities and tell them about your business, they'll send you far away for a long time."

"You idiot. That would be worse for you. What would you have."

"Don't worry. I have enough."

He knew she was not kidding. He had to be careful with her. He also knew she had had a lover for some time. The man had been a friend of Konstantin's, Doctor Zakharov. Her situation was exactly what she wanted.

Konstantin dropped the subject then and for the near future.

"It's important that Wanda not press me to marry her," he thought. Konstantin called Wanda his angel on earth. She was so gentle, sweet, and tender. She was everything in his life. It did not matter what mood he was in, she always took his mind off his problems, and he forgot about everything.

A year and a half passed. In the fall of 1932, the police captured a group of smugglers. A major trial followed. Konstantin remained untouched because it was another smuggling ring. He decided it was the right time to talk again with his wife.

"Did you see what happened? The government confiscated everything. I was right. We must get a divorce because if something happens to me, they will take everything. I'm not worried about myself. They can execute me as they did the others. Decide for yourself. I'll not talk about it anymore."

Now Konstantin's wife understood that everything he said had a reason, and she agreed to give him a divorce.

When they divorced, she went to Moscow to stay with her sister. Konstantin understood it was the time to cut himself off from the black market. He sent a message to all of his contacts telling them to stop all activity. Shortly after he notified his organization, all black market activity came to a halt. After his wife left for Moscow, Konstantin visited Wanda. He was cheerful and smiling.

"You'll never guess the news I have," he said.

"They've let you have a private practice again?" Wanda answered.

"No, this has nothing to do with my work. I'll have to tell you because you'll never guess. I'm free. My wife—my former wife—left for Moscow after we officially divorced."

He hugged Wanda, pressing her to him.

"I didn't want to tell you before it was over. Now we can be together forever. Are you happy, my darling?"

"I don't know what to say. This is so unexpected. Of course I'm happy. Why has this happened? Why are you divorced after so many years together? We've been together a couple of years. Why a divorce now?"

"All these years I've dreamed about it. But there were reasons why I couldn't divorce before, and you never pressed me."

"What has changed now?"

"It's a long story, and you don't need to know about it. What's important is that it's in the past. You can become my wife by law, Wanda Vlasova."

"No. I can be your wife, but I'll always be Stanishevsky. I hope you won't be disappointed."

"No, it's your right. If you wish to keep your maiden name, I'm not disappointed."

Wanda had never told Konstantin the story of her life. He did not know her first husband was Tadeush Stanishevsky and her second, Vladimir Chernov.

A few weeks later, they married in a civil ceremony. Wanda was officially Dr. Vlasov's wife. Nothing changed between them, only the formality. Konstantin was at home more often. After working at the clinic, he came home for dinner every day. He had found peace. After dinner, he spent time with Wanda's children. On Sundays, he sometimes painted. Wanda, as before, was always soft and kind. They talked about everything, music, art, life. Life with Wanda seemed to Konstantin easy and simple. But something had changed. They could go to the theatre together, as they could not before. Konstantin introduced Wanda as his wife. Wanda, at forty-two, was still beautiful, elegant; her lovely hair brought looks from everyone. She always looked fresh and cheerful.

Once, they went to the opera and ballet theatre and met Zakharov, one of Konstantin's friends from the medical academy. He was alone. His wife had died ten years before, and they had no children. Zakharov had never remarried. For a long time, he had been having an affair with Konstantin's wife. He did not love her, but stayed with her because he had no one else. He was happy when she left for Moscow and could no longer bother him and expose him to possible scandal. He knew that she and Konstantin were divorced and that she was planning to marry him. But he wanted nothing to do with marriage because he could not tolerate her uncontrolled, spoiled children.

Konstantin and Wanda met Zakharov in the foyer of the theatre, face to face.

"I would like you to meet my wife, Wanda," Konstantin said. "Wanda, this is Victor."

"I'm glad to meet you. Kostya, you devil you. From where did you bring your charming wife?"

"I didn't bring her from anywhere. She lived here in Odessa."

"Why haven't I met her before? Perhaps we went to the theatre at different times."

"No, Victor. Wanda was a widow for many years. She raised her children by herself and didn't have time to go to the theatre."

"Oh, I see. I'm a widower, too. But my wife left me no children. Why did Kostya meet you, instead of me?"

"My old friend," said Konstantin, "you've never had any tact. The signal for the first act has already sounded. We must go to our seats. See you later." Zakharov had blonde hair, light blue eyes, and a very light complexion, completely the opposite of Konstantin. Konstantin had dark hair, brown eyes, and a dark complexion. Their personal characteristics were also different. Konstantin was a risk-taker, quick to make decisions. Zakharov was precise, cold, and methodical.

Wanda watched the stage, paying no attention to the way Zakharov watched her.

Now Zakharov understood why Konstantin had divorced Irena. He was not stupid. The two women could not be compared.

"It would be interesting," Zakharov thought, "to find out if Irena knew why Vlasov wanted a divorce."

Zakharov paid no attention to the activity on the stage.

Intermission came. Konstantin and Wanda walked to the foyer. Zakharov met them there.

"How do you like this troupe?" he asked.

"Just fine," Wanda answered. "They came from Europe where they played with great success."

"Have you ever heard Shalyapin?" Zakharov asked. "No, I've never had the chance to listen to him sing."

"I heard him in Moscow twice, once in the opera Boris Godunov, and the second time in the opera Rusalka. It's hard to explain how well he played the old millwright in Rusalka[5]."

"Yes, I've heard about Shalyapin many times."

"Do you know that all the papers and magazines are saying that Shalyapin has no money, sings for almost nothing, and has asked for permission to return to Russia?"

"I don't believe a word of it," Konstantin interrupted. "It's nonsense. How can you believe those trashy papers? Shalyapin is the best. No one sings as he does. He's the greatest artist and singer. If Europe can recognize this troupe here now, how can they not recognize Shalyapin?"

"Yes, you're right," Zakharov answered. "But the media are noisy about him."

"Sure, there's a lot of noise after a Russian immigrant killed the president of France. Now all immigrants have a hard life. Many of them can beg for permission to return, but not Shalyapin, because he has the whole world open to him, not just France."

They had to stop talking because the intermission had ended. When they sat down, Wanda asked, "When did a Russian immigrant kill the president of France?"

"Not long ago," Konstantin answered. "He was deranged. He had no motive to kill the president."

"Why haven't I heard about it?"

"You don't need to know. In this world, so many crimes occur every day, every hour, every minute. You can't know everything that happns."

"But this is not an ordinary crime, and I believe everyone knows about it except me. I don't read the papers because I stay away from all politics."

"Good for you. It's better that way. Politics is a man's business."

The second act began. After it was over, they remained in their seats.

Zakharov did not want to disturb them.

"You know, Wanda, how jealous Zakharov is?" Konstantin asked.

"Jealous of what?"

"Of everything. I remember when, in the academy, it didn't matter how close we were, he was jealous of my success. If I scored better on a test or met a pretty girl, he always acted like my friend. But I saw through him. He was never my friend. Tonight, I introduced you as my wife, but he looked at you as if you were unattached and he wouldn't mind courting you."

"That's nonsense. He makes a good impression. Please, don't talk like that. You are old friends."

"No, we've known each other many years. I've never counted him as a friend. He came to our home after his wife died, and Irena felt sorry for him. She invited him for dinner almost every night. I knew they were very close for a long time. I didn't pay attention because it left me free. I wish they were married, but he's not stupid enough to let her harness him."

"Oh, God, what's happened to you? I don't remember you acting this way before. Calm down. You're upset about nothing. Pay attention to the stage. The play has started again."

Yes, Konstantin was upset. He knew Zakharov would not hesitate to tell Irena about Wanda. He knew also what could happen when Irena knew.

After the play ended, they walked out to the street. Konstantin asked Wanda to wait for him. He met Zakharov.

"Where is your charming wife?" Zakharov asked.

"She's waiting for me while I talk to you."

"Do you have a secret from her? Are you ashamed about what you want to talk about?"

"Hold your tongue, Victor. Stop taunting me. I have a question: Are you going to marry my former wife? If so, you have my blessing."

Zakharov's face turned blotchy red. He had not expected the question, and he knew Konstantin was aware of his affair with his wife.

"No," he said. "I don't want to marry Irena. She's not my type. If you were to ask about Wanda, it would be different."

The statement was a direct challenge. Konstantin answered, "You're disgusting. You are scum. I didn't know how low you were. You're lucky this place is crowded, so I can't slap you as you deserve. But I owe you."

"We'll see," Zakharov said as he left.

Wanda looked at Konstantin and saw how his eyes glittered. She grasped his arm, and they walked home.

Konstantin could not calm down. Wanda said nothing.

"The scum," Konstantin said at last. "He's good for nothing. I'll never forgive him."

At home, Wanda kissed him and asked, "Are you still upset, or have you forgotten about him? Come to bed. I love you. We're happy together. That's all that counts."

"You are everything I have," Konstantin said. "With you, I'm rich. You're my happiness. You're my whole life."

He kissed her forehead, her eyes, and her lips.

"Every man is a little boy," Wanda thought. "All I want in my life is to be with him. I don't want to be a widow again."

Wanda prayed every night before going to bed. Konstantin never interrupted her. She did not teach the children to pray. In school, the religious influences from home were discouraged.

After Wanda and Konstantin married, life was routine and quiet. But deep down, Wanda feared the experiences of her past. Her past had left its trace. She was happy, one day at a time, not thinking about the future.

Every day, she put fresh flowers on the table. She created a beautiful and quiet atmosphere in her home. Konstantin loved to come home from work. In the clinic he worked certain hours with his patients. He had overnight duty in the hospital once a week. Under all circumstances, however, he liked to be home for dinner. He became the children's friend and advisor. He told them stories about his work.

Gregory was a very talented boy. At school, the teachers found he had a facility for mathematics. He played chess very well. Even when he was eight years old, he could beat Konstantin, and Konstantin had been a good player in the past.

Masha had a beautiful voice and sang in the school choir. Wanda had no chance to teach her music and could not afford a teacher before. But even without instruction, Masha played guitar and sang gypsy love songs and romantic ballads. When Wanda listened to her, she cried and remembered how her sister Sophie had played the piano and sung.

"Mashenka," Wanda said once, "I want you to learn music. You're fifteen years old. It's not too late yet. What do you think, Kostya?"

"Of course, but only if she wants to. We can find a very good teacher and buy a piano."

"Thank you," Masha said. "I've always wanted to learn how to read music, like Svetlana from my class."

"You play better," Konstantin said. "You have perfect pitch. Only do it if you want to."

A few days later, Masha and Wanda went to visit a music teacher. When he heard Masha sing, accompanying her, he grew excited.

"Absolutely magnificent," he said. "And you say she has had no lessons. Unbelievable. I can give her voice lessons. At the same time, she can learn the piano. I promise you, three years from now she'll be a student in the conservatory."

Masha started her lessons. They purchased a piano from one of Konstantin's patients. It was old but a very good instrument. Wanda's happiness was unending. No real father could take better care of her children. If only Sophie would write a letter saying everything was fine with her and her family. But Wanda's letters were returned unopened. As long as no letter came, she could hope that all was well.

Time passed, and the everyday routine kept her mind off her worries.

The year 1932 was almost over. Masha was very successful with her music and school. During the short six months she had been attending lessons, she had learned to read music. In two weeks a concert would be held at her school. She would sing and play Glenka and Tchaikovsky. She rehearsed at home while Wanda and Konstantin acted as an audience, and they were pleased with her abilities.

The whole family would attend the concert tonight. On the morning of December tenth, snow fell and wind blew it into drifts. Everyone sat down to breakfast. Wanda poured tea into cups for all. Then someone knocked heavily on the door.

"Who could this be so early?" Wanda asked as she walked to the door.

She opened the door and saw two men in uniforms of the NKVD, the secret police. They walked in without an invitation.

"Does Konstantin Vlasov live here?" asked one of the officers.

"Yes, that's my husband. He's in the dining room. We're having breakfast now. Come in."

221

The children did not understand that Esther had died. Wanda told them she had gone somewhere else. Masha was ten and her little brother was six. At that age, children did not feel grief if they were not reminded constantly of their loss.

It took Wanda a week to find someone to watch the children when she was not home. When she found a woman, she called Konstantin. He agreed to pick her up the next day.

She replaced the receiver on its hook, returned to her apartment, and remembered the envelope Konstantin had given her. It was unopened, put away in the dresser. She opened the dresser, removed the envelope, opened it, and counted. One thousand rubles.

"Oh, God. Why so much money?" she thought. "He's mistaken. Perhaps it belongs to someone else. Tomorrow, I'll have to return the envelope to him." When she worked in the theatre studio, she was paid three hundred rubles a month. It was considered a lot of money. But now, a thousand rubles for a few days' work? It had to be a mistake.

Konstantin arrived on time. Wanda climbed into the passenger's seat, and Konstantin closed her door and got in behind the wheel. As soon as he sat down, she said, "This is your envelope. You gave me a thousand rubles by mistake."

"It's not a mistake. That's what your work is worth."

"Oh, no. You know exactly how much I made at the studio."

"Of course I know. But they paid you very little for your talent and your work. Calm down. You deserve this money. The work you're doing is art, not a craft. Very few people understand the difference, but I do, and I don't want to talk about it anymore. Take this money and spend it as you wish. Now we're going to an antique store. I called the owner in advance. He's waiting for us."

They drove to a large store packed with all kinds of furniture. A tiny old man walked around a glass partition.

"Hello, Doctor Vlasov," the old man said. "I'm glad to see you. Follow me to the other room. I'll show you all the Oriental furniture I have."

The other room was different, uncluttered. It was much easier to distinguish different sets of furniture.

They strode to the dining room, and Konstantin met them.

"Give us your passport, Citizen Vlasov."

Konstantin opened the desk drawer and gave them his passport.

"Has something happened to one of my patients?" he asked.

The officers looked at his passport, and one said, "We have been ordered to search your home."

He handed Konstantin a sheet of paper.

"What are you looking for?" Konstantin asked. "I'm a doctor. I don't even keep medication at home."

"We know what we're looking for. Everyone stay where you are. The children may leave."

Wanda told the children to go outside and gave them their coats.

"What's this all about?" Wanda whispered to Konstantin.

"It's a misunderstanding, my dear. I believe this is a mistake. It'll be cleared up soon."

"I don't like it. Why you? I know you're not interested in politics." Konstantin was silent. He knew this was not politics; it was something else.

He thought they might have captured one of his former associates and his name had been mentioned.

"But who could it be?" he thought. He did not consider that it might be his ex-wife's work.

The truth was that when Irena returned from Moscow, Zakharov met with her the same evening.

"Tell me, my dear," Zakharov had asked, "are you happy with your freedom? Now Kostya has left you behind, and he isn't worried about you or his children."

"What do you mean by that?" Irena asked. "We're divorced and we both agreed to the terms. There was no feeling between us. Sometimes we couldn't stand each other. But the children are grown. What's important, my dear, is what is between you and me now. Tell me, have you missed me?"

Irena smiled, walked to Zakharov, and tried to embrace him. He took her hands from his shoulders and motioned her to sit next to him on the sofa.

"Did you know," he asked, "that Kostya is married, and that's the only reason he wanted the divorce?"

Irena recoiled.

"That isn't true," she cried. "He couldn't marry anyone. I know the reason. Who told you that nonsense?"

"I saw them at the theatre. He introduced me to his new wife. Don't be upset. She's beautiful."

"No, no. You're confusing something. He introduced you to a woman, but not a wife. I'm sure of it."

"You're trying to change the facts. This is strange. I remember exactly how he introduced her. 'Please meet my wife, Wanda.' I also found out she's a widow and has two children. She's a rarity, an extremely beautiful woman."

"If everything you say is true, this poor widow will be a widow again. I still don't believe he could have done it."

"Why are you so upset? It was an agreement between you."

"Oh, no, you don't know the real reason," Irena said, smoking as she paced. "And you don't need to know."

"Now I understand. You still care for him. I've tried to understand what happened between you, but you haven't explained it clearly."

"No, there's no feeling between us. I don't care for him at all. But our divorce was supposed to be an honest arrangement. He lied to me, and now he has to pay for it."

"Come now, if you don't care for him, let him be happy. Let another woman love him. And remember how many times you lied to him—we both lied."

Zakharov spoke with a purpose. He knew Irena very well. He understood that her ego was talking and that she was capable of anything to destroy Konstantin's happiness. He had no idea what the actual reason was and how serious the situation was.

After that evening, events unfolded rapidly. Irena thought about nothing else when she discovered that what Zakharov told her was true. She went to the NKVD and explained the kind of business her husband had outside of his medical practice. She even mentioned the names of a few of his associates whom she remembered.

The search of Konstantin's home was almost completed. The NKVD found nothing. It was about two o'clock in the afternoon. The contents of the apartment were scattered and thoroughly disheveled. Only the foyer remained to be searched. Konstantin's briefcase lay next to a table. The officers placed the briefcase on the table, opened it, and removed a stethoscope, some papers, some patient histories, and opened a zipper on the side. From the pouch they removed money, a lot of money. They counted it —fifty thousand rubles.

Konstantin turned as pale as death.

"There were papers in the case. Only papers." he said.

"What is that?" Wanda asked, frightened. "What is the money from?"

"I don't know. It's not my money," Konstantin said, attempting to regain his breath.

"Citizen Vlasov," said one of the NKVD officers, "you are under arrest."

"Where are you taking him?" Wanda cried. "This is a misunderstanding.

How could a doctor have all this money? Please don't take him."

"It's our job. We have an order to search and arrest. The magistrate will let you know about the trial later."

They took Konstantin, who left without speaking. They told Wanda, officially, not to leave the apartment. She might be needed for questioning later.

Wanda collapsed on the sofa and wept despairingly. Later, when she had calmed, she washed her face and tried to pull herself together.

"This is a mistake," she thought. "Someone in his office put the money in his briefcase by mistake. Everything will be cleared up."

She paced the room and tried to understand. She thought about the money Kostya made and about the money he spent. She wondered how he had been able to decorate the apartment to make of her a kind of Cinderella princess. And then she thought about his wife. Why had she not thought about it before? It was true that he told her he made more money in private practice. She had never asked how much money he made.

Wanda was confused and frightened. She did not know whom to go to for help. Everyone had his own life and problems. And the NKVD told her to stay home. She could go nowhere. She lay down on the sofa and began crying again.

Konstantin's ex-wife, Irena, had gone not only to the NKVD but also to his office. She found time to put money in his briefcase. Konstantin's nurse saw her, but she knew Irena was Konstantin's ex-wife. Konstantin was in a consultation. Irena had brought the money in a prepared package. She had thought of putting it in his desk, but had seen the briefcase and slipped the money in the side pocket.

It was the end of the day, and Irena said to the nurse, "I'll come back later. Don't tell him I came; I'll give him a call later."

The nurse nodded.

And so the money came to be in Kostya's briefcase. At the NKVD offices, Irena explained that people came to Konstantin's office and left money, and someone else picked it up. The money was payment for smuggled goods.

When Konstantin left Irena, he took nothing except his clothes. All the money, jewelry, furniture and antiques he left for her and the children.

What a woman's ego can do! But Irena was not just a woman; she was an angry woman. She never considered that Konstantin might be executed, and that her children would have to live with the taint of a father who was killed for his crimes. She thought only of revenge.

Irena prepared to leave for Moscow and sent a letter to her sister.

"Kostya has been arrested," she wrote, "but he's already married. I don't know why he was arrested, and I don't know what will happen to him. But I know he wasn't arrested for nothing."

As she was gathering money for a train ticket, a messenger brought her a note: "Come to the magistrate for questioning."

At the magistrate's office, Irena asked, "What is this? Why are you talking to me? He has a wife. You can ask her the questions. I'll not answer any of your questions."

"Sit down," the magistrate said, "and remember, you have to answer. How many years were you married to Konstantin Vlasov?"

"Nineteen years. But we have an official divorce."

"I'll ask you about that later. Now, just answer what I ask. How long was your husband involved with smuggling?"

"He didn't tell me about it."

"But when you came here voluntarily and gave us information, you said he had the business for many years. Try to remember how many years. It's important to us."

Irena was nervous. "Damn," she thought. "Why is he asking all these questions? I'm not ready for them. But I have to answer."

"Maybe ten years," she said aloud, "he was associated with those people."

"That means you knew about it for all those years. Why didn't you tell us before?"

"Because he was my husband. Now we're divorced."

"That's what I thought. That means you were an accomplice for ten years. Only now you're turning him in."

Irena had not considered that the situation might be reversed.

"No," she said. "I'm not his accomplice. I helped the government arrest him. Why are you questioning me?"

"In this office, I ask the questions. You answer."

"I have to go to Moscow as soon as possible. I don't want to hear or see this anymore." Irena began to cry.

"You are either very naive or very clever. Really, you don't understand. You can't leave Odessa until the trial is over."

Irena sobbed loudly. Only then did she realize what an irrevocable mistake she had made by turning Konstantin in to the NKVD. It was clear that she could no longer be a bystander.

"Sign this paper, please," the magistrate said, handing Irena two sheets. "What is this? Why must I sign it?"

"First, this says you agree not to leave Odessa. Second, this is your statement."

"What happens if I don't sign? Why are you holding me here?"

"It is your right not to sign, but I must ask the prosecutor to arrest you for not submitting to the proper authorities."

Irena said nothing more, signed the papers, and swallowed her tears. She went home, shaking and walking drunkenly.

"How stupid of me," she thought. "How could I have done that? What will happen to me now?"

She had been completely blind to the consequences of her actions.

The same day, an inventory was taken of all Irena's property.

Wanda was interrogated the same day in the afternoon. Everything she said, the magistrate believed. She had been Konstantin's wife for only four months. Everything in their home belonged to him. She was a widow with two children and had no money. She knew Konstantin was a doctor. He liked art. She was grateful to him for all his help. She could say nothing bad about him.

Wanda did not cry. She was calm and asked no questions. An inventory was taken of her apartment. When she left the magistrate's office after signing the papers, the official said to his assistant, "Did you see the difference between the two women? This woman spoke the truth, and I pity her because they've taken everything in her apartment and the apartment, as well. But the other woman—I could swear she's hidden money, jewelry, and many other valuables. After they've taken everything she has, she'll still have enough to survive."

"You're right," said the assistant. "I think this woman has dignity. I believe Vlasov. He stopped the smuggling when he started a new life with a new wife. But he has to pay for his past."

"Yes, indeed, because his associates confessed. Millions of rubles have passed through their hands. It will not be a simple trial."

"What do you think? Will they be executed?"

"The court will decide. What we have to do is prepare the facts in this case."

The trial lasted more than two months. It began at the end of February, 1933.

Wanda tried to control herself, so that the children would not know how serious the situation was. She explained that it was a misunderstanding and that in a little while everything would be all right. She went to Masha's school for the recital. Her face betrayed none of her worry. Only her pillow knew how many nights she spent without sleep and how much she cried.

The trial began. The court was closed to the public.

Wanda did not understand why the court was in closed session. It was at the trial that she first met Irena. She looked at her briefly and turned away. She had too much to worry about already. Irena, however, watched Wanda very closely.

"Oh, now I see who he exchanged me for," Irena thought, "She is beautiful, and she has a beautiful figure. But now her beauty will fade without a protector like Kostya."

Paltry ambition had choked Irena. She was very slender, like a pole. She slouched and had a long nose and pointed chin. She had lost even more weight since she had turned Konstantin in, and her cheeks were sunken. Her black, short-cut, dyed black hair encircled her face. She looked like a witch.

"All rise. Court is in session."

The bailiff read the names of the accused and introduced the judge and the two jurors. He explained the nature of the trial.

Everyone sat down. The defendant, Vlasov, and his accomplices heard the charges against them read. Each of the defendants stood and gave his full name and date of birth.

Wanda looked at Kostya and her heart froze. He was pale, too thin, and she thought he would collapse. His voice, however, was strong.

"You, Citizen Vlasov, do you admit to the charges against you?"

"No, I do not."

"Do you plead guilty?"

"No, I do not. I do not plead guilty."

Konstantin's accomplices pleaded guilty. All witnesses were asked to leave the room and wait in the foyer. In the foyer, against the wall, stood long benches. Wanda watched the witnesses as they sat down. There was Konstantin's nurse, who had worked with him for many years, a few of his current patients and some from his private practice, the wife of the defendant Sukhov. The other defendant, Mogilenko, was a widower. Wanda counted ten witnesses in all.

All three defendants were accused of buying, holding, and selling smuggled goods. Witnesses were called. Wanda's turn came at two o'clock in the afternoon.

She was dressed in a brown coat and a small brown hat. On her feet were ankle-high boots. She walked straight, with dignity.

"Citizen Stanishevsky," the prosecutor began, "how long have you known defendant Vlasov?"

"He was my mother-in-law's doctor before she died. I saw him for two years but didn't know him. I knew him more closely for two months before we married, but by that time, he was divorced."

"He never told you why he divorced his wife?"

"No, I never asked, but he said they had had no feeling for each other for a long time."

"Did you know he was hiding a lot of money?"

"He never had more money than he made."

"How can you explain the fact that we found fifty thousand rubles in his briefcase?"

"I believe someone slipped the money into his briefcase. Only the night before, he opened that pocket and took a patient's history out. A piece fell on the floor. I picked it up and put it back. There was no money. The briefcase always stays in the foyer. If Konstantin were hiding a lot of money, he wouldn't leave it in the foyer. That's why I'm sure someone planted it for a reason."

"That's strange. Who would put this much money in your husband's briefcase? Do you know if he has any enemies?"

"I don't know, but I believe he did. What kind of friend would do this?"

"Do you think some of his old connections brought the money to pay for some goods."

"I couldn't tell you, but I know for sure that if he had that kind of money in his briefcase, he would not have left it in the foyer. He never went anywhere without me, ever since we were married. That's why I'm sure he had no smuggling connections."

Wanda was asked many questions, but her answers did not help the case against Kostya. It was true that she knew nothing about it. The two other defendants corroborated what Wanda had said. They had not seen him for some time. They knew him only from before as someone who bought some goods.

If not for the money found in his briefcase, the officials would have merely frightened him. If not for Irena's testimony, which she repeated to the court, he would have gone free.

The prosecutor read the charges and asked for the supreme penalty—death by shooting. The defense for each of the three accused tried very hard to argue for their innocence. Konstantin received life in prison and confiscation of all property. Sukhov and Mogilenko were sentenced to death by shooting.

Wanda heard the verdict and tears flowed down her cheeks.

"Oh, God," she thought. "Thank you for sparing him. He'll be back. Anything could happen." Her heart beat rapidly. She felt hope.

It was not easy to imagine how Kostya held himself together. When they asked him for his final statement, he said, "I ask the judge and jury not to take the property and apartment from my wife, Wanda Stanishevsky. This is not her fault at all. She has suffered enough in her life, and I did not mean for the things I have done to cause her pain. Please, help her and the children." His last words were spoken through his tears.

Wanda walked out of the courtroom. She saw the guard take Kostya away.

Wanda saw Kostya for five minutes in the jail.

"What have I done?" he asked, her. "How could I do this without thinking and incur all this for you?"

"What are you talking about? Things can change. What is important is that you are alive."

"Who needs this kind of life? In this case, nothing can change. It was a mistake to marry you, to make it legal. We should have waited, but now it is too late. . . What am I talking about? Where will you live? How will you find job?"

"Don't worry. I'll find something. No one will kick me out on the street."

"I love you. I don't know how I can live without you."

"Don't talk about it. It's important that you take care of yourself. I'll try to get permission to see you in prison. We have to have hope. Believe me, something will change."

PART VIII

"Listen, Wanda, try to find one of my patients. He can help you. I remember he's the manager of a meat processing plant. Maybe he can find you some kind of job. Now is a very difficult time."

Wanda did not answer. The guard said their time was up. She had to go.

"What is his name?" Wanda asked, as Kostya was led away.

He called to her. "Morozov. Nazar." It was all he could say. The guard took him from the room.

When Wanda reached the street, she wrote the name down.

After two weeks, Wanda received an order to move out of the apartment to a one-room basement apartment on Myasoyedevsky Street. It was hard to watch the children, crying, load their belongings into a one-horse wagon.

The driver helped Wanda move her few things into the new place. The two windows in the room were high up on the wall at ground level. The apartment was damp; mold covered the walls, and it smelled musty.

"This is temporary, until I find a job," Wanda told the children.

Through the Address Bureau, Wanda found Nazar Morozov. The next day, she knocked on his apartment door. It was opened by his maid.

"What is it?" the maid asked. "Does Nazar Morozov live here?"

"Yes, but he's not home. He's working."

"Where does he work? I need to talk to him."

"Who are you?" Morozov's wife interrupted from behind the maid. "What do you want?"

"My husband, Doctor Vlasov, gave me his name and asked me to find him."

"Come in," Morozov's wife said. "Sit down. What happened to your husband? He was a good doctor. My husband was very satisfied with him."

"An unfortunate misunderstanding. Someone reported him to the authorities and put money in his briefcase. The times are difficult. The court did not need much time to put the case together."

"What will happen to him?"

"The trial is over. The sentence was life in prison," Wanda said, and tears fell from her eyes.

"What a pity. How many children do you have?"

"I have two children. They took my apartment and all my property. They gave us a basement room."

Morozov's wife did not know that Wanda was Konstantin's second wife and that the children were not his. Wanda did not explain.

"You poor woman. My husband will help you. I'll send a message to him and give you the address where he works. Who could believe this could happen? He is a nice man and a very good doctor."

Morozov's wife shook her head. Her hair was full of curlers. She was heavy-bodied with a round face. She looked like an old-fashioned matron. Her long, silk gown with billowing sleeves made her seem even larger. But she had a kind heart and felt sorry for Wanda.

"Here is a message for my husband," she said. "I'll put the address on the other side. If you go now, you can find him in his office. Please tell his secretary I sent you. Good luck to you. I wish you well from the bottom of my heart."

"Thank you very much," Wanda said. "It's very kind of you. Good-bye." Wanda walked with the note in her hand and tears choking her.

"Again, I have to fight for my life and survive," she thought, "because people are starving and dying. Many do not have even a piece of bread."

A few days before, Wanda had received a message from the authorities to go to the government offices for food coupons for the children. Wanda herself was ineligible. She had to look for work, and each factory provided coupons to adult workers. There were coupons for bread, grain, and oil. There was a limit of one-half pound of bread for each child and a pound for adults. Wanda was reminded of 1921, when people died in the streets.

Why had it happened again? After NEP had blossomed and peaked, it collapsed, bringing hunger back to the nation. But it happened because the government took over all shops, stores, bakeries, everything privately owned. From the farmers, who had lived on the land from generation to generation, the government took the land that had been fed with the farmers' sweat—not from rich farmers, because all the rich farmers were executed during the revolution—but the middle class, who worked hardest on the land. First, the government sent out notices telling the farmers to give up their property. Whoever did not submit was called a "kulak," a tight-fisted person, unwilling to share his wealth. They took everything, anyway, and sent the kulak to Siberia. If they found hidden grain, the kulak was executed. The times were extremely difficult. The farmers fought and could not plant. There was no harvest. The year 1933 is mentioned in Russian history as a "no-harvest year."

Wanda walked, holding the message to the manager of the meat processing plant. She had eaten a piece of bread and drunk a cup of tea without sugar. She felt hungry and weak. When she approached the plant, she smelled the cooking meat. Her head began to spin. She walked into the office, her mouth watering.

"I have a message for Comrade Morozov from his wife," Wanda said to the secretary.

"All right, I'll let him know."

When the secretary returned, she opened the door for Wanda and ushered her in.

Wanda saw, behind the desk, a very slender, middle-aged man. She had thought he would be heavy and ruddy-cheeked. He was completely the opposite of his wife.

"Please, sit down," Morozov said, pointing to the chair in front of his desk.

Wanda handed him the message.

"Oh, you're Doctor Vlasov's wife? What can happen to people! What kind of work can you do?" Morozov walked around the desk to Wanda's chair.

"Any kind of work I have to, to feed two children."

"I can give you a job in the shop. The work is not very heavy, and you'll never be hungry. You can eat here but never take anything with you. The salary is very low because of the nature of the work. That's all I can do for you."

"Thank you very much. When can I start?"

"You have to go to the personnel department and fill out an application. Then you'll go for a medical examination. They'll let you know when you can start."

"Thank you again for your kindness."

"I'm sorry I can't do more for you. Good-bye."

After a few days, Wanda, wearing a white uniform, entered the sausage processing area. She had eaten nothing that morning, and when she smelled the sausage, she felt lightheaded and faint. She almost collapsed, but a woman walked up to her and caught her before she could fall.

"What's wrong with you?" the woman asked. "Are you feeling ill?"

"No, I'm fine. I didn't have breakfast, and I was a little dizzy."

"Nobody around here eats breakfast at home. We eat it here. Maybe you didn't have dinner last night?"

"You're right. I didn't. But I feel better."

"Follow me. I'm your supervisor. I had a call from the office to tell me I had someone new. What's your name?"

"Wanda."

"Are you Polish?"

"Yes, I was born in Poland, but I came to Odessa as a young girl."

"Sit down and eat. You have sausage and ham. Eat as much as you want. We need a healthy, strong worker. If you're hungry, what kind of job can you do? When you finish, come see me. I'll show you what to do."

"Thank you, but you've given me a lot. I can't eat all this."

"Fine. You can eat as much as you want."

Wanda took a bite of sausage. It was fresh and tasty. She felt as though she had never eaten anything so good before. Tears came to her eyes again.

"I won't be hungry," she thought. "I see that. But what about my children? I don't know that I'll make enough money to feed them."

She took a bite of ham. It was juicy and delicious. When she finished eating, she found the supervisor.

"My name is Luba," the supervisor said. "All the people here help each other. Everybody's friendly. We have a good working atmosphere here. You put the sausage in boxes, weigh them on the scale, prepare the invoices, and put the invoices in the boxes. I saw on your application that you know grammar. We have many workers here who can't read or write."

Wanda looked at Luba and smiled. Luba returned the smile. She had straight, light brown hair wrapped in a red kerchief, like a working woman on a government poster. But her dimples showed when she smiled, unlike the woman on the poster.

Morozov was right. The job was not difficult. The boxes moved on a conveyor to the scale. Wanda wrote down the weight of each box, and the box passed on through a partition to the shipping department. She was not used to being on her feet all day long. It was hard for her. But after a few weeks, she grew accustomed to it. She saw how her fellow workers put pieces of sausage in their pockets to take home. She did the same a few times. Then Masha and Gregory had meat with their bread.

Almost every day, the managers of the plant repeated the prohibition concerning removing meat from the premises. Everything belonged to the government. If anyone took even a small piece, he was picking the government's pocket. If all the pieces were put together, the pilfering was not a small problem.

Wanda asked one of her fellow workers, "Tell me, what would happen if the guard found a piece of sausage?"

"It depends on how much is taken. If it's a small piece, they will tell you not to do it again. If you take a pound, you can be fired and a note put in your file. It's important who the guard is, because different kinds of people do the job."

"Oh, God. Then it's much better not to take anything."

"Try, if you have hungry mouths at home. I don't remember hunger like this in my life. Food coupons given to me to cover two months lasted two weeks. And I have an old mother and two children on my hands. Try not to take from here."

The same day, Wanda decided not to take any more.

Every day, at the checkpoint, the guards frisked the workers. If they found a small piece of sausage, most of them paid no attention. But Wanda did not want to take a chance.

Once, she saw a guard find something on a woman. She put her in a room. The next day, Wanda found out the woman had been fired. She had taken a pound of sausage. When she heard about it, Wanda trembled.

When Wanda returned home, she explained to the children that she could bring no more sausage home. Her heart ached because she could eat but could not feed the children.

During the next few weeks, Wanda watched all the girls around her put pieces of sausage into their pockets, and she put a few pieces into her own pockets without thinking about it. When she was checked, the guards paid no attention and let her go. She breathed again. The children would have supper.

What hunger can do to people! They turn to all types of crime. Sometimes they are capable of things they would not consider in normal life. History shows how people tortured by starvation, kept from food for a week, and then shown a tray of food, with its delicious odors, and told it will be theirs if only they will sign something, even their own death sentence, will do it. People who have been hungry understand the temptation of food shown to the starving. This was the same. If someone was hungry at home, people would do anything to get food for them.

Wanda thought less and less about caution and sometimes took as much as a quarter pound. Once, when she was checked, the guard found the sausage in her pocket.

"What is this?" the guard asked. "You don't know the rules?" She put Wanda in a room.

"I took only these two little pieces," Wanda pleaded. "I swear I'll not take any more. I have two children at home. They're hungry. Please let me go."

"Sit here. I'll be right back. I have to check the others." Wanda was left alone. She trembled.

"What have I done?" she thought. "Now I could lose this job. I must beg this guard for forgiveness. But she doesn't look friendly at all."

The guard had tiny, deeply set eyes and a sharp nose. She looked at Wanda as if Wanda were her prey.

Fifteen minutes later, the guard returned. She was short of stature and had very short, almost white hair. Her cheeks were gaunt.

"You say you have two children at home?" she asked. "Where is your old man?"

"I'm a widow. I'm raising my children by myself. Please let me go. I swear I'll never take anything again. I must have this job."

The guard stared at her.

"You are beautiful. I've never seen beauty like yours in my life. But this is a depression. During a depression, everyone is the same. Beautiful or not, they're still hungry. I have three children, and I've raised them without a husband.

"Did your husband die?"

"Yes. He was a drunk. He drank like a dirty pig. I tell you the truth. I waited for him to die. He took everything we had and drank. He worked very hard, but everything he made he spent on vodka. Once—it happened two years ago —he didn't have money to buy vodka or wine. He found some lighter fluid and died on the street like a dog. My children and I started to breathe easier. I have three boys. I have to feed them and buy clothes. It's not easy. My older boy is twelve, and I have twins who are ten."

Wanda listened to her and thought, "Why is she telling me all this? I must be safe now. She has a heart. I thought I couldn't survive 1921, but I did. And now it's 1933, and again I stand at the edge of a precipice. But I feel I don't have the courage I had before. The only reason I have to survive is the children."

"I believe I can count on you," the guard whispered. "My name is Tanya, and I live on Kuznyechnoy Street. I'll give you my address. The building where I live is easy to find. You have to survive and save your children. So do I. We have to reach an agreement. I'm at this checkpoint three times a week, from eight in the morning until eight in the evening, Monday, Wednesday, and Friday. You can take two rings of sausage. One you take to my apartment; the other is for you. But you have to stay fifteen or twenty minutes after everybody's gone from your department because you don't have a second shift. Prepare your invoices; say you have to finish your job. Put the sausages around your waist. Put on your belt and then your sweater. Nobody can see what you're taking. Do you understand my plan?"

"I'm frightened. What will happen if someone sees me?"

"When I'm at the checkpoint, you don't have to worry about anything. If you see me in the morning, you can go ahead. If, for some reason, I'm not there, don't take anything. If somebody stays late and can watch you, don't take anything. When you walk through, just shake your head. And remember, we're doing it for our children. When better times come, we won't need their sausages. Do you agree?"

"I have to think about it. It's a big risk."

"Listen, my dear, you don't have the time or the chance to think. I told you my secret, what I haven't told anybody. I opened my plan to you. Now you could go and tell everything to the manager. I can turn you in for a few pieces of sausage."

Wanda looked at Tanya and saw a cruel light in her eyes. Wanda's skin crawled, and she said in a frightened voice, "What are you talking about? It never crossed my mind."

"People are different. I don't know you. I can't trust you completely. And you know how the times are. In times of starvation, people act strangely. But if something happens, we're both responsible. If I lose my job, you lose yours."

Wanda understood she had no escape. She felt trapped. She had to submit. "All right, I'll try. When do I start?"

"This is my address. I'll tell the children to be ready. They're smart. You can start the day after tomorrow. Now take these pieces home."

Tanya opened the door for Wanda and let her go. Wanda walked to the trolley stop. Her legs felt unsteady.

Someone touched her elbow. She turned around and saw a woman who worked with her. The woman had seen Tanya take Wanda to the room and had waited for her.

"What did that lowlife tell you?" the woman asked.

"Who are you talking about? I don't understand."

"Tanya—the guard. She's taken pieces of sausage from people before. Two women were fired, with her help. Now she's found sausage in your pockets. What did she say?"

"She said not to take anymore and let me go."

"That's hard to believe. It doesn't sound like her. I don't trust her or people like her. We all know nobody takes anything when she's on duty. You need to remember—don't take anything on Monday, Wednesday, or Friday. We call her 'skinflint.' I hate to see her ugly mug. She scared you to death. I can see you shaking."

Wanda's co-worker was named Nadya. She was about thirty with a nice smile, a round face, a double chin, full lips, and a figure like a matron's. However, she had no children. Her husband worked in a factory. She helped Wanda to learn her job when Wanda was new. They used the same trolley.

They had little time to talk at work but did when they waited for the trolley.

Nadya had waited for over forty minutes because she had seen Tanya take Wanda to the room.

"No, Nadya," Wanda said. "She didn't frighten me. I frightened myself.

She just explained that no one can take anything from the plant. She let me go because I told her I have children."

"I'm still surprised. It's not like her."

"But it's strange that no one told me before not to take anything when she's on duty."

The trolley arrived, and they changed the subject to a discussion about how hard it was to use food coupons. After work, nothing was left in the stores.

When Wanda arrived at home, she felt powerless and empty. She prepared a meal for the children and lay down on the sofa. She did not sleep. She thought about what had happened and what she should do. After a while, she realized that there was nothing Tanya could do to her.

Wanda felt better. She put Gregory to bed and began to read a book. Before she went to bed, she prayed to the Virgin Mary. She cried and asked the Mother of God to protect her and have mercy on her.

Despite what she had gone through in her forty-three years, Wanda continued to believe in God and to pray. Her Catholic beliefs, which she had held since childhood, were the most important things in her life. She could not renounce God.

Wednesday arrived. Wanda, shaking inside, went to work. She saw Tanya, shook her head, and walked through the checkpoint. Wanda worked, trying not to think about Tanya and her plans. She thought that her shake of the head would solve the problem.

When she left her department and saw Tanya again, she sensed that the guard was waiting for her.

"Come in here," Tanya ordered.

"Why do I have to go in there? You can check me here. I have nothing to hide."

Wanda was trembling. Nadya, walking next to Wanda, tried to protect her. "What do you want from her? She's right. You can check her here. If you find something, take her inside."

"Nobody asked you," Tanya said. "Go on. I have a report, and I have to check her. Or do you want me to take off her clothes in front of everybody?"

Surprised, Nadya looked at Wanda.

"You can take off my clothes in that room. You won't find anything. This is all nonsense."

Tanya opened the door, pushed Wanda inside, and said, "Wait for me." Tanya returned when everyone was gone. Wanda stood against the wall and looked at her.

"What, Wanda?" Tanya demanded. "You've decided to play cat and mouse with me? Remember, you're the mouse; I'm the cat. We had an agreement. Why have you changed your mind?"

"I had no agreement, and I don't want this. I won't take anything. Leave me alone."

"Oh, no. You don't know me well. I saved you from being fired. And now you try to do this to me? If you think you can walk away from this, you're mistaken. You're in my hands. I can bring sausage from the shop, stop you, bring you to this room, and report I found it on you. What can you say now?" There's nothing I can say. I'm frightened. I've gone through a lot in my life.

Please, let me go. I swear I'll say nothing."

"No, I never back away from a decision. Try to understand. You don't have choice."

Wanda was silent for a few moments.

"All right," she said. "I'll try. Let me go now."

"You can go. But don't change your mind again. I promise you, you'll be fired."

Wanda left the room, saying nothing.

If Wanda had had a strong personality, she would have gone to the manager to explain what kind of intrigue the guard had involved her in. She had always been timid, however. Her future was almost always in someone else's hands. She was a victim of her own beauty and her timidity.

She walked to the trolley as if she were a condemned woman. She did not see any way out of her situation. She walked, looking at her feet, and her tears fell to the ground. She could not see for her tears. She stopped, and then she heard Nadya's voice.

"Why are you crying? What does Tanya want from you?"

Wanda looked at Nadya. Only then did she realize she was crying. "It's nothing. Pay no attention. She didn't want anything."

"You don't want to tell me the truth. She never takes anyone without a reason. Something's wrong."

Wanda could not tell the truth. She had to lie.

"She knew my husband. She told me something about him."

"You're a widow. What can she tell you about your dead husband?"

"No, Nadya, my husband is in prison. The father of my children died years ago. I was married for four months before my husband was arrested and given life in prison."

"Oh, Jesus Christ, you poor woman. What you must be going through. What does Tanya know about him? How could she know?"

"Someone told her he's been sent to the Ural," Wanda lied, knowing well that Kostya had been sent to the Ural to prison.

"And I thought she couldn't talk like a normal person."

"Please don't ask anything more. I'm so tired. You see, the trolley's here." Two days later, at the end of the shift, Wanda left her apron on as the other women took theirs off.

"Finish up," Nadya said. "It's time to wash."

"I have to prepare invoices," Wanda answered. "You can go on without me. I have to go to the store and buy something with these coupons. They've almost expired. Masha is busy, and I have to go."

242

"All right, I'll see you tomorrow," Nadya said.

Fifteen minutes later, everyone was gone. The first time is hardest. Wanda took the sausages in trembling hands, seeing nothing in front of her. She put two rings around her waist and covered them with her heavy sweater. She walked from her department on shaking legs, almost falling several times. Then she saw Tanya. They looked at each other, and Wanda nodded her head. Tanya frisked her and said nothing. She could feel the sausages.

"That's better," Tanya whispered. Then she said aloud, "Go ahead." Wanda passed through the checkpoint. She did not remember experiencing such hammering in her temples. Now she understood very well that she had stolen. But she was like a mechanical toy. Someone turned the key and pointed her in a certain direction. She walked on for four blocks and found Tanya's building. She climbed to the second floor, found Tanya's apartment, and knocked on the door. Tanya's oldest son opened it.

"Follow me to the kitchen," he said.

Wanda walked to a very small, crowded kitchen.

"Are you home alone?" she asked. "Or are your brothers here, too?"

"No, they're playing outside."

"Can you leave me alone for a few minutes?"

He left and closed the door behind him. Wanda lifted her sweater and took both rings from around her waist, leaving them on the table. She felt lighter, more in her mind than in her body. As she left the kitchen, she asked the boy to show her the way out.

Fresh air hit her face when she reached the street. She wanted to run away from everything, but she knew she could not run. The children were waiting. She had coupons in her purse and had to get to the store before it closed.

In the store, she bought millet for hot cereal, oil, and soap. When she reached home, she saw Masha in the kitchen. She had prepared potatoes and was waiting for her mother to bring the sausage.

"No, my dear," Wanda said. "There is no sausage. There will be no more. I'll fry onions in the oil and put them on top of the potatoes. It will be delicious. Give thanks for the things we've got. People are starving. Thank God for saving us."

Wanda lay awake for a long time. When she did sleep, she had nightmares. She saw someone chasing her. She tried to run away, but someone stopped her. When she looked around, she saw Tanya holding her. The sausage around her waist fell to the ground. She saw people around her, all of them screaming and reaching toward her. She awoke many times, but when she fell asleep, the nightmare continued.

She awoke completely at four in the morning.

"What can I do?" she thought. Who can I talk to? I have no one to tell about what has happened to me. Why am I always alone in my sorrow? I can't tell anyone what is in my heart. I'm frightened. This is intolerable."

Wanda saw no escape from her situation.

The day for taking sausages came again. She left all the sausages on Tanya's kitchen table and went home.

At ten o'clock that evening, someone knocked on Wanda's door.

Who could that be, so late?" Wanda thought, as she moved to open the door. The children were asleep, and the room was quiet.

"Who's there?" she asked.

"It's Tanya. Open up."

Wanda opened the door and let Tanya enter. "Are you alone?" Tanya asked. "May I talk?"

"Yes, the children are asleep. We can go to the kitchen. What do you want at this hour?"

"I see you're playing the game not as I planned it."

Tanya took sausages from her coat and put a ring on the table.

"Why did you leave all the sausages in my apartment?" she asked. "Try to understand. You survive in these times. Listen, and listen good. You do that one more time and the game is over. If you see me in the morning, you take the sausage. But even if it's my day, and I'm not there, take nothing. Do you see how simple this is? Your children won't be hungry, and they'll have good food. If you have extra sausages, you can bribe somebody and find a better apartment. I have more experience with this kind of life. Your apartment smells damp."

"Yes, because it's in the basement."

"All right, I have to go. I believe you know better now. Remember, Wanda, if you don't fight for life, life will crush you."

Wanda closed the door behind Tanya.

"Tomorrow's Sunday," she thought. "I can breathe a little."

She felt better. She understood how desperate her situation was. She was alone again. She walked back into the room. The children were asleep, and she adjusted Gregory's blanket.

"They sleep in peace," she thought. "They don't know what their mother has done. Everything I do is for them only."

She sat on the sofa and covered her face with her hands. "Oh, my dear Sophie, how are you? I hope you're still alive. How is your family? I hope someday I'll receive some word from you. How is Kostya in prison? I hope he'll be a doctor in the prison hospital. Maybe he won't have to work like a slave. My happiness was so close, but it flew away forever."

Wanda did not sleep for a long time after she went to bed. She prayed, whispering.

When the new week began, after work Wanda took half the sausages to Tanya and kept half herself. Even though she saw Tanya at the checkpoint, she was still very nervous. Only when she had walked a few blocks from the plant did she calm down.

A month passed. It was autumn. The leaves had changed, yellow and crimson. The leaves fell and rustled underfoot.

The next time Wanda carried sausages from her department and approached the checkpoint, the wind blew into her face, and she squinted. Just before she reached the gate she stopped dead. She tried to catch sight of Tanya but did not see her.

"Is it possible I'm confused?" she thought. "I clearly remember seeing her this morning. I said 'good morning,' and she answered me."

Wanda had no time to consider further. She saw two men in NKVD uniform checking the people in front of her. Instantly, she knew what would happen next, something terrible, irreparable. She turned back sharply. She walked perhaps five yards before she heard someone call, "You! Woman! Come back here!"

"I left something in my department," Wanda said, starting to walk very fast. "I'll be right back."

A moment later, she heard footsteps following her, and a hand grabbed her shoulder. She jumped at the touch, frightened. When she turned, she saw a middle-aged man in an NKVD uniform.

"Do you have a hearing problem, citizen?" he asked. "Come with me to the checkpoint."

Wanda had nothing to say. Her legs were trembling, and she almost fell.

The NKVD officer held her arm tightly.

"This is the end," Wanda thought. "It's all over for me."

The search showed that Citizen Stanishevsky had stolen three pounds of sausage, which she had placed around her waist, under her sweater. The officer drew up a statement, put Wanda in a "blackbird," a van used only for prisoners, and took her to the NKVD station.

Her apartment was searched. One pound of sausage was found.

Wanda was kept in solitary confinement before her interrogation. She could think of nothing except what would happen to the children. They had no one else. They were alone in a dangerous world.

The NKVD held her through the night and took her to interrogation the next morning.

In a room with subdued light, the interrogator sat behind a table. He was young, about thirty, with straight, blonde hair, slicked back on his head. He showed Wanda the chair in front of the table.

"I am Investigator Nesterov, and I have a few questions for you. Are you in a condition to answer?"

He looked at Wanda, who was difficult to recognize after only one night.

Her face was pale, her eyes swollen from crying, her lips quivering.

"Yes, I can," she said.

"Tell me, with whom were you dividing the sausage that you took?" Wanda closed her eyes and thought about what she should say. The interrogator repeated his question, believing she had not heard him.

"With no one," she said. "I decided to take it because I have two children. I'm a widow."

"If you really did it alone, why were you not afraid to go through the checkpoint? This is not a little piece. This is two pounds."

"I took the risk. They don't check us all the time."

"How many times have you stolen, and how much?"

"Twice. Once, perhaps one ring, the second time, two rings. They caught me."

She spoke, knowing that her story could not be checked.

"Did you know what could happen to you for stealing from the state?" Wanda was silent, looking at the floor. After a few moments, she looked into the interrogator's eyes and asked him, quietly, "Tell me, what will happen to my children? I know I have to go to jail."

"The government will take care of them. You're not the first or the last to leave children alone after committing a crime. Now we have the Soviet authorities. We will take very good care of the new generation."

"What do you mean? What kind of care?"

"Your children will be sent to an orphanage. They'll go to school and live a normal life."

Wanda began sobbing loudly. Her handkerchief was wet, but she continued to dab at her eyes.

"Why are you crying? Your children won't be homeless. You should be grateful to the Soviet authorities."

"My children will live in an orphanage? This is what I've done to them?" Wanda sobbed uncontrollably.

"Listen, Citizen Stanishevsky, you can reduce the charges against you. All you have to do is tell me who your accomplice is. This won't be just your fault any longer. Your punishment will be mitigated."

Wanda answered immediately, pulling the handkerchief from her eyes.

"I did this alone. I can answer for anything I've done by myself. You may ask anyone I work with. I was in collusion with no one."

She answered the same as before because Kostya's trial was very fresh in her memory. Groups of criminals were punished more severely than those who acted alone.

"Well," the interrogator said, "if you insist. It's your choice. Sign this record of evidence."

He gave Wanda a sheet of paper covered with handwritten notes. "I can't see. Your handwriting is so small, I can't understand it."

"I'll read it to you."

He read everything he had written. Wanda signed, and he called in another officer to take her away.

"Where are you taking me?"

"To jail. Where else? You'll remain in your cell pending trial, and during the trial. Later, after you've received your sentence, they'll send you somewhere you've never heard of."

Wanda did not answer. "He can joke about it," she thought. "What kind of people are they?"

Wanda was placed in the "blackbird." Two men were inside, along with an NKVD officer. The men had been told not to talk to each other.

Twenty minutes later, the van stopped, and Wanda was allowed to go first. At the jail building, she passed through a gate. She followed the prison matron.

"Take this mattress and follow me," the matron ordered. "We'll go to the cell where you're staying."

The mattress was rolled. When Wanda tried to pick it up, she found it so heavy that she had difficulty keeping up with the matron.

"Oh," the matron said, stopping. "Wait. Damn. You haven't taken a shower yet. Go back. Why haven't they taken care of that yet."

Wanda almost fell. A few steps further, the mattress unrolled. She tried to hold it together. As she bent it, she heard the matron say, "What do you think, that you're here alone? No one will do your work for you, you weakling. Faster. Now I see you're a blue-blood."

Wanda pulled the mattress together. She had no strength, but the strength of anger at the matron's abuse. She placed the mattress on the floor in front of the shower room, removed her clothes, and stepped into the shower. Five minutes later, she was called to put her clothes on and go to her cell.

Cell number twenty-seven. Inside were two bunk beds. Women sat on each of the four mattresses. Another mattress lay between the beds on the floor. Another woman sat on it.

"Whre is my place?" Wanda asked.

"Your place is where you find it," the matron said, and she slammed the door.

Wanda looked around. The matron was right. She unrolled her mattress against the wall, sat on it, covered her face, and started crying. Her wet, braided hair, and her sorrowful appearance, in a different situation, would have inspired pity. But not in that situation. Not there.

These were women from a different world. They had no pity. Perhaps there it was right not to pity.

"Stop your howling," said a woman on one of the top mattresses. "Your tears won't help you here."

Another woman added, "And don't block the path to the slop bucket." Wanda opened her eyes. The woman whose mattress was also on the floor helped her arrange her mattress. Inside the rolled mattress was a cotton pillow, a sheet, and one blanket. Wanda lay with her head against the wall and her feet against the slop bucket. She understood what the slop bucket was then.

Next to the bucket was a cold-water sink. There was no partition to provide privacy.

Wanda covered her head with the blanket and tried to forget where she was and what had happened.

"Listen, newcomer, what's your name?" a woman asked. "What are you here for? You'll feel better if you talk."

Wanda remained silent, not moving at all.

"We're not the right company for you? Why do you turn your face away?"

"Leave her alone," said a woman with a low voice whose bed was one of the lower bunks. "Have you forgotten what you went through before you got here?"

Everyone was quiet. It appeared Wanda would be left alone.

A few minutes later, she heard someone whisper, "Maybe she's a decoy. Look girls, she's different, not one of us."

"You're stupid. If she's a decoy, she'd be talking too much, asking a lot of questions. Don't you have a brain?"

Wanda heard nothing more. After two days without sleep, she was exhausted and fell asleep.

An hour later, she heard someone call, "Wake up. Time to eat."

"I don't want it," Wanda said sleepily. "Leave me alone."

"It's a rule here," the low-voiced woman said. "You have to go by the rules. Roll your mattress back so we can get to the door."

Wanda could do nothing but obey. The meal was millet cereal. It was handed through a window in the door on metal plates. Each woman received two ladles full.

"You, with the braided hair," the guard said to Wanda, "give me your plate."

"Thank you, I don't want it."

The woman with the low voice took the plate from Wanda and passed it through the door. Then she said to Wanda, "Hunger makes everybody equal. You'll be eating just like everybody else."

Wanda took her plate and put it in her lap. She could not force herself to eat. She leaned against the wall and closed her eyes.

"Oh, God," she thought, "why am I punished like this? Have mercy on me. I know I'm guilty. I agreed to steal. But please, don't let me be punished like this. I swear, I'll never do anything like that again in my life."

She prayed silently and tears fell from her eyes. She left the cereal untouched on her lap.

"How long can you sit like a dummy?" asked the low-voiced woman. Wanda opened her eyes and saw the woman sitting next to her on the mattress. Wanda looked at her face. She was in her mid-fifties, with very short, gray hair. Her face was swollen, and she had bags under her eyes. Something in the woman's face frightened Wanda.

"Take the spoon," the woman said, "and start eating. You'll die like a dog before your trial ends. If you don't want to talk, that's your choice. But you have to eat to survive."

She handed Wanda the spoon, and Wanda forced herself to eat.

"That's better. Pretty soon we'll go to the courtyard for a stroll, if it isn't raining."

The woman whose turn it was did the dishes. The other women began to ask questions again, but Wanda did not answer. She believed what had happened to her was no one's business. She had not asked any questions of them.

"Yes," the low-voiced woman said, "stop chattering like magpies. What do you want? To find out everything in one day. Let her pull herself together."

"You have beautiful hair," she said to Wanda. "I've never seen such beautiful hair before in my life. But you'll have to say good-bye to your hair when you hear the verdict."

"What are you talking about?" Wanda demanded indignantly. "This is my hair. No one can touch my hair."

"Oh, no. Here, nothing belongs to you. Not yourself. Not your hair."

"I don't believe it. I don't believe this is happening."

"You'll see. This argument is pointless. The longer you stay here, the more you'll understand. People have lice and typhus. In jail, people are like cattle in pens. Who can save your hair? Now do you understand? I've been here before. That's how I know."

Wanda looked at the woman with wide eyes. She almost asked what the woman was there for, but she remembered not to ask any questions because she did not want to answer any herself.

"All right," the woman continued, "you can tell us your name, at least."

"My name is Wanda," she answered, and she looked into the woman's eyes.

Again, she saw something strange in her face. She saw the woman bite her bottom lip and nod her head slightly.

"What is your name?" Wanda asked.

"My name's Varvara," the woman answered. "We have one Nina here with dark hair and one Nina with red hair. And Marisa, on the floor between the beds, speaks with a Ukrainian accent, and we laugh. Are you a Pollock? Or is it just your name?"

"What's the difference? As you said, everyone's the same here."

"Oh, now I see you can talk, and I know you'll survive."

Varvara spoke and then returned to her bed. She lay down and said, "I want a cigarette bad. When are we going for a walk?"

Wanda sat against the wall as before. She did not cry anymore. She was terrified and felt cold all over. She asked herself no more questions about why she had done the thing she had done or what would happen next. She could not think about anything. She felt tense, and her body twitched.

A guard knocked on the door.

"Cell twenty-seven, time for your walk."

The door opened. Before Wanda could react, all five of the other women were at the opening.

"Stand up, beauty," Varvara said. "You can go breathe some fresh air now." She touched Wanda's shoulder.

The corridor was narrow. One guard walked in front, one behind. They walked out into a fenced courtyard. The courtyard was like a cage with a barbed wire ceiling. The guards left the women alone, and the six of them paced the cage like animals, from wall to wall, back and forth. Varvara walked next to Wanda.

"Tell me, what are you here for?" she asked. "Maybe I can help you untangle the mess."

"I don't need to be untangled. I don't need your help. My case is clear."

"It just seems that way. Are you in this alone?"

"Yes, I am."

"You see? You took the blame yourself. Somebody walked free and spit on you and your children."

"How do you know I have children?" Wanda asked, looking straight at Varvara's face.

Varvara's eyes shifted.

"I don't know for sure. But I think you do because of your crying. How many children do you have?"

"Two. A daughter and a son. Don't ask so many questions. My head is splitting. Please."

"Fine. But I'm trying to help you. I'm trying to be your friend. You can trust me."

"You don't know me. Why are you trying to help me? Tell me the truth. What do you want from me?"

"Now you're talking. Sure, I need something from you. If you're free, you can go find some people who could help me. You see? You can help me, too."

"I don't want to make any deals with anyone. One deal was enough for me.

If I have the luck to be free again, I'll make no more deals."

Varvara was silent. Wanda looked at her and saw her fingers tremble as she held her cigarette. Wanda also noticed how the other women, who had been walking, stopped to listen to the conversation. Nina, the red-haired one, shook her head, telling Wanda silently, "No." Wanda stepped away and began walking. The door to the courtyard opened, and the guard spoke.

"Cell twenty-seven, time to go back. That's enough for today."

"Why so soon, you son-of-a-_____," Varvara yelled.

"When you go to the prison camp, you can walk longer," the guard said, "but here we have a different system."

Again, they walked along the corridor, escorted by the guards. They came to their cell and went through the door one by one. Someone placed a piece of paper in Wanda's hand. She grasped it and hid it in her fist. Later, she put the paper under her pillow. She lay down, turned toward the door, and covered her head with the blanket. She took the piece of paper from under the pillow and read it.

"Varvara is an informer, a decoy. Beware."

Wanda began to understand. She turned over onto her back, uncovered her face, and watched the women. From her position, she could see all of them. She tried to discover who had given her the note. When she looked at Nina, she knew the red-haired woman had given her the message. Nina nodded.

Wanda sat down against the wall.

"Who knows what a decoy is?" she asked, looking for a reaction.

"If you stay here long enough," Varvara said in her low voice, "You'll find out."

"Why does she have to wait?" Nina asked. "She can find out now and try to be more careful."

To Wanda, Nina said, "A decoy is someone sent to a cell. The decoy asks a lot of questions, trying to get information to give the investigator."

"Why do they do that?" Wanda asked.

"You're so naive," said the dark-haired Nina. "For information, they cut time in prison. If somebody's in for five years, she gets three instead."

"You know too much," Varvara said. I see you've taken a lot of information to the investigator and tried to cut your time."

"Shut up, you. This is only my second time here, but you don't have enough fingers to count how many times you've been here."

"Will you be quiet, girls," said Marisa in her Ukrainian accent. "Maybe it would be better to sing a song together about home and freedom." Wanda looked at Marisa and felt pity for her.

"Why is she here?" Wanda thought. "She has such blue eyes, dark hair, and pale skin. She's not thirty yet."

Wanda kept silent because she was afraid to ask any questions. She knew very well that Varvara was the informer. An investigator had put her in the cell. That was all right. Wanda would give her all the information she would need, gladly.

During the next visit to the courtyard, Varvara gave Wanda a cigarette.

"I don't smoke, thank you," Wanda said.

"Try. You'll feel better."

"I won't feel better. It doesn't matter what I try now."

"You want to keep everything inside. That's why you're so hard on yourself. I'll tell you my story. In this world, if you don't steal, you don't survive. I stole a few items from a store. They caught me. I took the blame myself, and the scum who worked with me are walking free. People say you're only stealing if you're caught. And now I'm caught, and I have to pay for it. You see, I've told you my story. Why are you so afraid?"

"I'm not," Wanda answered. "Why should I be afraid? I just don't want to talk about it. But if you must know, I'll tell you. I'm here because I stole also, but I stole sausage from a factory. They caught me at the checkpoint."

"Oh, you stole from the government. Your case is not simple. Who were you working with? You didn't tell the investigator either?"

"No one was with me. I prepared invoices alone. I waited until everyone was gone, put the sausage around my waist, and covered it with a sweater."

"And you weren't afraid somebody would check and find it?"

"They checked me every day for a few months. They found nothing and stopped checking. The first time, I took one pound. Nobody checked. The next time, the NKVD was there. They checked everyone, and they caught me. Everyone was starving. I have two children at home. So I tried it."

Wanda told Varvara exactly what she had told the investigator. She paid no attention to the anxiety and signals of the women around her.

"Yes," Varvara said, "your case is not the easiest. The law's very tough about stealing from the government. Where is your husband?"

"He died. I'm a widow. If he were still alive, I would never do what I did." Varvara tried to find out if Wanda was trying to hide something, but Wanda gave her the same answer over and over. Wanda almost began to believe her own story.

A few days later, Varvara disappeared from the cell. She was taken at night; no one knew where. Perhaps she was placed in another cell as a decoy.

Wanda's investigation was brief, and her court date was set.

The month was October. The leaves were yellow and russett. Some, still green, lay on the ground. Wanda was placed in a closed van. Close to the door, on a bench, sat one guard, in NKVD uniform, watching her.

Wanda's was the only case to be tried that day. The guard looked at her and watched how she strained to see outside.

"How long have you been here?" he asked.

Wanda turned to him. "Three weeks. For me, that's a long time."

"Are you by yourself in this trial?"

"Yes. Why?"

"It's nothing. I just know this trial will be short. If it's a group of people, it takes months."

"What do you mean by short?"

"They might finish in one day."

"That would be better. I don't have enough strength."

The guard did not answer, only looked at her. Wanda had lost much weight.

She looked younger than she was, but tired.

When the van stopped, the guard opened the door, stepped out first, and helped Wanda down.

"All rise. Court is in session."

Wanda stood and looked around. There were a few people in the room behind her. She had never seen them before.

"This is best," she thought. "I'm glad they didn't bring my children here." The formalities began. Questions, similar to those asked during Kostya's trial, were asked and answered. Wanda answered as she had the investigator's questions.

"Call the witness Tatyana Struchkova," the judge said to the bailiff. Wanda's heart stopped.

"This is the end, she thought. "If she gives different testimony than mine, then I have to answer stealing and lying."

"Citizen Struchkova," the judge said, "raise your right hand and repeat, 'I will tell the truth and nothing but the truth.'"

Tanya repeated the words.

"How long have you known defendant Stanishevsky?" asked the prosecutor.

'I've seen her as I have a lot of other workers, but I didn't know her." Wanda began to breathe again. "Now I see that she didn't say anything," she thought. "Thank God for that."

"Did you check all the workers regularly?"

"I already said during the investigation that I check almost all the time. But sometimes, so many people go through at the same time, I can only watch and stop them if I see something suspicious. I hold people who take even little pieces of sausage. Three people were fired because of my reports. I remember checking this citizen, but I never found anything."

"How can you explain that she decided to take three pounds during your shift? Why would she take the risk?"

"You're right. She took a risk because the NKVD guards caught her. If they hadn't, I would have. I've got nothing to add. I can only repeat that I don't know her personally."

"She hasn't saved me," Wanda thought, "but she hasn't made things worse."

The prosecutor asked questions of two more of Wanda's fellow workers.

They had nothing to add.

At three o'clock, they announced a recess until the next morning. Wanda was returned to jail in the same van with the same guard. She sat with her eyes closed. She had only one thing on her mind. How were Masha and Gregory? They were big children now. In two years, Masha would graduate from high school. But what now?

Wanda did not cry. She felt only a dull pain in her heart. Her thoughts were confused. She saw, in front of her, Vladimir. He smiled and spoke to her. Next, she saw Grisha. She talked to him, but she did not hear her own voice. Then, she heard, very clearly, music, the same beautiful waltz that had been played at her wedding to Tadeush. Surely, this was Tadeush. He was waiting for her downstairs. She walked down the stairs in her wedding dress, her sister beside her. How happy she was! She felt weightless.

Suddenly, it was all gone. There was no music. She heard a shot, then a second, and Vladimir fell down on the floor. She saw blood puddled around him.

Everything was spinning, and then—blackness.

"Wake up, please. Are you all right?" Wanda heard the words as she regained consciousness.

Someone was slapping her lightly. She opened her eyes and saw the same young guard in the NKVD uniform. He looked at her with concern. Then he helped her get up from the floor.

"What happened to you?" the guard asked. "You fell down, and I thought you were dead. I slapped you, and then you came around. You're so young to die. How old are you?"

Wanda sat on the van bench and began to feel better.

"What happened to me?" she thought. "I thought I was asleep and dreaming. Why did I fall and feel nothing. Maybe I fainted."

The guard repeated his question.

Wanda raised her eyes and looked at him.

"Why do you need my age? It doesn't matter anymore."

"Don't talk like that. Everything will be all right. I can see you aren't a criminal. And I believe the judge can see it, too. They won't give you a long sentence. A woman made a mistake. She took some sausage during a time of starvation."

"You think they won't give me many years? How do you know?"

"I've seen so many cases in my three years in the service. I've seen so many criminals. You're just a harmless creature. The judge will give you a year, just in case."

"Oh, if your words could make it to God's ear. I fear they will give me more. A woman in my cell told me I would get no less than five years because I took from the government."

"She doesn't know anything, this woman. She tried to frighten you."

"Thank you very much. I'll try to believe it can happen as you say."

"Yes, I can see. You're thirty-five, no more. I'm right?"

"Almost."

The conversation ended as the van passed through the jail gates.

In her cell, Wanda ate her entire supper. She felt better. For the first time, she had a kind of hope. In her mind, she returned to her conversation with the guard. The more she thought about it, the more she wanted to believe it.

"He's right," she thought. "I'm not a criminal or a murderer."

That night was the first that Wanda slept quietly. In the morning, she ate her millet cereal and returned to court.

Today, a new guard accompanied her. He too was young but looked gloomy and sullen. Wanda tried to talk to him, but he answered, "Talking to the defendant is strictly forbidden."

Wanda sat down in the dock, alone.

"All rise. Court is in session."

The judge, a man in his mid-forties with a high forehead and wide shoulders, looked more like a wrestler than a judge.

The two jury members sat, one on each side of the judge, a man and a woman, young. The prosecutor was a young man also, in his thirties, with an open face. His appearance was attractive. His eyes looked kind. But it was only appearance.

Wanda observed everyone carefully. Her future was in the hands of these people.

The trial began again. The charges against Wanda were repeated, and the judge asked the bailiff, "Call the witness Maria Vinar."

Wanda's breath caught in her throat, and her heart beat wildly.

"How can she do this?" Wanda thought. "She's only sixteen, a child." Wanda felt pressure at her temples, and she gripped the arms of the bench tightly. "What now?" she thought.

Masha walked in. She was so tiny, pale, with a beret in her hair and her coat buttoned tightly. She looked around, and her eyes stopped on her mother. She looked for a long time at Wanda, and the tears standing in her eyes fell down her cheeks. She brushed them away and sat where she was told to sit.

"Do you remember how many times your mother brought sausages home?" the prosecutor asked.

"I remember we were starving. We couldn't buy anything with the coupons. I ate sausage one time, one little piece."

"Oh, God," Wanda thought. "She's clever, but I think she's had Tanya's help."

"Did you know your mother stole the sausage from the plant where she worked?"

"No, my mother never took anything that didn't belong to her. She always taught us never to do that. This is a mistake. My mother is an honest woman."

"You may step down. You're free to go."

Masha walked to the door, looking always at Wanda. Wanda lowered her head. She could not see her child with tears in her eyes.

"Call the witness Nadejda Smirnova."

Nadya came forward and Wanda, looking at her, did not understand why she had been called.

"Citizen Smirnova," the prosecutor began, "did you work with the defendant, Wanda Stanishevsky?"

"Yes, we worked together."

"Tell us, did you see how she hid the sausages?"

"God be with you. When I first heard that they caught Wanda with sausages, I didn't believe my ears. There's something wrong here. I know she's an honest person. She would never have taken sausages. Somebody forced her to do it. You have to find out, your honor, who forced her."

"Defendant Stanishevsky," the prosecutor said, turning to Wanda, "do you agree with what the witness, Smirnova said?"

Wanda stood and the room spun before her eyes. She stood straight and said, "No. No one forced me. I did it by myself."

"Why are you doing this?" Nadya cried. "Why are you taking the blame? I know this is wrong."

Wanda kept silent.

"You cannot speak to the defendant," the judge said. "You may step down. You are free to go."

Wanda was asked again if she had worked with someone else, but she gave the same answer, "I did it all by myself."

The judge, the prosecutor, and the jury left to confer. Thirty minutes later, everyone returned and took his place. Kostya's trial was still very fresh in Wanda's memory. Sometimes she thought her own trial was only a continuation of what had gone before.

The prosecutor began to read the final charges against Wanda. He enumerated them and repeated what had been said in court. He was sure Wanda had taken the sausages every day and had caused harm to the government during these very difficult times. In these hard times, the defendant, as if she had put her hands in the pockets of the hungry, and for her own profit.

Wanda saw his face as if through a fog. She did not understand exactly what he was talking about.

The judge asked Wanda, "Are you guilty or innocent?"

Wanda did not hear him, and he repeated the question. She lifted her eyes and stood.

"yes, I'm guilty," she said, and she again lowered her eyes.

It was absurd! Later, much later, she would find out what happened. She had no defense. She had no one to take her side or explain to her that she could not plead guilty to all the charges the prosecutor read. She thought that by saying she was guilty, she would receive a light sentence.

After Wanda answered, the prosecutor finished his speech.

"I ask the defendant, Stanishevsky, be given ten years in prison camp, ordinary regime."

She was dreaming. It was a nightmare. She felt frozen with fear. The court adjourned for deliberations. Wanda sat stiffly on the bench.

"I don't believe this is happening," she thought. "Why did the prosecutor ask for ten years? I don't believe the judge will agree. I thought I'd get one year, no more. I remember Kostya's trial. The prosecutor asked for the death penalty, and the judge changed it to life in prison. Oh God, I hope the judge will change this for me. He knows I have children."

The deliberations were brief.

"All rise. Court is now in session."

Wanda looked into the judge's face and then at the jury. Their faces were impenetrable. Wanda was trembling violently.

The judge spoke.

"In the name of the Ukrainian Federal Socialist Republic, for plundering what belongs to the government, over a long period of time, in the name of this Soviet court, in article of law number _____, I sentence the defendant, Stanishevsky, to ten years in prison, ordinary regime. The verdict is final, without right of appeal."

"It's not possible!" Wanda screamed, jumping to her feet. Her knees collapsed, and she fell, unconscious.

PART IX

Wanda regained consciousness lying on a stretcher in the van. She did not know immediately where she was, but she remembered what had happened when she saw the guard's face. She closed her eyes again.

"Why am I still alive?" she asked herself. "Why do I have to go through this?"

Wanda was sent to a different cell. It was in a different section of the jail where prisoners waited to be transported to prison camps. She was told she could not correspond with prisoners in any other jail or prison camp. That meant she could not locate Kostya or find out how he was. This time Wanda had the bottom bunk. There were three women in the cell before she came because, only a few days before, a large group of prisoners had been transported.

She was asked the same questions as before, but she did not answer. She lay on the bed and turned her face to the wall. Someone shook her shoulder, and she heard her name spoken. The woman explained that it was suppertime. The guard who brought the food had asked if she were in the cell. Wanda sat on the edge of the bunk.

"Are you Wanda Stanishevsky?" the woman asked. "Why don't you answer?"

"Yes, what do you want?"

"It's suppertime. Give me your plate."

"I don't want anything," Wanda said. "Leave me alone." She lay down again.

"No, the situation is different now. If you stop eating, they'll take you to the infirmary and feed you against your will," said the woman whose bunk was across from Wanda's. "Don't be a fool. It doesn't matter who you are. Take the food and eat. All of us have gone through this. I understand they gave you more time than you thought they would, and that shocked you. All of us received more than we deserved."

Wanda looked at the woman. She was very young, with short, dark hair and very dark eyes.

"How old are you?" Wanda asked.

"I'm twenty-two. What's the difference?"

"You look sixteen. You're very young."

"That's because she doesn't have much meat on her bones," said another woman. "Going from jail to prison and prison to jail, she hasn't had much good food."

"Nobody asked you," the girl said. "I can speak for myself." Turning to Wanda, she said, "I heard your name is Wanda. You don't look like you belong here. What sent you here?"

Wanda said nothing. She held the metal plate in her lap, kept her lips tightly closed, and looked down.

"We don't have secrets here. Sooner or later, we'll find out why you're here. But if you try to be friendly, maybe we can help you. We have some communication with the free world from here. But if you try to keep everything inside, there's nothing you can do by yourself."

Wanda heard the words "free world" and became interested.

"What's your name?" she asked the girl.

"Nusya. They called me that at home a long time ago, but here they call me Nuska."

"Listen, Nusya. You'd like to know why I'm here? I'll tell you, but not you or anyone else can help me. From the factory I took sausage to feed my two children. I'm a widow. Now they've given me ten years in prison, ordinary regime. Can you believe that?"

"Oh, Jesus Christ, how in the world could you steal from the government? I'm here for stealing, too. The first time, they gave me two years. After six months of freedom, I'm here again, but now I have five years. We just worked in personal property, apartments and purses. We took things from people who had more than they were supposed to. This time, they caught us because of foolishness. We were going to burglarize an apartment, and make enough money for a while. Mitka, our partner, told us it was one down, had a lot of stuff, and nobody was home. When we got there, they were waiting for us. All three of us got five years."

"How can that happen? You burglarized someone's apartment, took someone's property? And you got less than I did for taking sausages?"

"You're so raw. You don't know the articles of law. These are Lenin's articles of law: political crimes, smuggling, bribery, plundering from the government, and so on. Not all of the articles can be appealed, and some carry mandatory sentences. When you steal private property, it's a different article. Do you see the difference now?" Wanda nodded, saying nothing.

"It's not bad in prison camp. You can survive. What's frightening is going through transport."

"What's transport?"

"It's when prisoners are transferred from jail to prison camp. The journey is very long. But why should I tell you that? You'll see for yourself."

Wanda put her plate aside untouched.

"After all, Wanda," Nusya continued, "you don't understand anything. I told you you have to eat. In our world, nobody takes care of anybody else. You're on your own, and you need to understand—you survive or you die— it's all up to you. If somebody finds out you've stopped eating, you'll be sent to be force-fed. If nobody finds out, you'll just starve to death. You'll never be free. You have no one to live for?"

"You're so young," Wanda said. "How did you come by all this wisdom?"

"It's because I've been by myself all my life. I grew up homeless. I've known the streets from the time I was a little girl. I have enough experience of this dirty world."

"And you're not frightened of being alone in this life?"

"Everybody's frightened, if you think about it. Nobody wants to die."

"But what kind of life is this? Jail and prison camp."

"Everybody has a place. This is my destiny. Do you believe in destiny, Wanda?"

"I don't know what to believe anymore after all that's happened."

From the top bunk, a very slender, sickly looking woman, of middle age, joined the conversation.

"I'm an example. Believe in God. Pray every day. Observe all fasts. It was the work of the devil and God did not intercede."

"What are you here for?" Wanda asked, looking at the convicted woman.

"She's here for the 'wet business,'" Nusya answered.

"I can talk myself," the woman said, and she coughed heavily. She put a piece of cloth to her mouth, and Wanda saw blood on it.

"You don't need to talk," Nusya said. "You'll start coughing again. I'll get you some water, Raya."

Wanda whispered to Nusya, "She looks so ill."

"She is sick. She has tuberculosis. She can't survive transport." Although Nusya whispered, Raya heard her.

"I spit on that. Whether I live or not doesn't matter. They gave me twenty-five years in prison camp, strict regime. It's the same as a death penalty." She coughed again.

Wanda looked at Raya and began to see that others might have more difficult lives than her own.

"What is 'wet business?'" Wanda asked, "and why twenty-five years?" Raya started to talk, coughing frequently. No one interrupted.

"'Wet business,' as Nuska calls it, is murder. I killed my husband. He beat me like a dog. Three times I was pregnant, but never gave birth. He kicked me in the stomach. My last pregnancy lasted almost seven months. The child was alive inside me, but it was stillborn. I almost died."

Raya cried. Tears fell down her thin cheeks. She sobbed, coughing more and more. Nusya gave her more water.

"The judge didn't take into account that he beat you?" Nusya asked. "I told everything, but the prosecutor said it was premeditated murder."

"Why didn't you run away from him?" Wanda asked.

"I ran away several times. He always found me, brought me home, and swore he wouldn't beat me anymore. I was a fool and believed him. He wasn't a drunk, just a monster. If something didn't please him, he beat me. I loved him. He was handsome. He played the accordion. Women were always around him. Around other people, he behaved differently. Nobody could believe he would time to the bed and kick me. What do you think? I've always looked like this? I was healthy. I was happy and could smile. When I married him, I was eighteen. For a year, I had a normal marriage, but for seven more, I lived in hell."

"How old are you?" Wanda asked.

"I'm twenty-seven. But who could tell my age now?" She was right. She looked at least forty or forty-five.

Everyone was quiet, and Raya continued. It seemed she had waited for that moment to speak out.

"Last time, I stayed in the hospital for three months, but I lived. He didn't come to visit me once. Before, when he beat me, he visited me every day. I thought he felt guilty before and that this time he'd just left me. I went home, knocked on the door, and a young, fat girl opened it. She asked me, 'What do you want?' I told her, 'This is my apartment. I live here. What are you doing here?' She looked at me impudently and said, 'This was yours; now it's mine. Vanya lives with me now.' She pushed me so I almost fell down, and she closed the door.

"I had an aunt who lived in Peresip. I went to her and told her everything. She cried and told me, 'You're a fool, Raya, just a fool. He's taunting you. It's not easy to recognize you after what he's done. He'll get no forgiveness. If I were you, I'd kill him and send him to the devil.'

"Her words scared me, and I started praying. Such a thing had never crossed my mind. But bad luck doesn't come alone; more follows. After a few days, my aunt died. God rest her soul. On her deathbed she told me, 'Listen, Rayisa, now you'll be alone in this world. Nobody can protect you. He'll fool around and find you again and keep on threatening you. Don't let him put his hands on you. Take an axe and kill him, because if you don't, he'll kill you.'

"Those were her last words. I was left alone in her apartment, and I started to look for a job as a maid. I started working a few days later. I came home and saw Vanya sitting on the threshold.

"'I've waited over an hour for you,' he said. 'Where is your aunt? Where have you been?'

"He said it as if nothing had happened. I told him, 'Go your way and leave me alone. My aunt died, and I live here now.' The scoundrel said, 'I love you, Rayisa. No other girl can take your place. You're my first love and my last. I swear I'll never lay a finger on you again.' I told him, 'This is not the first time you've sworn that and then beat me again

267

and again. Now I have this apartment. I've started working. Finally, I have peace. God be with you, Vanya. Go your way.'

"But he didn't stop. He said, 'You, Rayisa, watch your tone of voice. You're my wife by law. If I say to go home, you go!' I knew there was nothing I could do. The more I talked, the madder he got. I was afraid he'd start beating me again. I put some things together and went with him. For two days, he was nice. He even cried. He told me how I'd lost weight, and he said, 'Now life will be different. I'll never beat you again. You'll gain weight and be beautiful like before.'

"But on the third day, he came home from work, and I called him for dinner. I saw right away he was in a bad mood. 'What's for dinner?' he asked. 'Borscht,'⁶ I said, 'and pilaf.'

"'Pilaf again?' he yelled. 'You know I hate it.'

"'Vanya,' I said, 'you should be thankful for it. People are starving. You've eaten it before, and you didn't say anything.'

"Then he said, 'Shut up, scum. You're grumbling.' He threw a chair.

I ran to the kitchen, from the kitchen to the back yard, and I hid in the woodshed. I thought I'd go away when it was dark. He was mad. He was screaming. A few times, he stepped out, called my name, then went back in. I waited until dark, left the woodshed, and walked to the gate, but he had watched me from the window. He caught me. He dragged me home like a puppy. I looked at him. His face was twisted like an animal's, and he was screaming, swearing. He tied me to the bed with a rope and beat me with a belt buckle. He beat me on the back and head. I was weak before he beat me. I don't remember anything more. I fainted. When I came around I was all wet. He threw water on me when I lost consciousness. I looked around, and in the light from the icon lamp I saw him asleep on the bed. I was tied like a dog to the footboard. I untied the rope and crawled to the kitchen quietly.

"I remember it was a Saturday. I had lit the icon lamp before he came home and prayed, thanking God for helping him to change. Somehow, God didn't hear me."

Raya coughed heavily. She stopped to drink and then continued.

"In my head I heard my aunt's voice: 'If I were you, I'd kill him and send him to the devil.' In the kitchen, behind the stove, was an axe. I felt around until I found it in the dark. I held it in my hands and went back to the bedroom. I don't know how I found the strength, but I walked to the bed. I could see very well, even though the icon lamp was dim. He was lying face down. I didn't think about anything. It just happened."

"I raised the axe over my head and brought the blade down on his. He didn't even scream, but it was as if I was crazy. I hit him over and over. When I quit hitting him, I had no strength left. I dragged myself to the kitchen and turned the light on. I was covered with blood, and so was the axe. I dropped the axe on the floor, sat down against the stove, and I remember nothing else.

"In the morning, my neighbor knocked on the door, but I didn't hear her. She pushed the door open and came in. She shook me, but I didn't come to. So she went inside and saw Vanya on the bed with his skull smashed. I heard all this at the trial, and they showed the axe as evidence.

"The neighbor called the militia and an ambulance. When the ambulance came, they used smelling salts and gave me some shorts. I came to. It would have been much better if I'd died then.

"They held me in the infirmary for a long time before I was able to go to trial. I heard so many good things about my husband from the people he worked with. He was a communist, devoted to the Communist Party, and had the true communist approach to his comrades. They said I was a kulak's daughter, but my parents died before I was sixteen. They never owned land. They worked for somebody. When they died I lived with my aunt until I got married.

"That's the end of my story. They gave me the maximum sentence, twenty-five years, strict regime. Nobody cared how he beat me, or how I got sick. If he hadn't been a communist, maybe everything would have been different." There was silence in the cell. It was evening, dusk. They could see only a small swatch of gray sky through the tiny, square, barred window.

Rayisa spoke again.

"What did you say, Nusya? I won't survive transport? You're wrong. I don't think I'll live until I'm transported."

"What are you talking about?" Nusya protested. "I just meant that transport is very long and difficult."

Raya lay on her top bunk and said nothing more.

Wanda sat against the wall on her bunk, frozen. In her mind's eye she saw Raya's fearful life, pictures flashing one after the other. She no longer thought about herself. Her kind heart was full with someone else's grief. It allowed no room for her own. Only as she fell asleep did she remember her children, and she drifted off with tears in her eyes.

In the morning, at six o'clock, the prisoners were awakened. Wanda awoke, washed her face, and sat on the bed, combing her hair. Nusya woke up next, and, after her, another woman jumped down from the top bunk across from Raya.

"I never saw such beautiful hair," the woman said. "It's so long and curly."

"Thank you," Wanda said. "I heard my hair will be cut, but now it doesn't matter."

"You, Sonya," Nusya said, "don't complain. You have beautiful hair, too. Go wash your face. It's your turn. We have to wake up Raya. She's still asleep."

Nusya pulled on Raya's pillow.

"Raya," she called, "wake up. It's time for breakfast soon. Wash up." But Raya continued sleeping.

"You have the whole day in front of you," Nusya said. "You can sleep all you want. You know the regime. The guard will check you."

Nusya stepped on Wanda's bed and touched Raya's arm. "Listen," she said, "how long will it take to wake you up." No sooner had Nusya spoken than she began screaming. "Oh, God! She's dead! Call the guard. Knock on the door."

Wanda and Sonya stepped up on the bed and looked at Raya. Wanda would remember how Raya looked for a long time. Her eyes were open. Her mouth was half open. Her hands were folded over her stomach as if she had been prepared to die.

Two guards came, put Raya on a stretcher, and carried her out of the cell.

"She was right," Nusya said. "She died before transport. She had a feeling. She had tuberculosis, I think, because her husband beat her and because she had to sleep on the floor in the winter. Now they can meet each other and compare notes."

"Can we change the subject, please?" Wanda asked. "It's frightening just to think about her. She was only twenty-seven years old. What a destiny."

A week passed and Wanda remained in the cell. She spoke very little and awaited the frightening transport. She remembered what Nusya had said about it.

Once, when the prisoners were walking in the courtyard, there were prisoners from five or six cells walking together. Wanda was next to Nusya.

"I've watched you all this time," Nusya said. "I like you. You don't talk too much, and you're a good listener. You said you have two children and nobody will take care of them?"

Nusya looked around to make sure no one was listening.

"Give me your address," she continued, "and the names of your children on this piece of paper. Try now, before we go back to the cell. After a few days, I hope we'll get some information."

Wanda asked no questions. Her instincts told her to trust Nusya. She wrote her address and the names, Masha and Gregory, and handed the paper back to Nusya, being careful to conceal her actions. She continued walking.

Nusya was right. A few days later, Wanda received a note: "Vinar, Maria and Gregory, were sent to an orphanage on Stepavoy Street. Your property was inventoried. The apartment is locked."

"Oh, God," Wanda thought, crying, "thank you. At least they are in the orphanage and not homeless, on the street."

"Thank you so much," she said to Nusya. "I owe you now. This was very kind of you."

"You're welcome," Nusya said. "And listen, do you have anything in your apartment that you'd still like to see in ten years when you come back?"

"This is possible?"

Nusya nodded.

"Only one portrait," Wanda said. "That's all that's left me from my past. I wrapped it in a pillowcase and sheet and put it in storage."

"All right. I'll remember that. We'll see an answer in a few days."

271

All Wanda's thoughts were outside the jail. She saw her children in the orphanage. They were not hungry, they had clothes, and for now they were all right. She had not believed in miracles for a long time, but, several days later, when she received a letter from the children, she began to believe.

Dear Mama,

We are healthy. We're going to school. I see Gregory every day, even though we're in different groups. We're not hungry. They feed us all right. The building is warm. We have enough clothes to go outside. Everything in the apartment was taken.

Don't worry. Take care of yourself. We miss you very much, and we hope we'll see you soon.

So kiss you and hug you.

Masha and Gregory

At the bottom of the letter, in different handwriting, was a note: "We were in time to save a picture and send it to the Boss. Everything's taken care of."

"Oh, Nusya," Wanda cried, "You're pure gold. Tell me, who's the Boss?"

"Be quiet," Nusya warned. "You don't need to know now. When you come back from the camp, you ask for the Boss. You'll find out."

"But whom do I ask?"

"Every thief in Odessa. You know how many there are. You have to destroy the letter before transport. They'll frisk you. Now tell me, how would you like to pay back the person who got you here?"

"No. I can blame only myself."

Wanda was very angry with Tanya, but she remembered she had children. She believed God would take care of everything. She would not feel better if something happened to Tanya.

Suddenly it came to her that she had forgotten to mention Marina's portrait to Nusya. Now it was too late. Everything had been confiscated.

Wanda was surprised at how a young girl like Nusya could have the kind of communications she had. Wanda was very far from understanding the reality of her new world. She had never known these circumstances before.

Wanda's situation was similar to an apartment - dweller's. People who live in apartments never think about pipes and sewers. The criminal world has a different system and that system exists in all levels of society. History shows how many times people in high positions ask criminals for help.

When the Soviet authorities came to power after the Revolution, there were more thieves and other criminals than before. In the name of the Revolution, the authorities took houses, private property, jewelry, heirlooms, everything. It was predatory, but organized. In the name of the Revolution, the authorities killed people only because they were aristocrats and of the noble class. The Revolution and its consequences begat terror and gave freedom to the hungry and brutal. Without law, they committed all manner of crimes because the Revolution gave them the license.

But now the Revolution was history. Years had passed. Promises of prosperity to a new generation, a new life, had not come true. The opposite had happened.

In 1933, the nation was in a depression. People starved. They felt anger, bitterness, and disappointment. People were pushed into all kinds of crime. The criminal world spread everywhere and became the greatest problem facing the Soviet authorities.

Who was the Boss that Wanda had heard about? He was the leader of gangs of thieves. Each gang worked in a different area, but the Boss rules all of them. The thieves brought him a tribute, a portion of each gang's take. If anyone tried to avoid paying tribute, he was taken to the "People's Court." The Boss was the judge and, in his suite, he held court with a jury. The jury decided whether to execute the offender or forgive him.

Over time, one Boss replaced another. The new Boss was elected only on the death or illness of his predecessor. The Boss was inviolable.

All thieves protected him and threatened each other by saying, "I will tell the Boss."

No one knew exactly where the Boss lived or where he hid his riches—all the tribute brought him by the thieves.

Wanda's portrait went to the Boss. Nusya had explained it: "You can ask any thief." But how would Wanda find out who was a thief? She asked no questions. She was happy just to receive the letter from Masha.

One afternoon, the guard opened the small window in the cell door and asked for Wanda Stanishevsky.

"Yes, that's me," Wanda said. "What has happened?"

"Nothing's happened," the guard answered. "Come with me."

Wanda walked to the door, turned to Nusya, and shrugged. She was taken to the shower dressing room. She had been there before. All the women showered together. A female guard came in and said, "Why do you still have long hair? Do you have a boyfriend who's saved it for you?"

"What are you talking about?" Wanda asked. "I said it's time to cut your hair. Am I clear?"

"Yes, clear enough. If it's time, it's time."

"Unbraid your hair."

"Why? It's much easier to cut it when it's braided."

"Do what I say. You're a convict. And don't forget to take all your clothes off."

Wanda unbraided her hair, and the chestnut waves fell down her back and down to the middle of her calves.

"Your hair is like something from a fairy tale," the guard said, and she left, closing the door.

Wanda stood, naked, but her hair covered her. She was not the young beauty she had been, but she was still very attractive, even in that situation. She felt cold, but she had to wait. No one came to cut her hair.

The door opened, and Wanda saw a male guard. He walked in and closed the door behind him. Wanda looked at him, frightened.

"Why doesn't a woman cut my hair?" she asked. "If you have to do it, please wait. I have to put my clothes on."

She picked up her clothes and tried to cover herself. The guard did not move. He looked steadily at her. Wanda instinctively understood what was going to happen. Her eyes pleaded with him.

The guard smiled, looking at Wanda impudently.

"I've come to admire you," he said, "before they cut your hair."

"You're a young man. I'm over forty years old. Please, let me go."

The guard was in his thirties, thick-set, of medium height, with a round moon-face. His face was splotchy, and he had bright red hair. He looked like a country boy.

"So what if I'm young," he said. "You look like a mermaid. And don't lie to me. You're not forty. I've seen forty-year-old women. Don't persist."

He came close to Wanda and continued, "Try to be nice to me. I can help you. I'm in charge of the transport. Any girl would be glad to spend time with me. All I have to do is whistle. But I don't need anybody except you. I spotted you in the courtyard."

He grabbed Wanda's clothes and threw them on the floor. Then he tossed her hair behind her and looked her over from head to toe.

"You look like a goddess," he said. "I've never seen a figure like that before in my life. It's like a picture."

"I beg you," Wanda pleaded. "Leave me alone. Please."

"Don't try to scream. It'll be worse for you. If you don't go along with me, I'll take you by force."

Wanda understood the horror of her situation. It was hopeless. The guard grabbed her shoulders and pulled her to him. She lost consciousness.

When she awoke, she was lying on a mattress that had been rolled up in the dressing room. The guard lay next to her, stroking her hair.

"If you wish, I'll save your hair," he said. "You'll have to wear a kerchief, so nobody will see it."

Wanda did not answer. She tried to move away from him.

"Lie quiet," he commanded. "I like you. It's a pity I met you here. But I know if we were somewhere else, you wouldn't even look at me. How many years did you get?"

Wanda closed her eyes and remained silent.

"I asked you a question. I'm trying to be nice." The guard's voice rose.

"Ten years," Wanda said.

"That's a lot, but I'll try to help you. You could be free earlier. I'll tell you how to act in prison camp. The authorities can give you two years for one. You could be free in five years."

"I'll tell you the truth," he said. "I know the rules and the law around here."

"What do I have to do?" Wanda asked quietly.

"For now, try to be kind to me. Later, I'll pay you back. You won't be sorry."

Wanda lay and said, quietly, "All right."

He embraced her, pressing his lips to hers. She felt disgusted, but she did what he wanted.

Later, Wanda understood how women become prostitutes, how they could begin to give themselves for money. She did it because he promised her freedom. She felt no moral responsibility.

"You have about a onth before transport," the guard said, lying on his back. "If you're obedient, like now, while I'm on duty every other day, you'll thank me for it. A girl like you, a prisoner, nobody sees as human. But I'm different. I like you a lot, and I won't hurt you."

Wanda was quiet, thinking about nothing. After a while, she asked, "May I put my clothes on?"

"What's your rush? You have time. I have a watch. We have thirty minutes. Why not use it?"

He turned to her, embraced her. She looked at the bare bulb on the ceiling, then closed her eyes and whispered, "Oh God, have mercy on me."

A half hour later, she put her clothes on, braided her hair, and went to her cell. She said nothing. The female guard opened the cell door for her.

When she entered the cell, the three women asked her where she had been. "They took me to cut my hair but changed their minds," Wanda answered, looking at the floor.

"Why did it take you so long?" Nusya asked.

"They asked a lot of questions." Wanda sat on the edge of her bed.

"That's strange," Nusya said. "Nobody is questioned after sentencing. I believe somebody cares for you. And you said you have nobody except the children."

"That's true. I don't have anyone except my children."

The window in the door opened, and oatmeal was brought for supper. The women stopped talking. Wanda felt humiliated, and she loathed herself. She could not talk about her feelings with anyone. To herself, she tried to say she had done the right thing.

"I did this to get my freedom," she thought. "I will pay any price for freedom, and this is my price." She could not stop thinking about it.

Five days later, Wanda was called again. When she heard her name, her heart was gripped with fear. The day before, she had tried not to think about it, but today, she had feared this moment since she had arisen. She was afraid; she knew she would again be taken to the dressing room.

When Wanda stood, Nusya said, "You've become very popular. Nobody else is called. Why you?'

Wanda did not answer and walked to the door. She was taken the same way as before. This time, the female guard opened the dressing room, pushed her inside, and closed the door.

"Hello, Wanda, have you missed me?"

Wanda did not answer. Ivan Stepanovich, the guard, took her by the hand and pulled her down on the mattress beside him.

"Don't be shy," he said. "You're still a proper woman. You've made love only to me, no one else. You didn't look for me; I found you."

He embraced her shoulders, pulling her to him. Wanda pushed him away. "Wait," she said. "I'm not used to it like this. Let me pull myself together."

"Don't be stubborn. I told you before. Try to be nice. I don't want to be rude. If you try to push me away, I can take you by force. Don't wake up the beast in me. At this moment, I could do anything. Oh, I almost forgot. I brought you something to eat."

He opened a paper wrapper. It contained a sandwich, two pieces of white bread with butter and cheese.

"You see," he said, "I've been thinking about you. And you try to resist me."

Wanda was hungry. After she finished the sandwich, events happened as they had before.

When Wanda returned to her cell, the guard immediately called the prisoners for exercise in the courtyard. Wanda walked next to Nusya and pulled on Nusya's sleeve. Nusya turned to her.

"I have to talk," Wanda whispered.

As they were walking in the courtyard, Wanda explained everything to Nusya. Nusya listened, throwing in an expletive occasionally. When Wanda finished, Nusya was quiet for about a minute.

"He's hooked you like a fish," she said at last. "Remember, nobody changes the verdict because the law calls for an exact term. He's a son of a bitch. He lied to you. Now we have to find a way to get rid of him."

Back in their cell, Nusya thought about a plan to get rid of the guard. A few hours later, the female guard escorted the women to the shower. Before they entered the showers, the women were given scissors to clip their fingernails and toenails.

"Listen, Nusya," Wanda said. "Cut my hair, please. That's the first thing we have to do."

"That's an idea, but I'll have to stand on the bench."

Nusya started to cut Wanda's hair. The scissors were dull, but little by little, she cut it. All the women watched.

"It's such a pity to cut hair like that," Sonya said.

"Do you have a picture, just to remember it?" another woman asked. "Maybe you've grown your hair all your life. You can cry, now that you have to cut it."

"If you lose your head, you needn't cry for your hair," Wanda said. "That's a proverb, I believe. I think it will be much easier and lighter for me."

Ropes of braided hair fell to the floor. A woman picked one up and gave it to Wanda.

"I don't need it," Wanda told her. "Please, Nusya, just cut it straight across. Then we can go take a shower."

"Wanda, I think you must have been extremely beautiful when you were younger," Nusya said.

Wanda smiled. They walked into the showers. The water was running; voices echoed. Wanda stood under the shower, and no one heard her crying.

Why was she crying? Perhaps subconsciously she knew that, like the hair she had lost and could not put back, her past was gone and would never return.

The next day, at the same hour, Wanda was called again. She walked to the door, turned, and looked at Nusya.

"Do what I said," Nusya commanded. "Don't be afraid."

The guard walked with Wanda and asked, "You cut your hair?"

"Yes. Yesterday."

"I don't know if Ivan Stepanovich will like that."

"Who is Ivan Stepanovich?"

"He's the chief of the guards, our boss, the same one who likes to see you when he's on duty."

"He's the warden?"

"No. He's what I told you. He's the chief of the guards."

"It's none of his business why I cut my hair. And I don't want to go to him. Take me to the warden. Do I have that right?"

"You've got no rights at all." The guard shushed Wanda. "Keep your voice down."

"I've got nothing to lose," Wanda continued. "I don't want to keep my voice down. Take me to the warden. I have something important to say."

Wanda and the guard walked as they talked. The plan Nusya worked out called for Wanda and the guard to stop a few doors beyond Wanda's cell. She was supposed to start screaming and ask to be taken to the warden. When she saw the warden, she would tell him how she had been raped. But everything Wanda said was said in a voice only slightly louder than normal. She forgot to stop and continued walking. The guard stopped at the dressing room. She opened the door and pushed Wanda inside. This time, the guard entered as well.

"What do you want, Vasilevna?" the chief of the guards asked.

"Ivan Stepanovich, she didn't want to come in. She asked me to take her to the warden."

"Go, Vasilevna. I'll find out what's going on."

He looked at Wanda, and then he said, "You cut your hair. Who did that, the infirmary?"

"No. I decide about my hair. It belongs to me."

"Why are you talking to me like that? I asked you to be nice. I don't want to hurt you. Don't rebel. You know what? In short hair, you're even more beautiful. Look at all these curls."

Wanda said nothing and looked at the floor. Nusya's plan had not worked.

Screaming now would be hopeless. No one would hear.

The chief of the guards pulled Wanda down beside him on the mattress. "I brought you another sandwich," he said. "Eat. It will give you strength." Wanda obeyed like a docile child. She took the sandwich. This time it contained sausage. She started to eat. The guard looked at her, smiled, and stroked her back.

"You're beautiful, very beautiful."

Wanda chewed her sandwich and did not answer. When she finished eating, he once again satisfied his brutal passion.

Wanda returned to her cell completely broken. Her arms and legs trembled. "Where've you been?" Nusya asked. "What happened?"

"The same place. I'm no hero. I'm good for nothing."

"All right. I'll take this into my own hands. You'll see. Things will change. You won't have to go to that red-haired beast. If I'm wrong, my name isn't Nusya."

"What are you talking about?"

"You'll see. I know the rules around here better than you do."

The next day, when the women were walking to the courtyard, Nusya suddenly began screaming at the top of her voice.

"Help! They're killing me! Help!"

Everyone stopped. The guard in front and the guard in the rear passed through the crowd of women to see what was wrong.

Nusya lay down on the floor and continued screaming.

"What happened?" asked one of the guards. "What are you yelling about?" Nusya sat up, pressed her hands to her chest, and screamed, "Take me to the warden. I'll tell him what happened."

"All right. I'll report it."

The second guard came and asked the first what had happened.

"Go tell Nikonorov that there's something wrong with this prisoner." Nusya lay down again and continued to scream for help.

The women walked on to the courtyard. A guard took Nusya to the warden.

He knocked on the door, asked to enter with the prisoner, and walked in.

"Please," Nusya said to the warden, "tell him to leave. I can't talk if he's here."

"Wait outside," Nikonorov said to the guard. "And you, come forward and tell me what happened."

Nusya waited until the guard closed the door and then started to speak quietly.

"I have to tell you a secret," she said. "Your guards are not doing what they're supposed to do. I heard you are strict but fair, and I decided to tell you."

Nusya lied. She had heard nothing of the kind.

"That's true," the warden said. "I'm strict and I'm fair. What do you know about the guards."

"We have a woman in our cell—Wanda Stanishevsky. She's about forty, but she looks a lot younger. She's beautiful and has a figure like a goddess. Her hair was so long it almost touched the floor. I helped her cut it. Your chief of guards, Ivan Stepanovich, rapes her every time he's on duty. He calls her to the shower dressing room about two o'clock in the afternoon and rapes her. She cries because she's so delicate. She can't stand up for herself. She told me this, and I decided to tell you about it."

"Are you telling the truth? Or is this your fantasy? You women here have vivid imaginations."

Nusya placed her hand over her heart and said, "I could swear, but I know I can't be trusted here. Tomorrow, when he calls her, you can see for yourself. You'll see I'm not lying."

"You're no dummy. You know what to say. All right. I'll check on it. But don't tell anyone else what you've told me."

"Thank you. I'm counting on you. She's a poor woman. A widow. She left two children, and she has nobody, no relatives, no friends. That slime just took advantage. ..."

"All right," the warden interrupted. "All right. I told you I'll check it out and I will. Go to your cell."

Nusya left the office, and the guard told her, "You can't stay in your cell by yourself. Go join the others in the courtyard."

"Fine. It doesn't matter to me. I walk, or I sleep. The time will pass."

"Tell me, did the warden help you? You won't be screaming anymore?" the guard asked as he walked with Nusya toward the courtyard.

"It's none of your business. He's the boss. I'll complain to him, not you."

"I asked you politely. Why did you bark at me?"

"Sure, he helped me," Nusya answered. "He promised, anyway."

Nusya spent twenty minutes in the courtyard, walking with Wanda, telling her everything she had said to the warden.

"Now," Nusya said, "it's important not to show anything. When they call you tomorrow, go."

"Thank you, Nusya. You saved me. How can I repay you?"

"Oh, maybe some time you can do me a favor."

"Tell me, can we trust the warden?"

"He looks like a reliable man. I believe we can."

Nusya was right. The warden was a reliable man, in more than looks. He was about fifty, taller than average, with a dark complexion and dark hair. He had worked in his position for about two years. Before, he was an investigator and prosecuting attorney. He was strict and principled. Those who knew him respected him. Even though Nusya had lied when she told him about his reputation, she was not mistaken.

The day came when Ivan Stepanovich was once more on duty. Wanda was anxious from early morning on.

"Don't be afraid," Nusya said to her. "Everything will be just fine."

"I'm not afraid," Wanda said quietly. There's nothing worse than what I've already gone through."

At about one forty-five, Wanda heard her name called. She walked to the cell door and turned to Nusya. Nusya nodded.

Wanda walked down the corridor to the shower dressing room. The female guard opened the door and let Wanda through. Ivan Stepanovich sat on a bench, waiting. He motioned for her to sit next to him. Wanda remained where she was.

"I brought you some fried meat," Ivan Stepanovich said. "I believe you haven't had meat for a long time."

The chief of the guards smiled, and Wanda's mouth watered.

"I don't want your meat, and I don't want you to call for me," she said. "I grieve in my heart and my soul for my children, and you call me only for your amusement."

"Who taught you to talk to me like that?" said Ivan Stepanovich, raising his voice.

"Nobody. I can speak for myself. And I have feelings too."

"All right. You asked for it. I can be nice, or I can be as rough as I am with other women. I have a different feeling for you. You're more intellectual, somehow. But now I see you don't understand good treatment. Come here and sit next to me. Now."

Wanda did not move. She was trembling and had difficulty breathing. He stood, walked to her, and grasped her shoulders.

"Go and lie down on the mattress," he commanded. "Don't forget to take your clothes off, if you want to keep them in one piece."

"No more," Wanda said, and she continued to stand.

"You're so stupid. You could have everything, but you choose to have nothing."

He pushed her down on the mattress. She fell and tried to get up again. He easily put her on her back. He grasped the front of her gray dress and pulled. The buttons flew. Wanda could not defend herself. His knees held her legs down. In another moment, her underclothing was torn away.

"When you resist, you're even more beautiful," Ivan Stepanovich said. "That's a good girl. I would give anything for you."

He was in ecstasy, tearing at her clothes, repeating obscenities over and over. He did not see that behind him the door was open and the warden had come in.

"What is this?" the warden cried. "What are you doing during your duty hours with the prisoners?"

When the chief of the guards heard Nikonorov's voice, it was too late for him to do anything. The picture was clear. Wanda was nearly naked on the mattress. Her clothes were in shreds. Ivan Stepanovich knelt over her with his pants down.

"Put your pants on immediately," the warden said firmly. "I want to see you in my office in five minutes."

To the female guard standing next to him, he said, "Bring her new clothes."

Wanda was crying from fear and from happiness that her torture was at an end. The warden sat on the bench, shaking his head. He looked at Wanda. She sat on the mattress, trying to cover herself with scraps of clothing.

"Don't cry," the warden said. "This will never happen again. I'm sorry about what you've gone through."

The guard brought new clothes. Wanda went into the shower room and put them on. The guard escorted her back to her cell.

"Did everything happen like we planned?" Nusya asked.

"Yes. Everything, almost. I'm glad the warden came in time. You, Nusya, you're a fine girl. God bless you."

Wanda lay down on the bed and closed her eyes. She saw before her the twisted face of the chief of the guards. Suddenly, she recalled how the warden had opened the door and taken in the scene. She began to laugh. She laughed as she never had before, loudly. The women jumped from their beds and looked at her. They thought something had happened. Wanda sat on the edge of her bed, crying and laughing.

"What are you laughing about?" Nusya asked. "I don't remember you acting like this before."

"I believe this is hysteria," Sonya said. "I've heard of people laughing and crying at the same time."

Wanda stopped laughing and sighed. "No," she said, "this is not hysteria. I just pictured how the warden opened the door and saw the chief of the guards on his knees with his pants down. I wasn't laughing then. I was frightened. But just now, I couldn't stop laughing. I couldn't help myself."

"That scoundrel got what he deserved," Sonya said. "I don't think this is the first time he's found a victim and done what he wanted."

"Don't worry," Nusya said. "The worst that can happen to him is that he'll get fired. We're nobody, just numbers."

"That's fine," Sonya said. "If he's fired, he won't abuse any more women. He's swine."

Three weeks passed. No one called Wanda anymore. Life in jail resumed its normal pace.

Once, after supper, the cell door window opened and someone said, "Prisoners Markova, Stanishevsky, and Zuitka. Tomorrow, early in the morning, be ready for transport. Put your clothes and things together. Be ready."

The women looked at each other.

"The time has come," Nusya said. "Bear up, girls. We have to survive."

"I'd almost forgotten about transport," Wanda said.

"But they didn't forget," said Nusya. "They care about us. They'll give only dry bread to eat. After that, you'll want a drink, but they give only one cup of water a day. You'll be thirsty."

Very early the next morning, while it was still dark, a knock came at the cell door.

"Be ready," a voice cried, echoing down the corridor. A pounding fist rumbled along the hall. The guards were passing from door to door to remind the prisoners to prepare themselves.

"What time is it?" Wanda asked.

"About three o'clock," Nusya answered. "It's the usual time for them to line us up and call roll."

Ten minutes later, the door opened, and the women walked from the cell to the corridor to join the other prisoners. In the prison yard, searchlights surrounded them. The prisoners stood in a long, single line.

"Listen to my commands," said the transport officer through a megaphone.

Everyone turned to face him.

"Step forward when I call your name." He began the roll call.

After everyone had stepped forward, the gate opened to reveal several large trucks. The prisoners passed through the gate and into the trucks to be taken to the railroad station. Each truck carried twenty prisoners and four guards, two of whom held German shepherds.

Wanda traveled with Nusya, sitting next to her in the truck.

"I'm so scared, Nusya," Wanda whispered. "It's night and these guards have snarling dogs."

"This is nothing," Nusya said. "These are only women prisoners. If they transport men and women together, there are more guards and more dogs."

The trucks stopped at a freight loading area. The prisoners walked to boxcars. They were specially made for transporting convicts.

Inside the cars, each prisoner had her own cage. Partitions kept them from communicating with each other. On the floor of each cage was a hay-filled mattress. When everyone was placed in her cage and the prisoners were counted, the train departed. Hanging from the ceiling was a single, dim lightbulb.

Wanda could not see Nusya, but she knew she was in the same car. She lay down on the mattress and covered herself with her coat. The car shook and swayed from one side to the other and she felt sick.

"I wonder how long this will take," she thought.

Through a small window, she saw the morning light. Soon, the train stopped. The women were escorted, one by one, back and forth from their cages to a toilet in the rear of the car. Standing, holding the bars of her cage door, Wanda saw Nusya pass.

"Nusya," Wanda asked, "How long will it take to get there?"

"This is a dead end. We'll be here until tonight. We travel only at night. Prepare yourself for three or four weeks of this. Transport has just started."

Wanda lay back down on her mattress. She closed her eyes and listened to the dogs barking, the prisoners calling to each other, trying to talk, the guards swearing.

"If this is God's will," Wanda thought, "that my children be raised in an orphanage, without me, maybe He wills that my life be taken. After ten years, when I come back, no one will need me because of my past. I'll be a shame to them. I know I'm finished. This is my destiny."

Tears flowed down her cheeks. The grief she felt overwhelmed her, and she cried out. She buried her face in the mattress and wept bitterly. She put her towel under her face and cried into it. The guard heard her, and he stopped.

"Why are you howling?" he asked. "You should have cried before you committed a crime. Now pull yourself together. You'll need strength to get through."

Little by little, Wanda calmed down, and she fell asleep. When she awoke, the car was shaking. It was dark outside. The dim light revealed the dirty ceiling.

"Oh, God," Wanda whispered, "Save my children. Don't turn away from them. They have no one in the world."

She asked herself many times what kind of life they had in an orphanage. There was no answer. Before she had left the jail, Wanda had learned that she would be able to receive letters in the prison camp.

What happened to the children when Wanda was arrested?

That evening, Wanda's apartment was searched. Two men in civilian clothes performed the search. When they finished, they explained to Masha that her mother had been arrested. Masha and her brother would have to stay, temporarily, in a children's shelter.

In the place where homeless children were taken, Masha and Gregory were kept in quarantine for forty-five days. After that, they were sent to an orphanage. Gregory joined a third-grade group; Masha joined the senior group. She had two years of high school left, but, because she missed forty-five days of school while in the shelter, she was kept out of classes and sent to work in the kitchen. She would miss one year. She scrubbed floors and huge copper kettles and washed dishes. She grew withdrawn and solemn. She seldom spoke.

Masha saw her brother only on Sundays. Gregory attended school because his absence from classes was less critical. When he saw Masha, he asked, "When do we go home, and where is Mama?"

"I don't know," Masha answered. "We have to wait." But she knew they would not see Wanda for a long time. She did not want to tell Gregory.

The orphanage was a place where children came from the streets. They were ruffians. They lacked discipline and education. Gregory learned very fast how to smoke, play hookey, and play kickball in the city streets. From a good boy, talented and well-behaved, he changed to become the same as the others.

One day, in the spring of 1934, six boys, aged fourteen to sixteen, ran away from the orphanage. With them, they took two younger boys; one of them was Gregory.

The orphanage director called Masha to his office.

"Where is your brother?" the director asked. "Did he tell you he was going to run away?"

Masha cried. She wiped her eyes with her apron, not answering. The director, a very short, fat man with pince nez glasses, walked around his desk and yanked the apron from her hands.

"Answer me, Vinar," he demanded, "when I ask you a question."

"What can I say? I don't know anything. He has been punished lately. They haven't let him see me on Sundays. The older boys get him in trouble. They're never punished, but he is."

"I'll find out about this. All right, you can go now."

"Please, tell me. Has there been a letter from my mama?" Masha asked, crying.

"If we receive a letter for you, we'll let you know. Go to the kitchen now." When Masha reached the door, she turned and said to the director, "Please find my brother."

"Don't worry," the director said. "We'll find him. Our militia know their job."

Days, weeks, and months passed, and the militia did not find Gregory. So Masha decided to carry on the search herself. Late one evening, when it was dark, she prepared a knapsack, filling it with clothes and other necessary items, and walked out through the orphanage gate. Children who worked in the kitchen were not checked in the morning or evening because their work prevented them from taking part in normal flag-raising and lowering ceremonies when the roster was read.

Masha was alone. She had no relatives, no close friends. She did not know where she was going, but she decided to start at the train station. She had no money.

She sat on a bench in the station with people waiting for the trains. By midnight, many of the passengers had left, and Masha had room to lie down.

She awoke early in the morning and could not remember where she was. But soon, she understood. Immediately, she had an idea about what she had to do. She walked to the restroom, brushed her hair and brushed her teeth. Then she returned to the station and began carefully observing the people. Finally, she found a family, a husband, wife, and two children. One child was about four, the other an infant. The family looked fairly prosperous. Masha decided to risk speaking to them.

"Excuse me. By chance, do you need a housekeeper? I can clean your apartment, do the laundry, and cook. I'm not afraid of work."

"Where are your parents?" asked the woman who held the baby in her arms. They died. I'm an orphan. Please, I beg you. You won't be sorry you've given me a job."

"Peter, what do you think?" the woman said to her husband. "We have to start in a new place. How will I manage?"

"It's all right," Peter answered, "but we don't know her. We have no references. How can we trust her with the children?"

Masha looked from one to the other, crying and sniffling.

"All right," the woman said. "We'll be leaving in an hour. You can go with us." To her husband, she said, "Peter, please go buy her a ticket."

Peter shrugged and left to buy the ticket.

Masha's future was settled. She traveled to Kharkov with the family of Peter Malukov, a civil engineer. Of course, she had no idea where they were going or how far away it was. She knew only that she had to be far away from the orphanage. She believed that later she could begin looking for Gregory.

When she was asked her full name, Masha responded, "Maria Vladimirovna Stanishevsky."

In Kharkov, an application was submitted for a new birth certificate for Masha. Homeless children found on the streets were routinely issued new birth certificates based on an age estimate determined by medical examination.

During this time, Wanda was in transport on the freight train. Every day, the situation grew more difficult. The dry bread scratched her throat. One mug of water a day did not help.

After a week, Wanda began to feel weak. Her legs swelled, and she contracted a fever. She could no longer stand at her cage door and beg for water. She lay on the hay-stuffed mattress listlessly.

One morning, a guard handing out dry bread called to her, but she did not answer. He opened her cage and entered. When he looked at her, he noticed right away that something was wrong. He called the chief of the guards.

At the next station, the train stopped, and a doctor was called. The doctor diagnosed typhus. The entire train was quarantined, and Wanda was taken to the hospital. The train could not leave for several days until it was known whether anyone else would fall ill.

All of Wanda's hair was removed. She lay in the hospital for two months.

She almost died, but her fate was to live.

Life had no meaning for her anymore. Only when she remembered, for an instant, her children, did she feel any hope at all.

A guard stood at the door of her room twenty-four hours a day.

After two months, the doctor told the officials that Wanda was ready to go to the prison camp. This time, she was lucky. She did not go by freight transport. She rode in a passenger train, escorted by two guards. After three days, she arrived at the camp. She had lost much weight, her face was very pale, and her hair had only begun to grow out in tiny curls. She was sent to a barracks, and Nusya spotted her immediately.

"Jesus Christ. What happened to you? I thought you were dead. I heard somebody had typhus. They sprayed the train. We couldn't breathe. I found out it was you who was sick. I'm happy you're alive. I'm glad to see you."

"Yes, Nusya," Wanda said, "I'm alive. And I'm glad to see you, too. The doctor told me that someone else had died on my mattress. That's why I got sick. They found out, and then they burned the mattress. I almost died, but I'm still alive. I don't know why."

"You've changed so much. No hair, skin and bones. You know, we've already started working in the rubber factory. Time goes faster than it did in jail. There's more freedom here. You'll find out pretty soon by yourself."

The next day, Wanda was given a letter from the orphanage.

"Your two children have run away from the orphanage," it said. "The militia are searching for them."

"Don't worry, Wanda," Nusya said. "Your daughter is a big girl. She can take care of her brother. An orphanage is the same as jail, but for children. And I'll tell you something else. An adult helped them escape. It's for the best. You'll see."

Wanda calmed down. Somehow, she trusted Nusya and what she said. She was worried because she knew nothing of her children's whereabouts. She did not sleep well, leaping up frequently with fright, and she could not look forward to any letters. Masha did not know where her mother was, either.

Wanda worked in the factory from eight in the morning until eight in the evening. In the rubber factory were chemicals. Acid ate away the skin on her hands and burned her eyes. Not long ago, in jail, Wanda was a pretty woman, but after a few months in the factory and her illness, she was difficult to recognize. Her hair grew back, but it was completely gray. Two deep wrinkles creased her forehead.

Her eyes grew red and inflamed. She visited the infirmary for eye drops, but they did not help. She developed an allergy to the chemicals. After six months of work in the factory, she was sent to the shipping department because, when she awoke in the morning, her entire face was swollen; she could not see. The move saved her.

In the warehouse, she packed galoshes in boxes. Little by little, her eyes returned to normal.

Once, Wanda met Nusya in the cafeteria. It was the first time in six months that Nusya had a good look at her friend.

"Wanda, you've changed so," Nusya said. "Listen, you have to pull yourself together. You've been here less than a year, and you've become an old woman. It's not easy to recognize you. You have all those years in front of you yet. You'll die like a dog, and they'll bury you like one. If you don't fight for your life, nobody else will. You're on your own in this jungle."

"Did you hear what happened in Barracks Six?" Nusya continued. "Some woman went crazy, and they shot her." Nusya was whispering now.

"What are you talking about?" asked a woman next to Wanda. "It's frightening to listen to you."

"I said what I heard," Nusya replied. "If you don't control yourself, the same will happen to you."

"I have no more strength," Wanda said. "If I die, that is my destiny— to die at age forty-four. The life I've had is enough for three people. I only have one wish, to see my children once more."

"Listen, Wanda," Nusya said. "I have a few years left here. I give you my word. When I'm free, I'll find your children. You know I have connections. Do you remember the letter you received from Masha? Do you believe me?"

"Yes, I do. Perhaps I'm still alive because I have some kind of hope. You're right. I have to eat, and take care of health, and survive."

The young girl from the streets explained to the well-bred woman how to survive in that kind of situation. Wanda now had hope. When Nusya was free in a few years, she would find Wanda's children. It was important to have a goal, and Wanda had one.

Wanda ate everything she was given and bought some groceries with the money she earned in the factory. In the barracks, she listened to the radio when she was free from work and on Sundays.

Three years passed. During that time, Wanda lost all her teeth and contracted scurvy. She received no letters from her children. But now, she had hope, because Nusya would soon be free.

Nusya was in prison only three years and nine months, instead of five years, because of good behavior. She was still a very young woman. Prison had made her stronger. She spent all her money for food. She never thought about saving for her freedom.

Nusya was called to the prison camp office to sign a paper that said she would be free in two weeks.

"Nusya," Wanda said, "You're my only hope. It has been my dream that you would go to find my children."

"I memorized the address where you lived before," Nusya answered. "I'll find the orphanage and see what they know. I'll send you a letter to tell you about everything. But it's not easy to recognize you, Wanda. You're not the same beautiful woman I met almost four years ago." Nusya shook her head.

"I know," Wanda said. "I look like an old woman. I have no teeth, gray hair. Believe me, I don't care."

"How old are you now?"

"I'm forty-seven, but I know I look sixty."

"When you're free, you'll get some false teeth, dye your hair, gain some weight, and you'll look completely different," Nusya said, laughing. "Maybe another Ivan Stepanovich will find you attractive."

The day came for Nusya to depart. Early in the morning, before wake-up call, Wanda walked to Nusya's barracks to say good-bye. They hugged each other and cried. Wanda gave Nusya a sheet of paper.

"This is for you," Wanda said, "from me."

When Nusya looked at the sheet of paper, she saw her own portrait.

"I drew you as I'll remember you forever," Wanda said.

Wanda had drawn the portrait so that Nusya's entire face, eyes, nose, mouth, were easily recognizable. But instead of short hair, Wanda gave Nusya very long hair, as her own had once been, and a beautiful, lacy dress.

"Oh, Wanda," Nusya cried. "You drew me so beautiful. Nobody could recognize this as me."

"If you had had a different childhood, you would look even more beautiful."

"Thank you very much. You're so talented. You're a real artist. Only you wasted your talent on nothing."

"Do you remember, Nusya, when you saved my portrait? All my sketches and paintings were confiscated along with everything else in my apartment. But that's past and gone, like so much of what I've loved."

Wake-up call sounded, and the women said good-bye one more time.

Wanda hurried to prepare for work. Nusya put the portrait with her luggage.

A few hours later, the train carried her from the far Ural to Odessa.

The year was 1937. It was a time of repression, Stalin's "cleansing."

The prisons and jails were filled with political prisoners. People lived in fear of tomorrow. Who would be next? Before, people had been sent to prison for their beliefs. Now, people with no political convictions at all, such as scientists, writers, professors, and engineers were imprisoned. Some were sent to jail because of a neighbor's report. Not even office clerks were immune. It seemed there would be no end to it. Fear froze all the people, fear for themselves, for relatives, for friends.

The authorities paid little attention to small squabbles. They had no time. They looked for enemies of the people, and everywhere they looked, they found them.

Nusya arrived in Odessa and very quickly found her connections. Her compatriots told her how things were going in the nation.

"You see, Nusya," said the chieftain of Nusya's former gang, "among our brothers, we don't have enemies of the people. We're the people's friends. The closer we stay to the people, the more we find out how much we're helping them."

"I had no idea you had become philosophers," Nusya replied. "I see many things have changed since I've been gone. Listen, I'm looking for somebody. I have business to take care of. I promised a woman in the camp."

"All right. Tell me, who wronged you?"

"Nobody. This is different. She's a good person. She has two kids here in Odessa. I have to find them."

Nusya was talking with an ex-circus performer, a magician who decided to change professions, to enter a field where he could better use his talents.

Nusya went to the orphanage and talked to the director. She said she was a relative who wanted to find out what had happened to the children after their mother was arrested.

The director was the same short, fat man with pince nez glasses. He listened and shrugged.

"Unfortunately, the children weren't found," he said. "It's very possible they're not in Odessa. Otherwise, the militia would have found them a long time ago. They searched for a year, and then they had to stop. I think some adult helped them because without the means for subsistence they could not have hidden so long. That's all I can tell you about Maria and Gregory Vinar."

Nusya thanked him and left.

"What sort of deviltry is this?" she thought. "Those nasty vagabonds. Where will I find them now?"

But Nusya showed her old energy and searched all over Odessa. The rest of the thieves' world also searched. They knew they were looking for a boy, fifteen, and a girl, twenty years old. What the militia couldn't do in a year, Nusya did in a month. Gregory was found in Peresip. He was living in an old thief's house. The thief no longer "worked," but he was teaching his trade to young boys. The boys brought their plunder to him and kept a share for themselves.

Gregory now had a nickname, "Grinya." No one in his world had a last name.

Nusya sat in the old, neglected house, talking with the thief, and waited for Gregory.

"How long has he worked for you?" she asked.

"Two years. He came to me after he worked the trains where he almost got caught. He's clever and bright. That's important in our business."

The thief stood and got himself some water. Nusya noticed that he was limping. She heard a knock at the door. It opened and three young boys entered. They were well dressed, clean; they did not look like vagabonds.

"How was work today?" asked the old man.

No one answered. They stared at Nusya, not understanding why he asked the question with her present.

"She's one of us," the old thief said. "Don't worry. You, Grinya, put everything on the table and see her out. She came to visit you."

Nusya looked at the small boy, whose face showed his astonishment. They walked out together.

"I brought you greetings from your mother," Nusya said. "We spent some time together. You know where. Can you write?"

"Yes, I can. Why?"

"I'd like to send a letter to your mother. You can give me yours, and I'll send them together."

"I'm not writing anything."

"Why not?" asked Nusya indignantly. "She's still alive only because she hopes to see you and your sister. By the way, where is your sister? When did you last see her?"

"I haven't seen her since I ran away with the other boys."

"Did you try to find her? She's your only sister."

"After we left, a few other boys ran away also. They told me Masha was gone and that they were searching for her. If she lived in Odessa, I would have seen her. I believe she went somewhere else."

"It'll be hard to find her. She could have married and changed her last name. But you write a letter because I promised Wanda."

"If I send a letter, someone might read it and find me. Now they won't send me back to the orphanage. They'll send me to jail."

"You're not dumb. You're smart for your age. Tell me, do you remember your mother?"

"Of course I remember. She was beautiful, with long hair. I remember her soft hands, how she stroked my hair. And I remember her voice."

As he spoke, Gregory looked at the ground. He was shy around Nusya.

This is good," Nusya said. "You remember her. Try to remember her like that, because when she comes back, you'll see her differently."

"Why?"

"She's changed over the years. She's been sick, and everything she's gone through has aged her. You have to understand what kind of life she's had. All right, I'll send a letter myself and try to explain everything."

Wanda received a letter from Nusya. It was the first letter she had received in years.

Hello Wanda,

I'm sending you this letter from beautiful, sunshiny Odessa. Life is much better now. We have enough bread.

I go to work pretty soon. A few days ago I met a guy. You know him very well. He's all right, healthy. But I couldn't find his sister, not yet. I think she's found a job out of the city. But I'll keep on looking for her.

How is your work? How is your health?

Say hello to the girls in the barracks. Answer me at the address on the envelope.

Your friend,
Nusya

Wanda read and re-read the letter many times. She understood that the "guy" Nusya mentioned was her son. Now she only worried about Masha. Where was she? Why did she leave town?

Wanda sent a letter to Nusya, thanking her for the good news. She was happy for Nusya because she was starting a new life. She asked some questions: "Please tell me. Where does our acquaintance, the boy, live? What school does he attend? Who takes care of him?"

Nusya could not possibly answer all the questions for fear of hurting Wanda.

"I don't know what she's thinking," Nusya said to herself when she read Wanda's letter. "I can't explain to her where he lives or what he does. Now it's important that I find Masha. Then everything will be fine."

Time passed, and Nusya could not find Masha. She knew, at last, that Masha was not in Odessa. She would have tried to find her brother.

What happened to Masha after she met the young couple in the train station?

She was taken to Kharkov, and the couple was not sorry about their decision. Masha was trustworthy, honest, of good breeding, a hard worker— what else could they ask for in a housekeeper? She took very good care of the children.

After six months, Masha received her new birth certificate. She was officially Maria Vladimirovna Stanishevsky.

The next summer, the whole family—husband, wife, two children, and Masha—went to the shore of the Black Sea. How Masha had waited for that moment!

Whey they arrived in Odessa, she asked several times to go to the city. She explained that she wanted to visit some of her mother's friends. But she was looking for Gregory.

All Masha found out was that he had not been found and that he was not in the orphanage. She looked in the train station, at the seaport. She asked some boys his age, explaining how Gregory looked. No one had seen him.

Masha's employer was a young woman named Lucy. She was taller than average and very slim. Her kind, light eyes always looked friendly. She pitied Masha, and for Masha's kindness she returned the same.

Masha grew very close to the family. She loved them as she would her own. She and Lucy seemed more like sisters, the younger trying to help the older care for the children.

It had been more than three years, and Masha could not imagine leaving the family.

In 1938, as they had before, in the middle of June, the entire family traveled to Odessa. In Odessa lived Lucy's father and his sister, an old maid and a lady with much education. She had graduated from a women's university before the Revolution. She lived in her memory, not remembering what happened the week before but able to talk for hours about what had happened thirty years ago. She was tall and big boned, and she used a walking stick for support. Always, she wore a lace collar or ruff that was yellowed with age. Her gray, but still thick, hair was divided down the middle and braided in the back. She lived with her brother, Lucy's father, who was a widower, Lucy's mother having died after Lucy was married.

Lucy's father was a very intelligent man. He was a professor in the university, and had been for ten years. He was tall, with salt and papper hair. He spoke slowly, thoughtfully, always weighing his words. He did not like to write letters. When his sister sent a letter to Lucy, he would add a few words, or he might send a card.

When Lucy's family arrived in Odessa in June, 1938, Lucy found out that a few days before her father was arrested and sent to jail. His sister could not orient herself. She told Lucy how they had come at night, searching, and took her brother. They told her, "Don't howl, old spinster, or you'll go with him." She repeated herself to Lucy again and again, unable to comprehend. Lucy told her to be quiet because Peter had gone to find out what had happened.

Peter discovered that Lucy's father, Samuelov Innokenty Alexandrovich, had been accused of espionage, sending information out of the country. He was a teacher of the German and French languages, so he had been accused of sending information to the French and German secret services. His case looked very serious, and there was nothing to be done until the trial was over.

"Listen, Mashenka," Lucy said. "You're like family to us. Can you do us a favor? Can you stay with my Aunt Nadezhda Alexandrovna? She cannot be alone. We have to go back to Kharkov. Peter has to go to work, and Sergei has to go to school."

"All right, Lucy," Masha replied. "I'll stay with your aunt."

Masha was happy with the turn of events. She now had more time to look for Gregory.

At the train station, before they entered the car, Masha hugged Lucy, Peter, and the children. They all cried. Lucy had to go, but in her heart, she could not leave her father's troubles behind.

Two months later, the trial was over. It lasted only one day. The sentence was read: "Twenty-five years, strict regime, in a prison camp." It was a terrible shock for Samuelov Innokenti Alexandrovich's sister, his daughter, and her husband.

Nadezhda Alexandrovna fell ill and spent most of her time in bed. Masha had to call the doctor almost every day.

During the two months before the trial, Nadezhda Alexandrovna had prepared a legal document allowing Masha to share her apartment with her. This formality was very important.

For more than four weeks, Masha cared for Lucy's aunt. She cleaned, did laundry, cooked, and changed the linens. Sometimes, Masha read the old lady her favorite short stores.

"Mashenka," the old lady said once, "You're such a kind, nice child. I'm so thankful for your kindness. When I feel better, I'll pay you back."

"What are you saying?" Masha chided. "I don't need anything. I'm glad to be in Odessa. I was born here and spent my childhood here."

Once, when Masha returned from the store with an armful of packages, she saw a young woman waiting at her door.

"Who are you looking for?" Masha asked.

"I'm looking for you, girl," answered Nusya, "if you're Masha Stanishevsky."

"Yes, I'm Masha. Come in. What can I do for you?"

"There's nothing you can do for me. But I think I can do something for you," Nusya said, smiling.

Masha looked at Nusya in astonishment. They entered the room, and Masha invited Nusya to sit down. She carried the groceries to the kitchen, walked to Nadezhda Alexandrovna's room, and gave her her medicine.

"Do you need anything?" Masha asked. "No, Mashenka, thank you. I'll try to sleep." Masha closed the door and returned to Nusya."

"I'm sorry. I had to give an ill lady her medication," she explained.

"Sit down, Masha," Nusya said. "We have to talk. I've looked for you for a long time, but Maria Vinar doesn't live in Odessa. Maria Stanishevsky I did find at this address."

Masha's face paled, and she asked quietly, "How do you know my name?"

"I'm Nusya. I spent some time with your mother. She asked me to look for you and your brother."

"Oh, God. How is she? Is she still alive? How is her health? My poor, dear mama. I miss her so much." Masha began to cry.

"She's alive, but it's not easy to tell about her health. She worries a lot about you children. You can send her a letter. You're twenty-one, aren't you?"

"Yes, I'm twenty-one. But I don't know what to write to her because I don't know where my brother is. How can I explain that to her?"

"You don't need to look for him. I've already found him. I can bring him to you any time it's convenient for you."

Masha was elated. She asked Nusya one question after another. Nusya interrupted her.

"Don't ask me anything. When you see your brother, you can ask him." Nusya promised to bring Gregory the next day.

The search for Wanda's children brought Nusya moral satisfaction. What made this young girl, raised in the streets among thieves and vagabonds, tie herself to the destiny of people unrelated to her?

She saw and felt in Wanda what had been missing in her own childhood— warmth, softness, and regard for others. She had stayed by Wanda's side, protecting her through jail and prison camp, letting no one harm the timid, defenseless woman. One look from Wanda was enough to calm Nusya when she was upset or angry. In her entire life, Nusya had cried only once—when she said good-bye to Wanda—and now she was glad to find Gregory and Masha. It was as if she had found someone very dear to her.

As she had promised, Nusya brought Gregory to Masha. When she saw them holding each other, the sight brought her to tears. They had not seen each other for four and a half years. Gregory was now a teenager; Masha was a grown, beautiful woman.

"You, Grinya, stay here," Nusya said. "Stay as long as you want. I have to go. You two need to do me a favor. Promise that you'll write a letter to your mother. Here's her address. You know how to write a letter."

Nusya left, very satisfied with her own actions.

Soon, Wanda received two letters, one from Nusya and another from Masha.

Nusya wrote:

Dear Wanda,

I have done what you asked. I found the sister of the boy you know. You're one lucky woman. When you finish your sentence and come back home, you'll have a new life. You won't cry anymore. I promise you.

I work in the factory. Everything is in order now, but I'll tell you the truth, I miss you a lot.

Hold on. Time flies. Half of your sentence is already over.

Say hello to the girls in your barracks.

Hug you, Nusya

In the other letter, Masha wrote:

Our Beloved Mother,

Try to imagine how happy we are to find out you are still alive and healthy.

Thanks to your friend, everything is fine now. But when you come home, it will be much better. I just want you to know that we are healthy and together. What happened is past now.

Write to us about everything you're doing. Keep your spirit. We are always with you, and we are waiting for you.

We kiss you and hug you very tightly.

Yours,
M. and G.

Wanda read the letter many times until she knew it by heart. She carried it with her everywhere, as if it were a treasure. It was the first letter she had received from her children in five years.

The boxes full of rubber boots no longer seemed as heavy. She felt heartened, strengthened because she had hope.

She sent a letter to her children. In it, she said that everything was fine. She was in good health and good spirits; she was working and had only one wish, to see them again.

Time passed, and the orphanage's search for Gregory was given up. He visited Masha almost every day, but he still lived with the old thief. Masha was busy looking after Lucy's aunt, whose health was deteriorating. She was slipping away. No medicine could help her. Finally, one morning, Masha walked into the old lady's room and found her dead.

Masha called the doctor and sent a telegram to Lucy. Until Lucy arrived, she worried constantly because she did not know where she would be going, or whether she could stay with her brother.

Nadezhda Alexandrovna was buried in Odessa's civilian cemetery. The morning was cold, and a light snow was falling. When Lucy and Masha returned from the cemetery, they were chilled to the bone. Masha prepared tea.

"You know, Mashenka," Lucy said, "I'm thinking that for you it might be better to stay here. You're like family. My children aren't so little anymore, and I can manage without you. You've grown up, and now you need to think about your life. You have this apartment. You can find a job, and you can be around people. In the summer, every year, we'll come, and we can stay here with you."

"Oh, Lucy," Masha said, wiping her tears, "I don't know how to thank you."

They sat and drank tea. Lucy told Masha about her father.

"It's strange, very strange, but we can't find him; we can't communicate with him. It's such a pity. He'll never know his sister is dead. I'm so frightened. What kind of future do our children have?"

After Lucy returned to Kharkov, Masha stayed alone in the apartment. She had two separate rooms and a kitchen and bathroom. She still could not believe it belonged to her. She had to find a job because she had to live and pay for the apartment. It was important to her that Gregory move into the apartment. Again, Nusya helped her.

Nusya found a job for Masha in the factory where she worked. She also helped Gregory move to his sister's apartment. As Nusya and Masha worked together, they grew to be friends. Sometimes, after work, they went to a movie. Masha had no idea who Nusya was or what she was. She had no idea what her brother was doing in his free time.

One evening, Masha was ironing sheets and listening to the radio. It was 1939, and the voice on the radio was describing the outbreak of war in Europe. The government was asking for volunteers to go to Spain to protect that courageous country.

Masha was listening very carefully. Suddenly, someone knocked on her door. Masha jumped.

When she opened the door, she saw Nusya with a young man. He was holding a large, rectangular package.

"Are you ready for guests, Masha?" Nusya asked. "We brought something for you."

"Oh, Nusya, you startled me. I was listening to the radio. There's war in Europe. There was a report from the war zone in Spain. I heard awful explosions, and at the same time, you knocked."

"This is Andre," Nusya said. "Can you show Masha what we brought?"

Andre began unwrapping the package. Masha watched curiously.

"Oh, my God!" Masha exclaimed. "That's my mama when she was young. I remember this portrait, but I thought it was lost. Where did you find it, Nusya?"

"You don't need to know. You have the portrait now before your mama comes home. You can look at her, see how beautiful she was—like a princess. I never saw anyone as beautiful as she was. It's unbelievable what life can do to people."

Before they left, Andre and Nusya removed a print from the wall of Masha's room and replaced it with Wanda's portrait. Masha walked up to the painting and looked at it closely. Tears fell from her eyes.

"Oh, Mama, Mama," she whispered. "This is you. You're so beautiful in that dress. I don't remember you like that, but I still remember you were beautiful. Maybe all mothers are beautiful to their children. How do you look now? Will I recognize you when you come home?"

There was another knock at the door and, again, Masha jumped. It was Gregory, returning from his "work."

"Look, Gregory, what Nusya brought today." Masha pulled Gregory into her room.

"Who's that?" Gregory asked.

"This is our mama when she was young. You don't remember this portrait?"

"No, I don't. This is her? She was rich? Bourgeois?"

"You didn't know our mother was from high society? Nobody talks about it now, but we need to know the truth."

"Look at that necklace. Where is it now?"

"You don't understand anything. The portrait was painted before the Revolution. Times change. After the Revolution, people were starving; they didn't think about jewels. They thought about food."

"Yes, I forgot. That was a long time ago. How does she look now? I remember her, but not very clearly."

"I've thought about this. In four more years, she'll come back home. Nusya told me she was very ill. She had typhus. But when she comes home, life will be different. We'll all be together."

Masha worked in the factory and saved her money. She explained to Gregory that the money would be needed when their mother came home.

Gregory worked in the factory and continued "working" in the evenings Sometimes, he gave Masha more money than she was able to make in an entire month. Masha had asked him before what kind of work he was doing, but he evaded the question. Finally, Masha stopped asking.

For some time, nothing special happened in the lives of Wanda or her children. They lived with the hope of reunion. It was the goal of their lives.

Young men asked Masha for dates, but she refused all of them. She kept her memories and feelings locked up inside her. She had started a diary some time before and wrote in it almost every day. She wrote not only about events but also her thoughts.

Two years passed. It was 1941. Wanda had two years and three months left to serve.

Gregory received his draft notice. In a year he would have to serve in the army. He had to report for a physical examination immediately. For almost a year he had little to do with his former world because the old thief died. Almost all his companions were in jail. No one had mentioned Gregory's name. He lived with Masha, who took care of him like a mother. He always had clean clothes and hot breakfasts and dinners. He helped Masha clean the apartment. The two of them were very close.

Masha and Gregory had no friends. Gregory stayed away from all the boys in the factory because his life had been so different from theirs. Like Masha, he kept his thoughts and his feelings to himself, sharing them only with her.

One evening, in the spring, Masha prepared dinner, put it on the table, and said to Gregory, "I haven't seen Nusya for a couple of weeks. I don't know where she lives. Maybe she's ill, but I can't go visit her."

Gregory sat on the sofa, leafing through a magazine. He put it down and said, "Tell me, do you ever think about why Nusya never told you where she lives or what her last name is?"

"No, it never crossed my mind," Masha answered from the kitchen.

"Come here. I'll try to explain something to you. … But maybe after dinner will be better."

After the meal, Gregory told Masha what he had been going through all those years, who Nusya was, and what she did for a living."

"Nusya was arrested," Gregory concluded, "a few weeks ago. She wasn't alone. There were a few people with her. You don't need to look for her. She's in jail."

Masha was shocked. She cried, covering her face with a handkerchief. "Don't cry," Gregory said to her. "It's all past now. Try to understand. I couldn't just leave that world. They would have killed me. You have no idea what I've been through."

Masha put all of Gregory's confession into her diary. She added her thoughts. As he told her more and more, she listened, and she no longer wept.

Wanda was allowed to receive one letter a month. She sent one each month to her children. In her letters, she described how she counted the months and the days until she could go home.

In one letter, Wanda received a photograph of Masha and Gregory. Masha sat in an armchair and Gregory stood behind.

"Oh, God," Wanda thought. "How they've grown. My son is exactly like his father, and Mashenka looks like Vladimir. Only her hair is the color of mine."

Wanda showed the picture to the women in her barracks.

"When you go home," said a woman whose bed was next to Wanda's, "Your daughter will be married and your grandchildren will be waiting for you in the train station."

"Oh, no," Wanda answered. "She's never said a word about a boyfriend. I'll ask her in my next letter."

In her letter Wanda wrote: "You're so beautiful, Mashenka. Tell me, do you have a boyfriend?" Masha answered the question, but Wanda never received Masha's letter.

N.TOREEVA

PART X

World War II began. Wanda almost had her life in order in the prison camp.

With the beginning of the war, however, she became increasingly uneasy.

According to the radio reports, the Germans had occupied Ukrainian cities, one after the other. The Russian Army was fighting desperately, to the last man, but they were forced to retreat.

War. Nothing can compare with the impact of that word. Panic. Fear. Cowardice. Heroism. Death. Everything was concentrated in that word. Trains filled with refugees from the Ukrain and Byelorussia traveled to the Ural and Siberia, deep inside Russia, far away from the German advance.

One morning, Wanda heard on the radio that the Russian Army had retreated from Odessa, and the Germans had occupied the city.

"Where are my children?" she thought. "I hope they have time to escape. Oh, God, let them be alive."

Wanda lived through more and more sleepless nights.

The factory where Gregory worked was quickly evacuated. Men eighteen years of age and older were drafted into the army. Although Gregory was not eighteen, he was notified to report for duty.

Masha saw him off and quickly prepared him for his trip. She wept. "Gregory, my dear," she said, "I beg you, write me often."

"I'll write. The war will be over soon. Take care of yourself."

The two parted. Later, Masha received a "triangle" letter, a special note without an envelope or postage. Gregory explained that he was in training and was well.

A few days after Masha received the letter, Odessa was occupied by the Germans. A few weeks later, the Rumanian Army took over from them. Odessa was a gift from Hitler to the Rumanian queen.

Life in the city was stilled. People were afraid to leave their homes because they did not know what to expect. Only women, children, and old men remained. Little by little, however, life returned to normal. All over the city banners proclaimed that "free trade" was allowed. "All Jews," other banners ordered, "must register with the gendarmes." The Rumanian authorities placed army officers in people's apartments wherever there was an extra room.

Someone knocked on Masha's door. When she opened it, she saw the yardkeeper and, next to her, a young Rumanian officer.

"You have an extra room, and you live by yourself," the yardkeeper said to Masha. "You must share your apartment with this officer. He speaks a little Russian. You're a quiet girl. You won't cause any disturbance."

Masha stepped aside without saying anything. The officer entered with his bags. Masha showed him to Gregory's room, gave him a key, and went to her room.

That evening, in her diary, she wrote down everything that had happened. Later, she went to the kitchen and made tea. The officer entered the kitchen and placed some packages on the table.

"This is something to eat," he said with a heavy accent."

"I don't need anything," Masha answered. She left the room.

The officer stopped her and gestured toward a chair. Masha sat down and looked directly into his eyes.

He was a good looking, dark complexioned man with brown eyes. If Masha had not know he was a Rumanian, she would have thought he was Ukrainian.

"I don't want to harm you," he said. "At home I left my mother and two sisters. I'll treat you like a sister. If you cook for me, I'll be very pleased. While I live here, you're safe. You're young and beautiful. You don't know soldiers. Sometimes, they're like animals. Let's have some tea."

He smiled. His Russian was not bad.

"Where did you learn Russian?" Masha asked as they sipped tea.

"In Bucharest. I was a student in the university, and I knew a Russian musician. He played and sang in a restaurant. He left Russia in 1921, and I practiced my Russian with him."

Masha was lucky. The yardkeeper had given her a good Rumanian. She was no longer frightened. She wrote down her conversation with him and her thoughts about it.

His name was Irzhy. He worked in the army's Odessa headquarters. He brought home groceries from the commissary, and Masha prepared the meals for both of them. Often, they spent the evening together.

More and more, Masha discovered what Irzhy's interests had been before the war. However, she told him nothing about herself.

Life in Odessa passed normally. People opened shops, small stores, and flea markets, where anything could be bought or sold.

No one knew where the Jews were kept. People only knew they were confined to some kind of ghetto. There was no communication with them. Masha wrote in her diary, "I met a woman from our block in the city market. She told me that all the Jews are kept on the edge of town. All the apartments they left have been taken over by neighbors who wished to move or wanted more space. Everything the Jews left behind was taken by the neighbors who often fought over possession, whether they needed the things or not. They grabbed furniture, dishes, lamps, anything they could carry away. I'm frightened just thinking about it. People never learn."

Masha hid her diary under her mattress, showed it to no one, and told no one what she wrote in it. Often, she made entries about Irzhy.

"He's twenty-eight years old," she wrote, "intelligent, and kind. Sometimes, we talk all evening, and I forget he's Rumanian and supposed to be an enemy. But I feel he's a good person. He treats me as an equal. We spend long winter evenings together."

In another entry, she wrote, "I catch myself liking Irzhy, and I feel he likes me, too."

The entries became more frequent, and they described her feelings and his behavior.

"Yesterday evening," Masha wrote, "we drank tea and listened to music. Irzhy took my hand and said, 'Masha, I like you a lot. I rush home to see you and spend time with you. If you can, come with me to Bucharest and meet my parents.' I answered, 'We can't even think about that.' He asked me what the reason was. I couldn't tell him. I was afraid to explain I have a brother in the army and that my mother is in a prison camp."

"He asked me, 'Maybe you have a boyfriend in the army? You've given him your word that you will wait for him?'"

"'I don't have a boyfriend,' I said, 'but my brother is in the army.'"

"Irzhy asked me, 'What are you afraid of? I'm not your enemy. War is war, and we're all soldiers.'"

A few days later, Masha wrote, "I must stay away from him and hate him. But I confess to myself that he's so close to me, and I love him."

A week later, she added, "I agreed to go with him to Rumania. I can just imagine how the neighbors will gossip about me if they find out. How can I explain to anyone that he's a good person, not an enemy. He promised me that we'll leave at night. I'll wait for him at the train station. No one will see us leaving together."

Masha went with Irzhy to Rumania, and they were married in Bucharest. Before she left, Masha wrote in her diary, explaining how Irzhy's parents were preparing for the couple's arrival.

In the last entry, she wrote, "My dear mother: If you only knew how happy I am. But I miss you and Gregory very much. Irzhy will be a good husband. He knows everything that happened to you. He feels sorry for me. We love each other."

The diary was filled to the last page. Masha placed it in a box, wrapped it, and tied it to the back of Wanda's portrait, the same portrait that showed Wanda looking like a princess. She put the portrait in a pillow case and wrapped it in the blanket.

When Masha left with Irzhy, no one saw them, but they guessed what had happened.

Odessa was occupied by the Rumanians until March of 1944. They retreated then, and the Germans returned, but for only three weeks. During that three weeks, every Jew in the ghetto was exterminated. Suspected communists, communist sympathizers, and partisans were lynched and left to hang from the light poles for several days to frighten the inhabitants of the city. Partisans hid in the catacombs. It was almost impossible to find them in that labyrinth.

On April 10, 1944, Odessa was liberated. The Russian Army marched into the city, hurling the Germans westward. All-Union Radio reported that Odessa was free.

Wanda received the news a year after she was freed from the prison camp. She had left the camp in the spring of 1943. Because Odessa was occupied, she had to find a job in a factory in Ural. She worked a year, saving every copeck[7]. Finally, when Odessa was freed, Wanda was free. She was free of overwork, humiliation, and fear for her life. She had survived because of her one hope—to see her children again.

Wanda bought a train ticket. With it, she received a pass, made necessary by the war and marshall law. She decided not to buy anything else and to take all her money with her. All her belongings she carried in a small, wooden trunk. In a small purse she kept her documents, letters from the children, and money.

The train took her from the severe cold of Ural to the Ukraine, but she had to change trains in Moscow.

She was very thin and looked exhausted. She wore a gray, coarse coat and a kerchief around her hair. She looked like an old lady, but she was only fifty-four. No one could have said she was the same Wanda that she was as an appealing, beautiful woman.

The train stopped. The controller checked her passport and her travel pass to Odessa. When he opened her passport, he saw the stamp that indicated Wanda had spent time in prison camp.

"I see you got what you asked for and served the full term," the controller said.

Wanda did not answer. She took her papers from him and put them in her purse. She knew that her past would not leave her.

But it was not important. What mattered was that she was going to Odessa and that she would see her children. After that, she could die.

Moscow. The train arrived late at night. Wanda walked to the platform. She had to register her ticket to Odessa. She approached a militiaman.

"Please tell me, where can I register a ticket to Odessa?" she asked.

"Do you see the crowd at cashier's window four?" he replied. "That's the place."

When Wanda walked closer, she saw hundreds of people at every window.

She stood in line and asked an older man in front of her if he was the last.

"How long will it be?" she asked him.

"I've already been here three days. The window will close soon and open again at nine in the morning."

"Oh, God. Is it possible to stand so long in line?"

"This is nothing, citizen. You should be thankful. Odessa is free. Thank God the Russian Army drove out the Fascists. We've waited this long; we can wait a few days more.

Wanda wrote her name on a list. When the window closed, people found places on the station benches to sleep until morning. Wanda found a space large enough to sit but not to lie down. She placed her trunk under her feet and put her purse inside her coat. She fell asleep.

She dreamed, and in the dream she saw herself walking on the seashore. Tadeush walked on one side of her, Vladimir on the other. It was spring. Acacias bloomed. She felt light, wonderful. The three of them stopped and watched the waves.

Suddenly, Wanda saw the waves carrying a doll from crest to crest toward them. The waves slammed the doll against the seacliff and carried it away again. It was the same doll she had thrown away years before.

"Save the doll," she screamed to the man walking with her.

"That's not a doll," someone said. "It's a child. How can we save it? The cliff is too steep."

"Please help. The child will drown," Wanda cried.

Wanda awoke to the sound of her own screams. A woman sitting next to her was shaking her by the shoulder.

"You had a bad dream," the woman said. "You were screaming, 'help.' Oh, this terrible war. We'll still be having bad dreams for some time."

Wanda looked at the woman, not understanding right away what she was talking about. She closed her eyes and thought about how she could explain that she had never seen the war, but that some things in life are just as frightening as war.

"They got rid of the Fascists in our city," the woman said. "Pretty soon the war will be over. Where are you going?"

"To Odessa," Wanda answered quietly.

"That's a coincidence. I'm going there, too. I was going on vacation to visit my parents when the war started. My vacation was much longer than I'd planned. You came from Ural also?"

"Yes. I worked there," Wanda evaded.

"You're by yourself, and I'm by myself. We can go to Odessa together and help each other pass the time."

"Yes, you're right."

They introduced themselves. The woman's name was Anna. When Wanda said her name, Anna asked, "Are you Polish by birth?"

"Yes. I was born in Poland, but I've lived in Odessa since 1905."

After an hour, Wanda knew Anna's entire biography. She had told very little about herself—only that she had a daughter and son in Odessa.

In only two days, Wanda and Anna had registered their tickets and found a place on the train. They were lucky. Some people waited for more than a week.

Wanda found a seat by the window. Anna took an upper berth. She began a conversation immediately with an older, gray-bearded man across from her. He called her "daughter."

Anna was very short and very petite. Her light hair was short-cut and made her face look like a child's. She was forty years old. Next to her, Wanda looked like an old woman.

The train rolled slowly from Moscow to Odessa. It made many stops at intermediate stations. After five days, it arrived in Odessa. The aisles were filled with bags and knapsacks. Documents were checked a few more times.

Anna had sent a telegram to her sister, and her sister was waiting for her at the station. No one waited for Wanda. After eleven years, she had returned to the city where she had been both very happy and very unhappy. She had been both very rich and very poor. What did the city hold for her now? Had it saved her children? They were all she had in her life.

She could tell no one the story of her life. If she were to start talking, she would have to relive her grief. It was better to remain silent. No one could help her anyway. Everyone had his own life and problems. She was used to being quiet. She never started a conversation.

The train arrived in Odessa late in the afternoon during a spring shower.

Anna recognized her sister on the platform, jumped up, and ran to her, crying.

They hugged each other, both of them weeping.

Wanda watched them with mixed feelings - - fear, happiness, pain, and hope. She did not say good-bye to Anna. Instead, she walked around her to the exit. Anna, however, saw Wanda, and she stopped her.

"Where are you going, Wanda?" Anna asked. "Let me introduce you to my sister. She was unfortunate enough to have to stay here during the occupation."

"I'm Valentina," Anna's sister said. "Believe me, occupation wasn't so bad. Life was much better than it is now. You could buy everything."

"Keep quiet," Anna whispered. "Somebody might hear you. That's just what we need."

"I say the truth," Valentina said, smiling.

"Maybe so, but nobody needs to hear it. Do you know how many people have spent time in Ural and Siberia for saying the truth?"

The three women walked to the exit together.

"Where do you live, Wanda?" Valentina asked.

"I don't know. I have an address where my daughter lives. I sent a telegram, but perhaps she didn't receive it."

Wanda gave Valentina the piece of an envelope containing Masha's address. She could not give her the entire envelope. It would have shown that Wanda had been in prison camp.

"We're going the same way, but you'll get off first," Valentina said. "The trolley line is not repaired yet. We use horses and carriages. One will be enough for all of us."

While they were riding, Anna gave Wanda her address.

Wanda left them at the address Masha had given her. The sisters continued on. Wanda had tried to pay them, but they would not accept her money.

"We don't need your money," Anna had said. "We're going the same way." The carriage moved away, and Anna said, "Let me know how you're doing." Wanda waved as the carriage left.

She approached the door to Masha's apartment and knocked. The door was half open. An old lady with a white kerchief on her head asked, "Who are you looking for?"

"I'm looking for Masha Stanishevsky. Does she live here?"

"No, she doesn't live here anymore. She's been gone for over a year, nobody knows where."

The old lady opened the door wider and said, "A young Rumanian lived here. When he moved out, nobody saw Masha anymore. Who are you to her?"

"I'm a relative. I came from far away. Did she leave anything? A note?" Wanda could barely breathe as she waited for an answer.

"Some of her belongings are still in storage. I haven't touched anything. Who knows? Things change. We've been through so many changes. You can follow me. I'll show you the closet where her things are."

Wanda followed her down a corridor. The woman pulled a bar back from across a door and opened it. The closet was large. On a shelf, Wanda saw dishes, pots, cups, plates. On the floor she saw some boxes, and behind the boxes was a large, flat package wrapped in a blanket. Wanda recognized the blanket.

"I covered her with that blanket," she said. "It's a child's blanket with animals on it." She began crying and slumped against the wall.

"Who are you to her?" the old lady asked again.

Wanda turned to her. Her face, which had been so beautiful before, now looked tortured. "I'm her mother," she said, whispering. "It's possible I've lost my children forever."

"Come inside," the woman said. "I'll make tea. You can rest." She guided Wanda into her apartment and helped her sit down.

"My name is Eugena," she said. "Gena for short."

"My name is Wanda Stanishevsky. You can call me Wanda."

It is not easy to explain what Wanda felt in her heart. All those years, she had hoped to see her children. She was so sure they were waiting for her and she would find them. What now?

Gena returned from the kitchen with tea and pastries.

"Sit down at the table," she said. "We'll have some tea and talk."

Wanda held her cup with both hands to warm them. It was not cold, but she felt cold inside.

"I'm a widow," said Gena. "My husband died before the war, and I lived with my sister in one, small room in this building. My sister died in the winter of nineteen forty-two. I couldn't live in that room anymore after she died. Her voice followed me. I felt as though her shadow was following me. I thought I'd go crazy. When Masha left this apartment, I moved in. Masha was a courteous, quiet girl. The neighbors gossiped because the young Rumanian lived in the same apartment, but nobody saw them together outside of the apartment. Tell me, how did it happen that you were so far away from Odessa when the war started?"

"I worked in Ural. That's all I can say."

Gena asked no more questions. She understood Wanda did not want to talk about herself. Gene saw how upset Wanda was.

"You can stay here overnight," Gena invited. "It's already evening. There's enough space, and you've had a long journey."

"Thank you very much. It's very kind of you. I have no place to go today. Tomorrow, I'll try to find something."

Gena prepared a bed for Wanda. Wanda freshened up, lay down, and fell asleep immediately. When she awoke, she saw light through the window. Gena was cooking something. Wanda fixed her bed and went into the kitchen.

"Good morning, Gena," she said. "What time is it?"

"It's ten o'clock. I didn't want to wake you. You were so tired."

"I don't remember when I've slept so soundly."

"Let's have breakfast. I've made fried potatoes and omelets. I have fresh bread and butter."

"Thank you, Gena. I have to wash. I'll be right back."

Wanda washed her face, and while she washed, she wept. She thought, "Where is Masha? Where is Gregory? The war is not over. I still have hope."

She dried her face and walked back to the kitchen.

The women sat at the kitchen table and ate breakfast, two women with very different pasts. Neither had had an easy life, but they held on to their warmth and their ability to care for people. They ate quietly, each thinking her own thoughts. Wanda was trying to decide what to do next, where to go.

Gena interrupted the silence, as if she had read Wanda's mind and was answering her question.

"Wanda, you can stay here. There's enough room for the two of us. You're alone, and I'm alone. Together, we won't be so lonely. Do you agree?"

Wanda's hand began to shake. Her tea spilled as she tried to replace the cup in its saucer.

"God bless you," she said. "I'll repay you for your kindness."

She stood, walked around the table, and hugged Gena. Both of them were crying. After the bitterness of their lives, each had a hope. They did not have to fear loneliness.

The war was coming to an end. People who had evacuated were returning. Wanda found a job as a school janitor. She lived with Gena as if she were a sister. They helped each other, sharing their time. They got along very well, each giving in to the other. Both were kind.

One weekend, Wanda was free from work, and she decided to clean out the closet. She threw away what could not be used and rearranged what could be used. In the closet, she found her portrait. When she unwrapped it, she found Masha's diary on the back. She was elated to have something of Masha's, and she read it through.

"Who's this in the portrait?" Gena asked.

"Me. I'm not easy to recognize. I was seventeen then."

"Oh, God. You were so beautiful."

"I don't believe I looked like that myself."

They hung the portrait. The room looked brighter for the addition.

"You're from rich society, Wanda," Gena observed. "I can tell from your clothes and the way you handle yourself."

"Yes, Gena. That was a long time ago. Now it's only a memory, and it seems like a novel I read many years ago. Someday, perhaps I can tell you about my past life, but not now. I can't talk about it yet."

When Wanda read Masha's diary, she knew Masha was in Rumania with Irzhy. She was happy to know her daughter was still alive and that God had sent her a good man for a husband. When the war was over, Masha would return to Odessa.

Wanda's spirits improved. She began to smile. Little by little, she returned to normal. She even went to the dentist and ordered dentures to replace her missing teeth. She began to eat and to regain her weight. Gena lived on a pension, but it was minimal. Wanda's small wage was twice Gena's pension. By combining their incomes, the two women managed to buy enough food to live. In the evenings, Gena knitted and Wanda read. They communicated very little with their neighbors, preferring each other's company.

Once, after evening tea, Gena sat in her armchair and Wanda turned on the radio. They listened to the soft music. Suddenly, Gena started to talk about the occupation, although she had not wanted to talk about it before.

"I'll never forget how very cold the winter was when the Jews were marched down the streets," she began. "There were old men, women, and children. As long as I've lived in Odessa, I don't remember such a chill wind and so much snow. The people walked with yellow, six-pointed stars sewn to their clothes. Some of the old people could barely walk at all. The gendarmes yelled, 'Schnell! Schnell!'

"I remember so clearly a woman walking and holding a little girl, maybe four or five years old, by the hand. On her other side was a bent old man with a long, gray beard. The little girl had a fur coat, muff, and hat. Everybody in the neighborhoods watched the people march, even though it was so cold.

"Where they took the Jews, nobody knows. The signs on the buildings said that all Jews had to report to the authorities. The authorities put the yellow stars on them. People on the streets whispered. Children asked questions and received no answers."

"Suddenly, from the crowd, a few steps from me, a woman ran to the little girl and tore off her coat and muff and hat and left her only her dress. It happened so fast that nobody realized at first what had occurred."

"The little girl's mother took off her wool shawl, wrapped it around the little girl, and tied it behind her. The column of people seemed to stop to let the mother tend to her child. The little girl was crying because she was frightened.

"The mother was a young, beautiful woman. When she finished wrapping the shawl around her daughter, she turned to talk to the woman who tore off the girl's coat.

"'I curse you!' she said. 'Do you hear me?'"

"The column started to move, and no one heard what else she said. The whole crowd looked at the woman who held the fur coat.

"I remember how everybody screamed at her, calling her names. She answered, 'What are you screaming about? All these Jews are walking to their execution. They don't need warm coats.'"

"The crowd would not let her get away, but she pushed her way through. I recognized. She lived in the building next to mine. When she left, somebody said, 'She's a school teacher. Can you imagine how she teaches children?'"

"Later, we found out they took the Jews to the ghetto." Wanda listened, and tears fell from her eyes.

"What happened to those people in the ghetto?" she asked, wiping her tears away.

"Two weeks before the Soviet Army came, the Germans came. The Rumanians had left. During those two weeks, they turned everything upside down. The gunfire was non-stop. Almost nobody went out on the street. All the Jews were exterminated."

"How could that woman look anyone in the face after stealing that little girl's coat in the cold winter?"

"She's not alive," Gena said. "A week after that happened, she slipped on the steps and fractured her skull. She was in a coma for ten days before she died. Try not to believe in damnation!"

"No I don't know what to believe in this world," Wanda said. "If everything happens by the law of requital, then why do honest people suffer, and nothing happens to cruel, mean people? I grew up a Catholic in a religious tradition. It's still inside me, but after everything I've been through, it's not as strong as before."

"My parents were not religious at all," Gena said. My father was in the Communist Party from nineteen hundred and five, and my mother was a communist sympathizer. Father died of tuberculosis when we were little, and Mother raised us by herself. Mother always believed in my father's ideas. Even in nineteen thirty-seven, when her brother, an old man, was arrested and executed for being an enemy of the nation, she said it was a misunderstanding.

"Soon after he was shot, she died. A few days later, we received a note to her from the KGB, telling her to report to them. Of course, my sister and I were shocked. We didn't think about reporting to the KGB that she had died.

"A day later—can you imagine—a blackbird stopped in front of our building. A few men in KGB uniforms came to our door and knocked very hard. I opened it, and they asked if Citizen Granova lived there. When they found out she was dead, they asked for the death certificate. When I showed it to them, I said, 'Mother was seventy-six years old. You'd arrest her if she were still alive?' One of them answered, 'An enemy of the nation is an enemy, no matter what age.' Then they were gone."

"Maybe it's better that Mama died of natural causes. She could never have survived arrest. I heard the conditions in jail were terrible. Some people died before their trials."

Wanda said nothing. She thought, "Gena is right. Jail is awful. But jail for political prisoners is much worse."

Gena and Wanda spent evenings together listening to the radio and talking. Gena liked to knit, and Wanda enjoyed reading. They had no one, no relatives or close friends.

Victory Day came, May 9, 1945. The radio announcer, Levitan, reported victory over Fascist Germany. People stood in groups in the square and listened.

A long awaited victory! With victory came hope of the return home of relatives and friends.

"I believe my children can come home now," Wanda said. "I'd like only to look at them. That's all I need."

Gena had no one to wait for, but she was happy for Wanda.

"I won't be in the way when your children come back?" Gena asked.
"Oh, no, Gena. You're like a sister to me. You won't ever be in the way." They waited every day for a letter, for any kind of news, but days and weeks passed and there was no word.

The soldiers came home. The sounds of harmonicas and accordions were heard in apartment buildings everywhere, celebrating the soldiers' return.

"Why don't you go to the military office and find out what unit your son was with?" Gena asked Wanda. "Maybe they know where he is now."

"I've thought about it," Wanda answered, "but I'm so frightened of what they will say. Perhaps it would be better to wait a couple more weeks. Gregory will come back."

After a few months, Wanda decided to talk to the military authorities. She and Gena went to the office together because Wanda was afraid to go alone.

The waiting room was packed with people. Gena and Wanda waited two hours before they were allowed into the office.

Wanda filled out a form, answering all the questions, except one. She did not know exactly when Gregroy entered the Army. An officer explained that she could go home, and they would let her know what they found out.

The days dragged by. Wanda cleaned classrooms and lobbies early in the morning and late in the evening. When she arrived home, she asked Gena the same question every day: "What's in the mail?"

Gena shook her head every day: "Nothing yet."

Two months later, when Wanda and Gena were both home, the mailman brought a letter from the military office. Wanda took the envelope and gave it to Gena.

"Please open it and read it for me," she said. "I'm afraid."

Gena held the envelope, hesitating, and looked at Wanda. After a minute or so, she opened the envelope and started to read: ". . . Gregory Vinar has been missing since January, 1943."

"How missing?" Wanda blurted. "What do they mean by 'missing?'" She dropped onto the sofa and began to sob loudly.

"Wanda, dear, calm down," Gena said. "'Missing' does not mean 'killed.' Maybe he was wounded and changed units. In this war, anything could happen."

Wanda wiped her tears away and said, quietly, "Why am I punished so? I suffered many times in my life, and maybe I'm still alive only because I had hope of being with my children. When I came to Odessa, I was sure they'd be waiting for me. But life is the master of my destiny."

"You've waited so long, Wanda. You wait a little longer. The war is over; that's important."

"I have to wait again and keep my hope. Oh, Gena, it's so hard. Maybe Mashenka will come home. I've got nothing left. All I can do is wait."

In the evening, they drank tea and listened to the radio.

"The war with Japan is not over yet," Gena said, "so much grief has come in our time. Do you remember the revolution, Wanda?"

"It would be much better if I could forget and remember only the good moments in my life. The revolution took my husband, took everything I had, and left me with a little child in my arms. Why didn't I die with Vladimir? Let's talk about something else, please."

"All right. What can we talk about? Maybe you know an interesting story. You read a lot. I like to listen to you talk while I knit."

"I remember a silent movie a long time ago. I'd like to see it again. I remember two of them very clearly. One was Alpine Flower, and the other was Monastery Bells. Do you remember them, Gena?"

"About love, beautiful and tender love. I recall those movies because they ended tragically."

"Why did they call the one Alpine Flower? Did it happen in the Alps?"

"No, Gena. The girl in the movie was so fragile and beautiful that she was called Alpine Flower. In the Alps, the flowers are unusually beautiful, but they're very sensitive. If you touch them, they fade immediately. That is the theme of the movie. I remember I cried when I saw that movie."

"That's strange. I don't recall that title. We're almost the same age."

"Oh, God, I forgot. I saw the movie in Paris."

"You've been to Paris? Where else have you been outside of Russia?"

"It was a long time ago, before the revolution, even before the first war. I took art lessons in Paris, and my honeymoon was in Italy. We spent a month there. Life was so different then. It seems like a dream to me, but I still remember after all these years."

"Wanda, I have a question for you. You're an educated woman. Why do you work as a janitor? You could find an office job easily."

"No, Gena. It's better as it is. A janitor doesn't need to explain her past in an application and answer all the questions about the society she came from. Cleaning classrooms is not very difficult. I'm used to it now. The money I make, thank God, is enough for us, but if we need to spend more, I still have the money I brought from Ural. I can add it to what we have."

During all their free evenings, Wanda told Gena stories from the books she had read and the films she had seen.

"You have an excellent memory, Wanda," Gena said once, "and a talent for storytelling. I like to listen to you."

"Thank you, Gena. What's important is to have someone who can listen." Months passed. There was no word from Masha or Gregory. Wanda began to lose hope. She understood Masha could not return because people who were captured by the Germans were called enemies of the nation when they returned. They were sent from the train station directly to jail. Masha was not captured. She left on her own. Perhaps no one knew, or perhaps Wanda only wished no one knew.

Wanda grew very nervous. She could not tell stories anymore. She read more and more, trying not to think.

Two years passed after the war. The year 1947 brought a bad harvest after the devastating war. A fearful hunger came. Food coupons were once again distributed to working people, fewer for dependents and pensioners. Money was worthless. A loaf of bread cost a hundred rubles. Everywhere people stood in line for everything. A bar of soap was like gold. People peeled potatoes and sold the peels.

In the market, American food products appeared: canned ham, coffee, and candy. The black market was booming. People traded their jewelry, fabrics, and shoes for food.

All the money Wanda had made in Ural, the money she had saved for three years, was spent on groceries in 1947.

"Wanda, dear," Gena pleaded, "this is your money. Don't spend it on me. I can survive on bread and water."

"Don't hurt my feelings," Wanda answered. "Why do I need this money? I saved it because I thought I could spend it on my children. Now I know they won't come back, even if I wait for them for the rest of my life. This money, Gena, can help us and be very useful. We can have a piece of meat and butter for our bread. I understand life differently now. I live today. I won't worry about tomorrow anymore. If I die tomorrow, that will be fine because my life has no meaning anymore.

"But that's enough philosophy. Let's have supper. We have herring, boiled potatoes, fresh bread and butter, and tea with honey. Even the manager of a factory would envy us for having a supper like that."

They survived 1947. When the year was over, the money was gone. Money had been devalued. For ten old rubles, one new ruble was given. The Soviet Union received help from the United States and bought grain. In 1948, the country had a good harvest. The economy improved, but people remembered the terrible hunger.

Wanda recalled 1921, 1933, and 1947. She and Gena welcomed the new year by sharing a bottle of wine.

"Happy New Year, Gena," Wanda said, holding up her glass, "and good health."

"Thanks to you, Wanda, we survived. May God grant we live a long time in good health. But I'm afraid to drink. I have high blood pressure. For fifteen years, I haven't touched alcohol."

"Just take a sip. This is a holiday, the New Year. It's not just any day. I can't remember the last time I drank, but today I want it."

Wanda drank an entire glass of wine, Gena only a quarter glass. Soon, Wanda felt inebriated and went to sleep.

In the morning, she went to the kitchen while Gena slept. It was a holiday, and Wanda would not work for ten days while the children were out of school for winter vacation.

She decided to prepare breakfast while Gena slept. On the kitchen table was the bottle of wine left over from the day before. She poured herself a glass and felt better after drinking it. She no longer felt the boundless sorrow. The night before, she had felt better after a glass of wine. Her mood improved; she could talk freely. She drank more and finished the bottle.

The liquor went to her legs. She found it difficult to walk, so she staggered to the sofa and fell asleep.

Gena awoke, went to the kitchen, and found the tea kettle boiled dry. Wanda was not there.

"Where are you, Wanda?" Gena called. "Today's a holiday. You're not supposed to go to work."

When she walked toward Wanda's room, Gena saw Wanda on the sofa, one arm hanging to the floor. She was frightened.

"Oh, God. What happened to you?" Gena took Wanda's hand and felt for her pulse. It was normal.

Wanda opened her eyes and saw Gena, as if through a fog. She did not understand what Gena wanted. She was still drunk. When Wanda rolled over on her side, Gena smelled the alcohol. She went to the kitchen and saw the empty bottle.

After a few hours, Wanda woke up and staggered to the kitchen. Gena prepared strong coffee and gave it to Wanda without speaking. Wanda drank the coffee and spoke first.

"Thank you, Gena, for the coffee. I finished the wine this morning. I was so depressed. When I finished it, I felt much better, but I fell asleep."

"Alcohol doesn't help anybody. It's not good for your health. But today is New Year's Day; it's an exception."

"Maybe Mashenka will come home this year. What do you think, Gena?" Wanda began to cry, and continued, "No, she's not alive. If she were still alive, she would have come a long time ago. She knew how I waited for her. And my son won't ever come home. All this is wrong. This year will bring nothing to me."

Wanda wept, sobbing loudly, and Gena let her. She knew Wanda would feel better afterward.

Little by little, Wanda calmed down. She washed her face and said, "Let's go for a walk. It's nice today. The air is fresh."

They walked slowly down the street. The sun was shining, and it was dry.

Only a few passersby were out.

"Winter is completely different in Ural," Wanda said. "There's a lot of snow, and the temperature can be forty below. Nobody walks on the street in January. Only young people are out, throwing snowballs for a short while. Then they run home. In temperatures like that, your ears and face can be frostbitten, and you won't even know it."

"I've lived all my life in Odessa," Gena said. "I haven't seen a big difference over the years. A few times, I remember, it was very cold, but only for a week or so. Most of the time, we only got light snow or rain.

I've always wanted to go somewhere else, see different places, but when he was alive, my husband always said, 'Everybody comes to Odessa for vacation. We don't need to go anywhere.'"

An hour later, they returned to their apartment. The next morning, Wanda went to the grocery store. The choices at the store were not large. She walked to the liquor section and bought another bottle of wine. Something inside her said, "Don't buy it," but another something told her, "Take a bottle. If you drink a little, you'll feel better and forget everything."

At home, Wanda took a box of spaghetti, bread, and sausage from the basket. She left the wine inside. She boiled the spaghetti, fried the sausage, and called Gena to eat.

Gena began to eat, but Wanda waited. She wanted some wine before dinner.

but she did not know how to explain to Gena.

"I almost forgot," she said. "I have a bottle of wine in the basket."

She stood, walked quickly to the kitchen, and brought back the bottle and two glasses.

"Why do you need the wine, Wanda?" Gena asked. "You had some yesterday and the day before. Today is an ordinary day."

"I've heard of people who live in the Caucasus who drink wine every day. Those people are very healthy, and everyone knows wine is good for you."

"Yes, I've heard of that. But they drink young wine they make themselves. There's almost no alcohol. You're drinking a strong wine."

Wanda opened the bottle and drank by herself.

Gena drank tea and said nothing. What could she say? Wanda was an adult and should know what she was doing.

Wanda felt giddy. She saw everything differently. She was not alone with her grief. She saw herself very young in Paris, drawing. In another scene, she was in Italy with Tadeush. It was like yesterday. She enjoyed her memories. She poured one more glass of wine and saw a different picture.

Jail. Prison camp. All the happiness was gone. She saw only the terrifying life before her. She began to weep and tried to speak, but she was incoherent. She motioned as if to push something fearful away.

Gena helped Wanda to her bed, and Wanda collapsed, drunk.

Wanda awoke at five o'clock in the morning with a terrible headache. At first, she thought she would make coffee, but she changed her mind. Instead, she filled a large glass with wine and drank it like water, as if to quench a thirst. She returned to her room, lay down on her bed, and asked herself, "Why am I drinking? What's happened to me?"

But the thought flew away quickly, and she fell asleep again.

Gena saw what had happened to Wanda, but she thought that Wanda would stop when she returned to work. It was true. When Wanda started to work, she did not drink every day. Early in the morning, she went to the school, moved desks, cleaned blackboards, and came home very tired, almost too weak to drink. Over time, however, she regained her strength.

Once, Wanda awoke at three in the morning and prepared to go to work. She heard Gena moaning. Wanda walked to Gena's room and asked, "What's wrong? Are you feeling badly?" Gena continued to moan and did not answer. Wanda thought Gena was dreaming. She turned on the light, looked at Gena, and began to scream.

Gena's face was twisted. One eye was half open, the other open wide.

"Oh, God. What can I do?" Wanda thought as she paced the room frantically, confused.

Finally, she decided to call an ambulance. She ran to the street. A pay phone was on the corner. Luckily, it was working. Twenty minutes later, the ambulance arrived.

The ambulance carried three people, a doctor and two attendants. As the doctor checked Gena, Wanda looked from one to the other. The doctor was a middle-aged woman with dark hair and an open, but tired, face.

"What can I say?" the doctor began. Then she sat down in a chair. She asked Wanda, "Who are you? A neighbor or a relative?"

"I'm her cousin. She doesn't have anyone as close as I am." It was the first thing that came to Wanda's mind.

"Is your cousin left handed?"

"Yes, she is."

"She's paralyzed on the right side, and she can't talk. Did she complain about anything recently?"

"Yes. Almost every day she told me she had a headache."

"Yes. She had a stroke. A blood vessel broke in her brain. I'm sorry, but we can't take her to the hospital. We don't recommend moving a patient like this. Can you take care of her?"

"Of course," Wanda said, and then she began to cry.

"I'll send a report to her doctor. In the morning, he will explain what you need to do."

The doctor and the attendants left. Wanda stayed with Gena. She did not go to work that morning.

At nine o'clock, the doctor arrived and gave Wanda a prescription for Gena. "Doctor," Wanda asked, "can you stay with her for ten minutes? I have to go to the corner to buy the medicine."

"Yes, go ahead. I don't have any more calls this morning."

Wanda almost ran to the drugstore. The pharmacist told her to wait for fifteen or twenty minutes.

On the same block was a grocery store. Wanda bought some wheat cereal for Gena and a bottle of wine for herself.

"I must not think about Gena's misfortune," she thought. "I have to drink a little and try to forget about it."

She went home soon afterward and talked to the doctor.

"Thank you for waiting, doctor."

"You're welcome. Give her this medicine every four hours. Feed her only liquids by teaspoon, bullion, puree, and wheat cereal. I'll visit her."

Wanda walked the doctor to the door and thanked her again. Then she cooked the wheat cereal, let it cool, and started to feed Gena. She had enough patience. She remembered Esther had suffered the same affliction.

Wanda slowly grew used to the change in her life. Early in the morning, she went to the school and cleaned classrooms. Then she returned home, washed Gena, moved her to prevent bedsores, and fed her. Every day, Wanda drank a bottle of wine.

She no longer fell asleep. The wine to her was indispensable. When she prepared meals for Gena, she poured a glass of wine for herself. She always ate something after she drank. She fed Gena as if she were a baby and told her stories she had read or that she had actually experienced in her own life.

"You know, Gena, how I love to read French novels," Wanda said once. "My favorite was by Honore de Balzac. In school, I took French, and when I lived in Paris I had practice speaking it. I know French better than Russian. Tadeush had a huge library, many, many French novels. When he left on business, and I was alone, I read and read."

Wanda finished feeding Gena, went to the kitchen, washed the dishes, and sipped more wine. Then she returned to Gena.

"Today's Sunday," she said. "I can tell you a story from Balzac's Human Comedy."

She sat on a chair next to Gena and started to relate "Father Gorio."

Wanda was drunk, but she began to tell the story. Her tongue was thick. She looked not at Gena but at the window where a geranium grew. She stared at the red flowers.

"Gena. Did you see? The geranium has started to bloom. A few years we've had this plant, and it has never bloomed. This is a special event. I believe you'll be feeling better. You've been in bed for seven months without any change."

She looked at Gena and knew immediately that something was wrong. Gena's mouth was open, her eyes were glassy, and she was very still. For a long time, Gena had been immobile, but Wanda could see emotion in Gena's face.

Wanda took Gena's wrist. There was no pulse. She put her ear to Gena's chest. Gena was not breathing. She had died very quietly as Wanda told the story.

"What will I do now?" Wanda said, weeping. "You've left me alone. Who will I talk to now?"

Wanda closed Gena's eyes and went to call a doctor.

It was late autumn when Gena's funeral was held. A few neighbors followed the coffin to the funeral. Wanda cried quietly. A strong wind blew, spinning the leaves; they fell on the coffin as it was lowered into the grave. Wanda dropped a handful of soil onto the coffin and stepped aside.

"This is it," she thought. "This was a person, but not anymore."

At home, she finished a full bottle of wine and fell asleep on the sofa. Someone knocked very hard on the door and woke her. She did not know right away where she was. She stumbled to the door.

"Who's there?" she asked, opening the door until the chain caught and held. "The Domicile Committee. Open up."

Wanda removed the chain. One woman and two men, looking very official, entered. Wanda believed she was about to be arrested.

"You live here alone?" the woman asked in a hoarse voice. She looked like man.

"Yes. I'm alone now, since Gena died." Wanda's head was buzzing. She did not know how long she had slept.

"That's why we came," said a short man in military boots and riding breeches. "You live in this apartment without an order."

Wanda looked at him and did not understand what he was trying to say. She blinked rapidly, trying to focus on him.

"All right. What can we do now? Can you give me an order?"

"You don't understand," said a hunched, balding, older man. "We can't give you an order because you live alone. This is a big apartment just for you."

"Furthermore," the woman said, "we have information that you spent some time in jail. That's another reason we can't give you an order."

Wanda's head cleared immediately. "Yes, but my sentence was finished. I had a pass to go to Odessa. I've lived here almost five years. I've harmed no one."

"Tell me, Citizen Stanishevsky," the hoarse voice went on, "a young woman lived in this apartment. She ran away with a Rumanian officer before the Soviet Army came. By chance, was she a relative?"

Wanda's heart beat rapidly. "How do they know?" she thought. Aloud, she said, "No, I have no relatives. I'm alone." She sat on the sofa.

The three looked at her and at each other. The man in riding breeches broke the silence.

"Citizen Stanishevsky, we of the Domicile Committee give you three days to pack all your belongings and find another place."

Wanda looked at him, not understanding.

"If you don't move in three days," added the balding man, "the militia will kick you out on the street."

All three turned as if on command and walked out, leaving Wanda sitting on the sofa.

Now she understood very well what they had said. In three days, she had to move out. But where would she go? She had no one. Her mind worked feverishly. She knew she would have to search for any available corner.

In the desk drawer, she found her passport with the stamp indicating she had been convicted. She had a temporary registration stamp, and another dated ten months later that gave her permanent registration. But the permit for the apartment was in Eugena's name. After Gena died, Wanda lost all rights to the apartment; she was not a relative.

In the drawer were other papers that Gena had saved over the years. Old bills covering the costs of the apartment showed that Gena had paid regularly. Wanda had paid the bills only for the seven months of Gena's illness. She had put the bills in with the others as she paid them.

She pulled the drawer completely out of the desk and put it on top. It was full of papers.

"Where do I begin?" she thought. Her heart felt empty, but she did not cry. She put aside all the bills and saw death certificates for Gena's husband and sister. She found home holiday greeting cards and envelopes from the military office. She remembered there were two envelopes, one letting her know what information the officials had about her son, the second informing her that he was missing in action. Now she saw a third envelope that she did not remember. She opened it and read:

". . . Gregory Vinar died bravely defending his country in November, 1943. ..."

Gena had hidden the notice from the military office, but Wanda had had a feeling all along that her son was no longer alive. She pressed the letter to her breast. She did not cry. Instead, she closed her eyes and imagined Gregory as a little boy. No, he did not die. He was still alive in his mother's heart.

Suddenly, Wanda felt hope. She pulled a shawl over her head and, carrying the envelope, went to see the Domicile Committee.

When she stepped into the lobby of the Domicile Committee's building, she saw the same balding man who had come to the apartment and told her that if she were not out in three days, she would be removed by the authorities.

"Excuse me, please," Wanda said. "When you came to my apartment, I was so shocked I couldn't talk to you. Now I've found this document. It says my son died bravely defending his country."

Wanda handed the document to the balding man and, with hope in her eyes, watched him read it.

"So what," he said, "if your son was killed in the army. Twenty million people were killed in the war."

"I thought," Wanda said shyly, "because my son gave his life for his country and I gave that life to him, I would not be thrown out on the street."

"Citizen Stanishevsky, we gave you three days to find a place to live," the balding man said, raising his voice. "I don't think you can cover your past with this notice."

Wanda ran out to the street and walked quickly away from the building. All the people in the lobby were, she knew, thinking, "What kind of past?"

When she reached her apartment, she began feverishly packing all her belongings.

"This is all," she said to herself. "I was so naive. I thought my grief was over and I would have a quiet old age. But who needs my life? Who could call this a life?"

She walked to the kitchen and found the bottle of wine. It was empty. She had finished it the night before. She found a few rubles in her purse and started to leave. Just as she reached the door, someone knocked. It was her neighbor who lived on the courtyard side of the building.

"Excuse me, please," the woman whispered. "I heard they're throwing you out. Is it true?"

Wanda stared at her and did not answer.

"Don't worry," the woman protested. "I haven't said anything to anybody. All the neighbors are saying they saw the Domicile Committee come here. You live alone in a big apartment. I know who wants your apartment—the Minaevs. They have two children. One of them is handicapped."

"It doesn't matter to me who lives in this apartment when I leave. I have to leave in three days."

"Oh, then it's true. It's not fair to throw somebody out on the street. Do you have anybody you can go to?"

The neighbor woman was fat with cheeks as red as apples. She talked without stopping. Wanda did not even know her name.

"No," Wanda said, "I don't have anybody, but I don't care."

"Where do you work? You can complain there."

"That's a good idea. Excuse me, I don't know your name."

"My name is Zoya. Your name is Wanda, I heard. Am I right?"

"Yes, you're right. Listen Zoya, thank you very much for the advice. Now I have to go to the store and buy something to eat."

"Sure, I just came for a minute. I feel so sorry for you. It's not right to give those people this apartment. Nobody likes them."

Wanda opened the door, and Zoya left. Wanda went to the store. When Zoya reached the courtyard, all the neighbors gathered around her, chattering.

"I found out everything," Zoya said. "It's true. The committee gave her three days. She was too proud, not neighborly. She only says hello, and then she's gone. Now she can feel how it is to survive without people."

"Why are you so cheerful about someone else's misfortune?" another neighbor asked. "So what if she didn't have much to do with her neighbors? She never hurt anybody."

The neighbors began arguing, some taking the fat woman's side, some Wanda's.

When Wanda returned, she heard bits and pieces of the argument and knew they were talking about her.

When Gena had become ill, the doctor had noticed Wanda's portrait and asked about it. After she had left, Wanda had taken the portrait down, wrapped it and put it in the closet. It attracted attention and suspicion because it contrasted so greatly with the apartment's plain, inexpensive furniture.

Wanda took the portrait from the closet and put it with the rest of her belongings. She drank a glass of wine and felt better. The wine seemed to give her new energy, and her mind seemed clearer, but after one more glass she fell asleep.

PART XI

Wanda knocked on the door of the assistant school maintenance manager's office.

"May I come in?" she asked, opening the door slightly.

"Please, come in," the assistant manager said. "I didn't see you."

"I have a favor to ask of you. I didn't know whom to turn to."

"Sit down. I'll help you if I can."

The assistant manager was a man of medium height and very slim build. His right sleeve was empty, and he kept it tucked into his pants. His straight, dark hair was slicked back, and his dark eyes were deeply set. He had lost his arm during the war, and when he returned home from the hospital, he discovered he had lost his entire family, his wife, her parents, and his three children. All were killed by a bomb.

Now he worked in the school and spent all his time there. He loved children. Everyone noticed how he enjoyed watching them. Only he knew what his thoughts were as he watched.

"Dimitri Nikolayevich," Wanda began, "they threw me out on the street. They took the apartment because the woman I lived with died and I live alone now."

Wanda did not cry, but she was so nervous that her hands shook.

"What did you say? They threw you out in November? It's almost winter. No one can live on the street in the winter. Which Domicile Committee is it?" Wanda told him which committee it was and the names of the three members with whom she had dealt.

"And there's more," she said. "I showed them a notice from the military office telling me that my son was killed. They told me that twenty million people were killed and that my son's death was not a good reason."

Wanda lowered her eyes, and her whole body shook.

"Give me that notice, please," Dmitri Nikolayevich said, reaching for the paper.

Wanda stood and gave him the notice in its envelope.

"He was a child," Dmitri Nikolayevich said, reading the paper. "Leave this document with me. Tell me, how many days did they give you?"

They gave me three days, but I only have two left."

"I'll try to do something today and let you know."

"Thank you very much," Wanda said, moving toward the door. "Don't thank me. I've done nothing yet."

Wanda walked down the corridor, thinking about how Dmitri Nikolayevich's life was not easy. He was an invalid and had lost everyone in the war. He understood her as no one else could. She was alone and no one in this world needed her.

She had worked as a janitor in the school since returning from Ural. She communicated with almost no one. She arrived earlier than anyone else and left before anyone arrived. She knew only one other janitor, Lili, who cleaned rooms near Wanda's own area. A few times, at meetings, she saw everyone together.

Throughout her life, Wanda had a reserved disposition. As a child and as an adult, she had spoken little. In jail and in the prison camp she had grown more distant and quiet. She had been raised a Catholic. She could pray fervently and believed in God. Her prayers were to the Mother of God.

But what was left for her now? She had no one, no relatives, no close friends. After life had beaten her many times, she had stopped praying. She would ask for no more help because she had no hope left in her heart. She had never actually renounced God; she knew God had simply turned away from her. She decided she needed no God and no people.

All of these thoughts Wanda turned over in her mind as she walked down the street. She headed automatically for the trolley stop. The trolley came, and she boarded it. She looked out the window and, after fifteen or twenty minutes, she saw the Polish cemetery. The trolley stopped, and she got off.

In all the years she had been back in Odessa, she had found no time or desire to visit her father's grave. She did not know what compelled her now to return. She remembered where the grave was; she remembered the monument. The last time she had visited was in the early thirties.

At the entrance to the cemetery, she bought a bouquet of asters. Then she began walking along the central path.

It was the end of November. Almost all the leaves were on the ground, and the wind tossed them. Crows sat on the bare branches, high in the trees, and shouted to each other, "Caw, caw, caw." Wanda looked at them. They were so big and black. With a rush of wings, the crows flew and cawed loudly, alighting on the path in front of her. Wanda walked around them.

She remembered when she and her sister Sophie had placed a small Rowan-tree next to their father's grave. On top of the tall monument was a cross. On the monument was her father's photograph on a brown, ceramic oval plate.

Halfway down the path, Wanda turned right. A few minutes later, she saw the top of the familiar monument. High grass and weeds surrounded the grave. If not for the cross and the picture, it would not have been easy to find the grave amidst the desolation. The weeds were so tall that Wanda could not read the inscription.

"Oh, my God," she cried. "How could I not visit you all these years, Papa?" She began to tear the weeds away with her bare hands. She did not feel the sharp thorns stabbing her hands. The weeds pulled easily because the ground was soft from recent rains. She pulled the plants and threw them away. They lay in piles around the grave. Finally, she could see the inscription.

"Oh, my dear papa," she said, kneeling. "Forgive me for not visiting you for such a long time. You were always in my heart. I miss you and Mama and everyone who was so dear to me, and my dear children whom you never had a chance to see."

Wanda wept loudly, unrestrained. She had to cry out, to throw everything off as she had not for so many years. She began to pray, remembering her prayers word for word. She felt that the Mother of God could hear her again and help her.

Wanda did not know how long she knelt at her father's grave, but she had felt chilly.

"I'll come to visit you, Papa," she said. "You're all I have left."

She walked to the exit quickly because it was growing dark. Her hands began to burn and hurt from the cuts and the embedded thorns. When she sat down in the trolley, she saw that her hands were covered with dried blood. The people sitting near her noticed and looked at her.

"I don't care," she thought. "I've found faith in my heart." She felt transcendent, above everything.

No one threw Wanda out on the street. The Domicile Committee gave her six square meteres in a basement close to the school where she worked. Her door was four steps down from street level. It was just a room, with no kitchen, no foyer. The stove stood in a corner. Next to the door stood a bucket with water in it. There was no sink or toilet. The toilet and water were available in the rear courtyard.

"Thanks for this," Wanda thought. "This is my corner."

The building next to Wanda's had been destroyed by a bomb during the war. Nothing had been done to rebuild it. Rebuilding began in the center of the city; this building was far from the center. First, historical buildings were rebuilt, then the transportation lines, hospitals, and schools, if they had been destroyed. Odessa sustained only moderate damage. The opera and ballet theatre was the pride of Odessa, and it was untouched. All the monuments also were unscathed.

Odessa is a very unusual city. Here live people of all nationalities—Russians, Ukrainians, Greeks. The Greek Plaza is still called by its original name. Many Poles remain, but their cathedral has been changed to accommodate a sports club and warehouses. The Germans had occupied a number of colonies surrounding the city. Today, only the names remain: Luzdorf, Boden, Strasburgh. When the war started, all Germans were evicted and sent deep into Siberia. Many of them died from the severe cold. Hadzhebay Estuary, an inlet of the Black Sea, still has the same name, a reminder that many years ago Tatar-Mongols lived there.

The streets of Odessa were paved with cobblestones and stone plates. Many years ago, Russia traded grain with other countries. The ships sailed in loaded with cobblestones and stone plates that served to ballast them until they could take on the grain. Little by little, almost all the streets of Odessa were paved with those stones and plates.

In the past, when trade with the East was at its height, Odessa was a noisy, happy city, unlike any other city in Russia.

People who were born and lived in Odessa spoke with a distinct dialect. Odessa was called "a city open to the world," and it is still known as the "pearl of the Black Sea." It was and is a place with a rich musical culture. It gave to the world some of its finest musicians and composers. It is a city of famous profiteers and swindlers. All of these things were and are Odessa.

After Cracow, for Wanda, Odessa was the second city. There she was both very happy and very unhappy. She had known Odessa before the revolution, in the twenties, and in the time of NEP. She remembered the depressions in 1921 and 1933. But after she returned from Ural, she almost never walked on the streets. She had not seen how the city had changed.

Now she lived in a very small room, without even a closet. She felt she would suffocate. There was no window, only a door with glass. When the sun was high, only a little light entered.

When she returned from work, she put soup on the primus[8], and that bread and sausage were her dinner. Sometimes, she fried a fish she bought from a fisherman on the corner, but not often, because she had to keep the door open for several hours. She had dinner and a glass of wine and then went for a walk. She was again drinking every day. One after another, she saw places she had not seen for years. The memories made her heart tremble.

Some people easily forget the past or do not think about it often, but even as she aged, Wanda's memory remained young. She remembered details of her childhood and young adulthood. The wine had a strange effect on her; it sharpened rather than dulled her memory.

Wanda had developed a habit. Every day in any weather, she walked. She could not stay long in her tiny room; she went to it only to sleep.

Once, after she had eaten quickly and was washing her plate, someone knocked on her door.

"Come in," she said. "The door is open."

It was the assistant school maintenance manager," Dmitri Nikolayevich. "I wanted to see how you're getting along here," he said, looking around. "Thank you. Sit down, please."

She showed him to one of her two chairs, which stood next to a small table. "What kind of place is this?" he asked, shaking his head. "I think this is temporary. Things will be better after a while."

Wanda sat down in the other chair and said, "Everything's temporary in this world. I'm used to it. You see, in my life, things are either the very best or the very worst. All of it has been temporary. I'm almost sixty. I've gone through much grief in my life, but somehow I'm still alive."

"Yes, you're right. It's all temporary. Nobody knows how long God gives you. I can't tell your age. You don't look more than fifty."

"Thanks for the compliment, Dmitri Nikolayevich. A year ago I got dentures. Without them I look like an old, old woman. I had the scurvy years ago and lost all my teeth."

"Excuse me, please, Wanda. Where is your husband? Was he killed in the war? I know your son was killed."

"No, my husband died a long time ago. He was young. His heart failed."

"All these years you were a widow, and you didn't remarry?"

"I had two children. My daughter has been missing since the war, and I have no information about her. Why are you asking about me? How has your life been?"

"Mine? It hasn't gone very smoothly. I was an orphan. My parents were killed in World War I. I worked and went to school and married very late. My wife was sixteen years younger than I. We lived with her parents. When the war started, I joined the Army and was badly wounded, but I survived. When I came back from the hospital, I found out the building where my family lived was destroyed by a bomb, and my whole family, my wife, her parents, and my children, were killed. After that, my life was as empty as this sleeve." He touched the dangling sleeve.

"I understand. It's a pity. It was a terrible war. Maybe you want some tea? I have some cookies and cherry jam."

"With pleasure. If it's not difficult for you."

"No, no," Wanda said, smiling. "It's no trouble at all."

She put the kettle on the primus and prepared tea. Dmitri Nikolayevich stood and walked to the bookstand next to Wanda's bed. He examined the titles.

"I see you have French and Polish books, not just Russian," he said. "Do you know those languages?"

"Yes. I'm Polish. I came to Odessa from Cracow when I was fifteen. I spoke Polish. I learned French in school and in Paris, where I lived for some time. That was a long time ago. I don't want to think about it."

The tea was ready. Wanda poured it into glasses held by metal servers. They drank tea and talked. Finally, Dmitri Nikolayevich stood and walked to the door.

"Thank you, Wanda," he said, "for your hospitality. I have one question for you. Why have you worked as a janitor all these years? You're an educated woman. You could find an office job."

"I'm flattered. Thank you for your opinion of me. But believe me, it's much better this way. Under the circumstances, this is better for me. Sometimes, we need only to survive."

"We can talk about this another time. Thank you again, and good-bye."

"Good-bye, Dmitri Nikolayevich. You're welcome any time. If you feel like talking to someone, I'm a good listener."

When he had gone, Wanda thought about how he knew more about her than she would have liked.

A few days later, he came to visit again. This time, he brought her a clothes rack and helped her attach it to the wall. Now she could hang her clothes. She covered the clothes with a sheet. She felt cozier in the room. Again, they drank tea. Wanda began to talk.

"I don't know, Dmitri Nikolayevich. What do you think? I would like to buy an icon of the Mother of God and put it in the corner. When I lived with Gena, it wasn't my apartment. I couldn't think about it. I knew she didn't believe in God. But she was a good person. And I'd like to show one portrait."

"What kind of portrait?" he asked with interest.

Wanda pulled the package from under her bed.

"It will be strange to put this portrait in this room," she said, "but it's all I have from my past."

"Can I see it?"

Wanda unwrapped the painting and said, "I don't have any other place to keep it. This little blanket I used to cover my daughter when she was a baby." She put the portrait on the chair, and the light reflected from the gilt frame.

From the portrait a young, smiling, richly dressed girl looked out.

"Who is that? Did you know her? Or is this a picture of great value?" He looked closely at the painting.

"Yes, I knew her very well," Wanda said, not really believing that the girl was she.

"I've seen this kind of picture in a museum but not in anyone's house. They took everything from you, and you hid this somewhere?"

"No, you don't understand. I didn't hide anything. This is not a picture for a museum. This is my portrait. I was seventeen years old, and it was ten years before the revolution. What do you think, that I didn't have a right to my own portrait?"

"No, of course not. This is yours, and it belongs to you. It's beautiful, just unbelievable. You can put this above your bed or over the table. It doesn't matter that it doesn't match the room. It will make this place different because it's a part of your life."

"No, it takes me back into my past."

"Who was the artist?"

"It was a long time ago. I don't even want to talk about it. It was in Italy— in Florence. The artist was Maestro R. It was on my honeymoon."

"You've had an interesting life, Wanda. You've been to Paris and to Italy."

"I don't want to remember that. It was a long time ago. No, I'll not put this portrait on the wall."

She wrapped the painting and replaced it under the bed.

"This is not right, Wanda," said Dmitri Nikolayevich. "This is not just a portrait. It's a work of art."

Wanda smiled sadly and said, "Look around, and tell me, please, does this place need a work of art? But for an icon, this miserable place is perfect."

"Tell me, Wanda. Before the revolution, did you have icons in your home?"

"We had a chapel where we kept an organ and icons on the wall. We prayed there. It was not necessary to go to the church."

"Now I understand. You were from very rich society. I'll tell you the truth. I don't know how you survived. Usually, women from high society were very fragile and suffered more than the men during difficult situations."

"You know, I don't understand myself how I survived and how I'm still alive."

"And what else is strange. ..."

Wanda interrupted him. "Dmitri Nikolayevich, excuse me, please, I can't breathe in this room. I have to go for a walk."

"No, please, forgive me. I've asked many questions. I have to go now. We've talked and I've lost track of the time."

"Thank you for the rack," Wanda said, walking him to the door.

She put on her coat and walked to the square. She walked, kicking the dry leaves and thinking. The wind spun the leaves away.

"Why did he ask me so many questions?" she thought. "Why does he want to know so much about my past? On the one hand, he's a nice man, but, on the other, he has something on his mind."

She sat down on a bench and watched the pigeons. The birds cooed and scratched, looking for food. In front of her, older women walked, pushing babies in open carriages.

"If my children were alive, I'd be a grandmother," Wanda thought, "and I'd be here walking with my grandchildren." She felt pain in her heart. "That was not my destiny."

She did not cry; she only felt deep pain. She closed her eyes and tried not to think about it. Little by little, she turned her thoughts to the search for an icon for her room.

"If I don't have anyone to talk to," she thought, "I can talk to God."

The next Sunday, Wanda went to the flea market. It was a big, noisy place where people bought and sold almost everything: old goods,

345

handcrafted toys, fried rolls filled with meat, jam, or peas. Shouts of "Hot pirozhki with meat!"

"Hot pirozhki with peas!" rang out from one side then the other.

Wanda wove her way through the crowd, searching for an icon. She had already walked around the market for an hour and had found nothing. She asked a woman selling crocheted doilies and mats, "Please tell me where I can find an icon. I've looked for a long time and can't find one."

"Woman, have you just fallen from the sky? Where have you seen icons displayed for sale? For selling those goods, people can go to jail. But I can tell you. … No, I'd better take you."

The woman selling doilies turned to another woman who stood next to her and said, "Hey, Dasha, look after my table. I'll be right back." She signaled for Wanda to follow.

They approached a table covered with junk—lamps, old pots, a few dishes. "Listen, Sergei," the doily lady said to the man behind the table, "this woman needs something." She turned to Wanda and said, "Explain to him.

But quietly. If he doesn't have it, we'll go somewhere else."

Wanda whispered, "Do you have an icon of the Mother of God with the Child?"

"Oh, the Virgin Mary?" Sergei said. "Sure I have. And I have St. Vladimir and Nickolaus. …"

"I don't need anything else," Wanda interrupted. "The Virgin Mary will be fine."

Sergei took the icon from a box under the table. The icon itself was set in a sterling silver mat within the frame. It was exactly what Wanda had in mind.

"How much?" she asked.

"Just for you—fifty rubles. If you want to know, they cost much, much more. This is hand painted on the wood. The mat is sterling silver, and this icon might be over a hundred years old."

Wanda gave him fifty rubles without speaking. Sergei wrapped the icon in pages of <u>Pravda</u>.

"Thank you very much," Wanda said to the doily lady.

"Why didn't you bargain with him? He could have given it to you for less. Who asks for icons now?"

"I can't bargain. It's only important that I found what I was looking for."

"Listen. Maybe you need some mats or doilies for your icon?"

"All right. You can show me what you have."

An hour later, Wanda had placed the icon in a corner of her tiny room, a mat draped around it, and an icon-lamp, which she had also purchased, sitting beneath it.

"Thanks to that woman who helped me," Wanda thought. "Next Sunday, I'll go buy some napkins from her. I didn't have enough money. She won't be hard to find, short and round like a ball, with a red nose."

Over the past few weeks, Wanda had tried not to drink at all. Perhaps she was ashamed. Dmitri Nikolayevich could come over any time for a cup of tea or just to talk. Or perhaps she had finally realized that life was worthwhile just because it is life. She spent much of her time trying to read. Books carried her to a different world, and she felt what the characters felt. She bought her books at a secondhand store. They were cheaper. Eventually, her book stand was full. In her free time, she read or prayed, if she was not walking.

The next Sunday, Dmitri Nikolayevich came, and Wanda showed him how she had displayed her icon.

"That's nice," he said. "It reminds me of the old villages, where my wife's relatives lived."

Wanda did not answer, but she understood. He saw her as old-fashioned. They sat down to the supper Wanda had prepared, fried potatoes and ham. "I'd like to ask you something and share something with you," Dmitri Nikolayevich said. "I don't have anybody. Somehow, I feel you're a good person to talk to."

"Please," Wanda said, "you can ask me anything. I'll try to understand. If I can, I'll help you."

He was quiet, thinking. Finally, after a few mintues, he began to speak.

"I met a young woman. She's a widow with no children. She's thirty-three, and I'm fifty-two, and I'm an invalid. She lives with her mother next door to me. They've gone to Leningrad to visit some relatives. The woman's name is Lana. She's so beautiful. She has long, ash-blonde braided hair and gray eyes. You know, Wanda, this is so painful for me. I'm in love, and she's young and beautiful. Why does she pay attention to me? Maybe she pities me. What do you think?"

"This is difficult for me. I don't know her. But I think she can love you, if she knows you well. She can love you for your kindness. Not so many men are left after the war. How long have you known her?"

Wanda examined him, trying to understand how a young woman could love him.

"We've known each other about six months," he said, "because we're neighbors. I've asked her twice for a date, and she didn't refuse. We went to the theatre and to a movie, and we had a good time. She's been gone three weeks now, and I miss her so much. If you saw her, you'd say she's too beautiful for me. Your opinion is very important to me."

"How does she act? Has she talked about her feelings?"

"No, she hasn't told me straight, but once she told me she likes my company."

"What can I say? When she comes back from Leningrad, try asking her directly."

Wanda knew he was lonely, had no one, just as she had no one.

One Sunday, when Wanda was walking in the park, she saw Dmitri Nikolayevich and a young woman in front of her. They were busy talking and did not see her. Wanda observed the woman.

"He was right," she thought. "She's young and beautiful. What could she see in him?"

The woman's complexion was darker than her ash-blonde hair and gray eyes would indicate. Her hair was braided into a crown. She was tall and looked quite elegant. Dmitri Nikolayevich was wearing a long leather coat and brimmed hat. He looked like the woman's father.

"What the devil can do when God's asleep!" Wanda thought when she had returned home. "Maybe she doesn't want to be alone anymore, either, and nobody else is available."

A few months later, Wanda heard from another janitor that Dmitri Nikolayevich was married. All this time, he had not visited Wanda. He had been busy with his new life. Furthermore, another janitor gossiped, Dmitri Nikolayevich had been an officer of high position in the Army.

He was wounded and so the government had given him a three-room apartment. Lana and her mother had had only one room and a kitchen. Now they had made a door and had four rooms. It was an excellent apartment.

He was a rich man, the janitors agreed. He had brought gold and fine fabrics and many other things from Germany. Not only did he earn a salary, but he had a very good pension. All of these things, they reasoned, had caused the woman to marry him.

Wanda listened but said nothing. She only thought, "People can talk, but I don't believe it."

Wanda saw Dmitri Nikolayevich in the corridor once. He passed her, greeted her, but he did not look at her. She saw the wedding ring on his finger. She understood that he now had a different life, but she felt somewhat rejected.

"Why didn't he tell me he'd married?" she thought. "He came by many times before and talked to me and asked questions. But people are strange. He helped me get the room where I live now. I'm thankful for that. Perhaps I should do something for him, too."

Months before, Wanda had started to knit a bedspread for herself. She had learned how to knit in the prison camp and, later, from Gena. She decided to make scarves for Dmitri Nikolayevich and his wife. She bought wool yarn, gray and red. Dmitri Nikolayevich's would be gray with one red stripe near each end. His wife's would be red with two gray stripes and fringe on the ends. Wanda was so happy with her idea that she began knitting immediately and enthusiastically.

The winter was rainy; the evenings were long. Knitting the scarves helped pass the time. After a few months, they were finished. She was satisfied with her work. She placed them in a shoe box, wrapped it, and took it with her to work. With the box under her arm, she knocked on Dmitri Nikolayevich's door.

"Come in," he said. "Who's that?"

"It's Wanda," she answered, opening the door.

"I haven't see you for a long time, Wanda. What's new?"

"Nothing's new. I believe you have a new life, though." She noticed that his face was rounder and looked more rested.

"Sit down, please," he said. "I can't imagine a better life. I'm so glad I married Lana. She's something else. So charming. And her mother prepares breakfast for me every morning. She doesn't let me go to work without a hot breakfast."

"I'm so happy for you, Dmitri Nikolayevich. I made these for you and your wife."

Wanda gave him the box, and he opened it.

"Thank you very much, Wanda. These scarves are so elegant. You knitted them yourself?"

"Yes. I remembered how you helped me when I didn't have anyone to take my side."

"What are you talking about, Wanda? That was nothing. I'll introduce you to my wife. I'm sure you'll like her."

"I'd like to meet her, but now I'll go."

"Thank you again for the scarves," Dmitri Nikolayevich said as Wanda nodded to him once and left.

It was spring. The air was fresh, and the weather was warm. Wanda walked slowly, thinking.

"This is strange," she mused. "Why hasn't he introduced me before?" She caught herself feeling his life meant something to her. She was concerned about him.

Time passed quickly. Summer came, and Wanda visited her father's grave regularly. She tried once to find Grisha's grave, but it had not monument and the records had been destroyed by fire during the war.

She planted flowers on her father's grave and watered them every Sunday. In a whisper, in Polish, she spoke to him, even though she had not spoken her native language for many years. She remembered that, to him, she had spoken only Polish.

It has been almost a year since Wanda had had a drink. Something had stopped her, but she did not know what it was. She was acquainted with a few neighbors but had no friends.

On the site of the building next to her, the one that had been destroyed during the war, a large hole had been excavated. Building materials had been hauled in.

Wanda asked one of the workers, "What are they building here?"

"A dormitory for young factory workers," he said, and he named a factory located several blocks away.

Every day, Wanda watched the building grow. The summer was pleasant, and the work went quickly. It was a two-story building with four columns on the facade and its entrance on the side.

The narrow end of the building faced the street. It was a strange structure for its location, far from the center of the city. People in the neighborhood came to call it the "philharmonica." It simply did not fit with the old, single-story buildings around it.

When fall was near, the outside work on the building was complete, and inside work was begun. Wanda entered the building and looked at one of the apartments. She saw three rooms, a kitchen, and across a hallway, a toilet and a bathroom. Each room contained a wood- and coal-burning stove.

"What is this?" Wanda thought. "They have to use coal even in the kitchen? There's no gas or hot water. And young people have to live here."

The building contained no central heating system and no hot water system. The workers who were to live there would use one stove for each apartment, no matter how many people occupied the three rooms.

"This is not smart at all," Wanda thought. "What were they thinking of when they designed this?"

When winter arrived, construction stopped; the windows and doors were barricaded to prevent theft. Almost seven years after the war ended, many people continued to suffer, without homes, or whole families, six or eight people, lived in one room and shared a kitchen with as many as five other families. Some people could not afford glass for windows and used cardboard instead. Some apartments had no water; toilets were luxuries. It was most important, though, that people had roofs over their heads and that the war was over. People grew accustomed to doing without many services.

In the spring of 1952, construction on the building resumed. By the end of May, the structure was ready to be occupied.

Once, as she was walking by, Wanda saw a sign on the builing: "Help Wanted: Stoker and Janitor." Below the advertisement was the name and address of the nearby factory. Immediately, Wanda went to the factory and asked for an application.

"I live in the building next door to this one," Wanda said to someone in the personnel department. "I can warm the rooms in the morning before the workers wake up. Since nineteen forty-four, I've cleaned school classrooms. And I can clean the kitchens and corridors. I do that kind of work now."

"Fill out the application," the clerk said, "and we'll let you know."

Wanda left the application and walked slowly home. She knew she could not work at the school anymore. From the previous fall until now, about eight or nine months, Dmitri Nikolayevich had been drinking heavily. It was painful to look at him. She had seen him once in the street, stopped him, and asked, "What's happened, Dmitri Nikolayevich? Are you not feeling well?"

He had looked at her with an expression twisted with pain. "Yes," he had answered. "I'm very sick, Wanda, but there is no cure for my sickness. I can't force her to love me. I'm a cripple, and I'm supposed to know my place in life. I forgot my place, and now I'm paying for it."

Wanda had tried to interrupt him, but he had brushed her words aside with a sweep of his arm. "You women don't understand anything. I love her with all my heart, but she doesn't even pity me. She leaves me alone all the time. Her mother goes to Leningrad to see her sister, and Lana spends most of her time there, too. Yes, she's young and beautiful. ... Why do you look at me? You, old woman, nobody needs you. Go. Clean. Do your job."

Wanda had stopped. He had continued to walk and talk. Wanda had turned around and walked back the way she had come. Her face had burned. She did not remember feeling so terrible for a long time.

"What does he blame me for?" she had thought. "I never harmed him." Wanda had felt very hurt, even though she understood he was drunk. But he knew her name and the job she did.

After that incident, Wanda saw him a few more times, but she avoided him. She heard from another janitor that he continued to drink a great deal and that he had problems with his wife. Wanda remembered that he had never introduced her to Lana.

All this time, she had thought about finding another job. She was already over sixty years old, but her work experience was not enough. Her ten years in the prison camp did not count. She was ineligible for any pension.

Now she had hope. Perhaps she would get the job in the new building.

In June, it was very warm. People dressed in summer clothing. Wanda received a note telling her she was hired as a stoker and janitor. She also received a description of her duties. In the winter, she was to keep the stoves burning and warm the rooms. She was also to clean the corridors, the stairs, the kitchens, and the hallways inside the apartments. She would make more salary than at the school.

Wanda went to the factory personnel department and took care of the formalities. She was told to start work in a few days.

She wrote her resignation from the school janitor position and took it to Dmitri Nikolayevich's office. Dmitri Nikolayevich took the paper and looked at it with bleary eyes.

"You're kidding," he said. "'Because I found another job.' What kind of job did you find?"

"I don't want to work here anymore," Wanda answered. "Where I go is my business. All I ask of you is that you sign."

"What happens if I don't sign?" he asked, screwing up one eye and looking at her askance.

"I'll leave anyway. I'm of retirement age. You know women retire at sixty. No one can keep me here, and you have enough janitors without me."

"All right, go. Maybe I wouldn't sign for somebody else, but for you, I'll sign."

Wanda looked at him. His words had no meaning. He looked so slovenly. His empty sleeve hung loosely, no longer tucked into his pants. She pitied him as a human being. His appearance stirred her compassion, but she remembered he had hurt her when she had asked him what was wrong. Wanda took her resignation, thanked him, and left his office. She had walked a few steps when she heard him call her. "Wanda. Please come back to my office." She turned and asked, "What do you want?"

"Come here, please. I ask you." His voice was different, as if he were no longer drunk.

Wanda returned to the office, and Dimitri Nikolayevich said, "Sit down, please. I need to talk to you."

"About what do you need to talk to me? I'm old, and nobody needs me. Why do you call me here?"

"Who told you you're old? Don't listen."

Wanda sat on the chair and smiled. "You told me that," she said. "After that, I decided not to bother you anymore."

"What are you talking about, Wanda?" Dmitri Nikolayevich sat down in front of her. "I couldn't have said that. I've always respected you, and I thought you respected me, too. I even remember the scarves you knitted for me. You see? I remember."

"It's good you remember. Thanks for that."

"Why are you acting like this? Why don't you ask me how I feel, how things are going in my life?"

Wanda looked at his face and saw his eyes sparkle feverishly. He was smoking a cigarette, and his hand shook. He inhaled the smoke deeply, blew it out, and began to talk.

"It doesn't matter about me, Wanda. My life means nothing anymore. You don't understand me. If you only knew how I love her. Have you loved anybody in your life? I don't mean just love; I mean complete madness. Why do I ask you? Not everybody can have this kind of feeling."

He fell back in his chair and closed his eyes. Wanda was frightened for him.

He sat with his eyes closed, and Wanda tried to distract him.

"Dmitri Nikolayevich," she said, "I remember everything. Believe me, I do. Even though it has been many years. As long as I live before I die, I'll remember my love. I was loved again later, but the feeling was different, more of the mind than of the heart. Do you understand? I was very happy for seven years. I married a man whom I adored. And you tell me I don't understand? If I could have died after loving him, not living another day, I would not have grasped at life. I would have died quietly, because I loved him with all my soul, and he loved me no less.

Not everyone can have that. You see, I live with my memories. They're always inside me. Life after him has not buried my feelings."

As Wanda spoke, Dmitri Nikolayevich opened his eyes, leaned forward, and gave her his full attention. When she finished, he asked, "What happened to your husband?"

"He was killed in a train wreck in Germany during World War One, 1914. It was a business trip. he never came back."

"That's awful. You said it very well: 'If I could have died after loving him, not living another day, I would not have grasped at life. …' This is true. Absolutely. Love is your soul. You can only know it one time in your life. If you lose it, nothing is left."

Wanda stood and said, "I have to go now. I wish you the best. I have to start my new job. Thank you again."

She walked to the door. When she reached it, he said, "You were lucky. Your love was reciprocated."

Wanda left without speaking.

PART XII

Wanda walked home slowly, thinking about her conversation with Dmitri Nikolayevich. Something about their discussion disturbed her. Why did he ignore what she said about her loving and being loved and, instead, concentrate on life when love is gone? He seemed fascinated by death.

She walked past the new building and noticed a large canvas-covered truck. From the back of it, young girls jumped. Wanda watched them. They carried small wooden trunks and rucksacks.

"Oh. I see who'll live in this dormitory," she thought. "They're just children."

She noticed they wore some kind of uniform—black. As she drew closer, she saw they were all girls, two dozen of them, no boys. They walked past her, carrying their luggage, paying no attention to her. One girl, however, stopped and asked her, "Do you live her, auntie?"

"No, my child. I'll be working here. I'll warm the apartments and clean."

"You're not retired yet?" the girl asked.

Wanda did not answer because someone yelled, "Hey, Rita. If you don't get going, you won't find a place next to the window."

"Excuse me," Rita whispered to Wanda. "I have to run. I'll see you later." She followed the other girls. Wanda stayed, watching the girl walk toward the building.

"Interesting," she thought. "How old is she? She couldn't be more than fourteen. She's so tiny, only two big, questioning eyes. And these children came to work? How could their parents let them go to another city at their age?"

Wanda's mind was occupied with the girls, and she forgot her conversation with Dmitri Nikolayevich.

The next day was Sunday. At seven in the morning, Wanda walked to the city market carrying a basket. She saw the girls who had arrived the night before jogging. They all wore the same gray running clothes. Again, Rita slowed to talk to Wanda.

"We're jogging after our morning exercise," Rita said. "Where are you going so early with your basket?"

"I'm going to the market," Wanda answered. "I need to buy some things."

"Wait for me. I'll come with you. All right? Give me five minutes."

Rita ran back to the building. Wanda had not itme to answer, so she stood and waited.

A short time later, Wanda saw Rita coming toward her. At the same time, the rest of the girls returned from their run.

"Rita, you've got nothing to do?" one of the girls asked.

"Listen," another girl yelled. "Buy me bread and a package of butter. I'll give you the money later."

A third girl chimed in. "For me, radishes and green onions, please."

Wanda and Rita had already crossed the street. They walked to the end of the block and turned the the corner.

"It's always like that," Rita said. "They don't want to go by themselves. I have to bring them everything."

"How old are you, Rita?" Wanda asked.

"Last April I was sixteen. Two months ago. How old are you? Why are you still working?"

"You look no more than fourteen years. You're so little and fragile."

"Nobody can tell my age. Just a year ago, I could go to the movie with a child's ticket. We children who grew up during the war didn't grow very tall because we didn't have vitamins and sometimes not even bread. But we'll grow now that we eat better. Don't you think?"

"Of course you can grow. My time was different. When I was sixteen, I looked like an adult. When I was fourteen, I looked seventeen. But that was a different time."

"You have some kind of soft accent. Did you live someplace else before?"

"You have good hearing. Not everyone hears my accent. I'm from Poland. I came here a long, long time ago. Where did you come from, and all these girls?"

"We're from different places. We went to the same community college for two years. The government sent us to work in this factory."

They walked in the early morning, two entirely different people, one older woman carrying the burden of her past life, and a young girl with the burden of a difficult childhood. The young girl, however, could still look forward to a future and looked at life through more cheerful eyes.

Wanda found out that there were twenty-four girls. None of them had parents. They grew up in orphanages. They received training in a trade while attending high school.

"You poor orphans," Wanda said when Rita had finished. "Now I understand the uniforms. How old were you when you went to the orphanage?"

"Since 1941. I was five. My sister was a year and a half, and my brother was eleven. The three of us were sent to an orphanage when Mama was killed by a bomb. My father was killed in the war, in 1944."

"What happened to your mama?"

"We were sitting in the train station, waitin for the train. Mama went to the commissary about two kilometers away from the station. She was standing in line. A German plane dropped a bomb, but we didn't know what had happened. We sat and waited until it was almost dark. My sister was crying. Then the soldiers came and asked us why we were sitting by ourselves. My brother explained where my mother had gone and that she hadn't come back yet. They took him to the commissary. He recognized her dress. She was killed along with many others."

"We were taken with the wounded soldiers to Novosibirsk, deep in Siberia. When we reached the town, we were sent to an orphanage."

"You poor children. I can imagine what you've gone through. What that war has done to people!"

"We're not poor children. The government takes care of us, feeds us, gives us clothes. When you lose your parents when you're little, you don't understand what you've lost. Only in the evenings did we miss Mama. Nobody told us stories; nobody sang for us. And we missed Father because nobody was there to hold us on his lap."

Wanda was crying. Listening to the story of this girl's life, explained so simply, as if she were talking about everyday things, touched her. Rita was sure of what she was saying about the good that had happened to her. But the story could not leave Wanda indifferent.

"Why are you crying?" Rita asked. "Everything is past. I'm sixteen now. I have a trade as a lathe operator. I'll make money, support myself, and get an education. In a year, I'll graduate from high school and go to college."

"Oh, you poor, poor orphan. You understand nothing about this life yet. Where are your sister and brother? Are they still alive?"

"My brother graduated from the university. He's a geologist. He was sent to work in Siberia. My sister lives with my aunt in Kiev, the city where I was born. We didn't grow up together, but we haven't lost each other."

Tears fell from Wanda's eyes. Rita stopped walking and took Wanda's arm. "Listen," she said. "I forgot to ask your name. Please, stop crying. I don't like it when people cry. You need to be strong and control your feelings. I don't cry, even though sometimes it is very difficult not to." Wanda smiled through her tears. She looked at the little girl. "My name is Wanda," she said. "Just call me that."

"Oh, no, I can't call you by your first name. You're older than me. They taught me to call older people by their full names."

"In your orphanage, discipline was very strict, like in a soldiers' camp. Did you say you don't cry? That must be the result of the way you were raised."

Wanda held Rita by the shoulders and said, "Listen, my dear child. If you feel like crying, cry. You'll feel better when you let it out. Sometimes, it's just necessary."

Rita looked at Wanda with wide eyes. Wanda smiled and continued, "I didn't cry for some time, but now after I cry, I feel better."

As they talked, they approached the city market. Wanda put all her purchases in her basket. Rita carried a fishnet bag. She bought bread, packages of butter, green onions, sausage. The long loaves of bread poked out of the top of her bag.

"May I call you Aunt Wanda?" Rita asked. "You didn't tell me your full name."

"Call me whatever you like, child."

"While we were walking to the market, I told you my life store. While we're walking back, could you tell me the story of your life? Do you have children, grandchildren? How many?"

Wanda did not know what to say. No one had ever asked her those questions so directly. She said, quietly, "No, I don't have anybody. Everybody died."

"Now I understand why you cried when I told you about myself. Forgive me, please. I didn't know you lost your family. I talk too much. It's too much excitement, coming to a new town. From the train, we jumped into a truck. We sat on the benches and sang. Monday and Tuesday, we have to have medical examinations. On Wednesday, we go to work. It's all new and interesting. I love new things."

Wanda understood that Rita talked as she did for a purpose. Before they reached the building where Rita lived, they had talked about the climate in Odessa and many other subjects.

Wanda noticed that Rita had an inquiring nature. She was well read for someone in her teens.

"Bye-bye, Aunt Wanda," Rita said. "Thanks for the company."

"Thank you, child. You've made my day." Rita ran to the dormitory.

When Wanda returned to her apartment, she boiled a potato on the primus and lay down on the bed. Somehow this girl had touched her deeply, in her soul. She could not remember anyone touching her that way so quickly. Maybe it was because Rita was an orphan. But Wanda had seen many orphans before. Most of them looked lost and frightened, and they were angry at the world because they were alone. This girl, though, was different. She was full of life. She did not see herself as a poor orphan. She blamed no one for what had happened in her life.

A knock at the door interrupted Wanda's reverie. Someone knocked persistently and called Wanda's name. When Wanda opened the door, she saw a janitor she knew from the school.

"Something terrible has happened, Wanda," the woman said, "something very terrible."

"What is it?" Wanda asked. "What happened to whom?"

"Dmitri Nikolayevich is dead."

"What are you saying? I just talked to him yesterday. This is impossible."

"Yes. He hanged himself last night. He was very drunk and hanged himself with his scarf."

"Like I said, this is impossible. He had only one arm. How could he tie a knot? And he was very drunk."

"I told you what I heard. Maybe somebody hanged him, maybe even his wife. She's scum."

"This is nonsense. Why would his wife hang him? Or anyone else?"

"You don't know anything, Wanda. He was a rich man. He brought a lot of valuable things from Germany. He had a lot of gold. That's how he was able to buy her. But she didn't stay with him long. He bored her—older, crippled. Maybe she just decided to get rid of him."

"Oh, God," Wanda cried. "What rumors people spread. When is the funeral? I must go pay my respects. He wasn't a bad man. I remember he helped me."

"There'll be a lot of people at his funeral. I heard it's scheduled for Tuesday at eleven."

When the woman had left, Wanda closed the door. The primus was making noise, the potato was boiling, and steam billowed from the pot. Wanda turned the primus off and walked out to the street.

It was still early on a Sunday morning. Not many pedestrians were out. She walked slowly, looking down. She could not get enough air, even though the morning was very fresh and the air clear.

"This is so frightening," she thought. "He hanged himself with the scarf I made for him."

"Aunt Wanda," Rita called. "Is that you? Wait for me."

Wanda turned and saw Rita running across the street toward her.

"Are you going to town?" the girl asked. "Can I go with you, please? I've never seen the sea. I want to touch the water. The real Black Sea. I'm so glad they sent us to Odessa."

Wanda stopped and said, "Listen, Rita, dear, I'm not going to town. I'm not going to the sea. I'm just walking. Someone told me some terrible news. A good person has died. I knew him well."

"I'm so sorry. Was he very old? How old was he?"

"No, Rita, he wasn't very old. He was about fifty."

"He wasn't young. Fifty is a lot."

"Yes, Rita, of course. If you're sixteen, even thirty years is old, it's a lot of years to you. But believe me, fifty is not old. I'll be sixty-two this year. In your thinking, I'm an old, old woman."

"No, you're not an old, old woman," Rita said with a shrug. "You're just not young."

"You're a diplomat. I believe I'll never be bored with you. All right, let's walk together. We can go to the park, if you wish. Maybe I won't feel so burdened if you're with me."

As they talked, they heard a girl from the dormitory call Rita.

"Rita! Come here! I need to talk to you."

The girl's name was Anna. Rita answered her. "If you need me, come here."

The girl approached but stopped a few steps away. "Listen, Rita," Anna said, "I can't talk in front of strangers. Come here."

"All right. What do you want?" Turning to Wanda, Rita said, "Wait for me, please. I'll be right back."

The girls whispered. Wanda heard only pieces of the conversation. After a few minutes, Rita dismissed Anna with a wave of her hand, and she and Wanda went to the park.

"Even though all the girls are bigger than you, they pay attention to you," Wanda said.

"Sometimes yes, sometimes no, but they like when I tell them stories. They don't like to read, but listen—yes. I can read books and tell them what I read. For two years, almost every Sunday, everybody has come together and sat on the beds. They listen very quietly. Today is Sundy. I promised I'd finish the story I started a couple of Sundays ago. I told Anna I'd finish the story today, when I come back."

"Rita, I heard the girl say, 'with some old woman.' Was she talking about me?"

Rita was embarrassed and did not answer right away. She explained later. "Yes, Anna said everybody was waiting for me, and I was going with some old woman. I told her your name is Aunt Wanda, not 'old woman.'"

"Tell me, Rita, why did you decide to come with me if everybody was waiting for you?"

"Try to understand. All the time I'm telling stories. For a long time, I've wanted to listen to someone who can tell me something interesting."

"I understand. If you come visit me, I'll give you something interesting to read."

"I like short stories by Lydia Charsky, but her stories were banned after the revolution. I found her books a couple of times. I also like short stories by Eliza Ozheshko. I've read only one of heer books. I think there are five."

"Now I know your interests. I have something for you from a second-hand bookstore. How does it happen that you're the only one who reads, and the other girls listen?"

"I've always liked to tell stories, ever since I was a child. Everything I read I like to talk about. That's how it started. Also, I like to write poetry. And you know, Aunt Wanda, when I write, nobody interrupts me."

Wanda listened to Rita and realized she liked the girl, and she liked to listen to her and talk to her.

"I believe someday you'll become a writer," Wanda said. "I think a professional writer. Would you like to be one?"

"I don't know. I've never thought about it. I like physics and calculus, but I'd like to know more about literature, what is already written."

"Can you read one of your poems for me, please?"

"My poems are not polished, I write them because I have feeling inside me."

Rita recited the poem she had written called "Wind."

WIND

The wind is caressing the wheat in the glens,
Singing and wailing 'til the day begins.
Now rambling in the field, to the forest he flies,
Lifting up from the earth, he races to the skies.
He restlessly passes the bankof the river
And causes the leaves of the willow to quiver.
He touches the hair of a beautiful maiden
Who sits under the willow, her heart heavy-laden.
Resembling Alonushka,[9] with a sorrowful look,

She hangs her head low, gazes into the brook.
It is said, though love is the essence of life,
The love itself can bring pain and inner strife.
Oh wind, please rest for a while, pause for a moment,
That she may send a message to relieve her torment.
But the wind is uncaring. He shows no concern.
He knows not of sorrows. Amusement he years.
He tousles the hair of the beautiful maiden.
Who cries under the willow, her heart heavy-laden.

"And you wrote that yourself?" Wanda exclaimed.

"Of course. I've written since I was ten years old. But like I told you, I haven't had enough school."

"You're so modest. Do you have something about love?"

"No. I don't write about love because I have to feel what I'm writing about."

"Have you ever had a boyfriend?"

"What are you talking about? I grew up under very strict conditions. Ours was a girls' school. Even in college, our group is all girls."

"What kind of rules are those? God knows what they'll turn you into. Tell me, have you learned how to think freely? Or do you think only what they tell you to think?"

"You're joking. What's bad about it, if we learn endurance and to have a strong will?"

"Sure. You'll grow up without endearments and kind words, all by command."

"It's not as bad as it seems. We children who grew up in orphanages did much better in school than children who had parents and lived at home."

"Someday, Rita, you'll understand what I'm talking about. When you start work and are making almost nothing, maybe enough for a dry piece of bread, and you see what it's like to live that way, we can talk about it. For now, we can walk and breathe fresh air, and smell the acacias."

For a few minutes, they walked in silence. Then Wanda said, "Next Tuesday I have to go to a funeral. When I think about that my heart trembles.

It's such a tragedy."

"Aunt Wanda," Rita begged, "take me with you. I've never been to a funeral. We go for our physicals in the morning, and I'll be free."

"Child, why do you want to see a funeral? You don't need that experience."

"Please, I beg you. I'll be very quiet. I'd like to see a funeral."

"All right. You can come with me, but I still don't know why you need to see that spectacle."

They walked for an hour in the park and returned. Rita asked many questions, and Wanda tried to answer her. Wanda felt much better after she got back because she was no longer alone.

On Tuesday, as agreed, Rita arrived at Wanda's room at ten o'clock. She knocked, and Wanda said, "Come in, Rita."

From the bright outdoors, Rita entered the dark room. For a moment, she could not see.

"I'll be ready in a minute," Wanda said, putting on her shoes.

Rita sat in a chair and looked around. In the corner, she saw the icon of the Mother of God. The icon lamp was lit. She walked closer and examined the display.

"I saw an icon like that in church. One time I saw an icon in clothes like that."

"You go to church?" Wanda asked.

"No. Oh, no. They don't let us go to church. I went once last year, at Eastertime. I'll remember it for a long time. This icon is beautiful. I like it."

"Let's go, Rita. I already bought flowers. We have to walk about thirty minutes."

As they walked out, Wanda gave Rita a bouquet of lilacs and tulips.

"Tell me, Rita, please. How did it happen you were in a church? You weren't punished for that?

"Nobody knew. I'll tell you what happened. I didn't know then that I'd be going to church. I bought some greeting cards for the holidays from a girl in a little shop. I always bought cards from her to send to my sister, my brother, and my aunt for holidays and birthdays. The girl's name was Irena. She knew me by name, too.

"I bought cards for May Day, and she asked me where I was going for Easter. I didn't even know what Easter was."

"'Listen,' she told me, 'come with me. My home is thirty kilometetrs from here by train.'"

"She knew I didn't have parents and that I lived in the community college dormitory. I had spring vacation, and she told me I would be gone for only three days. We would leave Friday and be back Monday.

"'You're an orphan,' she told me. 'You've never had a holiday like that. My parents would be very happy if I brought you with me.'"

"I asked the counselor if I could go with a friend for a couple of days. I lived in a west Ukrainian city called Strei. In the village where Irena lived, the people were religious, as I found out later."

"Irena was tall, blonde, and a beautiful girl. When we got to her home, she introduced me to her parents. 'This is Rita,' she said. 'She doesn't know what Easter is. She's never celebrated the holiday, and she doesn't believe in God. She's been raised in an orphanage.'"

"I said, 'Thank you very much, Irena, for that kind of introduction.' Irena just laughted. Her parents looked at me as if I were from another planet. I spoke Ukrainian, but even that was different. In their village, people spoke with a Polish accent."

"Irena had an old grandmother who lived with her parents. It was late in the evening, but nobody had eaten yet. I was so hungry, because I'd missed dinner at the school. I was ashamed to ask, though, and I went to sleep on an empty stomach."

"In the morning, I washed my face, brushed my teeth, braided my ahir, and then sat to wait until everybody was ready for breakfast. I saw colored eggs surrounding a tall cake on the table. My mouth was watering.

"I saw Irena's mother put everything that was on the table into a basket. She also added ham and sausage, and she covered it with a napkin. I just wandered around, waiting for breakfast, but nobody ate."

"I whispered to Irena, 'Tell me, are you hungry? When do you eat breakfast?'"

"She just looked at me funny and said, 'Rita! Today we fast.[10] Nobody can eat. Tomorrow we break the fast. For today, you suffer!'"

"What was this? I understood what it meant to suffer when there's nothing to eat. But there was a whole table full of food. I couldn't figure it out."

"In the backyard, a chicken clucked and a rooster crowed. A cow lay on the ground with her calf. I could see the forest not far away. Nature was beautiful there; the air was fresh and clear. Everhting was find, but how could I enjoy it when I was so hungry? I tried to keep my mind off my stomach. I petted the calf; he was so cute. That's how I spent my time until five o'clock that afternoon.

"At five, Irena told me it was time to go to church. The service would start at six. We had to walk instead of drive. My feet were so tired. I couldn't see anything except open fields and forest."

"I asked Irena, 'How far is the church?'"

"'Maybe two more kilometeres,' she said. 'It's in the middle of a cemetery. Are you frightened of cemeteries?'"

"'No, I'm not,' I said. 'The orphanage where I grew up was next to an old Polish cemetery. We used to play there after school. It was over two hundred years old, and nobody had been buried there for many years. Two years ago, the cemetery was destroyed and turned into a park. I saw how they opened the crypts and broke the coffins open and removed the jewelry with hooks.'"

"Irena said, 'Oh, my God, who would do that?'"

"I told her, 'It was the soldiers. I believe the government sent them. We children ran around, and nobody paid any attention to us.'"

"Irena was quiet, and we went on walking. My legs were so tired I couldn't go on, so I stopped. She took my arm and helped me. In a little while, I saw the church steeple and then the cemetery fence."

"At the church, people were standing outside, waiting. When the doors opened, we went inside. The church wasn't very big. The altar was surrounded by icons, so were the walls. I looked around and saw tall candles standing on the floor, and I could smell the burning wax."

"Irena whispered to me, 'I'm going to sing in the choir. We're to the left of the altar. You watch the people and do exactly what they do. When they pray, you keep quiet. This is vespers. Be prepared.'"

"I nodded my head, and she walked to the choir. I didn't understand what vespers were, but I decided to stay and wait and do what the people around me did."

"The service started, and the priest opened a big book on the pulpit. He started to read, and I didn't understand one word. The people around me repeated some of it. I looked around and saw that the church was packed with people of all ages. People knelt down, and I did the same."

"Up by the altar, behind the pulpit, was a big wooden coffin, and lying in it was a clay statue of Jesus. The statue was very brightly painted. The people crawled on their knees up to the coffin and kissed the statue's feet."

"I didn't want to do it, but the people behind me forced me ahead. When I reached the coffin, I didn't kiss the feet; I just looked and crawled away."

"After they kissed the feet, everybody stood up and walked behind the pulpit to a big stand with an icon on top of it. The icon was covered by glass. They kissed the glass. I couldn't do it. There were too many kisses all over it. Once they kissed the icon, all the people went back to their places, but they had to stand through the whole service."

"When everybody was finished kissing the statue and the icon, the priest continued reading, and the people continued to repeat some things he read. I looked around some more. Irena stood in the first row of the choir. When the priest stopped reading, the choir started singing. They started singing very quietly, then more loudly, then softly again. It was a beautiful melody. The choir stopped singing, and the people started to pray again.

"It was so stuffy in there. The smoke from the candles and the stuffy air made it hard to breathe. I took my coat off and held it in my arms. The coat was made of heavy wool; it was a uniform coat."

"I don't remember how long I stood like that, but I felt like I had no energy. I felt nauseous, and my head started spinning, amaybe because of the stuffiness of the place or maybe because I was hungry, or maybe both. For a minute, everything was completely silent. People stood with their heads bowed and prayed without a sound."

"Suddenly, I said, very loudly, 'Irena! Let's go.'"

"Maybe my voice was too loud. Everybody turned and looked at me. Irena's eyes were wide open. The next moment, somebody grabbed me by the collar. The church door was open, and they kicked me out."

"I walked into the middle of the cemetery. It was very late. All around me were crypts and graves. The moonlight was hazy. I walked down the paths. It was cold, and I put my coat on and put my collar up.

I heard an owl hoot in the trees. Leaves on the ground rustled. I was so tired and hungry, and I felt I didn't have the energy to walk anymore."

"To the right of where I stood was a grave covered by a flat marble slab. I took my coat off, put it down on the slab, lay on half of it and covered myself with the other half. I remember looking at the sky and seeing the stars, but I don't remember anything else. I just fell asleep."

"I woke up because somebody was shaking me by a shoulder. When I opened my eyes, I saw a man and a woman looking at me. The woman was holding a lighted candle. I stood up, took my coat, and walked away."

"I heard the woman say, 'Homeless and wandering around. What kind of place is this to sleep?'"

"When I got close to the church, I heard Irena calling me. 'Rita! Where are you?' When I came close to her, she shushed me, and then she said, 'How in the world could you scream in church? Don't you know how to behave yourself?'"

"No, I didn't know how to behave in church. How could I know? Nobody told me. But Irena didn't understand. I was so far away from religion and had no idea how to behave myself in that situation. If I'd known what vespers were, I would never have agreed to go. And to be hungry for a whole day before!"

"You make me laugh so hard I'm crying," Wanda said, wiping her tears. "We're going to a funeral, and you're telling me a story like that. You can finish it later. We're at the building where he lived."

They walked through a gate at the side of the building and followed an alley around to the rear courtyard. They saw a coffin lying on a table in the middle of the courtyard. On it were flowers, and around it were wreaths. Wanda put her flowers on the coffin and then took the flowers from Rita and placed them on the coffin as well.

Rita looked at the deceased and turned her face away. Wanda took her arm and said, "Let's go. I can't stay here." Rita nodded, and they walked back to the street.

"Now you've seen the spectacle," Wanda said. "But this is nothing. When the whole procession walks to the cemetery, you can hear crying, screaming, and lamentation. I don't think you'd like that."

"You're right," Rita said. "Let's go home. I feel sick." They walked quietly home.

Rita had wanted to see the funeral because she was curious, but she could not stand more than a few minutes. She could not look at the dead man's blue face and the mark on his neck.

Wanda had not thought there would be so many people. They were probably neighbors from the buildings around. And she had not expected so many wreaths. He had been in the Army and was a hero, but because he had committed suicide he received only a civilian ceremony, according to law.

Wanda thought about many things during the thirty-minute walk home. Yesterday, this was a person; today, he was gone. Rita walked next to her and asked no questions. Wanda was glad she was quiet.

"We're almost home," Wanda said when they stopped at the corner of their block. "Do you see your building? The one with the columns? I have to stop at the grocery store."

"Oh, yes," Rita answered, "I see it. Good-bye, Aunt Wanda."

Wanda turned right to the store. She had not had wine for a long time. She had not wanted it. But now something inside her craved a drink. Perhaps she saw life from a different perspective.

Like before, she bought a large bottle of wine and went home. She drank a glass, then a second. She became intoxicated at last and fell asleep with her head on the table. She awoke with a terrible headache, finished the wine, and felt better. Subconsciously, she knew she was an alcoholic. Any kind of stress pushed her to the bottle. She wanted only to forget her past and not think about her unhappy future.

The next morning, she went to work very early. She covered her head with a kerchief and pulled it low over her eyes. The girls walked past her and said hello. When Rita opened the door and saw Wanda, she asked, "Why have you covered your head like that? Are you ill?"

"Yes," Wanda said. "I have a headache. Why are you not at work?"

"I'm on the second shift this summer. In September, when I start school, I'll work one week on the day shift and one week on the night shift. I'll rotate between the first and third shifts."

"I see. But tell me, how can you work at night after you come home from school? You're so tiny. How will you find the strength?"

"Like I told you before, I'm strong. Your face looks sweaty. Did you cry when we got back from the funeral?"

"You see everything. Don't pay attention to me." Wanda walked away, carrying a mop and bucket.

Rita saw that she was bothering Wanda with her questions, and she walked to the back courtyard. She had known Wanda only a few days, but she felt drawn to her. Rita was an orphan. She was not used to having someone take care of her. No one had paid special attention to her. She always watched people, however, especially older people. She liked to ask questions because she knew older people could teach her. Rita had seen Wanda stop and watch the girls jump down from the truck that first day. Wanda had looked different, not like the janitors Rita had seen before. She saw a kind of nobility in Wanda's face, a soft smile. Rita caught herself thinking about Wanda often, and sometimes she felt as though she had known the lady for a long time.

Wanda cleaned the corridors and kitchens and walked out to the courtyard.

She saw Rita sitting on a bench, reading a book.

"Where does she find her optimism, her courage, and her stubbornness?" Wanda thought, looking at the girl. She put the mop and bucket away and sat down on the bench next to Rita.

The girl raised her head and looked at Wanda questioningly. "What are you reading?" Wanda asked. "Let me see the book."

"This is <u>Jenny Gerhardt</u> by Theodore Dreiser."

Rita handed the book to Wanda and added, "I finished <u>Jane Eyre</u> not long ago. It was a very good novel by Charlotte Bronte, very easy to read."

"That's good. You like to read. It's important that you understand what you read. Many people read all the time, but when you ask them what they've read, they can't tell you."

"As I told you before, I have to talk about everything I read to the girls. I don't know how we'll manage now that we're working different shifts. There's only one Sunday left."

"Tell me, would you like to be a writer someday, and write novels people will read again and again? What do you think about that?"

"Oh, no. I don't have anything to write. I don't have any interesting characters to write about. Also, you have to be in school for a long time to become a professional writer."

"You're right about that," Wanda said with a smile. "If you have a story and find characters for a novel, would you be able to write about them?"

"I've never thought about it," Rita answered, shrugging. "What can I write about now? It's a different time, and there are so many writers."

"I can give you a subject, and I believe you can write it someday. But I'm not sure this book will be published here."

"In a year, I'll graduate from high school and go to the university. I have to support myself. I'm not sure I'll be able to find the time to write a book."

"You're right. I don't know what I'm talking about. Come to my place tomorrow. I'll give you an interesting book I bought in the flea market. It's an old book, <u>Princess Kozansky</u>. I think you'll like it."

"Thank you. When I finish this book, I'll come over. I've never heard of that book."

"I have to go," Wanda said. "Good luck to you on your first day at work … Oh, I almost forgot to ask you to finish your story about your first Easter. How does it end?"

Rita smiled and closed her book. "I stopped when Irena told me that I hadn't behaved myself because I talked loud in church. I didn't answer her back because I was half asleep, hungry, and very, very tired.

"The people were standing outside around the church in a circle with their baskets of food at their feet. Irena's sister had come with her husband, and they had brought a basket, too. They joined the circle.

"I saw the priest's assistant, a man with a long beard and long hair, walking and swinging a container with smoke coming out of it. The priest walked behind him and dipped a brush in a bucket of water and sprinkled water on the food in the baskets. Some of the water hit me, and I tried to brush it off.

"Irena said, 'don't brush the water away. It's holy water.'"

"When the priest walked away, everybody picked up his basket and left through the gate in the churchyard."

"Irena said, 'He blessed our food. Now we go home and break our fast.'"

"I didn't ask any questions, even though I didn't know what she meant by 'break our fast.' I followed her and her sister and her sister's husband."

"The road back looked so long to me because I was so tired. When we finally reached their home, I had no strength at all. Inside the house, everybody started kissing each other and saying, 'Jesus has risen.' And everybody answered, 'Truly risen.'"

"I didn't understand anything they were talking about. I asked permission to lie down on the chimney seat where it was warm. They gave me a blanket and I fell asleep right away."

"They tried to wake me a couple of times, but I couldn't open my eyes. I slept all day and all night. I don't remember when I've slept that long in my life."

"The next morning I climbed down from the chimney seat. I felt refreshed. I brushed and braided my hair and sat down for breakfast. Everybody looked at me and then at each other."

"I can see everything you've told me. I think someday you'll be a writer. Remember my words."

"I'd like to be an engineer, but time will tell."

"Tell me, do you remember who your parents were?"

"No, I can't remember, but my aunt told me. My father was a physics and mathematics professor. He was a teacher in a military academy. That's why he went into active service the first day of the war. He was a volunteer instructor for a civilian aviation club, too. He was killed in nineteen forty-four. His plane was shot down."

"My mother was a pianist. We had a nanny who lived with us. I remember her much better than anyone else. When we evacuated, she moved to the village she came from, and we didn't see her anymore. Her name was Elizabeth."

"Of course. If there had been no war, your life would be completely different. It's the same with me. If there had been no war in nineteen fourteen, I would have lived a different life. All right. I have to go now. We'll talk more another time."

Wanda walked to her forlorn little corner and memories of her past gathered around her. She understood the girl whom she had left sitting on the bench with a book. She knew they shared the same grief brought on by war. But Wanda was from a different generation. She had had a different childhood. She had been raised differently.

She rushed home to have a drink and forget about everything. When she was drunk, her feelings were half asleep, and she saw things in a different light. Later, she fell asleep, and when she awoke, she felt awful. Her head hurt, and her whole body ached. Only more alcohol could make her feel better.

About two weeks later, after drinking some wine, one morning Wanda felt a little drunk. She walked over to the corner where the icon was displayed and fell to her knees.

"Maybe you can answer my questions," she said. "Even just one question. Why am I still alive? Please, ask your son to take me. If you can, beg him for me. Nobody needs me. Where is my daughter? Is she still alive? And my sister and her family? Why do I have this destiny? Why do I have to lead such a wretched existence? No. You look at me and say nothing. You don't have any answers. You don't have anything to say."

Tears fell from her eyes. Her face was wet with them. She sobbed loudly, in bursts of anguish. She had to release the pain she had held inside for so long. She did not hear the knock at her door or the door opening.

It was Rita. She had knocked, and when no one answered, she had pushed the door open. She saw Wanda on her knees in front of the icon. She did not understand what she saw and heard. Wanda's tears and her sobs confused Rita. She thought something terrible had happened. She walked up to Wanda and put her hands on the older woman's shoulders.

"Please," she said, "don't cry. Has something happened? Maybe I can help you."

Wanda jumped with surprise, and Rita continued, "I knocked, but you didn't answer. I opened the door and came in, and I saw you crying so hard." Wanda did not answer. She stood and then sat down in a chair at the table.

Rita sat in another chair and gave Wanda a handkerchief.

"No, thank you," Wanda said. "I'll wash my face."

She washed and then sat down, wiping her face with a towel. Rita was quiet. She knew it was no time to ask questions. Wanda looked at the girl and felt a burden lifted from her heart.

"You know," she said, "God himself sent you to me. I don't feel lonely when you're around. I have someone to talk to. How is your job? I haven't seen you for a couple of weeks."

"It's very hard, physically. The machine is very old and big. I don't have the strength to stay on my feet for a whole shift. I make very little money because I can't keep up with my production schedule. In a month, I go to school. I don't know how I'll manage."

"I think you're hungry. I have some potato soup and bread. Let's eat together."

Wanda was right. Rita was hungry. Her salary was enough to buy one summer dress, a pair of summer shoes, and a ribbon for her braided hair. The rest was only enough for stamps to send letters to her brother in Siberia and her aunt in Kiev. In the letters, she explained that she was happy and everything was fine.

They sat and ate the potato soup. To Rita, it was delicious. She noticed the half-empty bottle of wine on the table.

"Aunt Wanda," she asked, "do you drink wine?"

"Yes, I drink. What else did I have left?"

Rita was quiet. She shrugged one shoulder and continued eating.

"You remember I told you I'd like you to write a book?" Wanda asked. "Not now. Some time in the future."

"What book? About what? I don't understand."

"Finish your soup and all the bread I cut for you. I'll try to explain what I'm talking about."

Wanda walked to her bed and pulled out the package wrapped in a blanket. As Rita ate, she unwrapped the portrait and leaned it against the edge of the bed.

"Who is that?" Rita asked, startled.

"Look closer. Maybe you'll recognize her."

Rita walked close and then backed away, surveying the painting.

"No," she said. "I don't know who she is. All I can say is that she's a very rich and very young woman. How did you get this picture? And why do you keep it under your bed? The place for a picture like that is in a museum."

"Oh, Rita, you don't understand. Sit down, my dear. I'll try to explain." Rita sat, and Wanda continued. "This is my portrait. I was seventeen then.

This was painted in Italy. Do you see the date? Nineteen hundred and seven. It was my honeymoon."

Rita was mesmerized. She had read fairy tales and novels, but she had never seen a character from a fairy tale or novel.

Wanda looked at her and thought, "If only this girl can do what I want her to do."

"Listen," she said to Rita, "I don't know how long I'll live. I know my health is ruined. I drink every day. I'm an alcoholic. I have one wish— someday, when I'm gone, people will read about my life. I'd like to tell you the story of my life. Maybe, when people read it, they'll learn something from it. But I wonder. Maybe you could go to Poland someday, and they'll publish it there. Do you speak and understand Polish?"

"Yes. I was raised in the west Ukraine. Before nineteen thirty-nine I was in Poland. Of course we spoke and understood Polish, but we couldn't read or write it. Why do you ask?"

"I have a sister and her family in Poland. I've had no letters from her since the early thirties. Can you make notes and take down everything I tell you about my life? Someday, maybe you can write the book."

"I've never tried. Yes, I can make notes about everything you tell me. We can see what happens."

"That's good. But don't tell anybody. Keep this between us. Do you agree?"

"All right. What time is it? I have to go to work. I'm on the second shift. Thank you for the soup."

"Listen, my child. I think you have no money. I can give you some. I don't use it anyway."

"I'll just borrow it and pay you back when I get paid."

"That's fine. As you wish."

Wanda gave Rita the money and said, "Come tomorrow. Bring a notebook and a pen. At ten o'clock. All right?"

"Yes, that's a good time."

Rita left, taking with her some money and some of the warmth of this suffering woman.

At ten o'clock the next morning, as they had agreed, Rita knocked on Wanda's door. It wasn't clear to her what Wanda wanted, but she knew Wanda needed someone to hear her out. She would not feel lonely and unneeded.

On that morning, in July, 1952, Wanda started her story from her childhood. Rita listened with great interest. She made notes of dates, names, places, and events.

A short time before, Rita had told Wanda that she did not cry, that she was strong and tenacious. But now, Rita often brushed tears away from her childlike face. When she returned to the dormitory, she hid the notebook in her nightstand.

Naturally, the girls noticed how Rita had changed. She was quieter, more introspective. They saw she spent her free time with the old woman.

"Rita," one of the girls asked, "have you found a relative?"

"What are you talking about?" Rita responded, looking at the other girl anxiously.

"Everybody's talking about how you spend all your time with that old woman."

"Her name is Aunt Wanda. Why do you call her 'old woman?' That's not nice."

"You haven't read anything lately, and you don't tell us stories anymore, because you don't have time."

"Try to read by yourself. It's good for you."

"That old woman has cast a spell over you. We heard she has an icon. Maybe she's teaching you to believe in God and how to pray?"

"That's nonsense. We have freedom of religion. If she believes in God, she can pray. That's her right, but she never talks to me about that."

"Ok. Then tell us, what are you talking about every day?"

"It's none of your business." Rita walked out of the room, ending the discussion.

Very often, however, the girls bothered her with questions. Finally, though, all of them found their own interests, their own boyfriends, and left her alone. They went dancing, to the movies, to the park, and to the beach.

Some days, Rita went to Wanda's and found her very drunk, asleep with her head on the table. She never locked her door during the day. With difficulty, Rita dragged Wanda to the bed, removed her shoes, and covered her with a blanket.

Rita was always curious to find out what was next in Wanda's story. When Wanda was drunk, however, she could not talk, only mumble and then fall asleep again.

"You asked me to make these notes," Rita told Wanda when the older woman was able to listen, "but if you continue to drink your wine, I can't take notes. Maybe this isn't such a good idea. Maybe I don't need to come over anymore. What do you think?"

"You're right," Wanda said. "I have nothing to say. I drink. It's very painful for me to tell you about myself. I know very well what I've lost and whom I've lost. Please, be patient, my child. I'll be sober, and we can continue. Don't say this isn't a good idea. Try to understand, a little, how hard it is for me to go over and over my past and my grief."

"I'm trying to understand. I swear. But try not to drink like that. Your hands are shaking. You can't do your work in this condition. It hurts to look at you."

"I'll retire soon. I have eight months left. As people say, 'Drunks always wake up, but the stupid never do.' But you're right, of course. I drink more now."

All her free time, and she had little of it, Rita spent with Wanda. On Sundays, they sat for hours. Wanda told Rita the story of her life, and Rita took notes. Now Rita understood clearly that she could not write this book, and even if she did write it, it would not be published. This girl, who was raised by the Soviet authorities and who was still being educated by them, instead of by her parents who gave their lives for their country, understood life differently. She saw the world around her from a different perspective, with Wanda's help. She was no longer excited by the words from a popular song: "How beautiful life is in this Soviet country." She felt hungry and impoverished even though she worked very hard. She knew she had to do everything by herself, to fight for survival. Even though she knew she could not write a book about Wanda's life, she continued to take notes.

School started for Rita, and she had less and less time for Wanda. On the weekends, however, she always visited her. They ate breakfast together. Rita brought something, and Wanda prepared it. After breakfast, Wanda talked and Rita took notes. Wanda no longer drank until after Rita left.

On New Year's Eve, 1953, Rita celebrated with the young people from the factory. The next day, January 1, she visited Wanda.

The Soviet authorities had taken the religious holiday, Christmas, away, but they could not remove the custom. People celebrated New Years by decorating a Christmas tree and giving each other gifts on New Year's Day. Children had their school holidays after New Year's, and they were called the winter holidays.

Rita brought Wanda a pair of slippers. She knocked on Wanda's door with the box tucked under her arm. Wanda answered the door and smiled when she saw Rita.

"I knew you were coming," Wanda said. "I've been waiting for you. I made a wish yesterday, and I remember, in my time, when I was young, if we made a wish on New Year's Eve, it would come true. Come in and sit down. I have some lemon and some jam pastries. We'll have some tea."

Rita looked at Wanda, puzzled. Wanda's eyes sparkled, but she was absolutely sober. Rita had seen her drunk many times.

"Aunt Wanda, I brought these for you," Rita said. "Please try them on. I didn't know your size." She handed Wanda the box.

"Thank you, my child," Wanda said, "for your kindness. It's very nice to know that somebody remembers you."

She tried on the slippers. They were soft and comfortable, and they were the right size.

"I have something for you, too," she said, "but I'll explain it later. Right now, let's have tea."

"Aunt Wanda," Rita said, "I see you haven't been drinking, but you're in a very good mood. What happened?"

"I have a surprise for you. This year, you'll be seventeen, and I'd like to give you one special gift. You'll always remember me."

Rita thought, "Oh, I believe she wants to give me her icon. What will I do with it?"

They drank tea, and Wanda asked, "Did you bring your notebook and pen with you? We need to continue the story."

"Of course. I always have them with me when I visit you. Last time, we stopped where Esther passed away."

"I remember. We'll make notes later. Now, we should wish each other happiness during this year. For your success in school. You'll graduate this year with good grades. For your poetry, I wish your muse will often visit you."

"To your health, Aunt Wanda. I hope to come over and visit you for a long time to come."

They raised their glasses of tea, laughed, and drank.

"I'd also like to wish you—but I suppose it's just advice—never in your life will you smoke, and don't touch alcohol. I see your nature, your character. If you ever start, you'll never stop."

"I've never had a desire to drink or smoke. Almost all the girls in the dormitory smoke, and on the weekends, they pool their money and drink. Never has anyone asked me to join them. They know my principles."

"I know, but just keep it in mind. Now, my dear girl, I'd like to give you my portrait. That's all that's left to me from my past. Someday, you'll get married, have your own family, your own apartment, and you can hang my portrait on your wall. I was seventeen then, as you will be in April. This is my gift to you."

"No, no. This is a very expensive gift. I have no place for it. What can I do with your portrait in the dormitory?"

"You can leave it here, but remember, it's yours from now on."

"Thank you very much, but it will be years and years before I can take it." After discussing the portrait, they turned back to Wanda's story.

Historic events occurred in 1953. The people's leader, Joseph Stalin, died. It was announced on the radio on March 5. They recounted his many titles and his great services to his country.

Rita entered Wanda's room just as Wanda was pouring herself a glass of wine.

"Oh, Rita," Wanda cried. "I waited for you today. I even fried potatoes, your favorite. Now I have to have a drink because the great leader has died, and I hope he floats in limbo forever." As she finished speaking she put the glass to her lips and drank.

"How can you talk like that?" Rita protested. "What will happen now that he's dead?"

"Nothing will happen. The earth will spin as it has spun before, and life will be better than it was before. Maybe never again will his terror of the thirties occur."

"What are you saying? Stalin was our leader. He took the country after Lenin, and the people followed him. Thousands died in the war with his name on their lips. I know that everything isn't as it should be and needs to be changed, but it's the local governments that are the problem. Stalin was the leader. He was always right. In the orphanage, we called him Father."

"Rita, my dear, sit down. Listen. The time will come when you'll remember my words. Your great leader will be dethroned. You don't know anything about thirty-seven, thirty-eight, thirty-nine, and after. I met people and talked to them, people who were sent to jail during his 'cleansings.' In Ural and Siberia, many, many innocent people spent years. Many of them were exonerated, but only after death. Their relatives received letters saying that they had been sent away by mistake. Many of those who survived were made invalids. If you could hear how people in Ural and Siberia talked about your leader. Only the relatives and some close friends know exactly what happened. You won't find that story in any Soviet history book."

"What did you do in Siberia? Did they send you over there during one of Stalin's cleansings?"

"No. Something happened to me before that. Today, we start from nineteen thirty-three. Don't look at me with so much surprise in those big eyes. All right, I've had a drink, but my head is clear."

It was true. Sometimes, Rita was surprised at Wanda's ability to remember dates and events. On this day of Stalin's death, she found out what she had never known in her life. She believed Wanda. She trusted her. She knew Wanda had no reason to lie.

On the same day, she discovered Wanda had a daughter, Maria— Masha— somewhere in Rumania, and Wanda did not know what had happened to her.

Wanda gave Masha's diary to Rita. The diary's contents surprised Rita. She found out about a good Rumanian. Not all of them were fascist. But what had happened to Masha? Rita thought about it often. If she were still alive, why had she not returned? Perhaps she was afraid to come back because she had left Odessa with a Rumanian. Rita said nothing to Wanda and decided to look for Masha on her own.

In the factory where Rita worked was a young man from Muldavia, one of the Russian republics. It had been part of Rumania before 1940. He liked Rita and had asked her to go to the movie with him a few times. She always refused. She told him she was busy and had no time for dates. It was true. Her final examinations were approaching.

Recently, Rita had been promoted at work. She was no longer a lathe operator. She worked as a tool inspector. She no longer made parts; she checked them for quality control. She made a little more money. Like everyone else, she worked six days a week, with only Sunday free.

One Saturday, Ivan, the young Muldavian, asked Rita for a date again. Ivan was a good looking young man with full, chestnut-colored, curly hair, gray eyes, and a kind smile. Every girl would have liked to have a date with him, but Rita was not interested in boys then. She spent time at work, at school, and with Aunt Wanda.

But on that day, she agreed to go. Ivan was smiling. He was happy because the men in his dormitory had bet that Rita would never date him. They had been mistaken.

Rita and Ivan walked on the path in the park. He told her about Muldavia, and she told him about western Ukraine.

"Listen, Vanya," she said. "Can I call you that? In Muldavia, do people speak the same language as in Rumania?"

"Yes, the language is the same, but it's a different dialect."

"Can you read and write Rumanian?"

"Of course. I graduated from school in Kishenev, the capitol of Muldavia. Why do you ask?"

"Because I can speak and understand Polish, but I can't read or write it. My orphanage was in Strei City, close to Livov. It was in Poland before nineteen thirty-nine, and my language, Ukrainian, has many words that are the same in Polish. I like Russian, though, and I think it's the most beautiful language."

"No. Rumanian is a very soft and beautiful language. If you'd like, I can teach you."

"No," Rita said, shaking her head. "You can do me another favor. Can we sit down on a bench? I'll explain what I need."

She told him briefly about a woman who lost her daughter during the war.

The daughter lived in Rumania, and Rita was helping find her.

"I hope you can help me," she said, finally. "You could send a letter, in Rumanian, to the Red Cross. I've heard that that organization searches for people."

Vanya agreed to help her, if she would agree to go to the movie with him the next day.

"Only in the daytime," she answered. "If you don't agree, I won't go at all." He submitted and said he would prepare a letter in the morning. Rita said nothing to Wanda. Why make her worry? It was Rita's hope to find Wanda's daughter.

Rita figured Masha's age at about thirty-five from the notes she had taken. Masha's name was Stanishevsky. Rita gave all the information to Vanya for the letter.

When Vanya gave her the letter, he said, "The first of May I have some vacation. I'm going to Kishenev for two weeks. We have a Rumanian consulate there. I can give the letter to them."

"Thank you very, very much," Rita said. "You can't imagine how much you've helped me."

Rita had to pay for Vanya's help, of course. She went with him to the movies and to the theatre, where they watched Tchaikovsky's <u>Sleeping Beauty</u> ballet and the <u>Nutcracker</u>. They heard the opera <u>Iolanta</u>, also by Tchaikovsky, Rita's favorite composer. She went with Vanya even though she felt nothing for him.

Vanya had already told her he loved her, but he saw that his words got no reaction. Finally, he stopped talking about love.

Once, at the end of April, when Rita visited Wanda, she said, "You told me you were in love many times. You liked young men, and you had some feeling for them. Why don't I feel anything? I go with Vanya only because he is a good friend who takes me to the movies and the theatre when I have no money. I don't want him to touch my hand, much less kiss me."

"Your time hasn't come yet," Wanda told her. You'll meet someone later whom you will love. You're not grown up yet. You're seventeen, but you look like a little chicken. The war and starvation left an impression on you. Look at the girls around you. They have full chests, and you haven't had a bra in your seventeen years. You're just a late bloomer."

"Can we change the subject?" Rita protested. "I don't like to talk about it."

"You see. You're even ashamed to talk about it. This is a normal conversation. This is a result of the way you were raised in the orphanage. I was raised in a Catholic girl's school until I was fifteen. I didn't know much then, but later I discovered the world in a different way. Believe me, you've got your whole life ahead of you. If you don't like this boy, don't force yourself to go with him."

"Sure," Rita thought, "it's easy for her to say that." She waited for an answer from Rumania and hoped Vanya would be able to read it. She did not want to tell Wanda about her agreement with him.

In May, Vanya went home for vacation. He was eighteen years old and would go into the Army soon. All young men had to serve when they reached eighteen. Rita knew that when Vanya went into the Army, their relationship would end.

Rita's examinations began, and she took time off work so she could prepare. On Sundays, she still visited Wanda.

"Pretty soon, my child," Wanda said, "you'll be finished taking notes. In a few months, I'll be retired. I know my retirement pension will be half what I make now, but it will be enough for me to survive until I die. What I want to ask you is that, when I die, you will arrange to have me buried. I've saved a little money, enough for the funeral. I want to be buried next to my father. There's an empty space next to his grave. In a week, it will be Easter. Perhaps you can come with me to the cemetery and I'll show you."

"What are you saying, Aunt Wanda? You'll live a long life. You have to live, not think about death. I'll go with you to the cemetery, but where is it?" Wanda told her where the cemetery was and what kind of transportation she used.

Rita said, "Oh, no. That cemetery is closed. They don't bury anybody there anymore."

"But if there's space? You can do me this favor. I'm counting on you. I have no one except you."

Rita did not argue. Why should she? She knew it was only a wish. At that moment, she did not need to upset Wanda. "All right," she said. "We'll go to the cemetery together, and you can show me your father's grave."

Easter came. It was later that year and very warm. Acacias bloomed. Lilacs flowered, and tulips on the graves nodded their beautiful heads in the breeze. Wanda and Rita walked on the cemetery path, and Wanda said, "This is my destiny, to stay in Russia forever and walk on this path. Through the years of my grief I've returned here and talked like a madwoman to my father's grave. You see, my child, this is all that is left for me."

Rita walked quietly. Now she knew the entire story of Wanda's life. She was not frightened of the cemetery, but she felt chilled by Wanda's words. They reached the grave, and Wanda knelt. She crossed herself and began to pray silently. Rita stood aside and watched her.

The white-haired woman knelt on the ground facing the monument. On the obelisk, in its frame, was the brown-toned picture of the man who lay there. She knelt with her shoulders straight and her head held proudly. Her hair, still thick and wavy, was tied in a bun on the back of her head. Her face, thus exposed, was classic in profile. She had obviously been a very beautiful woman, but at that moment, Rita saw her differently than she ever had before.

Wanda did not cry. She stood and turned to Rita. "You see that empty plot behind you? I'd like to be buried there."

Rita listened without speaking. They walked toward the gate, and Wanda said, "Here everybody finds peace; all vanities are at an end. When we're young and healthy, we never think about it, but it is a fact of life, my dear. This is final."

"Aunt Wanda," Rita asked, "who planted the mountain ash beside your father's grave?"

"Sophie and I planted it. It was a very tiny tree."

They walked on without talking. Wanda thought her own thoughts. Rita could see the episodes of Wanda's life as they had been told to her.

On the envelope Rita had given to Ivan was her return address. She waited for an answer. Ivan returned from vacation. He had given the letter to the Rumanian consulate.

"I did everything you asked," Ivan told Rita. "They told me the letter would go to the Rumanian Red Cross. I have some news. In June I go into the Army for three whole years. Can we spend some time together before I go?"

"You're joking. I have final exams. July second is the last one. After that, I have a prom to attend."

"I forgot, but you can see me off at the train station, can't you?"

Rita said yes, that she would see him off, and she kept her word. As they said good-bye, Ivan kissed her on the cheek and said, "I'll write often. Do you promise to answer?"

"I won't promise anybody anything. Circumstances might change."

"You'll be married before I come back."

Rita laughed. "You're so cute, Vanya. I don't even date. I'm too busy. I work and I'll be going to the university. Look at me. Do I look like a girl who's going to be married? As Aunt Wanda says, I look like a little chicken."

"It's good, Rita, that you spend time with that lonely woman. I've followed you many times and then waited for you—sometimes for a couple of hours—

until you leave her room."

Rita stared at him surprised. She had no idea he had followed her. "And how long have you been watching me?" she asked.

"Come on, I wasn't watching you. I was just following you. When I saw you the first time, I fell in love, but you're not an easy girl to know. Very few boys can get close to you. If I had seen you with another boy, I would have been jealous, but I saw that you were with that lonely woman."

They stood on the platform, talking, and heard an announcement: "All recruits take your seats on the train."

"This is it, Rita," Vanya said. "I hope you find your friend's daughter."

"Thank you, Vanya. Thank you for everything. You're a good friend." Ivan tossed his rucksack over his shoulder and stepped up into the railroad car. Rita stayed on the platform until the train left and then slowly walked toward the trolley stop. She felt sorry that the train had carried this boy away. She had no special feelings for him, but he was not a stranger. She spent about an hour with Wanda on her way home, but her mood did not improve.

"I'm going home," she said to Wanda. "I feel so sad. My prom is coming soon, and I don't want to go."

"That's not right, my child. You need to go. It happens only once in your life."

Rita said nothing because her reason was not sadness. She had no dress and no money to buy one.

The next day, Rita sat at the desk in her room and studied for the mathematics examination. Someone knocked on her door.

"Come in," she said. "It's open." She did not turn to see who entered.

"Rita, it's me. Are you busy?" asked Wanda.

"Yes, I'm busy. I have an exam tomorrow. But if you've come, it must be because you need something."

"Look what I brought you. It's important that it fit you." Rita turned around and saw Wanda holding a package. "What is that?" she asked.

"This is a dress for you, and summer shoes. This is the smallest size dress for a girl your age, size one. The shoes are size five.'

Wanda unwrapped the package and gave Rita a white dress, simple but attractive, trimmed in white lace, and white shoes with half-heels. "Where did you buy these? How will I pay for them?"

"Don't worry, child. I bought them a few weeks ago from a woman who works at the school where I worked. Her son-in-law bought this dress for his wife. He's a sailor on a merchant ship, and he brought it from Bulgaria. It was too small for his wife. The shoes I bought at the flea market. Someone had them made to order and then didn't buy them. Don't worry about money. Everything cost only a few rubles. Let's try them on now."

Rita forgot how busy she was. She put on the dress and shoes. They fit perfectly.

"You know what?" Wanda said. "White is your color. You look beautiful."

"Thank you very, very much. You're just like Cinderella's godmother. You just touched me with your wand and my rags became a princess's clothes. The shoes are so comfortable, just like they were made for my feet. Thank you again."

She walked to Wanda, hugged her, and kissed her. Wanda wiped away her own tears.

Rita attended the prom and felt as though she were no different than anyone else there. Wanda had been right. It was a once-in-a-lifetime experience.

It was the middle of July. Rita was studying for her university entrance exams in August. She received letters from Ivan, but she did not answer them. When she talked to Wanda, she explained why she did not respond.

"If I start to write to him, he'll write back, and then I'll have to answer again. I'll begin to feel obligated. So I won't answer, he'll see that I won't answer, and he'll stop writing."

"No, that's no good. You must answer him and explain that you've graduated, and now you're busy with entrance exams. Explain that you're very busy, and wish him the best. He's in love with you, and he misses you. I understand you don't love him, but he was your friend, and you should act like a friend."

"Yes, you're right. I'll write him a letter. What would I do without you, Aunt Wanda?"

Rita wrote to Ivan. She closed with these words: "Please, Vanya, don't write to me anymore. I'm very busy. When I find time, I'll write to you."

In August, Rita passed her exams and was accepted to the university. She waited for an answer from Rumania, but none came. At work, she received a raise. She had more money and, when she was paid, she went to Wanda.

"Now I can pay you back," she said. "You've been so kind to me. I've been given a raise, and I make more money."

"You don't owe me anything, just the opposite. I don't know how to pay you back for your company. Please, keep the money. The dress and shoes were my present to you for your graduation. Don't forget, child, I don't have anybody closer than you who will listen to me. Don't hurt my feelings over such small things."

Wanda was no longer working. She had retired and was receiving a minimal pension. She managed, however. She had enough even for a bottle of wine a week. She was forced to drink less than before.

Rita asked questions about the notes she had taken. Wanda remembered additional episodes, and Rita wrote them down. It was strange. Rita loved to retell stories she had read, but she had no desire to tell anyone the story of Wanda's life.

One Sunday, Rita visited Wanda and brought a book by Cronin, The Citadel. She had checked it out from the factory library, and she thought Wanda would like to read it. Lately, on Sundays, they had been eating brunch together. Wanda made pancakes, and Rita brought jam and honey. They drank tea and talked.

Rita knocked on Wanda's door, but no one answered. She knocked harder and called, "Aunt Wanda. It's me." She saw one of Wanda's neighbors.

"Your aunt has been taken to the hospital," the woman said. "She collapsed in the bakery on the corner. Someone called an ambulance."

"Where did they take her? What hospital?"

"Go to the bakery. They can tell you." Rita thanked her and hurried away."

"Has she died?" she thought, "or is she still alive? It can't happen like this. I haven't told her about her daughter yet. Oh, God, make a miracle. Let her still be alive. If you exist in this world, and she believes in you, I beg you for her."

Rita spoke to God for the first time in her life. She asked that someone close to her be helped. She prayed without knowing she had done so.

At the bakery, Rita was told that Wanda had been taken to Jewish Hospital. "That's not possible," she said. "She's not Jewish. She's Catholic."

"No, no, that's just a name," a sales clerk told her. "The hospital was built before the revolution. The Jewish community gave the money to build it, but everybody used it."

She explained to Rita how to get to the hospital. Rita thanked her and left. When she arrived at the hospital, she put on a white smock, as required in all hospitals. She was directed to the cardiology unit.

Wanda had had a heart attack, but she was alive. She wore an oxygen mask and lay on her back in the bed. The nurse let Rita visit for five minutes, as if she were a close relative.

"Aunt Wanda," she whispered, "it's Rita. Do you hear me?"

Wanda opened her eyes and tried to speak. Rita put her finger to her lips, signalling for Wanda to be silent.

"I can talk. You just listen. All right? You're my aunt. I'm the only niece you have. They only let close relatives into this unit. You'll feel better soon. Now I'm going to go talk to the doctor on duty. There are only two visiting days, Wednesday and Sunday."

Wanda looked at Rita, and tears fell from her eyes. Rita wiped them away. "Don't cry, please, because they won't let me see you anymore."

Wanda nodded. The nurse walked in and said, "Your time is up. I have to give the patient a shot."

Wanda removed her oxygen mask and said to the nurse, "Please, let her stay a little longer, and give her my purse. I have a key to my room."

The nurse replaced the mask and said, "Don't do that, please. You've had a heart attack. Don't worry. I'll tell the people in admitting to give your purse to your niece." To Rita she said, "When you come during visiting hours, maybe they'll let you stay longer."

Rita bent, kissed Wanda on the forehead, and left. Tears choked her. She felt helpless and did not know what to do. She found a doctor, waited until he was free, and asked him about Wanda's condition.

"She's had a heart attack," he said, "but not a severe one. You can talk to her doctor on Monday." He gave Rita the doctor's name.

The next morning, Rita did not go to work. She was at the hospital at nine o'clock. She was given Wanda's purse. In it were the key, Wanda's pension documents, and some money. The doctor who was caring for Wanda was not free until eleven o'clock.

When Rita spoke to him, he said, "Wanda Stanishevsky has a bad heart. Even if she recovers from this attack, there's no guarantee she'll not have another. She must be very quiet; nothing must be allowed to disturb her. She cannot drink alcohol, coffee, or tea. In three weeks, if there are no complications, she can go home. As I said, though, she must be very careful with her health."

Rita could see that Wanda was very sick. From the hospital, she went to Wanda's room. When she opened the door, she saw an unfinished bottle of wine. The portrait was wrapped and standing next to the bed. On the nightstand was a note.

"Rita, dear, I'm not feeling well," Wanda had written. "I feel pressure in my chest, and it's not easy to breathe. I'm going out for some fresh air. If something happens to me, you know my portrait is my gift to you. Everything I have belongs to you. Thanks for everything. Wanda. P.S. I only wish. ..." The note was unfinished.

Rita threw the bottle of wine away, closed the door, and went to work.

"Is it possible she could die?" she thought. "Why is there no answer from Rumania?"

At the desk next to Rita sat Tina. She asked Rita, "Why are you so quiet? What are you thinking about?"

"I have something to think about, Tina."

"You can share it with me," Tina said. And she added, "What could you worry about at seventeen years of age? I have a lot on my mind. I'm divorced, and I have a child and an old mother on my hands. And now I've broken up with my boyfriend. You see? I have plenty to think about. What do you have?"

Rita looked at her wide-eyed. Tina had never been so open with her before. When Rita had transferred to that job, she had had a feeling she was not welcome because she was the youngest. The others had been very stand-offish, but after a while they had accepted her easy-going, very honest ways.

Tina was about thirty, heavy-set, with short, very curly blond hair. Her face was covered with freckles, and she had blue eyes with no eyelashes. She was not pretty, but very likeable. She had a beautiful, dimpled smile and very large breasts. Everyone joked with her. "Tina," they said, "You should give something to Rita. You have so much, and she has nothing." Rita blushed at their remarks, but she said nothing. What could she say? It was true. At seventeen, she still looked fourteen.

"I didn't know you'd had so much trouble," Rita said to Tina. "You smile almost all the time."

"We're not talking about me. I asked why you look so worried."

"A friend of mine is in the hospital. She's very ill. She had a heart attack. Also, she's alone. All her relatives are dead."

"How old is she? Is she one of your girlfriends?"

"No. She's about sixty-four, I believe. She was a janitor in our dormitory, but now she's retired."

"You have a kind heart if you feel that way about a stranger," Tina said, serious now.

"She's not a stranger. I've known her for a year and a half. We see each other often. If you only knew what kind of person she is, what kind of life she's had. I only hope she feels better soon."

"Today, when you were gone for a couple of hours, were you visiting her?"

"Yes. I talked to the doctor, and he told me she has a bad heart."

"If you have to go again, just let me know. I'll cover for you. I can talk to the supervisor. He'll let you go."

"Thank you, Tina. I really appreciate it. I can use the help."

In the evening, before Rita went to bed, she wrote a letter to her brother. Someone knocked on her door and entered. Rita turned and saw a girl from the apartment above her.

"Good evening, Rita," the girl said. "The mailman brought you this letter today. It's special delivery, and I signed for you. I think it's from outside the country."

"Thank you. This is the answer to my inquiry."

"Are you looking for your relatives?"

"No, it's not for me. I'm trying to help somebody."

"Oh, I see. You've got a lot going on. Good luck to you." She left Rita alone after handing her the letter.

Rita opened the envelope. The contents surprised her. The letter was not from the Red Cross and not from the consulate. It was from Masha.

Masha asked for Rita's help in finding her mother and brother. At the end of the letter, she wrote her address and phone number.

Rita could not believe her eyes. She had found Wanda's daughter. She sat down and wrote an answer immediately, although she wrote nothing about Masha's brother. She said that Wanda was not feeling well and closed by adding, "If you can come, it might help your mother recover from her illness. It's such a pity your mother received none of your letters. Now she is ill, please answer me at this address."

The next morning, Rita went to the post office and sent the letter airmail, special delivery. A few days later, she visited Wanda.

When she entered Wanda's room, she saw six beds, three on each side of the room. Wanda was in the first bed. Rita sat down in the chair next to the bed and asked, "How do you feel, Aunt Wanda? I brought you some apples."

"I feel better, my child. I'm so happy to see you. Have you been in my room? Did you find a note?"

"Yes, I saw your note, but it was nonsense. The doctor said you'll feel better soon."

"The doctor doesn't know how long I'll be alive. God knows, and I feel it will not be long. Believe me, the sooner the better."

"Don't talk like that. Try to be optimistic. When you feel better, I have some very good news to tell you."

"I'd like to feel better and still be alive on your wedding day. What is the good news? Have you met somebody? You can tell me now."

Rita shook her head. "Not now. You're still in the hospital, and you should rest and not move. We have time."

Wanda smiled. "I guess you're right. I should be in better shape. I must find out what's on your mind. I think it's a boyfriend."

"No, it's not," Rita said, laughing. "It's completely different."

"Oh, sure. You're still a little chicken. But your time will come, and you'll remember what I said."

Visiting hours ended. Rita had just enough time to peel an apple and cut it in pieces for Wanda.

"I'll be back in three days," she said. "What would you like me to bring?"

"I don't need anything, my dear. It's only important that you come." Rita kissed Wanda's cheek. "Be healthy. Everything will be just fine." Wanda was crying. Rita wiped the tears away and walked out, trying not to weep herself. She had never felt this way before. Wanda was very close to her, and Rita's affection for her was deep.

Rita had grown up an orphan without human warmth, and now, as she grew closer to Wanda, to Wanda's kindness and soft voice, she realized she could lose all of it. She hoped that when Masha returned, Wanda would be saved.

At work, Rita asked the woman who replaced her on the second shift, "Claudia, do you know, by chance, how long it takes for somebody to get a visa from Rumania?"

"You know somebody in Rumania?"

"No, it's for a friend of mine. She's in the hospital, and I answered a letter for her."

"Let me see. There has to be a permit from the Soviet embassy in Bucharest, and the Rumanian government has to give her a visa to leave the country. I can't tell you how long it will take, but there's some time involved."

"Oh, no. It will be forever before she can come."

"Listen, Rita, why are you so worried if it's somebody else's problem."

"It's a long story. You wouldn't understand. Thank you anyway. Now I know I've got no hope." Rita walked to the door. Claudia ran to her and took her by the arm.

"You look so upset," Claudia said. "Maybe I can help you."

"Thank you. Tina covered for me for a couple of hours when I went to the hospital. You are nice people here. But I don't think you can help me."

"I can try. I'm a good listener. I'm twice as old as you are. I have two children, a husband, and an old father who's been an invalid since World War Two."

"All right. Let's go to the locker room. I'll try to explain to you as briefly as I can."

Claudia had a dark complexion and a narrow face. She looked like she was from the south. Everyone called her Clava the gypsy because there was another Claudia in the same department. They called her Clava the blondie.

Rita and Claudia sat on a bench in the locker room. Rita was trying to decide how to begin. Finally, she started.

"This lady lost her daughter during World War Two. Later, she found out her daughter had gone to Rumania. The lady worked in another city. Now I've found the daughter through the Red Cross, and I've asked the daughter to come visit her mother because she's in the hospital. That's the story."

"It's not a simple situation," Claudia said. "I don't understand. If the Germans forced your friend's daughter to work in Germany, how did she get to Rumania?"

"Nobody forced her to go anywhere. She married a good man and went with him to his home in Rumania."

"What? She married a Rumanian during the war? Listen, my dear, this isn't a simple venture you've started on. How old was she when she went to Rumania?"

"I think twenty-five. What's the difference?"

"You don't understand anything. She was an adult. She's responsible for her actions. Rumania collaborated with Germany. That means they were the enemy. Now do you understand what can happen?"

"No, I don't. I read her diary. She loved this man. She married him because they loved each other. I believe it's more important that people love each other. Don't you agree?"

"You're lucky if you marry somebody you love." Claudia's face changed suddenly, and Rita noticed.

"What can I do now?" Rita said. "Should I send her a letter telling her not to come? When her mother is feeling better, maybe she can go to Rumania and visit her."

"I don't know what to say. How ill is her mother?"

"She had a heart attack, but it wasn't very severe."

"It's still a very serious illness. I don't think she'll be able to go visit her daughter even when she feels better. Would you like to visit another country and see how people live there?"

"I've never thought about it. I haven't seen Russia yet. I'd like to go to Moscow and Leningrad. I dream of seeing the Hermitage."

"I'd like to go to America, to Chicago."

"You're kidding. How can you go to America? Nobody will let you go."

"I know nobody will let me go. But I can wish. Thank God I can still <u>wish</u>. Nobody can stop me from doing that."

"You have somebody in America? Relatives?"

"No." Claudia closed her eyes and leaned against the wall. "My first love is there."

"You're married. You have children. I don't understand what you're talking about."

"How could you understand, if I can't understand myself? I was sixteen when I met him. I was in ballet school. Our group danced in the theatre. He lived with his parents close to the theatre."

"We met after the concert. He brought me a bouquet of flowers. He chose me out of the whole group."

"His father was an attache in the American consulate at the Port of Odessa. They had lived in Odessa for seven or eight years."

"John spoke Russian very fluently. We dated for a year. It was the best year of my life."

"You're a child. You can't know how I loved him—more than anything in the world. He was a tall, skinny boy with light red hair."

"Why didn't you get married?"

"Our dates were ended. His father was called back to America. It was nineteen thirty-seven. You don't know what kind of time that was."

"He came to the theatre after the concert, like always, with a small bouquet of roses, and he said, 'Claudia, we're going home to Chicago. I want to stay, but I can't. I love you, Claudia, very much. You're my first love.'

"I don't remember how I answered him, but I started crying. He put my head on his shoulder and stroked my hair. Then, suddenly, he took hold of my shouldeers, pushed me away, and looked into my eyes. 'Let's get married,' he said. 'Then I can stay, or they'll let you come with me.'

"How did he find the courage? He was always so quiet and gentle. I went home and told my mother—she was alive then. 'John and I love each other, and we want to be married.' I said to her.

"Did you say you grew up an orphan, Rita? It's better that way. You're your own boss."

"To make the story short, my parents wouldn't let me go say good-bye to him. He was gone forever. I didn't see him again. They kept me in the apartment for a week. My mother slapped my face. I still feel it now."

Rita listened quietly, and Claudia said, "It's time to go to work, and you should go home, Rita. But I must add, if they let me go see him, I would leave everything, my apartment, my family, and walk the whole way without looking back."

Claudia walked out of the locker room, brushing her tears away. Rita sat on the bench, perplexed. After a while, she went home. She had encountered something beyond her understanding. The government would not let a daughter see her mother? She knew only that she wanted to help and that she was deeply involved.

"I think everything will be fine," she thought. "People understand. The government is people, too. And as for Claudia's story, that's her parents' fault. Those were terrible years."

Before she fell asleep, she thought about Claudia's story. After she fell asleep, she dreamed of Claudia walking in the desert. Her feet were sticking, as if in quicksand, but she continued walking. Suddenly, Rita felt that it was not Claudia, but she, Rita, who was walking. She sank to her knees in the sand.

Rita awoke. Someone was shaking her.

"Wake up," her roommate said. "You were moaning in your sleep."

Rita lay in bed with her eyes open for a long time. Her dream had been so real that she felt the hot sand on her feet.

Two weeks later, Wanda was still in the hospital. Rita waited for the doctor and asked how Wanda was.

"I regret to say that fluid is collecting in her lungs and around her heart. We've done everything we can, but we can't change her heart."

"Tell me, doctor," Rita said, crying, "how long will she live?"

"Calm yourself now. She could live for six months. It's not easy to tell. You must be ready anytime."

It was a warm autumn. The geese flew south in beautiful wedges in the sky. Rita sat on a bench on the hospital grounds and waited for visiting hours. She watched the geese. They flew to warm places, and in the spring they always came back.

"The don't have borders," she thought. "They're free. They're born free and stay free. Only people create forbidden territories. People suffer so much grief from borders."

Not long ago, Rita had said she could not cry. She did not understand many things. All she knew was what she learned from school and from her counselor in the orphanage. Wanda's life had opened her eyes to another world, a world of injustice and the inhuman attitudes of world politics. It was all new to her.

At one o'clock, visiting hours began. Rita put on her white smock and went to Wanda's room. Wanda was lying in bed, high on two pillows.

"How do you feel today, Aunt Wanda? I brought you some honey, because yours is almost gone, and your favorite grapes."

"Thank you, my dear. God save you. I'm having trouble breathing, so they've put me up high on these pillows. Tell me, how are you? I count the days before you come."

"I'm fine. I go to school, and I work. I'm glad I don't have school on Wednesdays. I can come visit you. The girls have all kinds of news. They've started smoking; sometimes they don't come in at night. I've heard two of them are pregnant. It's frightening. They go dancing and to the movies, and they don't go to school. I go by myself."

"You're smart. At seventeen you're like an older woman. It's good you know how to behave yourself. But watch out. Don't let anybody hurt you. What time do you come back from school?"

"Very late. About midnight. I take two trolleys, but I'm not frightened of walking on the street where I live. The boys on the street joke with me. They call me Professor—the pride of the baggary of Muldovanka. What can I say?

I feel a little frightened when there's nobody around. It's so quiet, and I walk all by myself."

"I'm proud of you, and I think you'll survive. Do you remember you promised to tell me some good news? Is it not time?"

"You have a good memory. You remember everything. We have to wait a little longer."

"All right. You said wait, but I can tell you, my child, I won't come home from here. Don't look sad. Try to understand, my dear girl. I've lived a long and difficult life. I was so happy to meet you at the end of my life. Give me your hand. ... That's better. But don't cry. Do you remember you told me we have to be strong?"

Wanda held Rita's hand in hers and the girl wept quietly, her head lowered. "It's time to go," Rita said through her tears. "They've already asked visitors to leave twice. I'll be back on Wednesday. Please eat the honey. It's good for your heart."

Never before had Rita left Wanda with this feeling, perhaps because Wanda had held her hand and Wanda's voice was different. When she reached the street, Rita could no longer hold her tears back. It was Sunday. She did not want to go home. She went instead to the seaside boulevard. She took a trolley to Pushkin Street, and, when it stopped, she walked. In her mind, she pictured Wanda's past life.

Wanda had walked here, young and beautiful and so happy with Tadeush.

Over here, she had grieved and had seen death with her own eyes.

Rita walked and reached the shore of the sea. She watched the waves and thought, "Here she sat in a storm and said good-bye to her past."

"I promise you, Wanda," she said aloud. "Someday I'll write the story of your life. I'll write a book, and people can read it. Maybe they'll publish it in Polish as you wished. I don't know when, but I promise you."

Rita sat down on a bench and looked at the sea. She did not want to go home. She could not comprehend the immensity of the sea. She stared at the waves.

"Is the space next to you free?" someone asked. "May I sit down?"

Rita jumped. A man about forty with an almost bald head stood beside her.

He had tried to cover his bald scalp with a few strands of hair. Rita smiled.

"Did I frighten you?" he said. "Please, forgive me. Let me introduce myself. I'm Andre Vlasov. May I sit down?"

"Oh, please, sit down. It's time for me to go home."

The man's name seemed familiar to Rita. Where had she heard it? Then she remembered. It was the name of Wanda's last husband.

"That's a coincidence," she thought. She wondered about it and asked, "Is your father's name Konstantin?"

"Yes. But how did you know? I've never seen you before."

"And your mother's name is Irena?" Rita's heart beat rapidly.

"Her name was Irena. She died three years ago. But I don't understand. How did you know? If I'm not mistaken, you're the daughter of Feodor Nikolayevich?"

"No. I'm nobody's daughter. It's just a coincidence. May I ask you one more question? Where is your father? Is he alive, or did he die in the prison camp?"

Rita did not know what pushed her on. Something beyond curiosity forced her to ask.

Andre Vlasov looked at her without blinking. His pale face became more pallid. Rita did not know what he was thinking. He stared at her without speaking.

"You father was a doctor. Is that right?"

"You tell me who you are, or I won't answer any more of your questions."

"That's fine. You've already answered all my questions. I know you have a sister." Rita turned to him and said, "Good day."

"Wait. Where are you going? You haven't introduced yourself."

"My name means nothing to you. But if you must know, I'm Rita."

"Sit down for a minute, please, Rita. You intrigue me."

Rita thought quickly about how she could disengage herself from the sitaution. She sat down and remained silent, looking at him.

"You're right," he said. "My father was a doctor. He divorced my mother many years ago."

"I know," Rita interrupted. "He married Wanda."

"Oh, Lord. How do you know everything? Rita was quiet. She liked the game.

"My aunt, my mother's sister, told me Wanda was an extremely beautiful woman, and my father lost his head. Is that true?"

Now he was asking the questions. He realized Rita knew a great deal about his family.

"It's true that Wanda was extremely beautiful. She was also kind and soft. She liked to paint, like your father. Did you know he was an artist?"

"Yes," Andre Vlasov said quietly, staring at Rita, confused.

"Is he alive, or is he dead? Can you tell me that?"

"He's alive. He was freed because he was ill. He's in a nursing home here in Odessa. I visited him once."

"How long has he been in the nursing home? Just curious."

"About a year. I've answered all your questions. Can you answer one for me? How do you know the whole history of our family? You're so young. It's impossible that you could have known my parents. Perhps your parents knew mine?"

"You can think that. It's logical. What home is he in?"

"In Slobodka. He's an invalid. He's paraplegic. Why do you need to know."

"I'm sorry he's sick. His life wasn't easy. He's lucky he's still alive."

"Listen, how old are you, girl, fifteen, sixteen? You're reasoning like an adult with a lifetime behind you. It's strange. I want to add that my father risked his life for this beauty, and she never visited him in prison camp. No woman deserves to have risks taken for her."

"That's why you're not married?"

"You know that too? This is unheard of. You're like a little witch."

Rita laughed and stood up. "I have to go. Please don't keep me anymore. I promise you I'll be back next Sunday at four o'clock. Is it a deal?"

"All right. I believe you. I've never seen anything like this in my life. You are a riddle."

Rita smiled and walked away. She felt him watching her. She sat down in the trolley and thought, "I've played a trick on him. He really believes I'm a witch."

What a coincidence! If he had not introduced himself, nothing would have happened. Now Rita was very curious. She told no one about it. Instead, she decided to find the nursing home and see Vlasov.

The next day, the lectures at the university were not very important, so she decided not to go. She bought a bag of fruit and went to Slobodka. She found the nursing home and asked at the front desk for Vlasov's room. On the first floor, she walked down the corridor, found his room, and knocked. There was no answer. She opened the door.

The room was small and dimly lit. She saw two beds. One was empty, and in the other she saw an older, gray-haired man.

"Are you Konstantin Vlasov?" she asked.

"Yes, I am. Come in, girl. Are you from the Young Communist League?

Have you volunteered to keep us company?"

"Why do you say that? I came by myself. I just came to visit you, if you don't mind."

"No. Why? I don't mind. Sit down, please. What grade are you in?"

"I graduated from high school. I'm a student in the university."

"Just like that. What is your major? Can you tell me?"

"I'd like to be an engineer. You were a doctor. Am I right?"

"Oh, they told you at the reception desk?"

Rita did not answer. She watched him. He was slim, and his gray beard formed a crisp V below his chin. His hair was still thick, but entirely white. He wore pince nez glasses, and they made him appear intellectual."

"I don't know how to begin," Rita said. "I feel uncomfortable. I have a question for you. Did you know Wanda Stanishevsky?"

His pince nez glasses fell to the bed. He learned forward and stared at Rita.

"Who are you? What is your name? Why do you ask me this question?"

"I know Wanda Stanishevsky. She doesn't know you're still alive. She doesn't know anything about you since she visited you in jail the last time."

"Of course. Why should she remember me? She was beautiful then. I understand if she married. I don't blame her for my misfortune. It wasn't her fault. What is she doing now? Who is her husband?"

Rita saw his hands shake. "You know nothing, absolutely nothing. If you wish, I can tell you a little about what happened to her after your trial."

"Please, I beg you. I'd very much appreciate it. She was my dove. I always think of her with veneration. I'm only offended because she forgot me."

"After your trial, a few months later, Wanda was tried. She was sentenced to ten years in prison camp."

"That can't be true!" His voice rose, and Rita was frightened. She stood and walked to the window. She did not know what to do next.

"Oh, God," he cried. "My poor dove. What happened to her children? Where is she now? Is she still alive?"

"Yes, she's alive," Rita said gently. "But she's in the hospital. She has a heart problem. I don't know how to tell her about you. She speaks of you very warmly."

"Please, give me some water."

Rita handed him a glass and poured water from the pitcher on the table. He drank but nearly dropped the glass. Rita took it from him.

"Oh, my Wanda. She's alive. She's alive." He fell back on the pillows and closed his eyes.

"I'd better go," Rita said. "Here's some fruit for you. I'll come another time, if it's all right with you."

"Please, tell her I've always loved her. I still do. No. Please turn the light on. I'd like to write her a letter. Promise me you'll give it to her. Please give me the paper and ink. I have a fountain pen in my nightstand."

"I'll go outside while you write. Here's your paper and a book to use as a table."

Rita walked out of the room, feeling very agitated. "Why did I come here?" she thought. "What's happening to me? I've got no time for this. Why am I looking for adventures?"

She walked along a path on the nursing home grounds and saw patients, some without legs, others without arms. She saw one in a wheelchair without arms or legs. She felt nauseous and her head started to spin. She walked back to Vlasov's room, knocked on the door, and opened it.

"I have to go home," she said to him. "It's almost dark. Maybe you can finish your letter next time."

"No, I'm finished. I wrote what I could." He handed Rita a paper folded four times.

All right," she said. "I'll give your letter to Wanda. Stay well. Good-bye now."

He did not answer. Rita walked to the door, and he asked, "How did you find me? But it doesn't matter anymore, at all."

Rita left, heavy hearted. When she arrived at the dormitory, it was completely dark.

"Where have you been fooling around lately?" one of the girls asked. "Your briefcase is here, so you haven't been at the university. I believe you've found somebody."

"What are you talking about? I had some business to take care of. I'm not used to reporting to anybody."

"I just asked. You have a telegram. It came while you were gone." She handed Rita the telegram.

"Thank you, Leda. When did it come?"

"After work, but you didn't stop at home. I don't know who it's from. I didn't open it, believe me."

Leda was a plain girl. Her nickname was Pinnochio because of her very long nose and round, close-set eyes. Her straw-colored, straight hair completed her homely appearance. She was, however, the kindest girl in the group.

Rita opened the telegram: "Will arrive Odessa Oct. 20. Train 36. Car 5. Masha."

"Oh, God," Rita cried. "I don't believe this." She dropped the telegram and jumped with excitement. "What's the date tomorrow? October seventeenth. She'll be here Sunday."

"Who is it?" Leda asked. "Who's coming?" She picked up the telegram, read it, and asked, "Who's Masha?"

"Don't ask. I'll let you know later. Now it's time to wash and go to bed. Everything's in order now."

Rita put the telegram in her purse next to Vlasov's note to Wanda. Although she was very excited by the turn of events, she fell asleep almost immediately.

From early the next morning, Rita thought about how she would surprise Wanda. First, she would give Wanda Vlasov's note and watch her reaction. If Wanda reacted well, Rita would prepare her for Masha's visit on Sunday. She felt more excited than she ever had before.

After work, Rita, went immediately to the hospital. She had taken everything she needed to work with her. She stopped only to buy flowers— three white roses.

At the hospital, she put on the white smock and walked quickly down the corridor. When she arrived at Wanda's room, she stopped, confused. She stopped and looked again at the room number. The bed where Wanda had been was empty. The woman in the bed next to Wanda's called to her.

"Please, come closer. I can't speak loudly."

Rita approached her, and the woman continued. "Last night, your aunt felt very badly, and they took her somewhere. Ask the nurse on duty. She knows."

"Thank you," Rita said. "What happened to her?" She left the room, her heart trembling.

She found out Wanda had been taken to intensive care and was being monitored. She was alone in the intensive care unit.

"You can see her for only two minutes," the nurse told Rita.

"Thank you. That will be enough for me."

"But you can't take anything to her. Please leave your packages of fruit and your flowers here."

Rita walked into the room and saw Wanda lying high on pillows. She wore an oxygen mask and an IV entered her arm.

"Aunt Wanda. This is Rita. Do you hear me?" She took Wanda's hand. She felt Wanda grasp her hand lightly.

"I have good news for you. I have a letter. But I beg you, please, try to be very, very calm."

Wanda opened her eyes and nodded her head. Rita decided to take a risk. "This letter is from Konstantin Vlasov. May I read it to you?" Rita opened her purse, removed the letter, and looked at Wanda. She saw Wanda's wide-open eyes, and Wanda nodded again. Rita began to read.

"My darling, my dove, forgive me if I. ..."

"Are you still here?" the nurse asked. "Please leave immediately. I told you two minutes, and you're trying to read something." The nurse took Rita by the arm and escorted her out.

"Please," Rita pleaded, "let me finish this letter for her. It's very important."

"Are you out of your mind? Or don't you understand what I'm saying?" The nurse pushed Rita out the door and closed it. "Foolish girl. Your aunt is dying, and you've come to read something to her?"

"If my aunt is dying, you have to let me read this letter to her. It's from her husband. Please. You can come with me if you wish."

Rita was weeping and grasping at the nurse's hand.

"I could lose my job if I let you go in," the nurse replied. "That's all I can say. You can go to the doctor on duty. Maybe he'll let you go back in."

The doctor was in the emergency room. He had been called to meet an ambulance. Rita waited for more than an hour. She could not wait any longer and decided to go home. Sitting on the trolley, she was still upset. Tears choked her. She controlled herself only because she was in public. She could not read the letter even though Wanda would soon die. And she felt sorry for herself as well. She would soon be alone again.

As she walked home from the trolley stop, she whispered to herself. "Oh, God, keep her alive until her daughter comes and sees her. Please. I beg you.

She was a good Catholic. She prayed to you all the time. Have mercy."

Before she arrived at the dormitory, some of the girls stopped her. "Rita," one of the girls said, "are you sick? You're skin and bones. What happened to you?"

Another girl said, "I believe she's involved in something. If you're very smart, it happens sometimes."

"Leave me alone," Rita said. "You're just gossiping. Look after yourselves."

She walked to her room and lay down on the bed without removing her clothes. She felt shaky. Then she remembered that, in her excitement, she had not eaten all day. Lately, under the circumstances, she had often forgotten to eat.

Suddenly, she remembered Vlasov's letter and decided to read it herself.

She opened her purse but could not find the note. She checked her pockets.

No letter.

"What can I do now?" she thought. "I must have dropped it when the nurse pushed me out of the room. What a day." She began to cry from anger and self-pity.

At work, Rita tried not to show how upset she was, but everyone saw. They watched her and asked questions. Rita told Claudia about her friend's daughter coming Sunday from Rumania.

"How did you do it?" Claudia asked. "I didn't think it was possible."

"I didn't do anything. I think she did it all in Rumania, and her government helped her."

"How is your secret friend's health?"

"Oh, Claudia, it frightens me to think about it. They took her to intensive care. She's dying. The nurse told me." Tears fell from Rita's eyes.

"She must be a good person if you're so attached to her."

"It's not easy to explain, Claudia, but when she dies, I'll lose the best friend I've had in my life."

"I'll tell you the truth. I hope when I die, one of my children will be so concerned about me." Claudia shook her head.

On Saturday, Rita went to the city market and bought enough to prepare for Masha. Her roommate told her she would stay with friends and that Masha could use her bed if she had no hotel reservations.

Rita awoke very early on Sunday. She prepared breakfast and arranged to keep it warm. The train would arrive at nine, but Rita was on the platform at eight-thirty.

Summer was past, and few people were in the station. In the summer, it seemed as though everyone in the country came to Odessa, to the Black Sea, the golden sand. In Odessa, the prices in the city market doubled during the summer.

Now it was fall, the golden time. Rita paced on the platform and repeated Pushkin's poem: "I love luxuriant nature fading. The forests are crimson and gold."

Rita did not like fall because she did not like nature fading. She loved spring, when everything around her was waking up, blooming, blossoming.

Time passed quickly. She heard the train whistle and saw the locomotive rounding the last curve. Her heart beat faster, as if she were waiting for someone very close and dear to her.

The train stopped, and Rita walked to car five. She recognized Masha immediately. She had imagined Masha to look very like she did, above medium height, very elegant, wearing a brown suit. Her hair was chestnut colored and fell to her shoulders. She wore a narrow-brimmed, brown hat.

"Are you Masha?" Rita asked her. "I'm Rita."

Masha removed her gloves and said, "Thank you for meeting me here. Where are Mama and Gregory? I haven't received letters."

"I'll tell you on the way. Do you have hotel reservations?"

"No. I thought I'd stay with Mama."

Rita said nothing. She took one suitcase, Masha took the other, and they walked out of the station.

"Wait a minute, citizen," someone commanded. "Stop."

Masha and Rita turned around and put the luggage down. They saw two men in civilian clothes, one in a gray suit and the other wearing a raincoat.

"Are you Maria Vladimirovna Stanishevsky?"

"Yes, I am. What can I do for you?"

"You will come with us in our car. Who are you?" he asked Rita.

"Who are you to ask us questions?" Rita demanded.

"We're with the government secret service." He showed his KGB identification. "Valery Ivanov. This is my assistant."

"All right. What do you want? We have to go to the hospital. Maria's mother is very, very ill."

"Is that true?" Ivanov asked Masha.

"I don't know. No one told me about it."

"Yes, it's true," Rita said. "She's in Jewish Hospital, in intensive care. If you take us to your office and ask us all your questions, Maria won't have time to say good-bye to her mother. Do you understand that?"

"You know everything, but you're so little. Where did you come from?" Ivanov's voice was sharp.

Rita did not answer. She closed her mouth tightly.

"What do I do now?" Masha asked, confused.

"Get in the car," Ivanov said. "We'll go to the hospital and see if this girl is telling the truth."

"I'm coming too," Rita said.

"Of course," said Ivanov, smiling, "because if you're lying, you have to pay for it."

What a face Ivanov had! Worse than the way a fascist looked in the movies. Rita had been upset with people in the past, but she wanted to spit in this man's ugly face.

He had very thin lips, a straight, sharp nose, and eyes like daggers. His chin was blunt and jutting, his forehead low, and his hair was short-cut and bristly.

The other man, who had said nothing, was difficult to see. His full, dark hair tumbled over his forehead, and his eyebrows almost hid his eyes. Both men were built like heavyweight boxers.

Rita did not speak. They walked to the car. Inside the vehicle, Masha asked her, "What happened to Mama, Rita? You haven't told me anything. Where is Gregory? Can you tell me?"

"All right. I'll try to tell you, but I thought I'd be able to explain under different conditions. I've even prepared breakfast, and I have everything for dinner. Now is not the time to talk about it.

"How can I start? Your mother went into the hospital over a month ago. She had a heart attack. She's now having difficulty breathing, and she has to have oxygen. They've transferred her to intensive care. They only let me see her for two minutes.

"Your brother was killed in the war in nineteen forty-three. He was very young. Your mama has gone through so much. She lost you, and she lost her son. She became ill. After years, her sickness grew worse. This is the result. That's all."

Rita finished her simple explanation and looked at the man with the ugly face. He smiled.

"You tell good stories," Ivanov said. "Do you get good grades as a storyteller in school?"

Masha was crying. She covered her face with a handkerchief. She believed everything Rita had said and hoped only to see her mother alive.

"You know, Ivanov?" Rita asked, "even your face tells everybody you work for the KGB. I imagined KGB would look like you. Don't trust anybody.

Don't love anybody."

"You talk too much. I'll be asking you a few questions later. Right now, you can shut your mouth."

"You don't frighten me. I'm from an orphanage. My parents were killed. My father gave his life for his country. And you're trying to frighten me? We'll see."

Rita had lost control. By the time she stopped, it was already too late. The car was quiet. The only sound was Masha's crying until they reached the hospital. The car stopped, and they got out.

"All right," Ivanov said to Rita, "tell us. Who is sick in this hospital?" He spoke as if Rita were a child.

"Don't talk like that. Try to be serious. She's in the cardiology area. Intensive care. Wanda Stanishevsky. You can ask the doctor on duty. Visiting hours start at one today. That's why I wanted to bring Masha here. First, I wanted her to have breakfast and a little rest, but you're the boss. You've screwed everything up."

"What a tongue. Like a razor." Ivanov walked into the hospital lobby. They sat on the benches to wait.

Masha asked Rita, "Is there any hope Mama will get better? My poor mama. I remember her when she was young. You know how beautiful she was. I even remember her portrait."

"The portrait is not lost," Rita said. "It's in Wanda's room. I have a key. Your mama found your diary, Masha. That's how she knows about you. What has happened to you since you left Odessa?"

"My life is fine. Irzhy is a very good husband. We didn't have children, but we're raising his nephew. His sister died when the child was four years old. How did you meet my mother, Rita?"

"It's a long story. When we're alone, I'll tell you."

"Thank you. If not for you I would never have found my mother. I sent letters many times, but there was no answer."

"A friend of mine helped me get a letter to the Rumanian Red Cross. He's from Muldavia and knows Rumanian. I need to send him a thank-you letter." Ivanov walked over to them and spoke to his assistant. "She told the truth." He turned to Masha. "You can come with me. They'll let you see your mother now."

Masha stood and walked away with Ivanov. Rita started to follow.

"Nobody told you to go," said Ivanov's assistant.

"Nobody told me to sit and wait here. I'm not a defendant. Don't try to be bossy. And tell me, why are you guarding Masha? She can speak Russian. She's not lost. Do you guard all foreigners?"

He smiled and said nothing. Rita ran to follow Masha. When she caught up with them, she spoke to Ivanov. "Let me go first. I need to prepare Aunt Wanda. She didn't know Masha was coming. May I?"

Ivanov nodded. Rita walked through the open door.

Wanda lay on the high-piled pillows. Her eyes were closed. She was not wearing a mask, and no IV was attached to her. Rita heard her heavy breathing in the quiet, empty room.

"Aunt Wanda. It's me. Please, wake up."

She took Wanda's hand, but Wanda did not return the pressure. Rita saw the nurse at the door and asked, "Is she asleep?"

"No, girl. She's in a coma."

The nurse was older, not the same one as before.

"She has a short time to live," the nurse continued. "You can say good-bye. Maybe she can hear you?"

"Aunt Wanda, dear," Rita said, "I promised you I had good news for you. And I kept my promise. I found your daughter, Masha. She came with me, and she's waiting in the hall. She's beautiful, just like you described her. Please, wake up." Rita wept quietly.

Rita stepped into the corridor and called Masha. "Please come in. The nurse says she can hear. I told her you're here."

Masha walked into the room, leaving her hat and gloves behind in the corridor. She moved to Wanda's bed, looked at her, and sobbed.

"My dear mother. Is this you? I don't recognize you at all. If only you knew how long I've looked for you, how I've missed you. Look at me, my dear. This is your Masha."

Rita stood at the foot of the bed, weeping. The nurse left them alone, Wanda, her daughter, and the poor orphan Wanda had embraced with her warmth.

Masha kissed her mother's hand and touched her face. "Did you hear me? Please hear me."

Rita stopped crying, only sobbing gently. Wanda was not easy to recognize. She had lost a great deal of weight. She looked like an old woman. This did not look like the woman Rita had met two years before.

Suddenly, Wanda opened her eyes and looked at Rita. Her lips moved soundlessly.

"Masha! She's awake!" Rita cried.

Wanda moved her eyes to Masha and reached toward her. Just as their hands were about to touch, Wanda's fell to the bed.

"Mama, can you see me?" Masha asked. "I've come to see you. Say something."

"I see you," Wanda whispered weakly. "God sent you to me, my child. This is not a dream? Mashenka, is it you?"

"Yes, yes, it's me. Do you feel my hand, Mama?"

"Yes, I feel it. Gregory came with you, too?" Masha and Rita looked at each other.

"Kostya promised to come see me," Wanda continued. "I saw Tadeush yesterday. He brought me flowers. Your father cannot come because they killed him. You know, Mashenka, they shot him down."

Wanda's voice was clear; the whisper could be heard because the room was very quiet. Rita felt her flesh prickle.

"Mama," Masha said, "my dearest mama. Calm yourself. My father died during the revolution, a long time ago."

412

"No," Wanda answered, breathing laboriously, "they shot him. He was an officer." Her eyes moved to Rita. "Please tell Kostya to prepare an order for me for the next painting. I won't give anyone Marina's portrait. I'll put them on the wall in my living room."

Wanda was hallucinating. She spoke of her father and Sophie, asking Masha to bring them the next day. For a short time, her memory returned.

"Mashenka, I don't believe it is really you. I lived long enough to see you, my beautiful child."

Again, she began to call for Tadeush.

"Please, leave us alone," she said. "I need to tell him how I've waited for him all my life."

Then she spoke to Tadeush, raising her arms. "Come to me, my darling. Give me your hands."

Her hands fell to the blanket and her head fell to her chest. She had fallen asleep forever.

Masha tried to rouse her, but she did not respond. The nurse escorted Masha to the corridor where she collapsed in grief.

Later, Rita asked a doctor how it had happened that Wanda had been in a coma, but before she died, she had revived, talked, heard, responded, and hallucinated. The doctor explained that it happened often, that people in a coma revived before they died. It was a common phenomenon. For Rita, however, what she had seen was a mystery.

When Masha recovered, Ivanov explained that the funeral would be the next day. He did not let her stay with Rita or speak to her anymore. It did not matter that Rita objected. The two KGB agents took Masha to their car.

"Where are you taking her?" Rita demanded. "I have a key to Wanda's room."

Ivanov opened the car door and said, "Tomorrow, after the funeral, we'll go to her mother's place. Now go home." He slammed the door and drove away.

Rita sat on the trolley and closed her eyes. A hammer seemed to be beating inside her head. She was so tired, physically and emotionally. She was trembling.

"Tomorrow is the funeral," she thought. "They'll bury Wanda in the Second Cemetery. No one will allos her to be buried in the Polish cemetery, as she wanted. Why are these people from the government secret service guarding Masha all the time? Maybe that's how all people from foreign countries are treated. I was so naive to prepare food and a place for her. There's so much I don't know yet." She fell asleep, sitting in the trolley.

When she awoke, she discovered she had passed her stop. She left the trolley at the next stop and walked across the street to catch a car going in the opposite direction. As she stood at the trolley stop, she remembered that she was supposed to meet Andre Vlasov at four o'clock.

"Please forgive me," she thought. "Today, I have more important things to think about than meeting." Briefly, she thought of going to Wanda's room to take the portrait, but she felt uncomfortable going to the room when no one was there.

The coffin was closed. Rita preferred it that way. She did not want to see Wanda's face in death. At the cemetery were Masha, Rita, and a few of the women from the school where Wanda had worked. The two KGB men were also there. Masha cried quietly as Rita held her arm. Rita did not cry. The coffin was lowered into the grave, and the women dropped handfulls of dirt onto the casket.

Rita had ordered two flower wreaths. When the grave had been covered, she placed the wreaths on top of the mound of soil.

"I have to remember where this place is," Rita said. "I will be visiting." She wrote the path number in her notebook. "What are your plans?" she asked Masha.

"I don't know. I don't know anything anymore."

Rita looked at Masha questioningly. Ivanov and his assistant walked over to them.

"Do you have the key to her mother's room?" Ivanov asked Rita. "Yes, I have the key, but what do you want?"

"You come with us. You'll be a witness."

"Witness for what?"

There was no answer. They signaled Rita to follow Masha. The car door opened and Masha and Rita took their seats in the back.

Rita opened the door to Wanda's room. "Let some fresh air into this room," she said to the people following her. "It's been closed for a long time."

Five minutes later, they all entered.

"She lived here," Rita said. "Most people's closets are better than this room, but she didn't complain. I remember she said once, 'Life, Rita, is like a zebra. It has black and white stripes.' But I think she had more black stripes in her life."

"Tell me," Ivanov said, "where did you learn to talk?"

"The Soviet authorities taught me from my childhood to speak and fight for myself because no one will do it for me. You don't like it?"

"I'm just not used to little girls talking like that."

"I can be quiet if I want." She turned to Masha. "You can take this portrait, Masha. Wanda gave it to me, but I know it belongs to you." Rita unwrapped the portrait.

"Oh, Mama," Masha cried, "I remember this portrait. I wrapped it in this blanket before I left. Maybe someday they'll let me take it, but I don't know. ..."

"You can take this icon, too," Rita said. "Your mama prayed to this icon. It's a good memory." To Ivanov, she said, "tell me, will you let her take the icon, too?"

"You don't know what you're talking about. All of this belongs to the government."

"What? The portrait, too? Look at this note Wanda wrote." She showed him the part that gave everything to her.

"That is not an official document. It's not even notarized. A picture like that is museum property."

"This is Wanda Stanishevsky when she was young. This is Masha's mother.

Can you see that?"

"Where did you get that idea? This is a picture of a young, rich, aristocratic woman. Why should I discuss it with you? You can go home now. We don't need your help anymore."

"I'd like to go to the train station and say good-bye to Masha. When will she go home?"

"You can say good-bye here. That's all the answer you'll get."

"Of course. You're right because you have more rights. This is how it was, is, and will be." To Masha she said, "Good-bye. I'm so sorry we don't have more time to talk. I'd like to ask you many things about what Wanda told me. You know my address. You must write to me; I'll answer."

Masha nodded and walked to the bookshelves. "Mama had Polish and French books. My poor mama. She died and didn't know her sister was killed when a bomb destroyed her building. Sophie's husband Kazimir died before the war. I've been to Poland. That's all I could find out. I didn't find out anything about my cousins."

Masha walked to Rita and hugged her. "Thank you very much for everything. If I can, I'll write to you."

They held each other, and then Rita left.

EPILOGUE

It was late fall. A cold drizzle fell. It had been a month since Wanda's death. On a Sunday, Rita visited Wanda's grave. The wind caught her umbrella and flung it about so that her face grew wet from both rain and tears. She placed flowers on Wanda's grave. The mound of fresh soil had begun to wash away.

Rita began to speak to Wanda, just as Wanda had spoken to her father. "I came today to ask your forgiveness. What I did I did not do on purpose. I only tried to help you find your daughter."

Tears fell from Rita's eyes, and she sobbed.

"Now your daughter has been arrested and sent to jail. The authorities explained that she was arrested for political reasons. I understand it was because she left the country with a Rumanian during the war.

"If I'd only known! I was so naive. Your portrait was taken, but I don't know where, what museum.

"I'll miss you in my life, but you'll always be in my heart. I'll take care of your grave because I have no one else's grave close to me. Believe me, Aunt Wanda, the time will come when everything will be different. People's kindness will overcome evil and injustice. I don't know when. As you said, only God knows.

"I sent a letter to Masha's husband and explained everything that happened. I want to believe he can fight for his rights in his country because his country is on his side. I hope my letter went through. I also sent a letter to Ivan, but I couldn't explain everything. When he comes back from the Army, I'll tell him.

"I visited Konstantin Vlasov. I told him you're not in this world anymore. He kissed my hand and cried. That's all the news."

"I believe you'll forgive me for what I've done. You were always very kind."

Rita walked back to the gate. The rain was falling heavily. Water squished in her shoes. Her clothes were soaked through.

When she arrived at her dormitory, she felt feverish. Another girl called the doctor. He arrived and called an ambulance. Rita had double pneumonia, and she was emaciated.

For months, the doctors fought to save her. She survived, recovering slowly. She would live to write the painful, true story of Wanda's life.

THE END

ENDNOTES

1.   Mrs.
2.   Mr.
3.   Audience seating on the ground floor of the theatre.
4.   Mashenka, Masha - Full name Maria.
5.   Mermaid
6.   Borscht - vegetable soup.
7.   Copeck - penny.
8.   Primus - portable kerosene stove.
9.   Character from a Russian folksong.
10.   Christian Orthodox fasting before Easter.

Lightning Source UK Ltd.
Milton Keynes UK
UKHW011837280121
377874UK00001B/7